THE

DEAD

ENDERS

THE DEAD ENDERS

ERIN SALDIN

SIMON PULSE

New York London Toronto Sydney New Delhi

SIMON PULSE

An imprint of Simon & Schuster Children's Publishing Division

1230 Avenue of the Americas, New York, New York 10020

First Simon Pulse hardcover edition May 2018

Text copyright © 2018 by Erin Saldin

Jacket photograph copyright © 2018 by Anchly/Getty Images

For information about special discounts for bulk purchases,

please contact Simon & Schuster Special Sales

at 1-866-506-1949 or business@simonandschuster.com.

The Simon & Schuster Speakers Bureau can bring authors to your live event.

For more information or to book an event contact the Simon & Schuster

Speakers Bureau at 1-866-248-3049 or visit our website at www.simonspeakers.com.

Designed by Steve Scott

The text of this book was set in Absara and Frutiger.

Manufactured in the United States of America

2 4 6 8 10 9 7 5 3 1

Library of Congress Cataloging-in-Publication Data

Names: Saldin, Erin, author.

Title: The Dead Enders / by Erin Saldin.

Description: First Simon Pulse hardcover edition. | New York : Simon Pulse, 2018. |
Summary: Ana, Davis, Erik, and Georgie, bound together by tragedy, want nothing more than to escape the small tourist town of Gold Fork, but an arsonist and the return of long-lost family members force them to confront the past.

Identifiers: LCCN 2017056049 (print) | LCCN 2018000718 (eBook) |

ISBN 9781481490337 (hc) | ISBN 9781481490429 (eBook)

Subjects: | CYAC: Friendship—Fiction. | Secrets—Fiction. |

Arson—Fiction. | Summer resorts—Fiction.

Classification: LCC PZ7.S1494 (eBook) |

LCC PZ7.S1494 De 2018 (print) | DDC [Fic]—dc23

LC record available at https://lccn.loc.gov/2017056049

For Sylvie and Frankie

THE

DEAD

ENDERS

GOLD FORK IS . . .

But first, let me tell you what it isn't. This is not a fantasy. It's not even a love story. There will be no dragons, no spells, no visitors from worlds that look like ours but aren't, quite. There won't even be time travel. No one is carried away on an asteroid. No one's ancestors appear in a nimbus mist to hand over the key to the forgotten city. There will be no castle storming. We just aren't that lucky.

Or maybe we are. Maybe it is a fantasy, after all. Maybe—yes, definitely—this is a love story. But it's not the story you'd expect. It never is, in Gold Fork.

DAVIS

It's a regular firestorm of paper. I catch sight of some grades on the loose sheets as they float past me in the hall: C+, B, A-, a hastily scratched *Rewrite for credit*. The floor is carpeted with what we don't want. The janitors hate us. I make my way to my locker, listening to the shouting and the heavy clang of a couple hundred metal doors swinging shut for the summer. I'm trying hard not to look for Jane, but every time I see a corner of blue—blue shirt, blue skirt, even someone's blue backpack—I think it's her, and my breath catches in my throat.

It's never her.

Georgie's leaning against my locker door in jeans and some obscure band T-shirt. She looks like she belongs on one of those black-and-white movie posters, straight out of French cinema. Like she really should have a cigarette in her hand. She raises one hand in a lazy wave as if she hasn't actually been waiting for me.

"Georgie," I say, "don't take this the wrong way, but you really make the rest of us look bad. Just become famous already and let us all excel at normality."

She kicks a heel against the locker, pushing off. "I like your brand of bullshit, Davis." Then she looks around. "Where are the others?"

I shrug. "Ana was in pre-calc with me this morning, but I haven't seen her since."

"What about Erik?"

"You know we don't have any of the same classes." I don't have to say it, but she has to know what I'm thinking: I never see Erik at school—or if I do, we don't talk much. The only place our lives intersect is the Den.

"Bet he's forgotten," she says. "Of course."

My phone buzzes with a text just as Ana appears at the end of the hall, her head moving in a slow swivel until she sees us. She weaves through the crowd. Her hair is messy, and even from here I can see the ink smudge that's perpetually on her cheek—one of the drawbacks of being left-handed and using cheap pens.

I read the text just as she says, "Well, we made it. Last day of school."

"You guys," I say, and hold up my phone. I squint at it like I can't read the words, but I can. I can read them perfectly.

"A week's reprieve before the Weekenders get here," says Georgie. "I'll be spending it on my bed, asleep."

"You guys."

"I'll probably just try to see more of Vera," says Ana.

"How's she doing, anyway?" Georgie asks.

"She's—" Ana starts to say, but she stops when I grab her hand. I stare at it for a moment before letting go.

"You. Guys." I take a breath. "Dan just texted me from the newspaper office. The Nelson cabin burned down last night."

They don't say anything for a minute. The whole hallway

4

freezes, it seems—if this were a movie, I'd swear even the papers stop flying halfway through the air. No one else can hear us, but still. It's a collective breath, held.

Then we let it out.

"Shit!" Georgie's face gets red. "No. No fucking way."

"It burned. To the ground." I look at my phone. "Foundation and fireplace are the only things left."

Georgie kicks the locker, hard, with the toe of her combat boot. "Shit!" She covers her face with her hands.

"Are you okay?" asks Ana, even though we should be asking her that. She pulls her sleeve down over her left arm, covering the silver scar that winds—I know, I've seen it before, saw it even when it wasn't a scar yet and was just blood—from her elbow to her wrist, carving a line through her skin.

Georgie looks up and takes a deep breath. "Fine. Fuck. I'm fine." Then she adds, "It shouldn't have burned. That thing was made of steel." Her voice is still a little shaky. "I just—I'm sorry. But there wasn't any fuel around it. I mean, we took care of that."

We took care of that.

She's right, of course. When the chapel burned to the ground two years ago, there was nothing left on that plot of land but soot and char.

"The Nelsons never should have built their cabin there," I say. "Hallowed ground and all that. Maybe no one started this fire. Maybe it was just karma. Maybe it's just the universe saying, *If you can't keep a chapel from burning down here, you can't have anything.*" I'm trying to make light of it, but really, I'm just thinking of my mom and wondering if I should text her. The chapel fire is more than a memory to her. It's a haunting.

You know how people say, "I remember it like it was yesterday"? I've always thought that was so misguided. I mean, can anyone really remember yesterday accurately? Once the screen of sleep has fallen, events start to warp, take on different tones, different meanings. By the time we wake up the next day, yesterday might as well be last year.

But the chapel fire? I remember most of it like it's right now. And I always will.

Creeping out of my one-man tent at midnight, a feeling like rising water in my gut. Excitement. Nervousness. Georgie's voice still ringing in my head from after the cookout: "Meet in the chapel later?" Georgie, whom I hardly know except to know not to fuck with her. "Ana will be there."

Silently passing the other tents, some big, some small. I skirt my mom's tent—our fearless leader. The whole church youth group is here. Most of them are asleep. Not all of them have been chosen.

The chapel rises out of the dark, woods all around it, the cliffs beyond. When I enter, shutting the door quietly behind me, the air smells of incense and pine and dust. It's dark, but I turn my headlamp on and look around. Ana's standing with her arms wrapped around herself. She smiles, and the water rises another inch. Georgie says, "Good. You're here." And then Erik, looking as surprised to see me as I am to see him. I didn't know whom to expect, but Erik-the-track-star? Erik-the-guy-who-doesn't-need-this-because-he-already-has-everything-he-needs—girls-and-trophies-and-the-adoration-of-the-whole-damn-town? But here he is anyway. We nod at each other, two aliens whose ships have crashed on the same foreign planet.

I move next to Ana, and we bump shoulders in greeting. Then Georgie says, "A campfire's not a campfire without a little smoke," and she pulls from her pocket a perfectly rolled joint. Ana raises her eyebrows, and Erik says, "Thanks be to God."

It's my first time smoking, and I don't want anyone to know. But once I see Ana coughing and sputtering after her hit, I start laughing because of course. Only Georgie and Erik know what they're doing. Slowly—slowly—we relax. Make jokes, even. Georgie imitates Erik's expression as he inhales, and he laughs. Ana and I lean against each other, comfortable finally. I'll kiss her tonight, I know.

Everything is possible.

And that's where it becomes memory again. Because everything *was* possible in that moment. But then the moment after happened, and the moment after that. And by the end of the night, what brought us together wasn't the spark of new friendship and a cresting wave of maybe-finally-utterly-now.

7

All of that was gone. What brought us together—joined us for the rest of our time in Gold Fork—were screams and sirens and blood and ash.

ANA

"It doesn't make sense," Georgie's saying. "It just doesn't make any sense."

The noise around us is what I imagine the ocean sounds like: hollow and demanding. I look to my left to see if anyone's listening, but all I see are faces open in exclamation and relief. Then everything dulls and becomes blurry as Chrissy Nolls walks by, the collar of her thin jacket turned up around her neck. Even so, I can still see the way the skin folds over itself in strange ridges along the back of her hairline, a misshapen landscape.

I glance at Davis and Georgie to see if they've noticed her. They have. Davis is holding his phone so tightly that I can see the whites of his knuckles. I think about reaching over, touching his hand, and banish the thought just as quickly.

"Oh God," says Georgie. She closes her eyes for a long second. When she opens them again, Chrissy's at the other end of the hall. Georgie looks at me quickly and then turns to Davis. "They got out, right? The Nelsons."

His eyes follow Chrissy as she turns toward Tri High's main doors and disappears into summer. He clears his throat. "Weren't even there," he says, checking his phone again. "The structure's gone. That's it."

8

We all look in the direction Chrissy walked. "Good," I say, and we all take a breath as the panic subsides.

"Copycat?" asks Georgie.

"Who would copy us?" I say. "Besides, the chapel was two years ago."

"You're right," she says.

Davis takes a deep breath. "Two years ago today."

"Shit," says Georgie, and she's patting her pockets, searching for something. I can guess what. She pulls out a lighter, flicks it once. "I need to smoke." Then she adds, "Where's Erik? Where the fuck is he?" Georgie is usually cooler than this. Nothing fazes her. It's one of the things I admire about her. But she seems more rattled than I am, and frankly, I'm the one who should be crawling out of my skin. I touch my left arm with my right hand and breathe.

"Maybe he forgot," says Davis. "He's got his good-byes to deal with."

"Not like anyone is going anywhere," says Georgie. "Your girls will still be here all summer."

A guy—soccer player, I should know his name but don't—walks by, slapping Georgie on the shoulder. "See you at Fellman's?" he asks.

"Better believe it," she says.

"Good," he says, and laughs. "We'll party." He walks off, yelling at someone down the hall about *grab the wheels* or something.

Most people in this school speak a language I don't

understand. And I don't mean English; my mom may still retain some of the Spanish she grew up with, but she hasn't passed it on to me. I wish she had. I wish I knew what it was like to dream in another language. To have private conversations with my mom in the grocery store that we can be fairly sure no one else comprehends. To still belong to the world she ran away from.

No, for better or for worse, English is my first (and only) language. But the language of my school is more complex, more riddled with double meanings and hidden jokes. Even Erik can sometimes feel as foreign to me as the football players, the snowmobilers, the kids who go hunting every weekend in the fall with their whole families. I look at Davis and Georgie, my closest friends in this town besides Vera. And I feel, like I've felt a thousand times since that night exactly two years ago, the particular pain of owing everything good in my life to that terrible fire.

I don't know why Georgie invited me. But I'm not going to ask. I've watched her in youth group meetings—her easy way, her quick retorts. She's never had time for me until now, and the doubt I'd normally feel is eclipsed by the bright spark of pleasure when she asks if I want to meet in the chapel to smoke later. "Davis will be there," she says, and I wonder how she knows. Is my desire so clear? Can he see it too?

And then we're smoking, and it's easy. Davis, Georgie, and Erik—whom I don't know well but who seems, in this space, to be funny and friendly in a way I've never thought he could be. The moon, bright through the chapel's stained-glass windows, reflects off their faces so that they seem lit from within. Almost holy. And isn't that what friendship is? And isn't that what I've wanted for so long?

When we leave the chapel, the night is a quiet animal. We don't know what we've done.

Until we do. Erik first: a quiet "Oh." We turn around, and the cross on the door is burning, the chapel's windows filling with smoke. Georgie's voice: "Oh shit!" Davis's: "Ana! Come back!" But I've heard the other sound—a quiet crying, a desperate mewling. And I remember the cat, curled in the corner of a pew with her kittens. I'm already heading back in.

GEORGIE

"Looks like you'll be busy," says Davis, watching Chris (soccer player, kind of dumb, eight ball once a month) walk away.

"No rest for the wicked," I say, but I want to scream instead. *You don't even know!* I want to shout in their faces. *You don't even know what's at stake here!* But I add, voice totally calm, "Fellman's should be good for business."

It has to be.

"The Weekenders will all be here by then," says Ana, her expression a little wistful. She reaches over and pats a locker. "Good-bye, Gold Fork."

"Hello, resort town," says Davis. "Get ready for the costume change."

I look down the hall. It's almost cleared out by now. Most kids can't get out of Tri High fast enough at the end of the year. But I know what they're running toward, and it can wait.

"I don't think Erik's coming," I say. I look around once more, as though he's going to magically appear, sigh, and shake my head. Classic Erik. Always doing his own fucking thing. "I'll text him and tell him to just meet us at the Den."

"He wasn't in English this morning," says Ana. "I haven't seen him around."

"Bold move, missing the last day of school," says Davis.

"Yeah," I say, though I'm not surprised. The things Erik gets away with.

We head toward the big double doors. I inhale, letting the scent of old cafeteria food, rubber, and sweat wash over me. This is what I smell nine months of the year. This is what Gold Fork is, until it isn't. Davis is right: In a week, it'll all be replaced with newer smells. Better smells. The beautiful stench of wealth.

Those straight-to-DVD movies about gangsters or bank robbers? The ones where someone inevitably holds a wad of hundreds in front of his face, fans them and inhales, saying something stupid like "God, how I love the smell of money"? Those are bullshit.

You know what money smells like? Expensive tanning lotions and the exhaust of new speedboats. Lip gloss with the slightest hint of pomegranate or coconut, but not in an overpowering, corn syrupy, drugstore sort of way. Sunshine and possibility. That's what money smells like. For the Weekenders, at least.

It smells different to me, but not by much. Because summer is the best season for business. Always has been. That is, unless you stupidly hid your stash—the one you expected to sell at Fellman's—under the deck at the Nelsons' cabin, knowing they were out of town. Unless a couple thousand dollars' worth of drugs just burned up—incinerated, gone— in an instant. Unless you screwed yourself so royally that this summer has turned from a fun ride around the lake—one last round—into a mad scramble for money and lost time.

So maybe Davis is right. Maybe the Nelson fire is karma. And who better to point the cosmic finger at than me?

Watching them around the campfire: Davis, singing along to his mom's songs: "Jesus-Light," she calls them. Trying his best to look like he doesn't care, to not stare at Ana where she sits, hugging herself in the cold. She glances at him once or twice, but never when he's looking. Erik, scuffing the toe of his running shoe in the dirt, mouthing the words because no way in hell he's going to get caught with a song in his throat. A girl on each side of him. He looks at me and winks, everything already an inside joke between us, even the girls. Davis, Ana, Erik. I watch the three of them. I choose them carefully: the nerd, the nobody, the athlete. Not the friends a dealer would have. And so: the perfect cover.

And later: the cool of the night. The way the chapel envelops us as we smoke.

I like them more than I thought I would.

And even later: my shoe, grinding the joint against the floor of the chapel. Ana bending to pick it up and throw it away. Me saying, "Let's leave it. Let your mom wonder who the sinners are, Davis." Not knowing how right I am.

Only one sinner. Me.

ERIK

So I missed it. So what? Nothing happens on the last day anyway.

Here's what I missed: the sound of two hundred stampeding animals as they flee their prison and make for the light. Getting my grade for the Algebra II final I took last week. Fending them off—all of them—as they ask what I'm doing after.

After what?

That's the question.

When I get to the Den, hiding my bike in the bushes beside the lake road and climbing over the estate's wrought-iron gate, they're already waiting on the deck behind the big house, sitting comfortably in old Adirondack chairs that wouldn't have been dusted in decades if it weren't for us. They're all looking out at the lake, but they turn when they hear my tennis shoes on the deck's old wooden boards.

Ana and Davis raise their hands in greeting, but:

"What the hell, Erik," says Georgie, narrowing her eyes. "We waited forever at school."

"Sorry, George," I say, moving toward her and tapping her on her head with my palm—one, two—before letting my hand rest for a moment on her hair. Our little thing. "Couldn't quite deal with it, you know? All that bullshit noise." And I think, but don't say, that it's better to skip over the part about *another year gone* and *any summer plans?* and get right to the good stuff: summer and freedom and Weekenders and their clean, perfect lives.

"We got our finals back in math," says Georgie under her breath as I pull a chair closer to her. Ana and Davis are sitting on one side of her. All of our chairs face the water, and the sun reflects off of it like the blade of a knife.

"Bet you aced it," I say, and elbow her gently. "You know numbers."

"Yeah," she says, "I did. I—" She reaches down and pulls something out of her backpack. "Mr. Carlson said I could bring you yours." Then she looks away.

It's folded in half, once. I don't need to look to know what it says. I force myself to laugh. "Thanks, George," I say. "Chalk it up to more bullshit noise." And I stand and walk to the edge of the deck, which rises above a slope down to the water. I wad the paper up in a ball and hurl it toward the lake. Then I clap my hands. "That's better."

"Erik," Georgie starts to say, but then she shrugs and laughs. "Sure is."

"Tell him," says Ana. She has her knees pulled up to her chest—I guess it *is* a little chilly, though I haven't noticed

15

much, lately—and she nods at Davis. "About the fire."

"What?" I ask.

Davis points across the lake to Washer's Landing. "Nelson cabin burned down last night. Arson, they're thinking."

"What?" I ask again, like I can't hear him. I squint across the water. Sure enough, there's no glare of expensive windows, no glint off the solar panels that they had installed. No nothing, because there's no house there. "Damn," I say.

"First the chapel, now this," Davis goes on. "If it's a coincidence—if the problem was electrical or something—it's the freakiest coincidence I've heard of."

"Arson for sure," says Georgie. "Someone saw what we did and wanted to give it a try."

"Who would do that?" asks Ana, and I look away, but not before I see the scar on her arm.

Don't remember don't remember don't remember don't remember

The chapel goes up fast. One flame becomes five. And the four of us, watching at first, speechless.

Then Ana goes in.

I didn't think she'd go in.

And it's hazy—everything is muffled—but I can hear other people, too—Davis's mom and a few kids from the youth group. People are starting to wake up, climb out of their tents, as the chapel burns on.

And then it's really burning—burning in the way of colossal

16

mistakes, of no-take-backs. It's a wall of fire. And Ana's in there.

I can't even hear myself over the roar of the fire, but I'm yelling, screaming, my words lost in the flames. Davis is right next to me. Georgie—where's Georgie? Leaning over, hands on knees, coughing. I start to take a step toward her when Ana comes out of the chapel, her arms bleeding and empty. "I couldn't," she's gasping. "I couldn't save them."

Davis looks at me like he heard me say something, and maybe he did, but there's not time to think about it because I look up and watch as one of the shingles from the chapel roof flies off in a kind of slow-motion flutter, almost pretty, really, and lands on the tent where Chrissy Nolls is still sleeping.

JUNE

WHERE THE WEEKENDERS ARE ALWAYS JEALOUS

When you grow up in a resort town like Gold Fork, the Weekenders are always jealous. Those few that we meet at Grainey's or the public beach (we know they're slumming it, so far from their private docks, and we watch them carefully out of the corners of our eyes until they approach us with smokes or a hilarious story about that guy over there) want nothing more, they say, than to stay. "I can't believe you get to liiiiive here," they whine as their parents pack up the Tahoe and make sure all forty windows are locked tight in their summer place, that the cupboards underneath the sinks in each of the five bathrooms are open to deter mice or freezing pipes, take your pick. "I'd live here foreeeeever if I could." Then we watch from their driveways, hands in our pockets, as they wave from their cars, already settling down for the three-hour drive back to the city. Their parents' cautious eyes in the rearview mirror, watching to see if we're going to turn around and try the door to the cabin. We can almost read their lips as they say, "You sure about them?" And then, catching themselves, they cover. "They seem nice." Turning up NPR and whispering under their breath to each other: "Did you lock the sliding door to the deck?"

They always do. Lock it, that is.

But what the Weekenders don't get is that Gold Fork shrivels when they're gone. Like a child's bath toy that expands, plump and colorful, as soon as you add water, Gold Fork is a dry, hard thing when the Weekenders go home. We wave good-bye and walk back through town, wondering how someone would ever want to live here. Most of the stores are closed. The window of the real estate office is dark, so we have to squint to read the fine print on the ads that they've taped up for homes that none of our parents can afford. Through the glass front of Grainey's, Maria waves, holding up an empty coffee cup in question, but we shake our heads and keep moving. The sun is just as bright, the lake—on the other side of the street, practically lapping up against Chin's Chinese and Italian Specialties—just as blindingly blue. But the town has shrunk back to its former self. It's barely breathing.

We're a four-season town with only two that count. Once Labor Day weekend is over, we don't see the Weekenders until Coolidge Mountain opens for ski season. Then they come back, but we don't see them like we do in the summer; they're bundled up, too cold to talk, on their way to or from the hill or to and from the steakhouse downtown. They'll order their potatoes mashed, not baked, and return to their cabins for long nights of board games by the fire. If they run into us at Grainey's, we'll all pretend not to recognize one another, and they'll get their lattes to go. Once ski season is over, they won't be back until Memorial Day. They'll recognize us then. We'll welcome them with open arms, our faces contorted with something like pleasure. Because we need them.

What are the other two seasons like? Fall is loneliness and chill. Spring is mud.

So here's the ironic thing about Gold Fork. Even though we've lived here our whole lives, know back roads and hidden hot springs like they're our own, Gold Fork belongs to the Weekenders, not us. Because they'll keep coming back, weekend after weekend, summer after summer, for their whole lives. And we won't. Once we get out—if we get out—we're never coming back.

DAVIS

Erik's throwing rocks.

We've been hanging at the Den more often in the week since school let out. I mean, we were already the only ones to come here ("What's the point of a place like that if no one's going to use it?" asked Georgie the first time she suggested we all meet there after the chapel fire), but now, with the Nelson place on top of it all, it just feels more urgent.

"Burn, baby, burn." Erik stretches his legs out in front of him on the deck, leaning back. He lofts a rock in the direction of the lake. This one goes so far that I don't even hear it hit the water. "Good thing the Nelsons were in the city." He exhales, and a cloud of gray smoke dances out of his mouth and then stalls for one long second before disappearing. Erik passes the joint to Georgie. "Else they'd be toast points by now."

He laughs, and I shrug when Ana catches my eye. It *is* funny, in a way: We all know about the time Mrs. Nelson tried to order "toast points" at the Pancake Parlor. Wouldn't take no for an answer. So Erik's joke is good, I guess. But that's the thing about Erik: All his jokes have a tiny chicken bone hidden in the middle, just waiting to get stuck in your throat.

What I mean is, he's nice, but he's not always kind.

Who cares about kindness? That's what Jane would say.

Jane.

25

"What are the odds that the same place would burn twice?" asks Georgie. Her voice comes low from the back of her throat while she holds in the smoke.

Ana pulls a sweater over her long-sleeved shirt, and I see the wink of the silver scar on her left arm as she raises it over her head to tug it on. "Can we not talk about it?" she asks. "It's not exactly my favorite memory."

"Apologies in advance, Ana," says Georgie, exhaling, "but I think we're going to have to talk about it sometime. Davis has to write a fucking article about it for the newspaper. Isn't that what you told me, Davis?" She jiggles her leg and looks around. She's been nervous since we got here. Jittery. Really, she's been in a bad mood since I told her about the Nelson cabin burning down.

I'm sitting on the ground between her and Erik. Georgie passes the joint to me and I inhale. *Please don't cough. Please don't cough.* I nod. Exhale. Swallow. "Dan says it's too good to pass, and believe me, I tried. Two fires on the same site. Two years apart to the day." I try to shrug, but it looks like a tremor. "Too good to be true, if you're an editor."

"Great," says Ana, frowning. She catches my eye, and for a moment I'm back there, staring into the flames and calling her name. *Ana! Ana!*

I blink, and the memory's gone.

"What bullshit. It's not like anyone died," says Erik. But I see him glance at Ana quickly and look away again. "And besides," he adds, "there's no connection between the two.

26

The Nelson fire was probably just wiring. All that money, and they screwed up the electric."

"Let's hope so," says Georgie, and she squints her eyes and shakes her head like she knows something. And why not? She knows people. If anyone's going to hear something about the cabin fire, it's Georgie.

We all look again across the lake. At its base, Washer's Landing is gravel, sand, boulders, some nice ten-foot platforms perfect for a dramatic leap into the water. The cliffs get higher as you climb, though—there are places to jump from fifteen and twenty feet up. Above those, the thirty-five and forty-foot cliffs that no one would ever leap off of. And way above those, the skeletal, charred remains of the Nelson cabin. It's still midafternoon, and the cabin site above Washer's Landing seems lit up, its emptiness glaring. It was empty like that before, too, when the Nelsons bought the land from the town. Scarred and haunted by the ghost of what we did. But the Nelsons didn't care. They just wanted a good view of the lake. And a recently torched plot of land gave them that. Now it seems the ghost has spoken.

I look at each of them: Erik, staring across at Washer's Landing; Ana, hugging her knees; Georgie, pinching the joint between her fingers like she's trying to crush the memory of it all. "I have to interview Chrissy," I say. "For the article."

"Shit," says Georgie. Ana looks away.

"Why put her through that?" says Erik, turning toward me. "There's no connection. We're all just trying to create a

27

story here that doesn't exist." His eyes are dark. I watch as he curls one hand into a fist, his whole arm tensing.

I blink.

A second passes, and then he blinks back at me, expression flat as plywood.

"I heard she's going to State," says Ana. "She graduated this year, right?"

"Right," I say.

"It's always a surprise, isn't it?" says Georgie. "Realizing who's getting out. Chrissy Nolls—going to college. She must have flown under the radar all year, you know? Plotting her escape."

I nod. I don't have to say it. We're all thinking the same thing. From what we've heard, Chrissy Nolls never spoke in class. She never raised her hand. For all anyone knew, she could have been failing every subject. But here she was this whole time, getting ready to go.

"Well, good for her, anyway," says Georgie. "It's not like graduation changes anything for most people." Inhale. Long pause. Exhale. She holds the joint out to Ana, who shakes her head. "For, like, two-thirds of our class, graduation is basically just the end of one boring routine and the start of another." A dainty cough. I can see that her eyeliner, usually so meticulously applied, is a little smudged below her right eye.

"Hey," I say. "You kind of look like Rocky." And then—oh shit—I start laughing, which of course means I start coughing, which naturally means I look like a first-timer. Again.

Leave it to me to break a moment.

Georgie closes her eyes. She's probably reciting some catechism. Not that my mom's church prides itself on forcing its youth to recite Bible verses or anything—it may be a dog and pony show, but it's not *that kind* of dog and pony show—but we do have a few tried and true platitudes under our belts from our years of halfway paying attention in youth group. Like I said, it never hurts to cover your bases. So that's probably what Georgie's doing, reminding herself to love her neighbor, or that he who doeth something getteth something else. Verily, verily. Life is but a dream.

Whenever I get high, you see, holy wisdom starts to sound a lot like nursery rhymes. And that, too, maketh me laugh. And that, too, maketh me cough.

"You're such a virgin," Georgie says, rolling her eyes, and she's right on more counts than I'd like. "No more for you." And she takes one last drag and crushes the joint against the sole of her sneaker before dropping it in an empty Coke can that she pulls out of her backpack.

We don't ask her where she gets it, and she'll never tell. But even a dealer's got a dealer, and sometimes I wonder whether it's worth it—if this is really the job she wants. I'd never say that to her, though. You just don't ask Georgie those kinds of things.

"Shit." Erik looks at his watch. "Gotta go. It's almost six."

"Date with one of your adoring fans, All-State?" asks Georgie. She leans, elbowing him in the ribs. He leans toward her, too, and grabs her arm.

29

"No," he says, "just the Beast." Then he lets go of her and adds, "Can we quit it with the 'All-State' crap?"

"All-State," says Georgie. "All-State, All-State, All-State." Another elbow in his side, this jab a bit sharper than the first. "You have to let us be proud of you, son."

It's kind of amazing, actually. I've never seen the guy crack open a book, and yet here he is, college paid for in another year, and all he has to do is move his feet.

"I've told you," Erik says, voice suddenly tense, "it's not some big-deal state award. It's just some rando throwing money around, wanting to look good. Can we drop it?"

Even when he's annoyed, Erik looks like he belongs on a promotional poster for this town. *Adventure Awaits!* Something like that. We've all been hanging out for a couple of years, and I have yet to see him fail. At anything.

Cue the tiny violins.

"Okay," says Georgie, raising her hands. "Okay." Then she looks at each of us. "But what about you guys? Are you prepared for the onslaught? 'Double-shot skinny latte, no whip, extra caramel, hold the straw, spin it into gold, please.'"

I have to admit, she does a pretty good impression of a Weekender ordering at Grainey's.

"By this weekend, they'll all be here," Georgie continues. "So just remember: *That*"—she points directly at Washer's Landing across the lake—"is what we take to the fucking grave." She narrows her eyes at each of us, pausing on Erik. "Got it?"

30

Erik salutes her, but his eyes are serious. "Yes, Captain."

Georgie exhales. She turns and glares once more at Washer's Landing. Like she blames the land itself for what we did to it. Then she takes her aviators off her forehead and places them squarely on her face. "Okay, team. Disperse." She nods at me. "You first, Davis."

I make my way around the deck to the front of the cabin. From here, the driveway winds up and over a little incline before dropping back down to the lake road. Per tradition, I get all the way to the top of the incline, where there's a huge wrought-iron gate, before Ana starts following. Our bikes are hidden in the bushes on the other side of the gate. All four of us can climb over it and be on our bikes and cruising along the road in two minutes flat. We've timed ourselves.

Before hoisting myself over the gate, I turn and look back at the Den. It never fails to amaze me. The cabin is bigger than a grocery store, almost as big as the Walmart that just popped up along the highway into town. (Walmart. Otherwise known as the first sign of the apocalypse.) There's a tennis court at one end. It's all perfectly notched logs, huge windows, rustic touches everywhere. And three stories high. At least. Because it's built on a slope, the lower level isn't visible from where I'm standing, but giant pines appear to be holding up the deck on the lakeside. It's old, nothing like the newer cabins that look like their log siding and stone chimneys have been painted on. Ana calls the Den an "exquisite relic." Erik calls it a throwback. Georgie calls us, and then we meet her here.

The Den, aka, the Michaelson estate. More than sixty acres of private land, much of it waterfront. Some out-buildings, some broken-down docks. And everything totally, utterly abandoned. Though of course that's ridiculous. There are always rumors of it being sold—of some big deal in the works—so someone has to own it. Right? Someone named . . . let me think . . . Michaelson?

Fact is, there's not another house on the lake that even comes close. And nothing else is as old. There was only one other building that came close to it in terms of historical significance—Gold Fork's prized possession—but we took care of that when we burned it down.

I grab the gate, swinging myself up and over. I'm on my bike in seconds, pulling out onto the lake road and waiting for Ana and the others to catch up. I grab my water bottle from its holster on the frame and take a slow swig. Anyone who drives by will think it's just a routine water break.

Ana gets there first. She pulls her bike alongside mine, checks the road behind us. Nothing.

I turn to her. "Hey. You going to Fellman's this weekend?"

"Probably not," she says. "You?"

"I guess." Then I add, "You should come. It's the right kind of trouble."

"I bet," she says. "I've never been."

I gasp, put on a cheerleader's voice. "But it's *the* event of the year! First weekend of summer, first time the Weekenders come back, last blast for the seniors. You, like, can't miss it. It's, like, so totally amazeballs."

She laughs. Ana's laugh is low and sultry, not what you'd expect from her. I'm always surprised by it. "Well then," she says, and leans over her handlebars, stretching her back. "I didn't know you went to those things, Davis."

I shrug. "Gotta keep in the game."

Another laugh. "Right."

I used to see Jane at the party. Every year for two years, I'd notice her as she hung out around the bonfire with her friends or set up a tent far enough back from the road that hers wouldn't be the first the police would check if they decided to do a sweep.

I'm sure she'll be at the party this year. And I'll be there too, watching her from my spot by the trees while I nurse a single beer all night long. Thinking to myself, *Well done, Davis. You're right back to where you started, ol' boy.* Thinking: *Your story's already played out.*

"Well," I say, "think about it. It'd be good to have backup."

She gives me a strange look. "Backup. Sure."

"Yeah," says Erik, who's caught up and is doing that balancing thing on his pedals that I've tried maybe four thousand times and never gotten right. "You should come, Ana." He winks. "You never know what might go down."

"Enough," Georgie hisses as she passes us all on her bike. "Don't fucking loiter."

We head toward town. Georgie, then Erik, then me. I glance back and see that Ana's catching up. She's got her head down and to the side like she always does, kind of a puppy-with-an-earache move, when a red pickup flies around the corner from the direction of the campground at the north end of the lake. The truck is basically driving on the side of the road. The driver lays on the horn and swerves, nearly clipping Ana's back wheel. Ana's head jerks up and there's a look on her face of pure terror. I catch a glimpse of the guy's face: pierced eyebrow, everything pockmarked and hollowed out, like a moldy orange. Then the truck's gone, just the sound of its busted muffler trailing after it.

I pull my bike over to the side and wait for her to catch up. "Shit," I say. "You okay?" I want to reach over, give her a hug, but that's not who we are to each other anymore.

"Sure," she says, but her voice is unsteady.

"That totally killed my high," says Erik. He and Georgie have turned around and come back. "What a maniac."

I look at Georgie. Her face is pale, her mouth open slightly. Her chin is quivering. She looks almost as scared as Ana did.

"Do you know that guy?" I ask.

"No." Then she clenches her jaw. "Watch your backs," she adds, and there's a bite to her voice.

We bike back into town together and then separate. I'm headed to work—we go to print later tonight—and I watch Ana when she turns onto the airport road (though calling it an airport is kind of like calling a Happy Meal a "refined dining experience"). She and her mom live out that way. I take a deep breath before turning toward work. Try to shake the unease from my shoulders. Try not to think about the truck, pummeling toward her. The panic I felt, and something else—something related to the chapel fire, and the fact that more was lost that night than we ever talk about.

I've had my job at the *Gold Fork Roundup* for a few months now, though "job" feels too presumptive for what I do. Is it a job if you only work ten hours a week? Is it a job if what you're really doing is taking the editor's ancient dog on slow walks down to the lake and back? Is it a job if you don't get paid?

Which is not to say I don't like it. I mean, sure, I wish I were actually writing articles. And yes, I read the Letters to the Editor page (also known as "The Forked Tongue") and think, *Water rights? Again?* But this little weekly newspaper is the last holdout in a world of corporate greed. It only runs ads for local businesses. And it's five pages long on a good week. I love it the way you love that crazy substitute teacher who made every class period, be it European History or English, about climate change.

And, if I'm being honest, Harvard won't know any of that when they see "Reporter, *Gold Fork Roundup*," on my application.

And, if I'm being *totally* honest—

If I'm being *totally* honest, there's always the chance it'll be me who cracks the case of Gold Fork's fire starter. Me who writes the article about what brought down the Nelson cabin and gets his picture on the front page. Me who runs into Jane at Toney's and says, *It was easy, once I knew what I was looking for.* Me who shrugs, like, *whatever*, when she says she's sorry, asks if I'm busy, do I want to get coffee. Me who agrees once I see the look on her face—desperate, scared she's lost me for good. Me who gets it all in the end, gets the girl, just like the movies.

But, you know, that's only if I'm being *totally* honest.

I don't see Dan when I walk into the "office"—the main room of a small blue cottage just off Main Street. I throw my backpack down next to my desk and pick up a hard copy of an article from a small stack of papers next to the computer. Dan's old-school in that way; he likes to see the copy edits in red pen before making changes on the computer.

"Davis." I get through half of the article before Dan calls me from his office. "Got something for you." I glace at the edits I've made to the article—PLEISTOCENE AT IT AGAIN—and head to his office.

It takes five steps. This is because it's the only other room in the tiny cottage. I think there's a bedroom hidden some-where around here, but then again, Dan might just sleep on his office couch. He certainly looks like he does.

He's there now, feet up, pillow behind his head, papers spread over his chest. Some of his hair is plastered to his forehead, but he doesn't seem to care. His dog, Bernstein, is curled on the rug, snoring softly.

"The intrepid reporter," Dan says. "What news, what news."

"Holding steady at copacetic," I say.

He nods. "Sage words." Pauses. "How's the article going?"

"Fine," I say. "I'll have it in by tomorrow. Not much to report, actually. You know: *There was a fire a couple years ago, yadda yadda.*" I'm hoping he'll see just how boring it is and tell me to drop it—but no.

"Great," he says. "Make sure to highlight the lack of evidence. Make sure to stress that it's still an ongoing investigation."

I shift on my feet, trying to ignore the way my breath is caught in my throat. *Ongoing investigation.*

Nodding again, as though I answered him, he says, "Got a job for you."

"Great." I exhale. Dropping your rent check in the mail? Picking up a pack of hot dogs for your dinner? Or . . .

"Need you to check out a lead."

I lean forward, trying not to look too eager. "Sure," I say. "What kind of lead?" I'm thinking arson, thinking a trip out to the Nelson cabin, or what's left of it. Fingerprints in the ash. That sort of thing. A clue no one else sees. From there: article, picture in the paper, Jane. The romantic ending, filmed in sepia tones. I'd like to thank the Academy.

"Concerned citizen—wishes to remain anonymous"—

here he lowers his chin toward me so I know he's serious—"e-mailed to let me know that Toney's might start carrying organic chicken next month." He looks on steadily.

"Oh."

"So, I need you to snoop around, see what you can find out."

I laugh before I realize he's serious. "Sure," I say. "Okay."

"Could just be a rumor."

"Or it could be Toney's, trying to get free press without having to pay for an ad."

He looks surprised. "Huh. You think?" He runs a hand over his cheek.

I start to say more and change my mind. "I'll follow up on it," I say, in what I hope is a decisive and resolute way.

"Good, good." He's already waving me out. "Don't want to let any grass grow under this one."

I grab my reporter's notebook (empty, sure, but I'm ever the optimist) and head out. Text the others because they'll love how ridiculous it is. Ana writes back immediately: *Stop the presses!*

The whole thing takes about five minutes. I'm ushered back to the manager so quickly that it's almost like the people at Toney's were expecting me. They even have a sample of the new organic chicken for me to take back to Dan, but I refuse. "We don't accept free products," I say, trying to sound authentically professional.

I'm walking by the egg display when someone stops me.

"Sorry, do you work here?" It's a guy my dad's age. He's tanned and kind of leathery in that Weekender parent kind of way. Like maybe he has a bumper sticker that reads, MY OTHER CAR IS A SAILBOAT. He's holding on to a package of organic eggs, and he smiles at me and asks in a too-loud voice, almost like he expects me not to understand, "Do you know if these are from grain-free chickens?" He chuckles. "Sorry. I'm under strict orders from the ball and chain."

I know I must look as stupid as he thinks I am, because it takes me a minute to answer. I'm just staring at his face, trying to place it.

"Pretty much all chickens are raised on a paleo diet," I say, and then—

Then I remember where I've seen him before.

See, that's the thing about working at a newspaper this small. With nothing else going on, your editor might ask you to start going through old microfiche from the Stone Age and scanning articles, transferring those ancient newspaper editions to the website for easy archiving. And, while you probably won't read all the articles, you might read some, especially if your friend is mentioned. You might see, for instance, a photo from the Ice Carnival sixteen years ago, the caption describing how one family—mom, dad, newborn baby—were celebrating.

He's lost the beanie cap and mustache, but I swear to God it's him.

"Thanks," he says, and moves toward the cash register at the front of the store, eggs in hand.

If I were a real reporter, I'd follow him. Get him to talk some more, ask a few polite questions. At the very least, I'd see if he's with anyone, follow him to his car, write down his license plate number. *Something.*

But I'm not a real reporter.

Instead, I get out of the store as fast as possible. Make eye contact with no one. Maybe I'm wrong. I hope I am. Because I don't want to be the one to report to Erik that I think I just saw his dad, a guy who's been MIA for a decade at least, buying free-range eggs at Toney's like it's nothing.

WHERE YOU ALWAYS KNOW YOUR PLACE

We call ourselves the Dead Enders. What matters in Gold Fork—what's always mattered—is that you know your place and, more importantly, that you can classify others with just a few simple questions. This is crucial. No one wants to mistake a Dockside with a Toney. Would you confuse an astronaut with a janitor? Didn't think so.

If we were teaching a class on this subject, we'd start out by explaining that the first group, Genus Weekendus, got its classification not because it arrives on the weekend, but because, to those of its kind, every damn day of the summer is Saturday. This genus has a variety of species. Put down your beakers, we'd say. Shit's about to get real.

GENUS WEEKENDUS: THE SPECIES LIST

Docksides.

Those whose parents own one of the stately homes on the lake. Identifying characteristics include: a penchant for nautical stripes; a body that is already impossibly tan by the first hot day of the season; the ability to procure unlimited supplies of beer and gin; its own mode of transportation, which may or may not be referred to as the "camp wheels" (something with four-wheel drive and decals from various ski hills on the bumper that spends the off-season locked in its lake home's double garage); all the right water toys—stand-up paddleboards and Jet Skis and sailboats—and a way of looking like it was born knowing how to use them; perfect cheekbones; perfect hair; a perfect life. This species will be generous with the other members of its genus, hosting parties when its parents aren't home and taking those without on boat rides in the middle of the night where it'll blast music from a playlist that it created for Just This Moment. It will announce itself by saying something like "God, it's

43

so good to be back," stretching its arms out wide as though taking in all of the trees, the town, the lake itself. Its parents will announce themselves by looking around, smiling, and then, pulling the case of wine that they've lugged all the way from the city from the back of their Suburban, add, "But it could really use a decent wine bar."

Weeklies.

Similar to the Docksides with one glaring exception: Its parents don't own their cabin on the lake. They rent one, usually the same one every year, for a period of no less than one and no more than eight weeks. You will know a Weekly by the way it avoids telling you this. It will say things like, "My dad just wasn't able to take any more time off this year," or, "Let's meet at your place. Mine's a mess," or, "We were planning on replacing the dock, but you know . . . Why?" and you'll think, Weekly. Have pity on it, for its shame is greater than all other species'.

Toneys.

The lowest of the genus, marked by its ancestors' inability to procure one of the homes on the lake. Poor planning? Oversight? Or the hushed Financial Considerations? Whatever the reason, this species must weekend in town, usually in one of the nicer log homes in the neighborhood between Toney's Market and the lake. It, too, will wear nautical stripes and boat shoes, but will do so ironically, for it has no boat—or, if it does, the vessel must be launched from the humiliating public dock. For this reason, Toneys are early risers. You might see a Toney as early as six a.m., wrestling with the hitch

44

between its parents' pickup and the boat, legs submerged in the icy morning waters of the lake where the ramp descends at a gentle angle. A Toney usually has an older brother who is just this side of a fuck-up and who might spend a whole summer in Gold Fork waiting tables at the Burger Mill while he tries to get laid and thinks about dropping out of state college because what's the point? What's the goddamn point? He will be happy to buy you beer or anything else, really, and will stand around at Dockside parties looking like an early sketch of a pedophile. Toneys often suffer from one of the more embarrassing afflictions to attack Genus Weekendus, which is as easy to spot as smallpox: They start to believe that they are Dead Enders.

And this brings us to the other genus. Our genus, of which there is only one species. Who we are, for better or worse. Who we can never not be:

Dead Enders.

Have-Nots. Never-Wills. Do-Nothings. Go-Nowheres. Dead Enders don't summer. They don't weekend. They spend their summer vacation at home, wearing last year's swimsuits, last year's shorts. They're not all poor—a few of them may even live on the lake full-time, lending them an uncomfortable Dockside/Dead Ender status—but for them, summer in Gold Fork is another hot summer at home. And why would you buy a new suit for that?

We didn't come up with the name, obviously. That honor goes to a Weekender mother who was talking too loudly on her cell while she waited for her progeny to get their lattes at Grainey's. "I just can't even," she said. "I mean, it's heartbreaking to see. These kids here, the year-rounders. They're just . . ."—and we held our breath, knowing that whatever she said next would be ours, that we'd take it and use it like a weapon, like a weapon we chose—"on a dead-end street."

That's the thing with Weekenders: They're always giving us gifts, whether they know it or not.

But.

Dead Enders know things about Gold Fork that Genus Weekendus never will. They know how to get to the cliffs by Washer's Landing without using the main road; where to find mushrooms (of both salad topping and hallucinogenic varieties) the year after a forest fire; why the high school is painted that gaudy orange; why Grainey's espresso is better on Tuesday than Sunday. Trivial things that nevertheless mean you live somewhere. You're not just a visitor. You may hate it here eight months a year, may be planning on leaving and never looking back (except, we whisper to ourselves, low enough so no one else hears, maybe on the weekends), but at least you know it. And that's something, right?

ANA

My life began, like most things worth noting, with a fable. A girl, pregnant at seventeen, ten fifty-dollar bills clipped to the inside of her blouse, boards a bus for Portland. She has a family to speak of, but no family to speak *to*, which in some ways is worse. A quick glance behind her as she climbs on the bus, but there's no one in the waiting room of the station, no one running in, leaving the Mercedes idling at the curb, with a last-minute offer of forgiveness or home.

She's sweating already, and it's only going to get hotter.

On the bus: two college students from Walla Walla, heading down for a weekend of gambling. A migrant worker from one of the onion fields. Three old ladies, not sitting together—one with knitting, one with a Tupperware of prunes, one with nothing but her hands in her lap, twisting like eels. An army medic, on leave for a week. And one scared seventeen-year-old, trying not to cry as the bus rolls south out of Pasco, hoping that the contractions that started this morning will let up until she reaches Portland.

But of course, they don't.

The rest of the story is just what you'd expect. The bus driver, who's been wearing headphones even though it's illegal, finally hears her deep, animal moans about thirty miles from The Dalles, Oregon. Scared that there's another schizoid on his bus, maybe with a knife, he swings into the nearest rest stop, a wide parking lot on a cliff overlooking the Columbia

River. By now, the contractions are so close together that the girl thinks her body is about to rip in half. The medic, just a young guy, on his way to his first tour of duty, does what any good soldier would do: He washes his hands in the bus's cramped bathroom with a bottle of water and some hand sanitizer, nods at the young girl, and, without another word, reaches up inside of her to feel the baby. But he doesn't have far to reach, because the baby is coming out, fast and slippery.

The bus driver is already on his radio, calling for an ambulance, when the medic says, "The cord is wrapped twice around its throat."

The delivery is a miracle, the doctors say later. How the medic was able to bring that baby into the world and unwind the cord in the process—a miracle. But the fact remains that when the baby is out, five minutes later, her throat is free from the rope that threatened to pull her under, anchor her inside her mother's body.

The college students cheer, though their faces blanch at the metallic scent of blood and body that has filled the bus. The onion worker speaks quickly in the new mother's first language, offering up a rapid-fire prayer. The first old woman holds up her knitting: a tiny hat. The second old woman holds out a prune to the girl, who takes it. The third woman doesn't react at all. Her hands keep twisting, twisting, twisting.

It's the making of a country song. And it's easy to want to take something away from the story of my birth. A message, perhaps, about surviving against the odds. That's the way my mother's presented it all these years. "You fought your way here," she says. "I knew you'd always work hard for what you wanted."

Here's what I take away from it: My entrance to the world was a series of lucky coincidences. If the army medic hadn't been there, if my mother hadn't screamed so loud that the bus driver heard her through the Led Zeppelin playing on his headphones, if she'd hitchhiked, like she'd planned, I might not have made it. Everything about my birth comes down to luck.

Dumb luck.

When I get home from the Den, it's late afternoon. I don't see Mom. She's probably still at work. Some resort towns have more spas than restaurants, but Gold Fork's not like that. It only has one spa, located on the top floor of our town's tallest building—the Gold Fork Grand Hotel. Six stories up, you can sit in one of the Adirondack chairs around the glassed-in four-season pool and look out over the lake all the way to the mountains at the northern end and, beyond them, the jagged charcoal line of even larger peaks. When I was younger, they used to let Mom bring me with her on days she couldn't find childcare. She'd set me up in one of the massage rooms with some colored pencils and paper and a monogrammed towel to sit on—THE HARBOR SPA—and she'd come check on me every ninety minutes, between customers. I loved the smell of those rooms, jasmine and lavender and other essential oils staining the cuffs of my shirt when I reached into the little pots that each masseuse kept lined up neatly next to the extra stack of towels.

She works odd hours, sometimes not going in until noon, sometimes staying as late as ten. Wedding parties and national holidays are the worst. Last weekend, for example. Memorial Day. I haven't seen her since.

"Remind me never to book back-to-backs on Memorial Day afternoon," she says, surprising me by padding through the kitchen in her slippers. She looks hungover, but I know it's just fatigue. "Coffee?"

"I'll put it on," I say, moving to the pot by the stove. My stomach is rumbling, but I know better than to ask about dinner. I'll just make some noodles later. "I didn't think you were home."

"Been sleeping since noon." She sits at the table and rubs at her eyes. Her skin, darker than mine, looks worn and dull. Neither of us says much until the coffee's ready. I pour each of us a cup and sit next to her. "Thanks, mija." After she takes a sip, she puts the cup down and rests her forehead in her hands. "God. I was just about to walk out at six yesterday when we get a call from one of the rooms. Woman in town with her husband for some weeklong corporate retreat wants an eight p.m. massage. Carl looks at me—I'm the only one left at that point—and says I'll do it. He's on the phone with that woman and agreeing for me and I'm standing right there, shaking my head no. Can you believe that crap?"

I make all the right noises, but the truth is, yes. Yes I can believe that Carl, the slimy spa manager, would sign Mom up for more work when she's been putting in ten-hour days all weekend long. Because that's what he always does. But Mom will never quit. Why would she? Working at the Harbor Spa is one of the best gigs in town, as she likes to say. And, as she also likes to point out, it keeps a roof over our heads.

Some roof, I like to say in return.

Mom's still complaining about work. "I mean, the nerve."

"Yeah," I say.

She narrows her eyes at me. "You're not even listening." Then she smiles. "I guess I don't blame you." She stands and shuffles over to the pantry cupboard, opening it and peering inside at the ramen, cans of tomato sauce, boxes of off-brand mac and cheese that we brought back from Walmart's grand opening last week. She sighs and shuts the cupboard door. "I'm not that hungry," she says. "You?"

I shrug. "I'll get something later."

"Oh. Well, okay. If you say so."

Sometimes I think about telling her that she's a bad actor, that she's never been able to hide her relief whenever I say I'll take care of things. But what good would that do? She'd just feel bad. And I'd just continue to make dinner, do the shopping, make sure the apartment's all locked up before bed on the nights she works late. We each have our roles, as scripted as a fairy tale. Only this one doesn't have a magical godmother who fixes things with a wave of her wand. There's only me.

"You visit Vera today?" asks Mom, sitting back down.

I nod. Then, before she asks, I say, "The same. She doesn't remember."

I tried again today. Before I headed to the Den, I went to the Royal Pines Home for Assisted Living and Skilled Care. I usually go on Wednesdays and Fridays because that's what Abigail and I agreed on when she hired me, but lately I've been visiting more often. Vera had what the doctors called a "mini-stroke" last month, and even though she seems fine, I've been worried.

And besides, I'm trying to find her daughter, and Vera's the only one who can help me.

Vera is a lovely woman, even at ninety-two. She reminds me of French linens in a bed-and-breakfast—the kind with a canopy bed, a little tea set on a tiny round table. She's always wearing something pressed and tailored, like a filmy dress or a white blouse. She exudes care and wealth and manners. But the pictures from her younger days are just stunning. Someone (probably a nurse) has tacked a whole bunch of photos up on a bulletin board by her sink and mirror, and I like to ask her to identify the people in them. She can always identify herself, though she sometimes struggles with her daughters.

"Grand Canyon!" she said today, pointing to a black-and-white photo of herself on the edge of a cliff. "Lewis took me for our honeymoon."

"You're so beautiful," I said, like I always do. "You look

like royalty." And she did. She was a tall woman, perfect cheekbones, perfect hair.

"They called me Princess Grace," she said, "because I looked like Grace Kelly."

"I bet they did," I said. I took down another photo. "What about this one?"

The photo had the kind of orangey tint that pictures from the seventies tend to have. Vera, gorgeous in a summer dress, was sitting outside, one ankle crossed over the other. She was flanked by her young daughters, who stood behind their mother, a hand on each shoulder. I've seen this photo countless times, but I'm always shocked and mesmerized to see that one daughter is prettier than the other. Remarkably so. One girl is tall and thin, the spitting image of her mother, and the other is shorter, almost egg-shaped. She has dishwater-brown hair, not the lustrous mahogany of her mother and sister. Her smile in the photo is in the process of turning back.

"So this is Kathryn," I said, pointing to the tall one, "and that's Abigail."

Vera nodded slowly. "My daughters?" she asked.

We were two archeologists, sifting through the rubble. Making guesses. Naming bones.

"I think so." I pointed again to Kathryn, the tall one. "Does Kathryn live nearby?"

"Who?" she said. Her cloudy eyes focused on the egg-shaped daughter. "Abigail never was a beauty," she said.

I was shocked at how flat her voice was, like she was

stating an uncomfortable but necessary fact, like: *The toilet upstairs is clogged,* or *You're going to have to get a bigger bra size.*

"Oh," I said. "You know, I . . ."

"Who's that?" Vera pointed to the bulletin board.

"Where?" I looked at the pictures, touching each one lightly until she said, "Yes. There. Who's that?"

The picture was more recent—probably from the early or midnineties. Vera, seated, was holding a baby on her lap. Abigail, the egg-shaped daughter, was standing next to her with the same smile she'd had twenty years before.

"My baby!" said Vera, stretching a shivering finger toward the infant in the photo.

"Isn't that Abigail's baby?" I asked. "Isn't this when she brought her son to Seattle to visit you? And you and Abigail"—I tapped the photo—"had lunch together at that French restaurant?"

"I suppose it was," Vera said, doubt creeping into her voice. "Yes," she said more forcefully. "It was. But who is that?" she asked, pointing to the baby.

"I think you told me once that's Abigail's little boy," I said. "Your grandson." I nodded and smiled, encouraging her to claim this fact as her own. She's never been able to remember his name, and I've learned to stop asking her to try.

"He is," she said, nodding back at me. "That's right. He's . . ." She peered at the photo. "Oh, he must be around one and a half now." She looked again. "No, that's not right." She glanced up at me. "He's at least two."

I let her have it. What would it matter if she knew he's probably my age by now, if not in his twenties? Why remind her, even for a fleeting second, that she's as alone in this world as a person can be? More alone, in fact, than someone who never had a family. Because she had one—has one—and it's what the word "has" implies, and the pages and pages of blank spaces next to her name in the visitors' log, that makes Vera the loneliest woman at the Royal Pines.

"If she can just remember," I say to my mom now, "I can get in touch with Kathryn. I mean, Abigail made it clear she doesn't want to have anything to do with Vera—aside from paying me to sit with her—so it has to be Kathryn."

"If Kathryn hasn't come back to see her mother yet, it's possible she doesn't want to be found," says my mom.

"Maybe," I say, "but maybe she lives in another country. Or maybe she and Abigail had a fight, and she doesn't know where Vera is." It probably sounds far-fetched, but I don't care. "Vera knows where she is," I say. "I know she does. She just has to remember."

My mom smiles, shaking her head. "It's a fool's errand, mija. She doesn't even know what year it is."

"I know," I say. "But what else am I going to do?"

"Just enjoy your time together." She takes a sip of coffee. She doesn't look at me when she says, "Don't try to force family where it doesn't belong."

In some ways, I know, my mom will always be that girl on

55

the bus as it pulls away from the station, craning her neck to see if anyone is running in, breathless, to stop her. I've never met my grandparents, and never will. When my mom got on that Greyhound, she left behind a house that would make most of the cabins on the lake look shabby, a nice car, the promise of college, anything she'd ever want. She left it to have me, the product of a hookup with a rodeo cowboy who was offensive to her proud Mexican-American parents for both his profession and his anonymity. She could have everything, my grandparents made clear, as long as she put me up for adoption. *You're my best reason,* my mom tells me, over and over, and I try not to hear the pain behind the words. *We're all the family we need.*

But here's what she doesn't say. I'm the reason we live in an apartment building that was built in the sixties, all dark wood paneling and linoleum floors. I'm the reason we don't have a dishwasher, cable, dinners out, and *hey, let's order dessert.* I'm the reason there's a gray patch over my bed where the ceiling's been leaking for years. I'm the reason I sometimes hear her crying softly in her room after a long day at the spa, her door shut because she doesn't want me to know how much she misses the two people who should never have rejected her.

Who should never have rejected me.

Still.

Maybe it doesn't have to be that way for Vera. If I can return one of Vera's children to her, maybe she doesn't have to feel abandoned at the end of her life. Abigail's a lost cause—she's never been anything but a disembodied voice on the phone, hashing out how she'll pay me via direct deposit, and when. But Kathryn—wherever she is—lovely, sweet, oh she just has to be, the look on her face in that photo like she's delighted, like she'd do anything for her mother—Kathryn is the one I want to find.

"Hey. How're your friends?" Mom reaches across the table and ruffles my hair. "Been a while since we've checked in with each other."

"They're fine." I pause, thinking about this afternoon on the deck. The feeling I've had since Davis told us about the Nelson cabin, like there's something linking the fires that we can't see yet.

"Any romance?"

"Romance. Nice try." I close my eyes briefly. I've almost forgotten the truck that almost ran me down. The way Davis leaned toward me like he might hug me. How much I wanted him to do it. How he didn't.

"Who's that good-looking one? The town track star."

"Erik."

"Yeah," my mom says slowly. "What about him?"

I give her the same answer I always do. "Not a contender," I say. "I mean, like, seriously."

"Okay, okay." She raises her hands in mock surrender. "Sue me for being interested."

I know what she wants. She's so excited that I have

friends to tell her about that she wants even more. We don't get much time together, and she wants me to give her the whole package: drama, intrigue, a love story.

And I can't give her a love story—the chapel fire took care of that. Davis hasn't looked at me the same way since. But I do allow myself a half second of quiet pride. Friends. My friends. They may not be what I imagined, all those lonely days of junior high when I would go from apartment to school to apartment in one long, uninterrupted feedback loop, but, besides Vera, they're all I've got. And every Tuesday, rain or shine, we meet at the Den. On that redwood deck, the four of us shed our high school personas like starched uniforms and gather together to smoke and talk until the real world calls us back.

Still.

Our friendship was no accident. Or rather, it kind of was. We knew one another from the church youth group, but not well. And then one day a match was lit, and in the bright light of the flame, we saw only one another. We've been fused together ever since.

My mom's hand on my shoulder, shaking me out of my reverie. "Hey. That cabin fire, the one in the news. It must bring up some memories, mija." She pauses, then reaches down and touches my arm where the scar is. "We haven't talked about it in a while."

"There's nothing to talk about," I say. "I'm okay."

"You were hurt."

"I wasn't the only one." The whimpering, plaintive cry. Smaller sounds, too. And then the sound from Chrissy Nolls, smothered in her tent. I swallow.

"You couldn't have gotten them out. You'd have died trying." My mom's voice gets quiet. "You almost did."

That's all she knows—all any of them know. There was a fire. We happened to be outside—stargazing, we said—in time to notice. I went in after the cats. Chrissy's tent catching fire was a freak thing.

Still. Summer is a relief in one specific way: We don't have to see Chrissy at school every day. We hardly have to see her at all. And now that she's graduated? We can almost forget it ever happened.

Almost.

Mom's voice changes, becomes upbeat and cajoling. "How about you and I go to the Burger Mill? Extra order of crispy fries, split a huckleberry milkshake? I could eat, after all."

It's a treat, I know—something to make up for her long absences during the week. "Sure," I say, because I'm hungry, because I've missed her, and because I'd do anything to get away from the memory that flickers all around me. Heat. Smoke. The sound of Chrissy's screams. And always the pitiful, mewling cry. Fainter. Fainter. Gone. "I'll grab my sweater," I say, pulling it from the hook by the door and slipping it on. I glance at the silver scar that runs like a river from my wrist to my elbow, splitting my arm cleanly in half. Splitting it like a memory you can never escape: Before. And after.

The four of us weren't friends before the chapel fire. Not really. But after? We're tied together by that night in the chapel. We're tied together by our guilt. But more than that, we're tied by a friendship that emerged from the flames scarred, sooty, beaten-down, but stronger than anything any of us had before.

We don't make sense together. And that's its own kind of sense.

I know what everyone says about us—about all the kids in Gold Fork. We're Dead Enders. Hopeless. If we're headed in any direction at all, it sure isn't up. Davis makes fun of this. He says we'll be the ones asking burnt-out Weekenders for more cream in our coffee one day, that at least our skin won't be leathered by the tanning beds they go to all spring. He says the future is what you make of it, and then he laughs at himself because, what a dad.

And he's probably right. Davis is smarter than the rest of us combined. Probably smarter than all of Tri High. Georgie's got her business. Erik's got a full ride to the state university in a year. They're all going places. But me? I'm just waiting for the day when they leave me behind like a forgotten animal, trapped and crying for help that never comes. Like Vera, I'm not going anywhere.

I mean, just look at where I live.

I have a theory. I believe that we set what Vera would call our "unmentionables" as far away from ourselves as possible so that we don't have to claim them. That's why strip malls and bail bondsmen and prisons and trailer parks and ugly apartment complexes and old folks' homes lie on the outskirts of town, away from the nicer houses, the coffee shops—basically, civilization. I believe we secretly hope something will happen to the outskirts—tornado, tsunami— and we'll be freed of the unmentionables without having to answer for it. I believe we don't want to look at these places because we live in fear of someday finding ourselves living or working in one of them, and we want to imagine that, while this may happen to everyone else, it will never happen to us.

I'm lucky, I guess. In some ways, it's already happened to me.

WHERE THE SUMMER BEGINS

When the Weekenders come back in June, they come in stages. First, the retirees arrive in sedans, Oldsmobiles, RVs pulling their camp wheels. Next, the families with babies and toddlers, no one to pull out of school early, schedules that revolve around nothing but naps. Then the college students who are spending the summer at the cabin and who want to get here early enough to snag one of the few good gigs waiting tables at the steakhouse or pouring chardonnay at the Grand Hotel's lakefront bar. Most tend to forget why they arrived early, and by the time they remember that the whole point was employment, it's too late and they wouldn't want to mess up their own schedule of naps and eating, punctuated by lackadaisical swims from one end of the dock to the other. Finally, the weekend after school lets out across the state, the families roll in and we see everyone else.

They stop at Grainey's on their way into town for that first iced latte of the summer. We're there, of course, as we've been every afternoon since the last bell rang and we left our lockers hanging open to run down the halls toward the heavy double doors, papers flying everywhere. We headed to Grainey's that first after-noon, and we've been there ever since, waiting but not, if we're asked, waiting. Our eyes slide over them as they walk into Grainey's and pause next to the wire stands holding the *Gold Fork Roundup* and the free real estate magazine. They pretend to look up at the chalkboard behind the counter as though they don't know what they're going to order and maybe something's changed, anyway, since last summer, but nothing has. Nothing ever changes. And they order their iced latte again, this time with vanilla syrup but, they say, "Just a little bit, okay?" While they wait for Maria to make it, they look at their phone. Scroll down. Send a text. They lean into the counter with one hip and look better doing it than we ever have when we've tried leaning just like that at the end of summer. And we watch them without looking, our eyes trained on the horo-scope section of the *Roundup* or maybe on the big glass windows through which we can see across the street to the Grand Hotel but on which we can also see our own reflection and, just behind and to the side, the Weekenders, leaning.

We don't talk to them on the first day. We know that the first week of vacation is, to a Weekender's parents, sacrosanct. That, in order to earn what will surely be a summer of late nights on someone else's dock, the camp wheels borrowed and not returned until morning, they need to appease their parents for one intermi-nable week. Board games and dinners out, long talks about how the year went and whether soccer is really such a good option next season, what with their grades. What with the PSATs, the SATs, the IB exams, one hundred different ways to assess their potential.

The Weekenders are going places, and their parents won't let them forget it, not until that first week is over.

But finally, they let them go. Hand over the keys to the camp wheels and say, "Have a great night." Maybe: "Call if you're going to be late." And the Weekenders will call, those first few times, sneaking into the upstairs bedroom in someone else's cabin to use the landline or, if they're lucky, getting enough bars to call their parents from the edge of the driveway where their apologies (". . . so tired, think I'll stay at Mackenzie's/Blake's/Ryan's tonight.") can't be overheard by the people on the cabin porch who are, just now, debating the relative merits of keg stands. The first of a summer of lies both white and gray. Eventually, they'll stop calling with excuses. Eventually, their parents will stop expecting them to. And then the summer will really begin.

GEORGIE

I get invited to almost all the parties that the Weekenders throw.

Sure, some of them have their own connections in the city and bring what they need with them, but most don't. Maybe their parents have learned to check their bags before loading them into the back of the Suburban. Maybe it's laziness. I mean, they know I'm here. They might not have met me yet, but they've heard of me. And a business like mine relies quite heavily on word of mouth.

That's why, once everyone starts arriving for the summer, I'm the most popular Dead Ender in town. During the year, it's different. I don't go to as many parties. During the year, it's more of a job. During the summer, though, I can almost start to think of it as a hobby. Or, as my dad says when he sees me leaving for work tonight in my standard uniform of jeans and a T-shirt, "Ah. So every day is 'Casual Friday.'"

"Dad. It *is* Friday." I fold my jacket so that only the back is showing and lay it on the chair by the door before kneeling down to tie the laces of my combat boots.

He stops unloading the dishwasher and stands up straight. "Georgia, the way you present yourself equates to the way you wish to be respected." He looks me up and down. I watch him decide not to say the obvious thing. Instead, he says, "Remember to keep your eyes open. Anyone look suspicious, anyone acting strange . . ." It's a line from the police blotter, once news broke that the fire chief declared the Nelson cabin was definitely an act of arson. As though whoever burned it down is going to, I don't know, walk around in public, flipping lit matches onto the ground.

Light a fire in this town, and suddenly you're Charles Manson.

"I will," I say.

"Use your instincts," he says.

"Got it."

He looks up at the ceiling, thinking. "Your friend Davis— the one who works at the newspaper. He going to write about both fires?"

"Yeah," I say. "I think so."

"Good. He's a good writer." Dad glances at me. "You can invite your friends over, you know."

I shrug. "I know."

"I'd like to hear more about what he finds out."

And *that* is why I don't bring my friends over. I really don't need my dad, a born researcher if there ever was one, grilling Davis on the fire that was, until two weeks ago, the biggest news to hit Gold Fork in a decade. That chapel had been the first building erected in Gold Fork, back when it was settled. There were names etched into the pews from Dead Enders' great-great-grandparents. It was *the* wedding site in town; Weekenders reserved it two years in advance so that they could walk down the aisle in three-thousand-dollar dresses and have their reception out on the cliffs, everyone feeling rustic and content, feeling like they finally belonged here.

Oh yeah—and it was Davis's mom's church.

Dad turns to my mom, who's just walked in from the backyard. Her hands are dirty from pulling weeds in the garden. I see his frown of annoyance when he sees the dirt, but he tries to cover it. "Georgia's off to work again."

She smiles at me. "Have a good time with the kiddos." She doesn't look at my dad.

"You should charge overtime," my dad says, "for all the weekend nights they're asking you to work."

"Dennis," says my mom. "Stop. She wants to work, she can work."

He gives her a sharp look.

"I do charge overtime," I say, standing, my hand already on the doorknob as I grab my coat and fold it over my arm, careful not to crinkle the contents. Can't get out soon enough. "They're paying me well." And then, before we get into specifics, I'm out.

Gus and Dehlia, I remind myself as I shut the door behind me. What is it tonight? Right: parents going out for a romantic boat ride and then dinner in town. My nanny job's not the most inspired lie I've ever told, but it serves a couple of purposes. For one thing, it gets me out of the house from noon to six every day, not to mention the weekend nights when *hey, the Robinsons call, I haul.* For the past couple of years, my brother's stayed on to take summer classes at the state university, so I don't even have him to complain about our parents with. My job keeps me busy, and it keeps me away. But more importantly, it's setting the stage for the day in the not-too-distant future when I tell my parents that I'm dropping out of school and moving to the city and not to worry, I've got some savings.

"What price freedom?" The question is something of a joke between the four of us. We'll ask one another under our breath while we watch a Weekender haggling over the price of a pontoon rental at the marina, or when someone rolls down Main in a blacked-out Land Rover. "What price freedom?" we'll say, and then we'll laugh.

But I know the answer to that question: $8,920.30. That's exactly how much I figure I'll need to cover a month at a recording studio in the city, plus my third of whatever shithole the band and I can find to live in for three months. Three months is what I figure it'll take for me to find a job and start making enough to pay my bills. A new guitar would be nice, too, so I've factored in a Fender Jaguar and Big Muff effects pedal. Plus, you know, food and stuff.

That's the price of freedom. And, until the fire at the Nelsons' cabin, I had almost all of it.

It'll be a disappointment to my parents, I'm sure. *I'll* be a disappointment. But then, moving to the city with the band is a hell of a lot more impressive than what I'm doing now. And since all but one of the other members of the band just graduated, the only real option is for me to drop out of

70

school. It'll only be disappointing until they read about me in *Rolling Stone*.

Look. It's not like my parents ever imagined they'd be living in Gold Fork, working in jobs for which they're underpaid and overeducated. They didn't think they'd ever have to worry about being able to afford their kids' educations. But that's life for you. Dad doesn't get tenure and finds himself taking any high school teaching job in the state, any one at all, even when it turns out to be at— *gasp*—a junior high. Mom gets her nursing degree at night and starts looking for jobs at rural hospitals. And voila: Here we are in Gold Fork. As my dad has said, it's not what they wanted, but it's what they got. (Sometimes I think that's how they feel about their marriage, too.) Even with his swimming scholarship at State, my brother's still bled them dry. Which leaves me with nothing but the lot of the second-born: Think creatively.

I hop in Trusty Rusty—my beat-up old pickup that I bought with, you know, some nanny savings—and start the drive toward Fellman's Point, on the far side of the lake. And, just like clockwork, my chin starts to quiver.

It's been doing that more and more lately, usually right after I've met with Dodge. I don't feel like I'm going to cry or anything, but my chin starts quivering like an old lady's. For instance. It started shaking the second after he almost ran Ana down the other day.

And it started shaking when he slapped me.

71

Fucking Dodge.

I take one hand off the wheel and press it against my chin, willing it still.

I drive slowly through town, passing the hotel, the bars, the coffee shop, the mechanic on the corner who sometimes buys a teener because *you gotta keep in the game, right?* I begin to weave my way through the nicer neighborhoods on the other side of the lake, taking note of cabins I've visited, log homes whose doors are always open to me when the parents are gone. Cabins on streets with names that should embarrass you if you say them out loud: Meadow Larch Road, Sunrise Circle. Even—*Christ*—Turkey Lane.

Dodge likes to say that I'm a veritable yellow pages for the whole town of Gold Fork. Only, he doesn't say "veritable." His word of choice is more user-friendly.

It's been raining off and on for the past week. Not quite summer, even if the Weekenders *are* back. I drive out of town, following the lake road as the houses become larger and farther apart, hard to see in their nests of trees. (Davis was right when he said once that wealth is a kind of camouflage.) Eventually, even the cabins fall away as the road becomes dirt and I pass a couple of camps (the Boy Scouts, the Seventh Day Adventists) whose ramshackle buildings and threadbare flags stand out like broken thumbs. I pass a couple more big homes. The gated swath of land surrounding the Den. And then I'm on Forest Service land, the edge of the lake on my left lapping up against a wall of rock that separates the road from the water, dark woods on my right. If I turned in my seat now, I wouldn't even be able to see town. Farther ahead is the campground on the north side of the lake. But I turn off before that at Fellman's Point, taking a muddy fire road already cut deep with wheel tracks. I'm not the first one here.

The fire road curves away from the lake, ending about a quarter mile down in a wide meadow. I park next to a new Jeep. Next to it, a new BMW. How do I know they're new? Because each fleck of mud on their sides looks carefully painted by an artist for maximum effect. Trusty Rusty, on the other hand, doesn't look muddy at all—there's more of a general brownness from wheel to hood. There are about fifteen cars in all—early, still.

I get out of the truck, grab my jacket, and follow a trail down to the campground, where people are setting up tents in the trees and getting the bonfire going in a small clearing. I wave to a few Weekenders I know from last year. They're still in their urban woods attire: buffalo plaid shirts and designer jeans, Carharts that look too new, slouchy knit caps despite the fact that it's not that cold. Give 'em a week.

Erik's leaning over the bonfire with a long stick in his hand, but he straightens when he sees me and comes over. "Slim pickings." He puts his hand on my shoulder.

"Stick around," I say. "You know the ladies. They like to make you wait."

"You're here."

I rest my head on his shoulder for a second, then look up at him with a grin. "All business, no pleasure. You forget that I don't care about making you wait."

He shrugs. "Make me wait too long, I might not be here."

"A tragedy for all, I'm sure." And I take a small step back and swallow.

"You're something," he says, shaking his head. At least he doesn't look like he's modeling for an outdoor clothing catalog, though I note that he's in a flannel shirt too. If you can't beat 'em.

"Hey," I say, "you seen the others?"

"What? Davis and Ana? Have they ever come to this thing?" Erik laughs. "And what would Davis do here, anyway, besides write about it in his dream journal?"

"Something like that." It's Davis, a backpack slung over his shoulder.

"Where'd you come from?" Erik scowls, probably to hide his embarrassment at being overheard.

Davis jerks his thumb toward the trail leading to the cars. He looks at Erik strangely—almost sadly—for a minute, then blinks and smiles. "Or do you mean biologically?" He pauses. "You see, Erik, when a mommy and a daddy really love each other, they—"

"Oh my God." Erik punches Davis in the arm. It's playful... sort of. "These are not words I want to hear coming from your mouth."

"I may not be wise in all things, but . . ." Davis tries to sound confident, but it doesn't work. We know the truth. And, like the friends we are, we ignore it.

(Fun fact: Jane—infamous, heart-breaking Jane—is the only other member of my band who hasn't graduated yet. I know it, Davis knows it, and we never, ever talk about it. Because, what? He wants to hear how she's actually a pretty good drummer, all things considered? He wants to know when I've just come from practice and I saw her and she didn't ask about him? That she seems fine—good, even? Oh, *hell* no.)

"Kids," I say, "if you can't play nice, don't play at all."

Davis nods as Erik whines, "But, Mooooom."

I raise an eyebrow at Erik. "No after-school brownie for you." He tries to ruffle my hair, but I duck. "Keep it up," I say, "and you won't even get a carrot stick."

The place fills up as soon as the sun's gone down. There's a steady stream of headlights as the Weekenders and a few other Dead Enders arrive, blocking one another's cars in because there's no other way to do it. The unspoken rule is that no one parks anywhere near the lake road. The cops may know that we're out here, but we don't have to be assholes about it.

It gets cold, and I'm glad I brought my heavy motorcycle jacket, the one with all those useful little zippered pockets. I spend an hour or so working the party, greeting some of the Weekenders with nods, others with slaps on the back, a few hugs. Once it's dark enough, I start pulling little bags out of the jacket pockets, putting money into others, zipping them up.

God, I used to enjoy this.

Pills, teeners, caps, bumps. The pharmacist is in. Again.

And the night's just getting started. Some guy's brought speakers, and he hooks them up to his phone and leans them against a rock near the bonfire.

"Every year, just the same," I tell Erik. We're sitting back from the bonfire in the trees, having a smoke and squinting at the scene from the shadows. Pretty much everyone's here now, maybe fifty in all, and it's the time of the night when things start to get rowdy. I can see Davis and Ana, who got here late, sitting by some rocks closer to the fire. Someone turns the speakers up.

"I know," says Erik. He waves his hand toward a group of guys who are standing by the fire, a sea of plaid, denim, and perfect jawlines. He blows out a puff of smoke. The air around us is herbal and musty. "I mean, I'm pretty sure they don't listen to Neil Young all year long, but once they get to Gold Fork, man, it's 'Rust Never Sleeps' on repeat for the whole summer." He starts humming *"My My, Hey, Hey."* Then he turns to me. Sings, *"It's better to burn out than to fade away."* Even at this distance, the firelight paints hollow shadows on his cheeks. "That was in Cobain's suicide note, you know."

I know that—of course I do—but I say, "Watch it, All-State. You're starting to sound angsty."

76

"Don't call me that." His voice is brittle, and he closes his eyes and then opens them again. "Sorry."

"Touchy much? Here," I say, handing him the joint. "You finish. Clearly, you need it more than I do."

"Thanks." After he blows the smoke out again in a little puff, he says, "Tulsa."

"What?"

"I'm thinking Tulsa. Des Moines. Someplace like that."

He's playing Worst Case Scenario. Our little game. If you could get out, but the only place you could go was someplace worse, would you still go? Erik and I've been playing it ever since we burned down the chapel and getting out began to feel more necessary.

"No," I say. "Never."

"I'd do it," he says.

"You wouldn't. What, and be a mall walker? You'd go batshit crazy in a place like that," I say.

"Better to be bored crazy than just fucking nuts," he says, voice rough. He looks away.

I know who he's talking about, and I watch the side of Erik's face as he steadies himself. No. He doesn't want to talk about her. He never does. "Fair point," I say. "Well, you don't have long to worry. You're out of here in a year. I am too." I don't tell him that if I play my cards right, I'll be gone sooner than that.

"Hey," he says, smiling, "here's an idea. Why don't I come with you?"

"Yeah, right. To the city?"

"Sure," he says, and studies something on his shoe. His voice is too casual when he adds, "Could be fun."

I'm flustered by his tone, but I say, "Keep dreaming. I don't think your scholarship is transferable." I laugh. "Don't worry," I add, leaning over and resting my hand on his head, tapping twice. "I won't forget the little people when I'm famous. I'll still take selfies with you at my concerts."

"Asshole," he says, and looks away. When he turns back to me, he's smiling and loose, the old Erik.

I take the joint and rub it against the sole of my sneaker before slipping it into a pocket. "Well," I say, "that took the edge off."

The light from the bonfire flickers across his face, and I can see his eyes, rimmed red like a little mouse. I pull a bottle of Visine from my back pocket.

"Here," I say. "For your condition."

He laughs, tipping his head back and squeezing the drops into the corners of his eyes. When he looks back at me, a single tear trails down his cheek.

"Don't get all sentimental," I say.

He gives me the Visine and catches my hand, pulling me toward him. His eyes crinkle, and he bites his lip before whispering, "You bring it out of me."

For the briefest moment, we pause, foreheads touching. I feel myself sinking toward him, a forceful *yes* rising in my chest. A *yes* two years coming. Then I pull away. No. Not now.

Not when I'm so close to getting out. "Erik, dammit," I say, trying to keep it light. "You have me confused with someone else." This isn't how we are. It might be Erik's routine, but it's never been his routine with me.

"Georgie." He swallows. "You're ridiculously beautiful." He puts one hand on my cheek and tries to draw me in again.

I tip my head down. "And you're high," I say quietly. But I'm breathing fast, and I know I could just turn my face up an inch and give in, just this once. *Erik*, I remind myself. *This is Erik. It would cost too much.* I don't move.

There's a pause. Then he whispers, "What? You've never—" His voice is low and husky.

But I know him too well. I've seen him with the other girls. This is all part of his game.

"No," I say. "I never have." I let the lie rest between us for a minute. "Erik," I add, trying to catch my breath, "you're not ready for a girl like me." Never mind whether I'm ready for a guy like him. Sure, I love him, but I love him like you love the cousin who wrecked your uncle's car and shrugged when he told you about it. I have to love him at arm's length. Right?

So that's what I put between us. I push away from him and smile. "Besides," I say, just to smooth it over, "if we hook up, you'll have no one to complain about it with." And then I smile, a smile I didn't know I had in me. The smile says, *There'd be nothing to complain about.*

He rubs his hand over his cheek. Shakes his head, stands up, looks away. When he glances back at me, I'd swear he

79

looks sad, if I didn't know him better. But this is Erik, and he finally says, "I swear to God, Georgie, you are one tough bitch." His voice cracks a little, but I pretend not to have heard.

"Compliment accepted."

He's smiling, even though I can detect the faintest blush on his cheeks. It can't be every day that Erik gets turned down. "Well, all you have to do is let me know," he says.

"Noted." I'm trying—we're both trying—to sound normal.

"Day or night." He steps toward me. "Georgie, I—" He swallows. "Rain or shine."

"Got it. You're a man for all seasons." My voice sounds unfamiliar and loud.

He turns to head back to the fire.

"Hey," I say, and he wheels around. "You know Andrea?"

Erik nods. "Toney with a place near the bank?"

"Yeah. If you see her, will you send her over? There's something I gotta talk to her about."

Erik winks at me. "Sure." He turns back again. Says over his shoulder, so soft that I almost don't hear him: "Georgie, I—" I see him shake his head. "Sorry." Then he's gone.

For a minute, then, I'm alone in the trees. What just happened? The way Erik looked at me—

No. After all this time? Just when I'm about to break free from this place? When you see the light at the end of the tunnel, you have to ignore the hands that reach out to you from

80

the walls, grasping at the corner of your shirt, trying to pull you back. Does that sound heartless? Maybe it is. Or maybe it's easier to think of it that way, instead of considering what I'm missing. Those hands. His particular hands. Leaning in, pulling me close, doing the thing I've been thinking about for two years. Fuck the consequences.

No.

It would cost too much, with Erik. We know each other too well. Every summer, I allow myself a fling—some nice-enough Weekender who wants nothing more than I do and who doesn't want to know me or be known by me. That's what's safe. That's what works.

Erik and I wouldn't work, and he knows it. We'd go up in flames. So why did he try something now?

I shake my head and pull my knees up to my chin, letting myself sink into the music. With each drumbeat, I let go of what just happened until the music is all there is. No more Neil Young now. There's a heavy beat, insistent and repetitive, thrumming through the speakers. The party's on.

This town is shit for music. It's one of the most glaring divides between Weekenders and Dead Enders. You know exactly whose party it is as soon as you drive up and hear the music blasting from the deck. Weekenders are Neil Young before the party gets started, hip-hop once things are moving; Dead Enders are country all night long. And during the summer, all the restaurants with anything even resembling outside seating host live bands that always fall somewhere between folk and rockabilly. Usually it's a pair of sisters, or an orphan, or a family of banjo and tambourine players.

Never what I want to hear.

My music's different. There's rage in the music I like. Rage and grit. All the musicians sound like they eat sand. It's the most real sound there is. Broken Social Scene. Japandroids. Car Seat Headrest. And the older bands too: Neutral Milk Hotel. The Breeders. Nirvana, of course. *Those* are the people whose lives I want—not the Weekenders. And I was almost there. $8,920.30. I had eight thousand of it already—until the Nelson fire.

So now I'm starting over, kind of. After paying Dodge for the lost product, I've got $5,500 left.

But maybe I can still do it in one more summer. That's all I need, if I hustle. One more summer of my fake nanny job.

One more summer of Dodge.

Dodge. The classic example of what not to do. What happens when you stay in Gold Fork past its expiration date. I think at one point he was even the guy you might see up on the ski hill after the last chair has gone up, carving the final figure eights of the day into the mountainside, no poles, just arms. In one hand, a joint. Voice just this side of comatose.

And then he went away for a couple of years. To the city, I heard. And when he came back, he wasn't the kind of lovable, reckless stoner I remembered. He was hard. Flinty. Hung out in the alley behind Grainey's in that old jacket of his, those old scuffed boots. No more afternoons on the mountain. Different powder, now. Because when he came back, he had product. Better product. People started talking. So when he cornered me by the gas station and told me that my previous supplier was out of the business and it was time to step it up and could I fucking deal with that, I knew he could make things either really, really easy or really, really hard.

It was just a slap. That's what I keep telling myself. Dodge slapped me in the face when I asked about dialing it back a bit for the summer. *Summer's the best season. You don't dial anything back,* he said. Of course. So stupid of me to think I could just cut my hours, like I'm working at Walmart or something.

Just a slap. Right.

That's when I did the math. Figured out what I need to go. That's when waiting until graduation didn't seem so important anymore.

The others don't know about Dodge. I mean, they know there's someone—obviously there has to be—but they don't know who he is. They probably think my supplier is, like, my friend or something. But I've worked hard—really hard—to keep my business life and my social life separate. And Dodge is no friend of mine. Also? They don't know how close I am to leaving—how close I *was*—and they definitely don't know that Dodge is both my ticket to freedom and the chain around my ankle.

That's the thing about lies. Even the most authentic

friendship can be based on one. The trick is to bury that lie so deep that no amount of digging can ever touch it.

I scan the crowd: bodies leaning in and away, swaying, trying for a touch here and there. Everyone hoping for something. Am I the only one who knows they're not going to find it here?

God. That's what I should've told Erik. *You're not going to find it here.*

Or should I have—

No. Light at the end of the tunnel. Remember that.

I'm just about to stand up and look for Andrea myself when a guy kind of flops down next to me. He's tall and rangy, all legs and arms. Messy blond hair. Lip ring. Combat boots like mine, but they look somehow more authentic on him. Like he's had them for a decade, not half a year. College kid, maybe. I haven't seen him before.

"Whoa," I say. "Steady on."

He looks at me, turns on a smile. "Georgie, right?" He's got a beer in one hand, and he holds it out like an offering.

I can almost hear Davis in my head: *Ah, another supplicant.*

I nod, ignoring the beer. "That's me."

"Yeah, Jonas told me about you."

Jonas . . . Jonas . . . Oh, right. Goes to the university with my brother. Gets in touch when he's in town. Dime bags, mostly. Pretty typical.

"Sure," I say. "I know Jonas."

He looks relieved. "We know each other from school. He told me to find you."

84

The guy's staring at me, waiting, and I want to say, *Dude, there's no password.* But I say, "Yeah," instead, and stare right back. I know I could make it easy on him, but these little moments of awkwardness? Another perk of the profession. Plus, if I'm being totally honest, I don't mind the view.

Then he laughs—a quick bark—and claps me on the back. "You're good," he says. "Jonas said you're all right. So," he adds, "how 'bout a QP."

Jesus.

But the way he says it, drawing out the words, makes me think this is just a warm-up.

There's always the risk. The risk that *this one*, this totally harmless, and sure, fairly hot guy could be the narc. The plant. The *whatever*. Imagine every gritty detective show where an undercover cop says things like, "They won't even see me coming," or, "Whatever you do, don't get involved," and you've basically got the soundtrack to my nightmares.

So. The test. "No problem," I say. "Tomorrow soon enough?"

"Really?" His face is pure wonder, like he thought it'd be harder. A+. Cops can't fake this look—they wouldn't want to. On a cop, this kind of Christmas-morning excitement would be a giveaway. They'd never risk looking like they want it. But on this guy, it's kind of cute.

"A grand."

"A grand." The smile dissolves and he leans back. "Resort prices."

"You pay for the ambience," I say.

His laugh is quieter now. "Jonas didn't say you were funny."

"The more you spend, the funnier I get." I realize that I've been leaning forward, filling the space between us, and I roll back my shoulders, settle my palms into the dirt.

He nods like he's deciding something. "Henry," he says, holding out his hand.

When we shake, I can feel it all the way down into my low belly. I close my eyes briefly, then open them again. "A pleasure," I say.

He nods at my jacket. "Nice throwback. Who are you— Sid Vicious?"

I laugh. "Something like that." I look him up and down again, taking my time. "What brings you to Gold Fork, Henry?" Time to figure him out: Toney? Weekly? Dockside? "Where are you staying?" The underlying question: How hard will it be for you to come up with a thousand dollars in the next twenty-four hours?

Henry smiles. Puts on a detective's voice. "'Or is your name even Henry?' Lots of questions from someone who should value privacy." He pauses. Raises his eyebrows. "Look. I'm the one taking a risk here. Jonas didn't give me much to work with."

"Oh?" Now I'm interested.

"Said you'd be the hot girl who looked like she'd rip you a new one if you got out of line." Another smile.

"And?" I say. "Think you got the right girl?"

"Maybe," he says. "Half of what he said is true, at least." He shifts his shoulders toward me. I feel the pull toward him. Just like a fucking magnet, just like a fucking cliché. But I don't care. Erik is too risky—too much at stake. I don't know what he wants. But this guy? He wants what all Weekenders want, ultimately: a good summer story. I can give him that.

Our flirtation is easy. And easy is what *I* want. He'll do just fine.

"Hey," says Andrea. She's standing next to us, eyes nervous. "Is now, like, a good time?"

I smile at Henry. Feel the magnet break apart. I catch my breath and say, "Good as ever," as he stands.

"See you later, Georgie," he says.

My name sounds right coming from his mouth.

I watch him leave, joining some friends and giving someone a slap on the back. He's in a black T-shirt, black jeans. A fucking QP.

"Some party," Andrea's saying.

She's anxious, but I don't have time to make her feel better about her first buy. I reach into a pocket and pull one of the white baggies that I so carefully measured out this morning. The kind of Ziploc you'd put a pair of earrings in so you don't lose them in your suitcase. "Just a taste. Twenty," I say. She hands over a Jackson, and I hand over the baggie. "Enjoy."

"Thanks." She looks at the coke. "Should I just place another order now for next month?" God. Such a fetus. She heard from Lisa who heard from John who bought some from me last summer, and now she wants to become a regular. Will probably try to order something ridiculous like an ounce—something she can't possibly get through by the end of the summer. But she likes to think she would.

"No," I say, still watching Henry. "Wait till you're done with this one."

She crinkles her brow. "But how will I find you?"

Henry turns back around. Even from the shadows, I can see his smile. His lip ring glints in the firelight. "It's Gold Fork, Andrea," I say. "You're going to see me everywhere."

WHERE YOU GET WHAT YOU WANT WHEN YOU WANT IT

We take what we can. From the Weekenders, sure, but also from the town, the land, ourselves, other Dead Enders. We take unchained bicycles, sex, Peppermint Patties, forgotten sweaters, firewood, friendship. We take what we can because we know that we don't have time to waste. If we want it, we want it now. If we need it, we have to take it. And once we have it, we hold it close, knowing that we could lose it at any moment. Wildfire. Avalanche. Recession. Guilt. In this place, everything is both a gift and a weapon. Our only hope lies in knowing what can wound us.

ERIK

I go through the motions. That's easy enough. It's all I ever do. School, track, the Beast of Burden, Dead Ender girls like Kelly, Mischa, Jessie, and all the others—I know exactly what's expected of me. I perform.

After I leave Georgie, though, I can't. Not yet.

I walk away from the party, away from where Georgie's sitting, hair tucked behind her ear, waiting for her next client. My hands are shaking, and I stuff them into my pockets. I head up the rutted fire road until I hit the main lake road and, beyond it, the black skin of the lake itself. And I stand there, feet planted, looking out over the water, wishing I could take it all back.

All of it.

All of it.

The cold air stings my cheeks, and I breathe out, heavily. Shit. Why the hell did I try to kiss her? And the other question—the one I don't want the answer to.

Why doesn't she want me?

I could hit myself. I came this close to ruining everything. Georgie knows all my bullshit. She knows about my mom. She'd probably call me out on all of it. Why would I want that?

Because, the voice in the back of my head says. *Because it's Georgie.*

Another breath. Steady, steady. I can't blame her for not wanting it either.

Better to stick to the Kellys and Mischas and Jessies of

Tri High. The Dead Ender girls I hook up with aren't stupid, exactly, but they're no Georgie. No one is, really. When it looks like they might actually start liking me, I gently tell them that, because we understand each other so well, I know it's time to let go. Yes, I use that stupid saying about how if you love something, you have to set it free. But I never say the rest: *If it comes back to you, it's yours forever.* I never say that.

Because those girls—they've got no idea who I am, what I'm capable of. To them, I'm just the local track star. Going places. Getting a sports scholarship and blowing this town. And that's one story, sure.

But it's not my story. It's not my story at all.

Georgie. I wanted you to be my story. Georgie. God. I almost told her, too. Almost said what I've been thinking for the past two weeks, ever since I found out: *There's no scholarship, Georgie. Not anymore. Now there's only you.*

But instead of telling her, I just went for it. And now I know. There's no scholarship in my future. There's also no Georgie. I tried—finally—for the thing I've wanted ever since we met, and she made it clear. She doesn't want me. And can I blame her? Who'd want my baggage anyway? No one's taking me with them.

I'm just turning to head back down the fire road when a pair of headlights swerves around the corner on the lake road and heads toward me. I don't flinch, don't move. The car—Land Rover, of course—skids to a stop in front of me. Staccato blare of the horn.

"What the—" A girl's voice comes from the driver's side of the car, yelling. "Man! Didn't you see—" But the voice stops. There's a long pause. I peer through the glare of the headlights to the shadows within the vehicle—two, maybe three other girls, heads bent together, conferring. The door opens, and I see brown cowboy boots, scuffed. Upscale-vintage-store variety. Two tanned legs, thin sundress, a sweater that wouldn't keep a housefly warm. Leather bracelet wrapped around one arm like a snake. Long brown hair—like Georgie's. Curly—not like Georgie's. Pixie face.

She walks toward me. "Hey."

"Hey." I'm watching her, the way she moves, like she's got time. Like we're not standing in the middle of a road. "Sorry," I say. "You caught me by surprise."

She shrugs. "That's okay." We're close enough now that I can tell she's a foot shorter than me. "Hey," she says, "you going to Fellman's?"

"Just came from there." And I jerk my thumb toward the fire road off to the side. "You're almost home."

Her face opens in a smile. "Good. It's my first time," she says, and then laughs at how that sounds. Her laugh is bright and unburdened. She probably laughs at most things, most of the time. What that must be like. "First time here," she adds.

"I don't think you'll be disappointed."

"No," she says, looking at me, "I won't."

Then she moves back toward her car, taking her time. I step out of the way as the Land Rover turns down the fire road. She pauses as she passes me, and leans out the window. "See you down there?" she asks.

I nod.

That smile again. "Good."

I give them ten minutes to park their car and get drinks. Don't want to look too eager. But something's fluttering around the edges of the night, something like hope, and I don't want to wait too long. Give it too much time and it might burn away.

By the time I get back to the party, it's probably close to twelve thirty. I haven't missed much. It's louder now, the group moving around more fluidly. I recognize most people. Someone's rolled a keg down from the parking area, and a group congregates around it, filling plastic cups or water bottles with beer. I don't see the girl from the Land Rover. Georgie's hanging out by the rock where the speakers are set up. She's chatting with a group of younger girls, and she looks up when I come back. It hits me like it always does—a fist to the gut. Georgie's not blandly pretty, like the Kellys of Tri High. She's not basic. She's something else. I know some guys think she's hot because she deals—not giving a shit can look sexy. But I don't care about that. To me—and God, if I ever said this out loud—she's just *interesting*. And that's beautiful. I watch her a second, give her a little wave. She gives me a thumbs-up and a smirk. I push back my disappointment. That girl.

I wave at a few people, get the requisite high fives, the handshakes. It's a good group, but I keep moving.

Davis is sitting on a log that someone dragged over to the fire and talking to Ana about something. He's got a book on his lap. I walk over.

"—on it for a couple of months," he's saying.

"Can I see?" Ana holds out her hand. The scar on her arm is long and thin, like an accusing finger. I look away before she catches me staring.

Davis starts to pick up the book and then catches me watching. He puts it back in his lap. "Hey, Erik," he says. For a second, he leaves his mouth hanging open like he's going to say something else, but then he snaps it shut.

I nod at him. "Hey. Hi, Ana. Surprised to see you here."

She shrugs. "Davis talked me into it." Looks at him. Smiles.

"What are you cats up to?" I say.

Ana laughs quietly. "Cats?"

She's pretty hot. I'll give her that. She's no Georgie, but Ana has curves in all the right places and skin the color of caramel topping. (I described her that way once to Georgie, and she said, *Oh yeah? What color is ignorance?* Then she stared hard at my hands.)

I nod. "Yeah, you know, you cats?"

Davis taps the log next to him. "Pop a squat?"

"I feel like I'm in a nineteen-fifties sitcom," Ana says, and Davis laughs.

I have no idea what's so funny, but I laugh too. Sometimes,

talking to Davis is like stepping into the conference hall where a giant nerd convention is taking place. But honestly, I didn't think I'd see Ana there too.

"So, what's that?" I ask, pointing to the book. Out of the corner of my eye, I watch as Kelly and a group of her friends arrive. I made sure to cut things off with her long before school got out. Don't know what I thought might happen, but I sure as hell knew it wouldn't happen with her. She scans the crowd. Says something. Her friends will all be looking over here in five . . . four . . . three . . . two . . .

"Why are all those girls looking over here?" Ana pushes her hair off her forehead. "Is something wrong?" She glances down at her outfit, as though maybe she spilled beer on it earlier.

"I don't think they're looking at you," Davis tells Ana. "They appear to be watching their prey quite carefully."

"I'm nobody's prey," I snap, just as Ana says, "Oh, I know. I'm not, like, a narcissist or anything."

Davis pats her knee, just like a grandfather. I swear to God. Nerd convention. "It's a book I'm working on," he says.

"What?"

"You asked what this is." He holds up the book. "It's a graphic novel."

"Let me see."

"When it's finished." He puts it back in his lap. Then, watching me watching him, he zips it into his backpack. "I'll show you when it's done."

I don't think Davis trusts me much. And why should he? Lately, I've caught myself watching him—his easy life, brains and money and two parents who'll make sure he gets where he needs to go—and I've been filled with a hot rage that I can't control. It's not fair to him, I know. (Then again, nothing's fair—that's become painfully clear to me recently.) But Davis has a habit of looking at me like I'm about to steal his lunch money or stick a Post-it on his back that says, "Tell me I'm your bitch." He probably thinks I hooked up with Jane or something. But I didn't. I didn't even try. Because Davis is all right. I wouldn't exactly call him to help me move furniture or anything, but he might be the guy I'd call if I had a broken heart. It's hard to imagine, but yes—I think I'd call Davis.

Not that I'll tell him about Georgie.

(I've sometimes wondered how he got a girl like Jane to go out with him in the first place. I mean, he has all the moves of a born-again—doubt he even got her shirt off. I heard that's why Jane broke up with him. She got tired of waiting for him to grab her ass. But that's just a rumor. I would never tell Davis that.)

"Okay," I say. "So what's it about?"

"High school."

"It's not about aliens? What do your people call them? Cyborgs?" Davis is always lugging around some sci-fi or fantasy book, usually something the size of the Bible. He probably gets through one a week. And really, what other kind of person do you see at a nerd convention?

Davis shakes his head. "I dabble in realism."

"It's not about—" I don't have to say it.

"No. It's not about the fire." He shakes his head. "I'd never write a book about that."

I try to imagine the description. Ana's arm, dripping blood. The sound of her voice as she screamed, *I can't get to them! Someone, help me! I can't get to them!* How she fainted just outside the chapel before she could try again.

The sound of Chrissy's screams.

Don't write about it. Don't think about it. Pretend it never never never happened.

Ana smiles. "It's really good, Erik," she says. "I saw the first page."

"Oooh," I say, too loudly, "a whole page!" It comes out harsher than I intended. Most things do. I try again. "Okay. I'll wait for the finished product." Then I add, "But you better show me."

"I have a feeling you'll be my toughest critic," says Davis. He's looking at me intently.

"What?" I say.

"Nothing. Just—" Davis does a kind of fake shrug.

"God. What?"

"Anything new going on with you? Like, any interesting Weekender sightings?"

"Nothing more interesting than what's going on here." I glance around. Still no sign of Land Rover. "Why?"

He's about to answer when Georgie joins us, planting her

feet so that she blocks the light of the fire. I can hear a few Weekenders calling her name behind her, but she raises one hand and turns her wrist, and they shut up.

"What, are we meditating now?" she asks, jabbing her finger at the way Davis is sitting, legs crossed like fucking Gandhi. She squats down in front of us but doesn't make eye contact with me, and I wonder if she's still thinking about what happened earlier. I'm not a blusher—no one but Georgie would call me sentimental—but I feel my cheeks burn for the second time tonight, and I look away from the fire. Shit. What if I ruined *this*?

"Just Davis," I say, then turn back to her. I don't care if she can see me blushing. *This* is all I have.

"Well, he's certainly the most enlightened one here." She rocks forward and hits the back of my head with the heel of her hand. She lets her hand rest there for a minute, then pulls it away.

So we're okay, then. I swallow.

"Davis is writing a book," Ana tells her.

"About us, " I add.

"Wrong," Davis says. "Not about you. About life."

"And therefore us. What, is it some advertisement for church youth groups everywhere?" I say.

Davis looks down at his lap. "No." And I know he's thinking about the fire, his mom's church burning to the ground. I know he blames himself. And yet again, I've made him feel bad. Great work, Erik.

"Whatever," I say. "The only good thing the Beast's ever done was to let me join your mom's youth group."

"That's sweet," says Ana, just as Georgie says, "Awww. You wuv us."

I can't look at her.

"Doesn't seem like that would've been a hard sell," Davis says.

"You don't know the Beast of Burden." And I remember the two days of asking, of trying to make it seem like my mom's idea instead of a favor. How I understood, even then, that Georgie was the only person I wanted to know in this town and the youth group was the best way to know her better. "But," I add, "she thought it would look good on my college applications. She thought the big names would want a 'scholar-athlete'"—I make air quotes with my fingers—"but it's not like I was suddenly going to inherit a brain." And then I laugh, so they know it's okay.

"Your mom was thinking about these things in junior high?" asks Ana. I watch her expression turn from incredulity to pity. "Wow. Mine just wanted to make sure I wasn't sitting at home watching telenovelas with the subtitles on."

"The Beast never sleeps," says Georgie, putting her hand on my shoulder.

"No," I say, trying to ignore the warmth of her hand, trying not to want more, "she doesn't."

"Well, I'd say it worked out," says Ana. "I mean, you got that award, after all."

100

"Home free," adds Davis.

"Yeah," I say. "Yeah."

But I don't tell them about how I called the coaches at my dream schools last week and they said sure, they'd gotten my information, and they'd be happy to have me walk on, no problem, but there wouldn't be any money, not with my grades and my measly District Championship. I don't tell them that being the Tri High track star and winning District is nothing like winning State. That coming in fourth at State is the same as wearing a shirt that says I CAN'T RUN FAST ENOUGH. I don't tell them that without this award, I don't have jack.

Really, when it comes down to it, I don't tell them anything.

Davis laughs. "Don't worry, Erik," he says. "You might not be in my book, but one way or another, you'll leave a legacy. I'm sure of it."

I don't know what he means, but what's new? So I laugh with him. He's looking around the party but trying not to, eyes darting here and there, his fist grasping one strap of the backpack like he's afraid I'll reach over and take it.

Or maybe he's not afraid of me. Maybe he's afraid someone else will see his book. Or that he'll have to see someone else. And suddenly I get it.

"She's not here," I say to him.

Davis nods. "I know," he says. "If she were, I'd have gone home a long time ago."

"Ah," says Georgie. "Still pining."

"'The path of love never did run'—whatever." Davis shrugs. "At least I've got my support group." He knocks his knee against Ana's. "And no shortage of subjects for my sociological study on the cross-cultural mating habits of Weekenders and Dead Enders."

Nerd. Convention.

"I mean, this is so strange," Davis continues.

"What do you mean?" Ana smiles.

Davis waves one arm around. "Just that everyone's still so cautious. Have you noticed how they pretend to have forgotten one another's names? It's like no one can quite admit that they might have"—gasping, clutching his chest—"missed one another."

"I don't recognize anyone," says Ana.

"Really?" Georgie raises her eyebrows. "I know about half of them." And she raises a hand in greeting at some guy on the other side of the fire. He's standing next to a dark-haired girl with braids in a too-thin sundress and a sweater. The girl from the Land Rover and I lock eyes. Her smile shifts a fraction of a millimeter, and the meaning totally changes, becomes a message only for me. She turns and walks away, but I know she knows I'm watching.

"Well," I say, standing up, "it's been real."

"Where are you headed?" Georgie glances around her and then shakes her head. "Never mind. I'll use my imagination." She pats her pockets and stands. "I'm heading home anyway," she says. "I'm all sold out. It was a good night." She catches my eye and looks away.

"See you both later," says Ana.

Davis is already leaning over his backpack, unzipping it again. He looks up. "Call if you need us," he says to me.

"What's that supposed to mean?" He's been acting strange all night, and now this. "Do I need a babysitter? What are you, like, Mary Poppins or something?"

Davis looks like he's going to say something else, but then he just shakes his head and turns away.

I try not to think about the way Davis sounded as I walk away from the fire. Like a TV dad. Like a TV dad who knows about a dead grandmother and doesn't want to say anything yet. Whatever. He doesn't want to tell me? Fine. If we're friends, it's by tragic circumstance. The four of us are a strange mix to begin with, but Davis and I are oil and water. If we didn't have Georgie reminding us every week to meet up at the Den, if we didn't have the fire and our secret (*my* secret, I remind myself), we wouldn't even nod at each other on the street. He's never trusted me much anyway—and he shouldn't. In fact, the last thing I need is Davis focusing in on my lies. He's the kind of guy who'll keep digging until he finds the box you've hidden in the ground, so far down you thought no one would ever touch it. Davis is not someone I need to be near right now.

Besides. I've got better things to do anyway. The party's almost over. I head toward the cars. It's just a matter of time now (I hope), of waiting and pretending not to wait, of looking like I'm taking a break from the action when really, action is what I've come for. Because I think—no, I'm pretty sure—that, in five minutes or maybe ten, the dark-haired girl in the too-thin dress will follow me here. And then things will start to get interesting.

Georgie—I push the thought away. She was probably doing us both a favor.

Again, I let myself feel the smallest flare of hope. Maybe this Weekender has what I need. Dead Ender girls never stop wanting more, but Weekender girls don't *want*. They *have*. What they don't have, they *get*. And that's almost beautiful.

It's the one lesson my dad passed on to me before he left.

DAVIS

In *She Woke Before Me*, Jane is always wearing the same thing: a threadbare blue T-shirt, old jeans, men's oxford shoes that are scuffed at the toes. She's always wearing this because that's how I always think of her, because that's what she was wearing when we first kissed and it's also, coincidentally, what she was wearing when she told me that I was awesome and great but just not quite *it*, you know?

I twirl my pen in my hand. Behind the park bench where I'm sitting, I can hear the occasional rumble of a motor as cars cruise down Main, looking for parking. In front of me, though, it's all silence and water. The lake stretches north from the edge of downtown, bushes and trees and rocky shoreline giving way to cliffs and granite and, eventually, wilderness at the far end. Some city planner was smart enough to draw up a little park at the southern shore, sandwiched between the Gold Fork Grand and a little string of gift shops. There are a couple picnic tables, a volleyball court. A handful of benches. I think they trucked in the sand.

Here's the panel I'm working on now: Jane sits at a table across from me. She's looking to the side. Her hair is kind of tossed behind one ear in a sexy way that insinuates that my hands were just touching it. She's wearing the outfit. Eyes large and round. Conversation bubble: *I'd like to spend just one day inside your head, Davis.*

Somehow, it doesn't sound quite right, coming from her.

I've been working on the book for a couple months. It's a graphic novel. About Jane. About things she's said, ways she's looked at me, funny quirks she has, like how she glances at the ceiling and shakes her head in a quick little shimmy whenever she's trying to find the right words for something. (For instance: Her head shimmied like that after she said I wasn't quite *it*.)

More and more, though, the book includes things she *might* have said, given time. That's what happens, I guess, when you only date for a couple months. In my find-the-arsonist-win-back-the-girl dream, there's always a kind of slow-mo scene where I present the book to her and she basically evaporates in tears of regret about the time she wasted thinking I wasn't *it*. My hope is that she'll be so busy being sorry that she won't notice where I've taken creative liberties.

Creative liberties. That's generous.

I shut the journal and toss it into my backpack as I stand and look at my watch. Almost noon. Damn. Two weeks of summer break gone and what have I got to show for myself? Another solitary morning. Jane's hair. A stomach that's telling me I'd better eat something before the meeting I've got soon. The meeting. I've been avoiding it all week. I turn my back to the lake and trudge across the street toward the Open Six Hours.

Honestly, I just love living in this town. I mean, it's a place where a store calls attention to itself by bragging that it's open for *six hours!*, as though most places are only open for a measly three or four. Sometimes I think that Gold Fork is a tiny town that aspires to be an urban metropolis, despite the fact that it has the ethos of a Ukrainian hamlet. My mom has told me more than once about how she used to take me outside in the winter without a hat, back when I was a baby, and how women would stop her on the streets to yell at her. One woman, I believe, went as far as to kick off her boot, pull off her own sock, and try to wedge it onto my cone-shaped head.

(It's no longer cone-shaped, by the way. Now it's just kind of round. Like a squash. I try to break up the monotony of my head with square glasses, interestingly collared shirts. Does it work? You'd have to ask Jane.)

When I walk into the Open Six Hours, Ana's there. She's

just standing in the candy aisle, looking lost. She's wearing some sort of sweaterdress, even though it's the second week of June, and she's staring at a Peppermint Pattie in her hand.

"Tough decision," I say. "Go with what's familiar, or try something new?" I reach around her and pick up a PayDay bar. "Retro, classic, and hearty," I tell her. "Could totally reinvent your day."

"Hi, Davis," Ana says.

Are her eyes always this sad? I look at her until I realize that I'm just standing here, holding the PayDay like an idiot. So I keep going. "The question you have to ask yourself is, do you want to feel the wind in your ears as you swish down an Alpine slope"—I point at the Peppermint Pattie—"or do you want an afternoon of good, clean fun, helping your dad fix up his old Mustang?" I hold the PayDay a little higher.

"Alpine slope," she says, and opens the wrapper to take a bite.

"You gotta pay for that," the girl who works the register calls from across the store. She talks like she's stored chewing gum in each cheek. "You can eat it here, but you gotta pay before you go."

Ana nods, keeps chewing.

"Rebel," I say. The candy bar is starting to feel heavy in my hands. I'm weirdly nervous, not sure what to say. It's like we're the only people in the waiting room at a doctor's office. And there's only one magazine, and it's *Better Homes and Gardens*. "So, Fellman's was pretty good."

"Yeah," she says, chewing. She's a dainty chewer.

"Thanks for—" I don't know how to finish. "You know, thanks for listening to me talk about my book. For not saying it's, you know, navel-gazing. Which I guess it kind of is."

She laughs, takes another bite. "I wouldn't. It looked good—from what I saw of it."

It had been so easy to talk to her. She'd told me more about Vera, about their lazy afternoons together on the patio at the Royal Pines. I'd told her that I didn't know many people who could work in an environment of diminishing returns—that was the phrase I used—and she hadn't gotten mad. Instead, what had she said? *I'd like to spend one day inside your head, Davis.*

It sounded good. So good that I let myself imagine what it'd be like if Jane said it.

And for a quick second, I let myself remember what it was like to first get to know Ana. How excited I'd been when she joined my mom's youth group—the quiet girl I'd seen in the halls but had never had the guts to talk to—and how surprising she was, subtly funny and kind. How she told me about her desire to learn her grandparents' language, even though her mom said there was no need, since it was just the two of them. How I'd harbored a hope that—

That was then, I remind myself. This is now. If there'd been a question mark at the end of a sentence about me and Ana before the chapel fire, the flames wiped it away and started a new chapter. You don't get the happy ending when you've caused that kind of damage. You just don't.

"Well, thanks," I say again. "Hey. Did you think—" I pause. "Did you think something was off with Erik?"

"Not really." Then she adds, "What's going on?" She swallows. "At Fellman's, you kind of seemed weird. I mean," she says quickly, "that's not exactly the word I want. Off, at least. Around Erik." She takes another Peppermint Pattie.

"That's two," says the girl behind the counter. "Third one's free."

Ana raises her eyebrows and tears open the package. "Want my third?" she says.

"Yeah." I grab one too. Hold it in my hand. "Thanks. I needed this." Then I say, "It's going to sound stupid."

Ana grins. "I doubt that."

"Okay. Well, what do you know about Erik's dad?"

Ana tilts her head. "Not much. Erik's not very forthcoming about personal stuff. But he's been gone for a long time, right?"

"Since elementary school, at least." And because two hours of searching through old files and even, at one point, a box of old microfiche didn't give me anything other than that one photograph of the young family, I try to think back. Because of course I can remember Erik, fast even in elementary school, the best at PE when being best at PE was the only thing that mattered. (Not that that's changed.) But his parents? Book fairs and parent-teacher nights. Always Erik's mom, looking flustered and alone. Always a raised voice. Someone's fault—the teacher's, the principal's. Something wrong. Always. "He must've left when we were really little—

like kindergarten or earlier. I don't remember him."

"He wasn't here by the time Mom and I moved in. Do they keep in touch?"

"Don't know. I kind of doubt it, though." I pause, and then I say, "I think I saw him at Toney's."

Ana steps back. "What? How do you know?"

"He looks like him. Even kind of sounds like him, if you can believe it."

"You talked to him?"

"For a second. About nothing."

"But why hasn't Erik said anything?" she asks. "At least to Georgie, you know?"

"I don't think he knows," I say, and take a bite of my Peppermint Pattie. "And I can't be the one to tell him. *If* I'm right about this."

"Yeah," she says. "It can't be you. Sometimes the two of you are"—she waves the wrapper in the air—"just fine. And then other times . . ." Ana shrugs.

"I know." For a second, I'm back at the chapel again, standing outside the blaze, yelling for Ana. Erik's next to me, yelling something I can't quite hear. The sound of broken glass. Ana coming out, blood dripping down her arm. And later, when the fire trucks were there, the chapel already a pile of smoking rubble, Erik turning to me and saying, "Never mind. What I said earlier? I was kidding. Forget it."

Forget what?

The fire may have brought us all together—we started it,

after all—but that moment, when Erik thought I heard some-thing I didn't hear, has kept a screen between the two of us. I don't think I'll ever know him. Not really.

"Thing is," I say, "I'm never quite sure that he won't slip a muscle relaxant into my drink or glue my sleeping bag shut or something, just for a laugh. He's never seemed to want my feedback."

But she doesn't seem bothered. "I think you've watched too many of those eighties high school movies," Ana says. "That's the only time anyone actually wakes up with gum in her hair or gets out of the shower in gym class to find his pants hanging from the basketball hoop." She laughs.

"I respectfully disagree," I say, taking another bite of my Peppermint Pattie. "May I present a snapshot of my seventh-grade year. One: snowballs down the back of my sweater. Two: porn in my locker. Three: fake notes from cheerleaders asking me to meet them behind the Dumpster after school." I don't tell her that the porn was the worst—so much more humiliat-ing because puberty was arriving at a rather glacial pace.

"That's bad," Ana admits. "But that wasn't Erik, was it?"

"Not that I know of," I say. "All I mean is, Erik doesn't talk about his life outside of"—I hold up one finger—"track." Two fingers. "Girls." Three fingers. "Other girls. And maybe that's all his life is. But it doesn't make me the ideal candi-date to tell him about his dad."

Ana looks at me. "You're always counting in threes," she says. "Why is that?"

"Because it makes sense," I say. "It makes things make sense." I blush, then add, "A little order is in order, you know?"

Ana's nodding. "I get that. It's got to be nice, looking at any given situation and dividing it up into equal parts. Then you can take them one by one and not have to worry about the whole." She crumples the Peppermint Pattie wrapper in her hand.

I stare at her. "Right." It's how I've felt about most things. School, Gold Fork, even Jane. If I could graduate in three years, I would. If we could drop a season—summer, probably—and end up with only three to deal with, I'd be happy. Relieved, even. And if I had been able to figure out Jane, understand her dimensions, annoyances, her *reasons*, maybe I'd have had a chance, instead of addressing her whole person and thereby screwing it up from the beginning,

It takes me a minute to pull myself away from the image that's appeared in my mind suddenly of Jane walking away. Always walking away. "Also," I say, "three is a prime number. And therefore, inviolable. You don't fuck with three."

"I've always said." Ana smiles. Then she says, "I have to pay for these," and holds up the crumpled wrappers. "What're you doing now?"

I think about the meeting I've got in a few minutes. No way I'm going to tell Ana about it. "Nothing," I say. "Just—work."

"Okay." She squints at me but doesn't say anything else.

"Until next time," I say, saluting her. "Go forth and, you know, whatever."

"Bye, Davis."

As I head down the street to Grainey's, I wonder how often Ana's at the Open Six Hours. I know where the others usually hang out in the summer. If Georgie's not working, she's in the alley behind the art store, hanging out with her strange group of harmless stoners, a bunch of guys (and a few girls) who all have long hair and sweet, kind of clueless smiles on their faces at all times. Erik's in the high school's weight room, even in the summer, or off somewhere with some girl. Jane is probably finishing lunch with her best friends at the diner on Third. She goes there almost every day. Has a grilled cheese with tomato soup. Cuts off the crusts and dunks them in the soup before working through the rest of the sandwich. Eats with one hand propped on her cheek, like she's considering each bite. Crosses her ankles under the booth, smiles at me, and says, *You're just not quite* it, *you know?*

But Ana? Aside from the Den and Vera, I don't really know what she does. After the fire, something about her shut down. We were so busy hiding what we'd done that we couldn't waste time with the what-could-have-beens. And now, two years later, I'm pretty sure I imagined the whole thing. Ana was never interested. That was a fantasy, like everything in my life.

She shifts uncomfortably in the chair across from me at Grainey's. I don't blame her: We've been avoiding each other for two years. Me, because of the obvious. And she, because

113

I think when someone's heard you screaming from inside a burning tent, you tend to want to keep some distance.

This is the closest I've been to Chrissy Nolls since that night at the chapel. I have to fight the impulse to jump out of my chair and flee.

"What do you want to know?" she asks, and looks at her phone. Swipes up, swipes down, like she's almost too busy to be here. Adds, "My mom said this would be quick."

"Um." I look down at my open notebook, which is obscenely blank. I was so nervous about this meeting that I didn't even bring questions. For a second, I wish I'd followed Ana wherever she was headed this afternoon. Anything to avoid this interview. I try to remember what Dan told me to ask. "Do you think there's a connection between the two fires?" I write the question as I ask it so that I don't have to look at her.

"No."

A long pause while I wait for her to say something—anything—else. Finally, I say, "Oh. You don't?" to my notebook. A question about as professional as a whisper.

"No." Her voice is certain. I look up at her, and she's leaning forward against the table, her hand on the back of her neck, covering the burn. "The chapel fire was an accident. Ember from the campfire, most likely. Why would anyone think the two were related?"

"Good point." It's hard to look her in the face like this. She's right—the fires can't be connected. Because we definitely didn't start the Nelson fire.

"I can't believe I let my mom talk me into this interview," she says. "Like talking about it's going to help. Thank God I graduated. Now I can get away from this place. That's what you want to ask me about, isn't it? How the fire's affected me?" She slowly pulls her hand away from her neck like it's hard to do, like the hand is stuck fast, which it probably is. She's been covering it for two years. (*Like Ana,* I think, and push the thought away.)

The burn is worse at the back of her neck, I know, but I can't see it from where I'm sitting. From here, I can only see the way it weaves up the sides, stopping before it gets to her ears. The pink ridges of skin, puckered and puffy, disappear at the bottom into the collar of her shirt.

"I can't wait until I can leave in September. State university," she says. Her mouth is set in a grim line. "Where I'm just the Burned Girl, and not *Our* Burned Girl." She rests her hand against her neck again. "So yeah," she says. "That's how the fire affected me."

"Oh. Okay. Good." I write that down, even though I know none of it's going in the article.

"It's funny, though," she goes on. "You're not the first person to interview me."

"I'm not?"

Her smile is a straight line. "The police. Can you believe it? Wanted to rule me out, they said. Me: a suspect. What crap."

I raise my eyebrows. "I didn't know that."

"You wouldn't," she says, and I'm hit by a vague memory of Chrissy-before-the-fire. Easy laughter. Pictures of kittens and puppies up in her locker.

That's not the girl sitting across from me now.

"Doesn't matter," she says. "It wasn't me. You think I ever want to go back up there? That's the last thing I'd do." She glances around Grainey's, taking in the Weekenders and their iced mochas. "Screw this place. Once I leave, I'm gone."

I don't get anything else out of Chrissy—not that I expected to. I doubt Dan'll see my notes and think there's an article in here somewhere, and that's fine with me. I bike home through town in the midafternoon heat, following the lake road as it turns toward the west side.

And here's where my dirty little secret comes out. Because, see, while *generally* only the Weekenders have places on the lake, and *generally* this leaves the rest of us to mock their wrap-around decks and stone fire pits and fleets of boats and other, as they like to say, "water toys," *specifically*, that's not exactly the case. *Specifically*, in fact, one of us lives on the lake. *Specifically*, me. An old house, sure, built in the seventies, when Gold Fork was just becoming the destination that it is today and therefore lacking that sort of log cabin appeal that everyone's always clamoring for, but a house on the lake nonetheless.

I lean my bike against the side of the house and go in around the back, by the kitchen. "Home," I call.

A muffled shout from upstairs. I toss my backpack on the kitchen island and go to the fridge. I still haven't really eaten since my fruitless trip to the Open Six Hours, and I'm starving. I'm slathering some mustard on a mystery-meat sandwich when my mom walks into the kitchen.

"We thought it was you," she says. She turns and yells up the stairs. "Darling, our beloved son has returned from work." Then: "So, how was your day? Work? Friends?" She scrutinizes me. "Did you see Jane?"

It never surprises anyone that I'm close to my parents. I wish it would. I wish people—okay, Jane—would look at me and think, *I bet he has a really strained relationship with his parents,* instead of what they really think, which is, *I bet his mom knows all about his feelings of inadequacy,* or, *I bet he and his dad stay in on Saturday nights to refinish midcentury dining chairs.*

"Mom," I tell her, "Gold Fork's small, but it's not that small." *I wish I wish I wish it were.*

"Hmm." Mom's not really listening. There's a copy of the newspaper with an article on the Nelson fire on the dining room table. She's been reading it. I glance at it, and she catches me looking.

"Do you think there's a connection between the two fires?" she asks.

"No," I say. "I don't." I walk over and put my arm around her. "The chapel was an accident. You know that." As always, the lie lands like concrete in my gut. "Embers from the campfire . . . or something."

117

She sighs, looking suddenly very tired. "I want to believe it was an accident—the chapel. Not vandalism or—worse." Mom picks up the article and studies it, then puts it back down. "I want to believe that people are inherently good, Davis, even when they do bad things."

"Hey, Moose." My dad comes downstairs, wiping his hands on the front of his "house jeans." (He really only has two pairs of jeans, because he's more of a chino-and-button-down guy when he's working at the real estate office in town during the week.) "Anything new?" He sees the newspaper and flips it over so that the article is hidden. He looks at my mom, but she gives him a quick smile to let him know she's okay.

"No Jane sightings," she says. Turns back to me. "Want to talk about it? Shake out the emotional cobwebs?"

You wouldn't guess it from the dirt roads and burger joints, but Gold Fork's a bit of a hot market for a good counselor. And who better to trust with your darkest secrets than a minister who wears blue jeans under her robe and won't turn down a scotch at Christmas? A minister who never, ever minces words. My mom is that guy at the party that you keep inviting because he brings the booze, but then you have to deal with the fact that he's gonna say something like, "Damn, man, what's that on your *face?*" My mom's like that, except she says things like, "Lord God, please help us to see what others can't, and to press for the change that you find fitting," all while standing at the pulpit and staring so directly at her *own son* that everyone else starts staring at you and they, too, notice the stupid baseball hat you insisted on wearing this morning.

She's no wild one, my mom, but she's just wild enough to be real. And her congregation loves her.

They certainly loved her enough to try to raise money for a new church in town when—unbeknownst to her or anyone else—her son and his friends burned down the old one two years ago. They had to sell the land at Washer's Landing, of course—it was worth too much, and the profit paid for a significant portion of the new building. It broke her heart.

"Things will come together, Moose," my mom says now. "They always do. Sometimes in the most fantastic ways. Have faith in yourself." She looks down at the table, shifts some random papers around. "Anything else I should know about?" She looks up again, and I swear she's sizing me up. "Work . . . the fire . . . and friends?" Her tone is off.

But before I can answer her, ask her what she's getting at, my dad laughs.

"What this family needs is some sun and sand," he says. "Why don't you and I head down to the dock, Moose, and work on that new extension I'm putting in? I could use a hand."

My phone buzzes with a text from Dan. *Piece of paper found at Nelson site. At least one legible word, according to fire chief.*

"Great idea," Mom says. Her tone is normal again. "It's been a while since we've had a Dock Day. You guys head down now, and I'll bring some snacks in a few."

Another text: *Nelsons coming back to town in a couple weeks.*

Need you to do follow-up interview. Standard questions. Up for it?

Sure, I text back. Interviewing the Nelsons is a far cry from following up on organic chicken. It's hard not to be excited about that.

"Sounds good," says Dad. "Davis?"

"Okay." I put the phone on the counter. "Let me grab something first."

I'm rereading the first book in Pierce's The Song of the Lioness series (for the twentieth time), and it's still in my backpack from last night. Once I get it, I step over to the kitchen window and peer down at the lake. From here, I can't see much—just a fingernail of blue. But from down on the dock below our house I know I can see a few of the nicer cabins on the other side of the water, the Den in particular with its log siding and tennis court. The Sea Rays, a few people in the bows, making their way from cove to cove to pick up friends for an afternoon of drinking and tubing. The Weekenders on their Jet Skis, curls of white foam skimming the lake, turning to larger plumes of white as they get closer to our dock. Is Jane on the back of one of them, her arms circling the waist of some Apollo? Yelling over the sound of the motor, *Are you sure your parents won't be back until next week?*

I mean, when you think about it, there's only one reason why I'm not running into Jane at every street corner. Why I didn't see her at Fellman's. Because there's only one reason anyone skips that party.

She's moved on.

ANA

There are moments you don't forget. This one was just after Mom and the Colonel (that's what I called him) broke up a couple years ago—and we were sitting on our thrift-store couch, picking the burnt kernels of popcorn out of a big plastic bowl. We both like the burnt bits. She'd been crying, and I'd been saying the empty, trite things that I thought you were supposed to say in these situations. He was the only guy she'd dated for as long as I could remember. I didn't know how to respond.

"You'll find someone better," I said, not even sure if I believed it. Not even sure I wanted her to.

Mom looked at me. I remember how her mascara had streaked around her eyes so that she looked like an evangelical from one of those shows that are always on when you watch TV at one in the morning. I was just kind of patting her arm like I was a Red Cross volunteer after an earthquake, and she said, "There's only one Better, mi cielo." She laid her hand on mine and squeezed and said, "The rest is all bullshit. All of it."

I didn't know what to say.

"Know this," she said, her voice suddenly angry. "You can love as many people as you want. But there will only be one who is better than the rest. Only one guy will get you—really get you. And if you lose him, or if you don't even see him in the first place, you'll feel it forever." Then she started to cry again.

At the time, I didn't think it worthwhile to point out that, from where I stood, the Colonel sure didn't seem like "the Better," and that frankly, I was glad he was gone. I just let her put her head on my shoulder and cry, and I said more empty, trite things and chewed slowly on the burnt kernels and willed that night to be over so we could get on with our life as just two.

But I haven't forgotten what she said, because, on one level at least, she was right. I don't think that we can trade love around like baseball cards. I don't believe that a heart, once broken, ever fully heals. I think we love once, and fiercely.

And I think I might not get love the way other people will. I think Vera might be my Better. She may not know my name, but she knows *me*.

And. Even if she doesn't remember me telling her, she knows the truth about the chapel fire.

That's why, after I run into Davis at the Open Six Hours, I decide to go visit her. For some reason, seeing Davis made me uneasy. He was talking about someone who looked like Erik's dad and I couldn't concentrate because I was remembering how he showed me his novel about Jane at Fellman's. How I watched his face. Saw the way he looked at each page like he wanted to disappear into it and *be* the story. And I tried not to think about how things might have turned out. I tried not to think about the weeks leading up to the chapel fire and the way Davis had—still has—of capturing a moment that appears nondescript to everyone else and making it somehow hilarious or strange or lovely. How we'd started talking, finding dumb excuses to sit together, sharing sidelong looks, inside jokes. And I thought—I hoped—that the overnight at the chapel would bring something more.

I got my wish, I guess.

I didn't wear short sleeves for a whole year after the fire. Even now, I rarely do. The scar is more than just a reminder. I'm marked by the ugliness of what we did. It defines me. And it holds me hostage.

Davis hasn't looked at me the same way since.

We were fourteen, I remind myself again. Whatever we had? It didn't mean anything.

I jump on my bike and head for the Royal Pines. Down Main Street past the hotel and the coffee shop, the lake glistening. The water's surface out toward the middle is dotted with the tiny wakes of water-skiers, even though the water must be only barely above freezing. It's June, after all—not exactly the height of summer. I take a left onto Rollins, a back road that skirts the town. The houses get smaller, and the front porches, which are all wicker furniture and fresh flowers closer to the lake, start to sag under piles of tools, metal benches with lead paint peeling off. The pine trees out here even look bedraggled. It's hot, and I'm sweating by the time I arrive at the nursing home. My shirt is sticking to my back, my dark hair a frizzy mess around my face. The sky is growing dark and I feel like I've just ridden through a cloud of gnats, but as soon as I walk in the sliding doors and pick out Vera's calm face in the solarium, it's all worth it.

She's my person. My Better.

"Hi, Vera." I kneel down by her wheelchair. "It's me."

She looks confused. "Isn't it always you?"

I nod. "I guess so."

"Well, take me away, then." She glares at one of the nurses, who's walking toward us with a cup of juice, and the nurse turns on her heels and walks away. Vera sweeps one arm in front of her. "Let's go. This room isn't doing anything for my complexion."

I keep my laughter low as I push her back to her room. Erik says that, viewed from the air, the Pines probably looks like a swastika. I disagree. I think it resembles an insect, with four or five hallways stretching out from the main nurses' station like legs. Each hall is named for a tree, naturally. Vera lives in a single apartment halfway down Larch Hall. She doesn't have any roommates, unlike some of the residents. When we get there, I park her next to her bed and side table and then move around the room, opening the blinds and straightening things up. "There," I say, grabbing one of the visitors' chairs from the corner and pulling it next to her. "Fresh and cheery."

"That you are," she says, per our routine. She reaches over and pushes the bowl of nuts on the side table toward me. "Would you like a snack?"

"Thanks." I take one and chew. I always take one, even

though I know they're the same nuts that were here last week, and the week before that, and the week before that.

She's never called me by name. She remembers me, of course—my face, sometimes even my stories. Maybe when we've lived as long as Vera has, certain things don't matter anymore. The words we use to set ourselves apart from others might seem frivolous. "Names are just accessories," she said once, and she was right, as always. She's never mentioned my darker skin and hair—has never called me *Lupe* like a couple of the other residents who came up with it one day and still call out to me as I walk by their wheelchairs like we're all in on it together. *Lupe! Lupe!* All that matters to Vera is that I show up, eat her almonds, listen to her breathe.

We chat for a while, covering the basics. This leads, like it often does, to Vera saying something about the dining room in her old house, how you could seat twenty around the table if you needed, and me saying, *Twenty? I don't know twenty people to invite!* and Vera laughing lightly. I'm just picking up her Harry Potter book to start reading chapter one for the fortieth time when I hear someone talking loudly by the nurses' station.

"—a list of medications. That's all I'm asking for." Short pause. "Well, I don't care if you don't know me. I know my rights." It's a woman's voice, and she sounds tired. Tired and angry. "What? I have to call ahead? Is this a spa? Do I need a reservation?" There's a mumbled response, then finally: "Thank you. I'll do that."

125

I raise my eyebrows at Vera. "Did you hear that? Sounds like there's some drama."

She blinks. "Hear what?" She rests her hand on my arm. "What were you saying?"

I hold up the book with my other hand. "Never mind. Should we read a little?"

Vera peers at the cover. "That looks interesting."

"It sure does," I say, even though we had this exact same conversation four minutes ago. "It's called—"

"Excuse me."

I turn my head at the voice. It comes from a short woman in the doorway. Stocky. Compact. Her dull brown hair falls to her shoulders, and she's wearing an orange and purple caftan that makes her look like she just stumbled out of bed and brought the sheet with her.

"Excuse me," she says again. "Could you leave us?"

"What?" I close the book.

"You know, could you leave us? Go work on another room?"

"Another room." All I can do is repeat her words.

"I can take it from here," she says. "You can leave now."

I grab Vera's hand with my own and squeeze. Then I look back at the woman. "I don't work here," I say slowly, enunciating so she'll understand. "I'm a visitor like you." I can't believe I'm explaining myself. I want to ask her if the color of my skin has anything to do with it. My mom's told me about the sorts of things she hears at the spa. Beyond the ordinary half-joking requests for happy endings ("Joke!" they say when she steps back, reaching for the doorknob—"I was just joking!"), there are the other ways people can make her feel small. The uglier ways. Practicing their Spanish on her—dinero, por favor, final feliz. Asking her if she's got her papers. So yeah—I wonder if this woman looked at me and thought, *Chica probably cleans the bedpans*. But then, something about her voice is familiar. A voice I heard over the phone, almost two years ago, asking me for more information about myself.

She looks at me steadily for a moment and then says, "You must be Ana."

That's when I realize that I've seen her expression before—annoyed, looking down and to the side like she'd rather be anywhere but where she is—and I glance at the family photo next to Vera's bed.

"Abigail," I say.

"Abby. Abigail's a name for a dead president's wife." She takes a step into the room and looks around. "No one calls me that except my mother. She always refused to call me Abby." Her gaze flits back and forth between Vera and the room, never resting on the woman in the wheelchair for long. It's as if Vera's not even here.

I squeeze Vera's hand again.

Abigail—sorry, *Abby*—starts moving around the room, picking up things and putting them back where she found them: a cardigan, the small potted cactus I brought Vera last month. "It's not the shithole I was imagining," she continues.

127

Her voice is flat, a little gravelly. She speaks with the careful precision of someone who doesn't talk often.

Vera's been watching us the way a cat watches two birds from the window. Her head moves from my face to Abby's and back again. "Hello," she says finally, holding out her hand. "Welcome. You must be the help."

Abby snorts and looks away, and I think about the only other conversation I've had with her, over the phone more than a year and a half ago. I'd answered the ad in the *Gold Fork Roundup*. I was probably the only person who did. *Companion needed*, it had read. *Elderly woman. No poachers.* And I'd wondered why the person placing the ad was concerned with getting an elk out of season until I talked to Abby on the phone. *My mother is addled,* she'd said, almost before I'd finished telling her my name. She'd clipped the ends of her words as though they were fingernails. *Old and addled, and she won't know you from day to day. She certainly doesn't know me.*

I remember thinking that mothers never know their daughters.

She'd kept talking. *What I want to know is, what's in it for you? I have control of her assets,* she'd added, as though that meant something. *So there's nothing to gain there.*

That's when I almost hung up the phone. But I didn't. I told her that I liked old people, that I didn't have a grandma, that I needed a job. All true. I didn't tell her that I needed something to keep my mind off the memory of the fire, of the sound that came from within the chapel as I fought my

128

way back in, slicing my arm and searching for something that I wouldn't—couldn't—find. But by then those weren't the only reasons I wanted the job. By then, I just wanted to see the woman whose own daughter thought about her in terms of assets—of gains and losses. What kind of woman could Vera be? And, I'd wondered, what kind of daughter was Abby?

Now I see. I watch as Abby slowly moves forward and shakes Vera's hand as if they're being introduced in a conference room. "Mother," she says, addressing her for the first time. "It's Abigail."

"Thank you," says Vera, and drops her hand to her lap, where she begins picking at lint on her skirt. "That's all right, dear."

Abby catches my eye. *See? Addled,* her expression says, and I want to tell her that Vera's not always like this. She has good days and bad days. Like all of us.

"Abigail," Abby repeats, more loudly. "Your daughter."

Vera looks up. Peers into Abby's face. "Kathryn!" Her smile is pure delight.

Abby reacts as though she's been slapped. She wheels around and steps away from Vera's chair, moving quickly to the window. I can't see her face, but her voice, when she speaks again, is a taut line: "No. Not Kathryn. Abigail."

Vera's smile becomes uncertain. "Kathryn," she says, "will be back soon. Won't she?" Then she looks at me, and I take down the photo from the wall without speaking and hold it out to her, pointing to Abby. But it's clear that the photo doesn't register. In Vera's mind, this is probably just another of those things that she doesn't understand but assumes she should. So she rolls with it. "How nice to see you," she says finally to Abby's back, and pushes the bowl of nuts forward. "Would you like a snack?"

There's a sigh of resignation as Abby walks back over to Vera. She grabs some almonds and chews. "Terrible," she says, her mouth full. But at least it's something.

"Well," I say, standing, "I guess I should go." What I don't say is, *Who are you why are you here and what do you want with Vera after all this time don't hurt her don't you dare hurt her.* The last thing in the world I want to do is leave Vera with Abby, but I can't get in the way of a family reunion—if that's what this could even be called. "You two probably want to catch up."

"Stay," Abby practically barks. Then she adds, "Please." Her jaw is clenched, eyes blinking a little too quickly, and I realize I've seen this face before on the family members of other residents, those daughters and sons who visit only once a month, maybe less. She's frightened by this place. People who aren't comfortable in hospitals are usually pretty uncomfortable at the Royal Pines. It's lovely enough for what it is, but what it is generally smells like urine and antiseptic spray and sounds like forty souls' worth of memories echoing against the white walls in a constant, tumbling murmur.

I want to tell Abby that the trick is to listen for only one voice in the murmur, to learn its cadence, to add her voice to

Vera's own until Abby's words fill in the gaps and what her mother's saying becomes clear and bright and whole.

I want to tell her all of this. But as I listen to Abby create and fill silences, I know it would be useless. Abby doesn't want to hear what Vera has to say. I don't know why she's here now, or what she wants, but it's clear that, when it comes to her mother, Abby would rather not hear anything at all.

We walk out at four, just as one of the nurses comes in to wheel Vera down to dinner. I'm lagging behind so I can text Georgie (*You won't believe who showed up at the nursing home today*), but Abby slows and waits for me.

"Ridiculous time to eat," she says as we walk through the sliding doors into the rain. "They must go to bed at six."

I slide my phone into my pocket, pull my shoulders in, and huddle against myself. Of course she doesn't know that Vera is asleep by seven at the latest. She doesn't know anything. But I say, "Yeah." The rain, which started while we were inside, is thick and insistent.

"She has a doctor's appointment tomorrow," says Abby. "A follow-up on the stroke."

"Mini-stroke," I say.

"Tomato, toe-mah-toe," says Abby. "It's still a serious medical event."

"Is that why you're here?" I ask.

Abby peers at me through the rain, and I can't tell if she's glaring. "Partly, yes," she says, and then doesn't say anything else.

131

I can barely see my bike through the sheets of water. "Well," I say, "I have to go." I can feel my phone vibrate in my pocket. Probably Georgie. She knows no one's visited Vera since I started working here. When I describe Abby later, I don't think Georgie'll be surprised at all.

Abby doesn't offer me a ride. Instead, she says, "Remind me of your schedule."

"Wednesday and Friday," I tell her. "During the school year, I come in the afternoons. But now—" I shrug. "Anytime during the day, really."

"And that's what I'm paying you for," she says.

"What?"

"I mean, that's all I'm paying you for. Today's Monday. Not your scheduled day."

"I was in the neighborhood."

"I just want to be clear. I'm paying for two days." Abby wipes at the rain dripping down her forehead with the sleeve of her caftan. She looks annoyed at the rain, annoyed to be having this conversation. *Well, fine,* I want to say. *Let's not, then.* "I'm only paying for the hours we agreed on. Nothing more. Today was an exception, of course. I asked you to stay. I'll pay you for that hour."

I don't answer her for a minute. I look away toward the far end of the parking lot, where the nurses have to park. Then I say, "Where's Kathryn?"

"You didn't answer my question."

"I didn't hear a question." I blink at her. "I only heard an accusation." I don't want to have to tell her that yes, I do visit Vera at other times—almost daily, actually. I don't want to have to tell her that I don't charge her for it—that I'd do it all for free if I had to.

She takes a deep breath. Lets it out slowly. "I'm sorry," she says. "Travel, you know? We just got in a few days ago and the place is a mess, and—" She waves her caftan so that it catches more rain. "Not your problem."

I shrug and turn toward my bike. "No," I say, "it's not." *What place?* I want to ask. *Where are you staying?*

She starts to say something else, but decides not to. In a minute, I hear the slap of feet as she moves toward her car. Then the engine starting, the wet squeal of wheels on pavement, and I'm alone again.

I'm almost home, soaked through to the bone, when I remember what she said about travel. *We got in a few days ago.* She's been here for days—and this afternoon was the first time she visited her mother.

Kathryn, I think, *where are you?*

WHERE THE LAKE IS ALL YOURS

That man behind you in line at Toney's, buying twelve frozen chicken breasts and a case of beer. The Weekender mom who's trying on end-of-season tank tops at a shop downtown and saying something embarrassing to no one, like, "One last hurrah." The ten-year-old at the public beach, staring at the Jet Skis and biting his lip, ignoring first his dad, then his mom as they yell his name. The girl at the ice-cream shop, standing behind the counter on one foot and looking for all the world like she has not one goddamn left to give.

They each have a lake.

Their lakes look the same on a map, but they're composed of different roads. Over the span of a single summer, new roads take on the heft of memory, the burden of hope. Fishing spots, swimming coves, empty and serene meadows: Each have the potential to redefine the whole summer for any one person. And when that happens, nothing looks the same again.

And the thing is, it keeps shifting for each of us. We may watch together as a flock of geese lift and fly, sounding their good-bye across the water, but none of us see the same thing at that moment. Someone hears the geese and thinks about what her mother has told her about how her grandfather could mimic their call so perfectly, and her heart, in that moment, snaps taut. Someone watches them and wishes for the courage to put his arm around the girl he's standing next to so that this moment, this lake, might be theirs together. Across the lake, a Weekender stands on his dock and thinks about the market, and whether it will rise like the geese or fall like his son yesterday, when he dropped him in the water and yelled, "Swim, dammit!"

And the geese themselves fly onward, water dripping from their webbed feet. Transients, all of us.

GEORGIE

Be interested, but not too interested.

That's the plan.

Once I got the QP from Dodge, I texted Henry and set up a meeting. And now, as I make my way around the corner from Grainey's and duck through the alley, I remind myself of my Weekender rule: Don't take anything too seriously.

He's waiting next to the Dumpster behind Grainey's. When I hand him the brown paper bag with the mason jar of tightly packed weed inside, he slips it in the messenger bag that he's got slung across his chest.

Henry laughs quietly and shakes his head. "Well, that was fast," he says. "Resort towns. Everything's both easier and harder here."

"You got that right," I say, and hold out my hand for the money.

Crisp Franklins. Straight from the bank.

"Looks like someone just drained his savings account," I say.

"Who said anything about 'drained'?" He winks. "I might still have a few dollars. Let me buy you a coffee." He tilts his head behind him at Grainey's. "Since we're here already." Then he laughs again, touches my shoulder.

Shit. Not too interested? Nice try. He's wearing a Ramones T-shirt, threadbare enough for me to know that it isn't just one of those novelty shirts that companies in China make just to capitalize on the latest infatuation with punk. There's a hole up by his armpit. It's the real thing.

What? A T-shirt isn't enough? How about this: When I handed him the brown bag, our fingers touched, and fuck if it wasn't a scene from the cheesy movies that I'm pretty sure Davis watches on the DL on Friday nights. Stars and confetti and all that.

It's funny that I thought I was immune to that sort of stuff.

Erik's forehead against mine. Everything suspended. Everything electric. "You've never—"

I wanted to be immune.

Henry and I get iced coffees and sit across from each other at a table by the window. He leans toward me.

"Thanks for this," he says, patting the messenger bag next to him. Then he adds, "I don't usually order in bulk."

"Big Costco shopper," I say.

"Funny," he says. "Again." He leans back, stretches his arms over his head. The hole near his armpit winks. "You might be the most"—he pauses—"*interesting* person in this town." A smile. "So. What's there to do around here, anyway?"

I set my coffee down. "What, you're not a regular?" I already knew that, of course. But I'm thinking maybe he's been here before and I haven't noticed. Weekenders often take breaks from Gold Fork for a few years—run out of money, wait for a new cabin to be built. That sort of thing. "What are you doing in the Fork?"

138

He pats his bag again in answer. "What do you think?" Then he laughs. "I'm helping my mom and stepdad out with some stuff. Nothing too exciting. Beats getting a job, right?" He shifts in his seat. "I mean, aside from what you do. The perks must be pretty good."

I shrug. "Not as great as you'd think." And as soon as I say it, I swear I see Dodge out the window, shuffling down the street toward the water like some sort of tourist. Has he seen me? He knows I'm delivering the QP today. Is he checking on me? But then I blink, and he's gone.

God. So paranoid.

"But really," Henry's saying, "what else do you do?" He glances around the coffee shop. "Besides this."

"We walk around," I say. "We go to parties that we don't throw. We drink coffee." I don't tell him about the Den.

He laughs and leans in. "We?"

"My friends and I."

"Ah." He leans back again. "Sounds good to me." There's something I can't put my finger on—laughter just under the surface of everything he says—that makes me want to keep him talking. Makes me want to lean closer. Makes me wish there wasn't a table between us. "What about music?"

"What about it?" I wave my hand around. "It's shit, unless you like people basically whispering vows to one another while they strum their guitars."

Henry laughs. "Hell no."

"Do you play?" I ask, even though I already know the answer by the way he asked.

He nods. "Bass. We haven't exactly taken off yet or anything, but I think we've got a sort of Sonic Youth–meets–The 1975 thing going on. I don't know," he adds, and looks down. It's the first time I've seen him look anything but certain, and I want to leap over the table to him.

There's nothing sexier than the tiniest flash of insecurity on someone who has absolutely nothing to feel insecure about.

"What about you?" he asks.

"Yeah," I say, "I play." But I don't want to tell him about the band quite yet. Music—it's my best thing. I don't want it to seem small when I talk about it.

I'm saved by the scream of a fire engine. I put my hands over my ears, and we both watch as it tears down Main and heads in the direction of the lake's west side.

"Maybe our pyro is at it again," I say. My heart thrums in my chest, and I try to quiet it, focusing on my breath. *Probably nothing,* I tell myself.

"What's up with that, anyway?" Henry asks. "They know that cabin was torched. How hard can it be to catch someone around here?"

"Have you seen our police station?" I laugh. "It's basically a cubicle."

"Wonder what it was this time," he says, and pulls out his phone.

"You're not going to find anything on there," I tell him. "Even our breaking news doesn't hit the web until a good twelve hours have passed." *Probably nothing.*

"The Stone Age," he says, and I laugh, but I'm nervous. I'm thinking about Davis's place, out in the direction the fire engine was going. The Nelson cabin was on the west side too. Before that, the chapel. I shiver, hugging my arms around myself. Paranoid. "Hey," I say, "you said you were helping your parents out. What are you helping them with?"

Anything to change the subject.

Henry rolls his shoulders back and shifts in his seat. "Don't you know?" he says, smiling and making air quotes with his fingers. "The 'family business.'"

"Stepdad's business?"

"Not really," he said. "I don't even know why I call him that, though—he and my mom got together when I was six. He's just my dad, I guess."

"What about your—" I'm not sure how to ask.

"Bio dad? Never met him. One-night stand, I think, when my mom was in grad school." He laughs. "Not that I like to think about *that*. Kyle's all there is."

"So what's the business?" I ask. "What are you doing for them?"

"I was kidding," he says. "I'm basically doing jack shit this summer. I'm coasting on my parents' good graces. Just like everyone else around here."

"Not everyone," I say. "Some of us can't afford to coast."

He leans in. We're close enough that he has to lower his voice when he says, "Coasting is overrated."

I'm looking so intently at Henry, drinking in every word, that it takes me a second to feel it. But then I do. A burn on my right cheek, like acid. Like a slap. Someone's staring at me from outside the window. I turn, very slowly.

Dodge is so close to the glass that I can see a tiny fog of breath against the pane. His eyes—little, mean—narrow at me, and he holds up a phone, wiggles it in the air.

"Who's that loser?"

"Town drunk," I say, but I'm already reaching in my bag for my phone. New text message.

Do your fucking job.

"Shit," I say aloud.

"What?" Henry glances again at Dodge. Dodge widens his eyes, opens his mouth, barks out a laugh that we can hear from inside. A pretty good impression of a crazy drunk, even though he doesn't know what I just said.

"I have to take this call," I say, holding the phone close to my chest. "I'll be right back."

I walk out of the coffee shop, phone to my ear, and round the corner toward the alley.

He meets me back there a minute later.

"Amateur hour," he says when he shuffles over. He's not smiling.

"Let me do my job, Dodge." I glare at him.

"Is that what this is? Seems to me you're fucking

around." His hands are in his pockets, fumbling with something.

"I just sold a QP. Excuse me for getting some coffee." I try to sound tough, but I can't see what he's holding, and a crazy part of me thinks it might be a gun.

"Getting coffee. Sure." He brings his hand up and tosses something at me. It hits my face before clattering to the ground, and I flinch. Dodge laughs. "Weak."

It's a key, attached to a miniature red lifeguard tube.

"What's this for?" I ask.

"Driving the boat," he says. "We're expanding. New way of getting people what they want." He smiles, though calling it a smile is generous. I can see gaps in the back where teeth should be. "So many docks, so little time."

"No thanks," I say. "I'll stick to meeting my customers on dry ground."

Dodge steps forward, grabbing me by my arm and digging his fingers into the bone. "Like hell you will. I'm expanding, which means you're expanding. And besides, I don't know how to drive a boat."

"I don't—" I start to say, but he digs his fingers in deeper, and I whimper instead.

He lets go and grabs the key, stuffing it back in his pocket. He starts to walk away, and then turns. "Next time we meet, you'd fucking better know how."

When I walk back into the coffee shop, Henry looks up. "Everything okay?" he asks.

I will myself not to touch the sore part of my arm. "Yeah," I say. "Work stuff."

"Ah." He looks like he wants to ask more, but instead he stands and holds out his hand. "Come on, then. Let's make this town work for our approval."

We spend the rest of the afternoon doing the things that Weekenders do when they want to think of themselves as Dead Enders: scouring the thrift store on Fourth Street for cat-eye sunglasses and a ridiculous sweatshirt with MARGARITAS ARE FOR DRUNKS (front); I TAKE MY TEQUILA NEAT (back). Laughing at all the doilies. Thumbing through the sad CD collection at the drugstore, both of us amazed when Henry pulls out a Neutral Milk Hotel album for five bucks. Eating pizza at the city park as we watch the water-skiers, rating each fall like we're judges at the Olympics. We're having such a good time that when Henry slings his arm around me on the park bench, pulls me in for a little half hug, turns my chin toward him and kisses me, I don't exactly pull away.

I can't. Not with the magnets holding us together.

Not going to be interested, Georgie? Fuck that.

By the time I get home, he's already called and left a message. "Hey. Georgie." Pause. A rustle—paper? Not sure. "Good to hang out today. Thanks for helping me out." His voice so smooth, not an ounce of worry. "Just calling to see if you want to hang out sometime. Dinner or . . . something." I can almost hear his half-crooked smile. "Text me if you want."

I listen to the message three times, wondering when the best time to call back would be. In an hour? A day? A few days? It's summer, after all—the time to play games is decidedly shorter. Play a game too long and you lose. And I don't want to lose.

I know what Ana would say. *Be careful.* Because she knows what I know: The Weekenders are always trying to claim us. I've seen Ana around the Weekenders—especially Weekender guys—she's circumspect, not particularly interested. She doesn't want to give them anything they want. But me? Everyone's my friend in this town. Everyone wants to be the person who knows me best. *Oh yeah, Georgie,* they'll say. *She and I are pretty tight.* Or, if they're smarter, they'll do the slow nod when someone asks about me, say something like, *Why do you ask?* like they're my gatekeepers, my bodyguards.

They think we've got something. An understanding. Probably even think I want to be like them. But the Weekenders aren't my friends. They've always been business. A means to an end, and the end sure as hell isn't paddleboards and Jet Skis. What I want costs more than their *toys*.

But. Even though I know I'll call Henry back, even though I already feel the slow fall toward him, like I'm standing on a hill and he's below me, his arms an invitation, that doesn't change the fact that, when I got home tonight, before I even listened to his message, I pulled out my little notebook. Entered amounts from the previous week of work, added in my cut from his QP, did the math. $2,700 to go.

ERIK

Something a teacher said this spring. Health class, I think, which we all had together. The teacher (this old guy who should have retired about four decades before we were born) said, "Part of growing up is realizing that your parents are real people, too, with real strengths and real weaknesses."

Davis leaned over toward me and Georgie and whispered, "You think?" Because we all knew by then that our parents were real people. Real as in: people who have sex when they think their kids are going to be gone all afternoon (Davis); people who don't get tenure at their university and have to move their family to a small town so they can teach junior high school history and read important books after dinner (Georgie); people who work nights and weekends because everyone knows that's when you get the best tips (Ana). And then there are people like my mom.

"How's yours?" The Beast reaches over and takes a forkful of my mac and cheese. We're sitting at our kitchen table, the radio on in the background so that we have something to listen to while we chew.

"Same as yours," I say, but she's shaking her head.

"Yours is better. Did you add something? Pepper?"

"Salt."

"I never get it right." She looks down at her plate, and then over to mine. "Yours is so much better."

And, because this is our dance, I reach over and switch plates with her. Then I grab the salt.

The others all know their parents are real and flawed because they've seen them do strange or embarrassing things over the years. But they don't know their parents like I know my mom. This is what I know: My mother is the kind of person who cleans Weekenders' houses for a living and complains about the things she's not asked to clean—tennis rackets and computers and long silk dresses—as though just the fact of them in those huge houses is enough of an imposition. She's the kind of person who stays home on Saturday nights in a quilted bathrobe and these wretched blue slippers that you got her one year in the miscellaneous aisle at Toney's because you'd forgotten to go shopping and it was already Christmas Eve and you couldn't deal with the look on her face if there was nothing under the tree again. I call her the Beast of Burden because it's true. She's always frazzled, puttering around, looking like she hasn't showered for worrying about me.

Most importantly, she's the kind of person who will never, ever, ever be happy with what's on the plate in front of her. She's never ordered the right thing at a restaurant. She's never seasoned her food correctly. And even when it's the same goddamn thing as what she's eating, she will want what you have.

I'd take walking in on sex or professional failure or a string of lame father figures any day over our nightly ritual of me handing my plate over and my mom looking ashamed and then relieved.

But the true athlete doesn't trip on small pebbles lining the track. He runs right over them, knowing they might even make him faster.

The Beast is chewing happily, glancing at me now and then with the briefest blink of guilt. "Hey," she says, "have your grades arrived yet?"

"No."

All I do is lie.

"I bet you got an A on that algebra final," the Beast says now. "I bet you got straight A's."

"I told you. I don't know yet."

"Well, it's an A. I guarantee it."

I sigh. "Something like that."

"You got an A."

"Yes," I say finally, "you're right. I did." It's that time in the meal when the walls start to close in around me.

From the living room, I hear the radio announcer's metronomic voice. . . . *Fire started in a trash can outside of the brewery yesterday afternoon . . . no serious damage, though the fire inspector is wondering if this could be connected to . . .* I push my plate aside.

"Something wrong?" She didn't hear it, then.

"No, just full."

She looks me over, eyes narrowed, and then she nods. "You've been under too much stress," she says. "And you deserve a break."

I nod.

"It's good that you're not working this summer," she goes on. "Enjoy yourself. But not too much," she quickly adds.

"I'll behave," I say, trying to sound sincere.

"After all," she says, "you've earned it. Nothing to save for now."

I don't say anything. I spent the past three summers working at the marina—boat maintenance, Jet Ski rentals. Later, after town clears out, I help pull the docks onto shore at all those private beaches so they don't buckle in the ice. Glamorous work, all of it.

When I got the scholarship, I quit my job. Called the marina that day and told them I wouldn't be coming back this summer.

I was so stupid.

Now, instead of making money, I spend the first hours of the day in the library. I don't have a laptop—of course the Beast can't afford one—so I have to use the computers that are tucked behind the audiobooks and across from the Kids' Korner in the Gold Fork Public. That's why I go early, as soon as it opens at eight. I don't need to be working on my résumé to a soundtrack of fifteen screaming toddlers ripping pages out of their favorite books. That, and I don't want to run into anyone. I guarantee that none of the Weekenders have résumés—or, if they do, they're just college résumés. Not—horror—job résumés. And working on a job résumé at the public library basically makes you homeless.

"Anyway," the Beast says, "I was going to tell you what Mrs. Jensen said. You won't believe it."

I'd beg to differ. I'm never surprised by what my mom's clients say while she's cleaning their sinks or scrubbing the wine stains out of their carpets. It's usually something along the lines of shock at the price of their neighbor's new car, or outrage if the county threatens to raise their property taxes. Money. Always money. And never enough of it. Typical Weekender bullshit.

She's looking for a response, so I say, "Yeah?"

"Well, she wanted to congratulate you, first of all. She'd heard from Chris Foster—does their landscaping—and ooh la la, was she surprised. Couldn't *believe* my son was the track star." The Beast makes a dismissive huffing sound. "I wanted to tell her you don't need her congratulations. That you don't need anything of hers." She crosses her arms over her chest, triumphant.

"Was there something else?" I feel itchy. I can't get away fast enough.

"Oh. Yes. Turns out Mr. Jensen knows the fire chief. He was first on the scene at the Nelsons', you know."

"Oh, that. Right."

"So far, they don't have a name. But Mrs. Jensen said they're getting close. Something about a footprint near the burn site. But I don't know. I wouldn't put it past the Nelsons to just torch it themselves if they were having troubles. God knows they were stingy as hell with me." She shakes her head.

"Never a tip, in five years of working for them. Never once. Not that I'll get one now." And she laughs.

The fist of my stomach clenches and unclenches at the sound of her laughter. I stand, pick up my plate, take it to the sink. "I'm going on a run."

She frowns. "After eating?"

"I didn't eat."

She follows me and touches my arm. "Sorry to bore you."

"You didn't. You don't." Deep breath. "Really."

When I get upstairs to my room, I close the door. Lock it. Check the lock, then check it again. Send a text. Wait for the reply. Then I sit on the edge of my bed and take off my shoes, dusting dirt off the soles before sliding them under. Take off my shirt and fold it. I stand, and make my way to my dresser. I open the top drawer and grab my running gear. I lay my shirt on the neat stack inside. Reach underneath and pull out a small box. I hold the box in my hand, feeling its weight. I could shake it to hear the gentle rattle, the clunking as the contents hit each side.

I could, but I won't.

I put the box back and get dressed in a hurry. I can't get out of here fast enough. Why did I say I was going running? Now I have to put on the whole show—lacing my shoes before doing stretches by the door, drinking my obligatory glass of water. It looks like I'm getting ready, but all I'm doing is wasting time. When I finally hear the click of the front door behind me, I exhale. Start off at a slow jog, but once I round the corner, I walk again.

I watch my feet as I move. Why bother looking around? I'd only see shitty streets, shitty houses, shitty little lives. You want to talk about dead ends? The Beast and I live on one of those side streets that the Weekenders never even know about. It's not far enough away from downtown to be in the woods, not close enough to be attractive. It's just row after row of run-down clapboard houses, built back when Gold Fork was more logging town than resort. No matter what time of day, there's always a dog barking somewhere. Always a car motor sputtering in someone's yard. No one's got a chandelier made out of antlers on my street. We're lucky to have electricity.

Everyone here thinks I'm after fame and glory. Everyone thinks I have Olympic-size dreams. They couldn't be further from the truth. When I think about being twenty, twenty-five, here's what I want. A truck. A laptop that I don't have to work all winter to buy. My own plate at dinner. Boring conversation with a pretty girl about what we're going to do tomorrow. Soft carpet and a quiet dog waiting for scraps under the dining room table. I want to fall asleep listening to the sound of rain on a roof, knowing that when I wake up, the coffee maker won't be broken and I'll drink a cup while getting ready for my job at a bank or maybe an accounting firm. Every Sunday, phone calls from my imaginary family, just checking in.

All I want is a normal life. That. Is. All. I. Want.

But even that seems like a stretch. Normal's not for me.

If Normal were for me, I wouldn't have lost my scholarship. I wouldn't be sitting here with jack shit, pretending that I'm going to State for free in a year, when really, I have no idea where I'm going, or how. I wouldn't be living a lie.

I'm always going to be living a lie.

Maybe Georgie did us both a favor when she turned me down. Because I wouldn't be able to lie to her for long. Not about everything.

I start running. It's what I do whenever I want to escape the memory of Ms. Henderson, the guidance counselor, on the phone: *I know you won the award . . . The bylaws stipulate . . .*

Faster, faster.

They're sorry. But adamant.

I don't have to be at the skate park for a couple hours. I let my feet carry me—out of my neighborhood, away from this two-timing town. The familiar road along the west side of the lake, paved until it's not. Four miles out, four miles back. I know this road by heart.

When I get to Washer's Landing, I turn off. Run across the gravel driveway toward the ghost of the cabin. I stop and lean over, breathing heavily. Can imagine the smoke and soot, flames shooting from every window. My breath steadies, and I walk past the large fireplace—the only thing still standing now. I cross over toward the cliffs and stand at the edge, looking out over the lake.

There are a handful of boats out, a couple wakeboarders, some kids on tubes. The water ripples green and inviting from here. The shadows on the trees across the lake are a comforting hand. It's peaceful. And the memories of Henderson's voice fade away like they always do, replaced by the steady sound of my own breath.

Then I turn around and start running back.

I was just a kid when my dad left, can barely remember him, really, but I can imagine him—can picture the way he left. I like to think he was an athlete, like me. That, like me, he was the fastest in his class. And I like to think that, when he left, he didn't just leave—he sprinted. Because that's how I'll have to go, one of these days. I'll have to run so fast and so far that my lies can't catch up with me. Mom, Kelly, all the other Dead Ender girls I've hooked up with—they won't be able to keep up. They've never had what I need. I'll be gone before they even hear the starting gun go off.

Four miles out. Four miles back. I get to the skate park just in time to meet her.

Layla's waiting for me at the entrance. I had to give her directions. Of course she hasn't been here before. When I walk up, she looks just like she did the first time I saw her— willowy and light, like a painting of a girl. She's wearing the same cowboy boots, same leather bracelet wrapped around her wrist. Layla starts to look real the closer I get: real brown hair, pulled away from her face, real eyes, real smile.

A Weekender. *Maybe*, the little voice in the back of my

head says, *my Weekender*. I immediately regret the run—now I look sweaty and disheveled.

"Hey," she says, and her voice is real, too. "What's up?"

"Not much." Funny, for me to be tongue-tied. I try to remember how easy it was with her body pressed against mine as we stood between cars in the makeshift parking lot at Fellman's, kissing at sunrise. But the conversation with the Beast has left me rattled, and I can't stop thinking about the scholarship. My only ticket out.

Layla's no Dead Ender. The street this girl lives on is straight and narrow, pointing all the way to a perfect future on the golden horizon. Coffee in the morning. Carpet underfoot.

She's looking at me, waiting, so I say, "Wanna walk around? Get an ice cream, maybe?"

Layla laughs. "An ice cream?"

"Well, I mean . . ." I'm stumbling—*God, get it together*. "If you want."

"Sure," she says, and links her arm through mine. "We'll get an ice cream." She's smiling, but I don't think she's laughing at me. I don't think so. "And then maybe we can pick up where we left off."

She's got one hand in my hair and the other against my back before I know it, pulling me toward her. Her mouth is soft. I open my eyes to look at her as we kiss—her eyelashes, her nose. Everything just right. I close my eyes again, and give in to the momentum. Her hands are everywhere. Mine are, too. It feels inevitable. Unstoppable. Now now now.

But I break away and take a breath. "Let's get that ice cream." And when she looks surprised, I add, "And then come back to this."

"Ice cream."

"Yeah."

She pauses, and then shakes her head, kind of smiling. "Okay," she says. "I guess." She reaches over and hooks her finger in my waistband. Pulls me toward her an inch. "Ice cream's fine."

It takes everything I have to start walking. But I do, and she comes with me, sliding her hand into mine.

"You're a gentleman," she says, smiling. "I didn't expect that."

"Neither did I," I say, and listen to her bright, warm laugh.

But I am. At least, I want to be. Because I don't want this to move too fast. I want dates, ice cream, meeting her mother, impressing her little brother. I don't want Layla to be like all the others. If I'd met her last year, it'd have been different. Last year she'd have been just another girl—maybe the best one, sure, but still just another one.

But that was last year. Last year I hadn't gotten—and lost—the scholarship. Last year I hadn't tried—really tried—with Georgie. Last year I didn't know that Normal was as much as I could hope for, as far as I could dream. And I didn't know I'd want Normal so bad I can taste it.

DAVIS

Frame One: Jane, on her parents' landline. Cord wrapped around one wrist. She says, *I know, but that's the thing. I've never met someone so . . .*

Frame Two: cord stretched between her two small hands. She looks into the distance, eyes searching, the phone propped between her ear and her shoulder.

Frame Three: She's leaning forward a little, intent. The cord lies slack. *Inimitable,* she says.

Inimitable? I put my pen down. Is that what I want my girlfriend to call me? I shake my head. Correction: girlfriend on paper. That makes it sound like we're legally bound—married, or filing a lawsuit or something. It's not the actual truth, which is that I have a girlfriend, and she's made of paper.

This book is the only thing I've got going. My week has been a blur. Not a blur as in: getting-wasted-every-night-what's-a-weekend-for-when-you're-in-Gold-Fork-anyway-Wednesday-is-the-new-Saturday-every-night-all-night. Definitely not that kind of blur. More like: Hey-it's-Monday-wait-now-it's-Saturday-guess-that's-how-life-passes-you-by. The fact that I actually have a job—okay, okay, *unpaid internship*—puts me leagues above where I was last summer,

157

which basically consisted of riding my bike around town, "looking for excitement" (in the words of my dad, which should indicate exactly how successful I was).

But the problem with an unpaid internship (besides the obvious, you know, *lack of payment*) is that the hours aren't exactly robust. I still have time to kill. So, I do what any respectable sixteen-year-old boy with a broken heart and five dollars in his pocket would do: I get on my bike and head to Grainey's.

Now. You may be saying to yourself, *Self, I'm concerned. Isn't that the coffee shop where Jane and her friends hang out almost every single day?* To that I would reply, *Yes. Yes it is.* But in Gold Fork, our options are limited. If you want to break up with someone, you have to deal with the fact that you'll probably see him everywhere. I mean, you can't claim the only decent hang-out spot other than the diner just because you have enough friends to fill a table and he doesn't.

You can't, Jane. You just can't.

Grainey's is on the far end of Main Street, exactly one-point-one mile from my house. I'm fine when I first get on my bike to ride over, but my heart starts pounding as I coast onto Main. I'm sweating by the time I find a spot for my bike in front of my dad's real estate office across the street. My hands are clammy, and I have to try three times before I can get the combination right on the bike lock. I'm trying to look busy, in case Jane's watching. Busy and competent. When I finally turn to walk into the coffee shop, though, I can see myself in the door's thick glass, and I look disheveled, Saturday-morningish. I run a hand through my hair and walk in.

The thing to do.

The thing to do when walking into a coffee shop where your ex-girlfriend may or may not be hanging out is to:

1. Look straight ahead.

2. Affect a preoccupied air. A furrowed brow helps. So does a slight frown and a shake of the head, as though you've just realized that you've booked not one, but two dates that night and *now* what are you going to do?

3. Exhale. By now you've made it to the counter. In just a minute, you'll have your coffee in hand. You'll take it black even though you'd like to add some cream or soy milk at the very least, because you know what happens to a guy's image in the five seconds it takes him to unscrew the top of a milk thermos. When Maria hands you your coffee, it will be time to scan the room. You'll act like you're looking for a table, but really, you'll be on high alert. Chances are, you'll see her at the first table your eyes land on. Be prepared. She will be more beautiful than she was on the last day of school, the last time you saw her. She'll probably be wearing The Outfit. She might be with a guy. Even if she isn't, the specter of another guy will be there, just to her right, like a promise she has to keep.

A scan, a smile, and then you walk right by her. That's the thing to do.

But Jane's not here. When I get my coffee and do the turn-and-scan, the only person I see is Ana, because she's right in front of me.

"Davis," she says. "Hey."

"Oh." I almost fall backward from the surprise, so I lean forward. For a second, I kind of toggle back and forth. I must look ridiculous. I take a quick glance over her shoulder. No Jane. The coffee shop is only halfway full. I recognize a few of the people here. One guy with a lip ring, sitting at a table with two cups in front of him, catches my eye and then looks away. "Hey. How's it going?"

"Good." She smiles. She's wearing a blue long-sleeved dress with tiny white flowers all over it, and her boots.

"You look nice," I say, and then catch myself. "I mean, very Americana. What do they call that look? Prairie chic?"

"I think they only call something a 'look' when a celebrity wears it."

"You're probably right. Well, in any case, it's nice." Why in God's name do I keep saying "nice"? The pressure of maybe seeing Jane, I guess.

Or maybe it's just Ana. Because she *does* look nice. Nice nice nice nice nice.

Ana laughs. "Thanks." Gestures kind of vaguely behind her. "Well, I should go." She starts to turn.

From a table nearby, we hear a guy say, "I mean, it's just a little too coincidental. Two fires in the same place. And then that new one—over by the brewery."

A woman's voice answers, "That one? Wasn't it small potatoes compared to the others?"

"Fire is fire."

Another woman's voice. "Frankly, it's a little scary. What if this is just the beginning?"

"Of what?" the man asks.

"Of a Stephen King novel." She laughs, and then we hear her say, "No, but seriously."

Ana and I look at each other. Frozen. She says quietly, "Did you know about the brewery fire?"

"Yeah," I say. "There'll be an article tomorrow. But it's nothing, really. Trash can outside—brewery wasn't touched."

"Fire is fire," she whispers, and smiles, though it's a sad smile. And then she starts to walk away.

"Wait." I touch her shoulder, and she shivers like I've shocked her. "Sorry."

Her eyes widen, but then she smiles. "It's fine. You just surprised me."

My hand is still on her shoulder, and I stare at it like it's a Rorschach test. "Sorry," I say again, moving my hand away. "But . . . Have you heard from Georgie at all? Or"—pausing, hoping she doesn't notice—"Erik?" I step over to the cream station and Ana follows. I pour a little into my cup. (Whatever. Jane's not here to see that I actually like my coffee the color of suburban carpet.)

"No," she says. "Not really since Fellman's. I've missed you all," she adds, then coughs. "But—why do you ask?"

"I just—listen," I say. "Yesterday I found something about his dad." I lift my coffee in the direction of a table, and she follows me and sits, tugging her sleeves carefully over her wrists.

"What did you find?" she asks, leaning forward.

"The divorce notice in the paper," I say. "They got divorced when we were three." I take a sip of my coffee. I like this: Me and Ana, scheming. Collaborating. It feels . . . well, *nice*.

"Does it say anything?"

"No. But I did find—" I pause, not sure I want to go on.

"What, Davis?"

"It was a legal notice. Something about child support nonpayment. That was the term it used."

"Oof. A deadbeat dad," Ana says, "is worse than a nonexistent one." Her cheeks flush.

"I'm sorry," I say.

"Don't be. Seriously." Then she says, "But why would he even come back if he isn't going to—"

I hold up my hand and clear my throat. Ana turns to look. Georgie's just walked into Grainey's. I'm about to wave, but it's clear that she doesn't see us yet. She walks straight over to the guy with the two coffee cups in front of him and puts her hand on his shoulder. He stands, hands her a coffee, and they lean against each other for a quick second. It's such a small gesture you might miss it, but Ana looks at me and mouths, *Who's that?* and I know she saw it too. It's weirdly intimate, coming from Georgie.

We watch them leave.

"So that's new, I guess," says Ana.

"Where did he come from?" The guy looked vaguely familiar, but then, everyone does in Gold Fork.

"Fellman's," she says. "I saw him there, I think. But," she adds, "I didn't see him hanging out with Georgie."

"Gotta hand it to her," I say. "She moves fast."

"Yeah," says Ana, and the look on her face is almost wistful. She glances at me and then away. "When you know, you know, I guess." She pulls at the sleeves of her dress again.

I try to think of what to say to that, but I've got nothing but questions. Georgie and a guy? Since when? How is it so easy for everyone else, and so difficult for me? And more importantly, what the hell am I supposed to do when I run into Erik? My ability to act like everything's fine has the life span of a housefly.

But I don't say these things. I don't need to. Because then Ana's gone, too, a quick good-bye before she heads the other way down Main on her bike. And I bike toward the marina, thinking about the way Georgie and her guy leaned against each other like a physics experiment.

Jane never leaned against me like that, not even in those days after she first asked me out in art class. Back when we were meeting after school at the park, doing homework on a blanket she kept in her locker and talking about our plans, our hopes, the ways we imagined blowing this town off in two years to only ever come back at Christmas with a fabulous haircut (Jane) and a graphic novel that's getting small but significant attention in an underground and decisively cool sort of way (me) and yes, okay, sometimes leaning. But not enough. Never enough.

Oddly, the only person who would really understand this, I think, is Ana's old lady, Vera. I went to see her once with Ana this spring. The roads were muddy and I was borrowing my parents' car for the day to run errands and hit the Den, and Ana was going to walk all the way from the Den, otherwise. I thought—okay, I was *sure*—that it would be an exercise in lethargy, that I'd have to prop my eyelids open with toothpicks while Ana read to her or something. But that wasn't the case. Vera was more alert than I thought she'd be. Plus, she had this bowl of really delicious nuts by her bed. She'd nod whenever I took one, like I was doing her a favor, which is how I ended up eating half the bowl.

And then Ana noticed that Vera's emergency button was somehow disconnected, and she went to the nurses' station to tell them about it and I was alone with Vera and I smiled at her, all *Isn't it funny that we're alone together with nothing to talk about?* expecting, I don't know, to just sit there until Ana came back and filled in the silences, but Vera grabbed my hand instead. Her eyes were slate.

"Love can miss you," she said, voice matter-of-fact. "It can just chug right by you like a passenger train." She must have seen something in my expression, because she squeezed my hand a little. Her fingers felt like chicken bones around my palm. "Not always, young man, but sometimes. Don't believe those who tell you to give it time, that *it* will find *you*, because"—she let go of my hand and shrugged—"sometimes it doesn't. Cupid's Arrow. That's what we used to call it." Her voice went high and girlish. "'Have you been hit by the arrow?'" And then she giggled, remembering some inside joke from another time. "Oh, but," she said, sitting straighter in her chair, "what would I have done with a husband, anyway?"

I asked Ana about it later. I didn't tell her everything Vera said—just the last bit. I told her I thought Vera'd been married. *She was,* said Ana. *But maybe it's better to forget what you no longer have.*

I've thought about that conversation with Vera a lot in the past few months. And now, seeing Georgie with Henry, I remember it again.

Here's what's going through my head as I start biking toward the marina:

Jane. Were you my train? Jane?

When I get down to the beach, it's crowded with Toney's and Dead Enders, toddlers and dogs. Friday afternoon. Everyone appears to have a snow cone from the little cart that's set up on Main Street. Not exactly an inspirational setting. I turn and walk along the park path that leads to the marina.

I see them before I know what I'm looking at.

They're standing on the marina's dock. At first, I take her for a Weekender. Her hair's lighter than it was on the last day of school, and she's tan, wearing only a bikini top and shorts.

A different kind of uniform than the one I've been imagining all summer. I watch as she leans against the mannequin she's standing with, pulls him closer, and says something into his ear.

Jane.

A woman from the rental shop pulls up alongside them in a Jet Ski and hands them the key. Well, that's something at least. Her Weekender doesn't own his own toys. But then I see the mannequin turn and call to the end of the dock, where a huge speedboat, basically a yacht, waits idling. It's filled with people, and one of them, a youngish guy, jumps out, runs down the dock, and grabs the key, which the mannequin gives with a slight nod. The guy jumps on the Jet Ski and heads toward the middle of the lake. And Jane wraps one arm around the mannequin's waist as they walk together to the end of the dock and climb into the boat, where he turns the speakers up full blast and takes the wheel.

Naturally. Because it's his boat.

Three things come to mind as I'm standing there watching the wake that the boat makes behind them as they speed off. First, there's a certain amount of gratification in knowing that I was right, after all. Of course she found a Weekender. Of course he looks like that. Of course she looks happy. Didn't I predict all of this?

Give yourself a pat on the back, Davis.

Second, she never even saw me. I was staring at them so hard that my vision got fuzzy, and she didn't even notice me there on the beach.

And third.

Third, I can breathe.

Whenever I've imagined this moment, I've thought that I'd freeze. That even my lungs would betray me. But here I am, standing by the water, and—

I can breathe, Jane.

I reach into my backpack and grab my journal and my pen, turning to a page I haven't known how to finish.

Jane's on a deck looking out over the lake. One leg curled under her, the toes of her other leg barely touching the ground, pushing her chair back a little. The person she's talking to is just outside of the panel. Note: It's not my deck. This one is much nicer. The view, for one thing, is million-dollar, not "penny-ante," as my dad says about the sliver of blue that you can see from our kitchen window. Conversation bubble above her head, empty.

And I remember, like I do at least twelve times a day, the look on her face when she told me I wasn't quite *it*. There was something there. Regret, I always thought. Preemptive regret, the kind that says, *Oh, this is going to bite me in the ass someday*. That's what I wanted to see. Because she did like me once. I always thought it had to do with the way, in those old movies I watch with my parents, the cheerleader finds herself mesmerized by the science nerd who wears safety goggles whenever he drives. She had to like *something* about me enough to ask me out that day in art class and to not run away when I stumbled over my yes.

But now I think I know what it was she liked, and it wasn't me. I start writing. Don't stop until I'm done. I look down at the page. *He lived on a lake,* the conversation bubble says. *I thought he was a Dockside.* One more sentence. *Turned out the emperor had no clothes.*

Jane was never interested in me. She was interested in my view. And when she saw it, she did the only thing a Dead Ender with Weekender aspirations can do: She got the hell out.

ANA

"Did I ever tell you about the summer I hitchhiked to British Columbia?" My mom is washing potatoes in the sink, and she turns to wave one at me. "One or two?"

"One," I say. I'm sitting at the table in our kitchen, grating cheese into a small bowl. There are already four other bowls on the table filled with condiments: sour cream, green onions, broken pieces of bacon. It's Sunday, which means one thing: u-stuff baked potatoes. My mom's specialty.

She turns back to the sink. "I think I was sixteen. Your age, can you believe it? At first, it was me and my friend Jill—we were going to make our way up to the fishing lodges, get some seasonal work. I think we had an idea of ourselves as great adventurers. I know we thought we were heart-breakers." I watch the back of her head as she shakes it, laughing. "But Jill backed out at the last minute. She said she got work in town, but I think she broke down and told her parents what we were planning, and they refused. It's a wonder they didn't tell my mom and dad. They'd have locked all the doors. As it was, they didn't know I was gone until they got the first postcard. By the time they'd calmed down, the summer was almost over and I was on my way home." She smiles, then turns away before I can see the sadness in her eyes.

"What's Jill doing now?"

My question has caught her off-guard. She turns to face me again. "Jill? God, who knows? She got married out of high school. I know that much. Tim. Nice enough guy. She's probably doing something like I am, you know?" She shoots a smile over her shoulder at me. "Living and loving and generally maintaining."

It's her catchphrase. Whenever anyone asks my mom how she's doing, she always says the same thing: "Living and loving and generally maintaining." She'll say it no matter what—even if, say, the rent's due and her hours just got cut at the spa. Even then.

"Anyway," my mom says, "it was wild. I went by myself—what else was I going to do? You wouldn't believe the people I met on the road. Truckers, families, an orchestra conductor. People were friendlier back then. They had less to be scared of." She looks at me. "Now, of course, I wouldn't hitchhike if you paid me."

"Uh-huh," I say. As much as Mom wants to appear young

and free in her stories, she doesn't want me to start getting ideas. But she's got nothing to worry about. She's got to know that I'll never do anything crazy or dangerous or thrilling. I've learned my lesson.

Sometimes I think my mom tells me these stories so that I'll believe her when she tells me she wasn't always like this: struggling and lonely in a wood-paneled kitchen. I think she wants me to know her as Linda, not Mom. She wants me to know that, even now, she's not *just* my mom. And I'd like to know her that way, but I can't tell her the truth: It's impossible. At least, right now. Because she *is* just my mom— the person I curled against in one twin bed after another, in one town after another, her stomach my pillow, my hand in hers. I didn't understand then that her body was her own, and even though I know it now, it's still not real to me. We are connected by silver threads, she and I, so translucent you never see them unless the sun is shining in just that way, and we always will be. Her body is not her own because my body is not my own. She'll never see me as the Ana I know I am. She can't. I'm hers, just like she's mine, and it makes us blind to each other.

"Oh," she says, opening the oven door and placing the potatoes on the rack, "mija, I forgot to tell you. A woman called for you yesterday. Said it was about your abuela."

"Vera," I say. My mom's retained the language her parents used around the house while she was growing up, but over the years it's been pared down to terms of endearment, a handful of nouns, and the occasional swear word that she thinks I might not understand.

(Sometimes I wish she hadn't felt the need to leave everything behind, including so much of the language she shared with her parents. She's told me they learned English when they moved here with her as a child, but they were always more comfortable with the language of their home country. And so I've always worried that I won't be able to talk to them if they ever find us. *If they ever try to find us*, I remind myself. *If they ever try*.)

"Vera. I always forget her name." Mom smiles. "I think the woman was her daughter?"

Why would Abby be calling me now? I haven't seen her since she first came to town, and frankly, I didn't think I'd hear from her again. "Did she say anything?"

My mom laughs. "On the contrary. She hardly said a word. But her voice—it was what you'd expect. Like she—like it's hard for her to *stoop*."

"Like she's not used to asking for things—" I begin, but Mom finishes my sentence.

"Because she hasn't had to ask." She laughs again. "Exactly."

I make a mental note to tell Davis about Abby. She's the quintessential Weekender, and Davis always likes to know when people fit the mold. He calls himself a cultural anthropologist. As for me, I don't like to know that people can be only how they appear. Especially if how they appear is kind of awful.

"She left her number," my mom is saying. "Sorry I didn't tell you earlier—I don't know how I forgot."

Actually, the same thought has occurred to me. I get so few phone calls that my mom practically has the number memorized for me whenever someone does leave me a message. I can think of only one reason my mom would forget. "Mom," I say, "have you met someone?"

The blush is instantaneous. She giggles, just like a girl. "Mayyyybe," she says, drawing the word out. "It's probably too soon to tell."

I wait.

"Well," she says finally, "he's a contractor. Zeke. A pretty regular customer at the spa, actually." She glances up at me. "You'll like him, Ana. He's sweet."

Sweet. The second guy she's brought into our lives since I was born, and all I get is *sweet*.

"That's great, Mom," I say, trying to sound sincere.

"Well, you'll meet him soon, I expect." Her eyes are hopeful, asking me a question I can't answer. "He's taking me to the city next weekend, actually. I already got the time off. He's got some business there, and he thinks I deserve a break." She laughs. "And I guess I do!"

"That'll be fun." I try to smile, though I don't feel like it. She just met him, and they're already going to the city for the weekend? I feel a quick shiver of betrayal when I think about the possibility that she's been seeing him for a while and not telling me about it. Biding her time. Because optimism is a form of currency with my mom—with work, with money, and I guess even with guys named Zeke. And she expects me to spend it as freely as she does, never mind the fact that it always runs out.

When I arrive at the Pines on Tuesday, Vera's not waiting for me in the solarium. I scan the faces in their chairs once, twice, try to push back the panic that's rising in my throat. I check her room, but she's not there either. I walk back to the solarium, but if there's music playing over the loudspeakers (usually Sinatra or Holiday), I can't hear it. Not over the drumming of my heart.

I go straight to the visitors' desk and sign in. Try not to sound worried when I ask, "Is Vera around? I don't see her," but my voice is high and tinny. I've tried to call Abby back a couple of times since I got her message, but she's never picked up. And suddenly I wonder if she was calling to tell me the thing I never want to hear.

(I talked to Davis about this once. We were hanging out at the Den after Georgie and Erik had gone home, just watching the sunset. He asked how Vera was, and I was surprised that he remembered her name, and I told him that I panic when I don't see her waiting for me. He paused, then nodded. "Ah. The great fear of all who visit the elderly. Russian roulette. One day—someday—we all arrive to an empty chair.")

The desk nurse—Gloria—smiles at me. "Hello, Ana. Don't worry," she says, and turns her gaze toward the exit. "She's fine. Better than fine. It probably has something to do

173

with her handsome chaperone." Gloria laughs. "Youth enlivens us, you know."

I turn to see a guy pushing Vera toward us. Combat boots, lip ring. It takes me a second because it's so incongruous, but then I place him: the guy who was with Georgie at Grainey's. Vera hasn't noticed me yet, and I watch as she looks down at her lap and smiles. It's true: She looks younger than usual.

"Hey. Ana, right?" he says, stopping in front of me. "We just got back from a little drive. I didn't want Vera to miss your visit." He leans down to Vera. "Grandma, Ana's here."

Grandma.

"Of course," says Vera, lifting a hand, which I press between my own. "Hello, dear."

"Oh," I say. "Um, where did you go?" I try to keep my voice steady. I try to keep it together. But. *Grandma.* I always knew Vera was someone's grandma. I just never thought they'd come claim her.

"The most lovely place!" says Vera, answering my question. "The ocean!"

The guy and I exchange looks.

"It was beautiful, wasn't it, Grandma?" He squeezes her shoulder, and she reaches up and grabs his hand.

"The people," she says, "were all in blue."

"Well," he says, "why don't we get you to your room? Then the three of us can talk."

"Yes," she says, "and I can nap until Mother comes."

We head down Larch Hall, the guy pushing the chair. He

174

leans over and whispers to me as we walk. "Is she always this confused?"

"No," I say.

He shakes his head. "I don't get it. I drove her up to the parking lot at the top of Coolidge Mountain so she could see the view. We didn't even go by the lake. I didn't notice a whole bunch of people in blue, either." I can hear the tinny clang of teeth on metal as he bites on his lip ring.

"Maybe she's tired," I say.

"I bet she is. She slept in the car on the way back." He pauses. "But this is strange."

How would you know?

When we get to her room, she's already asleep, hands folded on her lap, chin lowered toward her chest. "Catnap," she says when we wake her. She looks at the two of us and blinks. "Henry," she says. But then she adds, "And Kathryn. Thank you for coming."

So now I know his name at least.

He's about to say something, but I reach down and place my hand on hers. "It's so good to see you," I say. *My abuela.*

She blinks at me again. One eye is drooping on one side, and it makes her look sad, on the verge of tears. She says, "I've been waiting for you to come back. Why did you stay away? I've got all this space. Extra bedrooms. I could make one up for you."

"I'm sorry," I say. "I'll try to do better."

"What the—" I hear Henry mutter under his breath.

175

Louder, he says, "Grandma. That's not Kathryn. That's Ana. Ana, remember? Your friend?" He kneels down so that he's face-to-face with her. "Ana visits you every week. Kathryn hasn't been here in a while."

She studies his face. Then she unfolds her hands and wrings them together. "I'm sure I've put them somewhere," she says.

"What?"

"The nuts. You must be starving."

Once the nurse gets her settled in bed, fluffing the pillows so that she's sitting up, Vera tries to make conversation. Her eyes keep closing, though, so Henry and I finally help her scootch down until she's on her back. She's completely asleep within a minute.

"Well," says Henry, closing the door behind him as we retreat into the hall, "sorry to ruin your visiting time. I didn't expect her to get so tired. Or confused." He turns to me. "I would've taken her out another day if I'd known. I mean, my mom told me how close you two are."

"What else did your mom tell you?" The anger that I've kept at bay since I saw him come through the doors with Vera is spilling over. Anger and relief—relief that she's okay, that today wasn't the day, after all. I know that's part of it, but I still can't help the crest of fury that starts at the top of my head and rushes toward my shoulders. "No, really. I'd love to hear."

He takes a step back. "I don't know what you mean."

"Pretty easy to pick me out of a crowd, I bet." The ease with which he walked over to me, pushing Vera's chair. The only Latina girl in the room.

"Look. My mom told me that there was someone who visited Vera, and I . . ." He stumbles over his words. "You didn't look like a nurse."

"I'm sure." *How did I look? How did Abby describe me? Did she even say Latina? Or did she say something else?*

I try to calm down. I remind myself of the way he looked with Georgie—like he cares for her. Henry probably doesn't know that Gold Fork actually has a pretty big Latino population, and how would he? Weekenders don't think about what they don't see.

But then he says, "Man, what's the big deal here?"

"What's the big deal?" I jerk my chin toward Vera's door. "What's the big deal?" My voice is a furious whisper. "Maybe you could start by telling me where you and your mom have been for the past—oh, I don't know—twenty years. Or why you're here now. Or where Kathryn is. Or what you think you're doing with Vera. She's not stupid, you know." Tears are pricking at my eyes, and I swipe at them with the back of my hand. "Sometimes she knows who you are." Then I lean toward him. "And that's going to make it even worse when you leave."

"Whoa," he says, taking a step back. "Sorry." And he does look sorry, sort of. "I can't—it's not easy to explain," he says. "My mom and Ve—Grandma—they aren't close."

"I gathered that." I'm not letting him off the hook. "So why are you here?"

He won't meet my eyes. "You should ask my mom that." It must sound as weak to him as it does to me, because he adds, "Look—I don't get the whole thing between my mom and my grandma, okay? But my family is no more screwed up than anyone else's. We have our secrets and our fights, but what is that? Totally normal. Fact is, I hardly heard a word about Vera until this summer, and suddenly, here we are." He shrugs. "Worse places to be."

"So why now?"

He shakes his head, exasperated. "Like I said: Ask my mom, okay? She and my stepdad are tying up some stuff."

"That's what your grandmother is to you?" I say. "A loose end? A thread?"

"I didn't say that."

"You didn't need to."

I stick around after he leaves, hoping that Vera will wake up. I sit next to her bed, holding her hand while she sleeps, safe in her world of dreams and filtered memories. I want her to wake up and tell me that it's all going to be okay, that she's not going to leave me, that it'll always be the two of us, sitting outside in the sun as she smokes a pipe.

When I first started visiting Vera, it surprised me that she smoked a pipe. The only people I'd seen doing that before were the old men who hang out at Grainey's right after it opens in the early mornings. And she was so polished, so constrained that it seemed improbable at first. But Vera could pack her own pipe with sweet tobacco and light it herself with quick pops of breath. It gave her such pleasure, then, to puff on it or clamp it between her teeth, making me laugh. Now she forgets that she has a pipe—kept safe at the nurses' station. She rarely asks for it anymore. But when she does, I push her outside and we sit under the hanging plants near the back entrance. I pack it myself and help her hold it to her mouth. I remind her that she's still here.

(We only talked about the chapel fire once, while she was smoking her pipe. I'd just started visiting her, and the scar hadn't calmed to silver yet—it was still a raised red seam down my arm. It was hot, and I took off my cardigan after looking around to make sure no one else was watching. Vera reached over and ran her fingers across the seam like she was reading braille. And then—I don't know why—I told her everything. When I was done, she put her hand on mine. *Some things never leave you*, she said. *Some things you never forget, Ana.* She'd smiled. *Not in five years, not in fifty.* It was the only time she's called me by my name.)

But she doesn't wake up, and I stop at the nurses' station before leaving to ask them to call Abby. "Tell her something's different," I say. "Probably nothing, but . . . different. She's more confused than usual." Gloria nods. She's noticed too.

I bike home in the evening light, something clawing at my neck, my hands. Something's wrong. It wasn't just the strangeness of seeing Henry at the Pines, of connecting the little baby in the photo to the guy who is maybe—probably—hooking up with Georgie.

Because even though Georgie and I don't usually share this stuff with each other—*girl talk*, my mom calls it, as though what we do with our hearts and bodies is a childish pastime—I still have to think there's something I'm missing, something I don't see. Georgie and I've never had any use for girls like Kelly, the ones who always look perfect and vacuum-packed and who spend their summers hooking up with as many Weekenders as they can, like they're trying to build a backlog of memories for the years ahead when they're shackled to a run-down two-bedroom near the Gold Fork skate park, three babies, maybe, definitely a husband whose voice sounded like a different kind of promise when he told her he forgot the condom. We don't talk about it much, but I know—that's not Georgie.

There must be something about Henry that's worth it.

So it's not that. It's this: All I can think about as I weave through Gold Fork's quieting streets is how jealous I felt when I saw him with Vera. Once the fear that something had happened to her dissipated, I just felt raw envy. Because I've always wanted to be able to do those things for her too: Drive her around, show her the town and lake. Get her out. Give her air. Let her breathe.

But I don't have a car. And now that Abby and Henry are here, laying claim to her time, her life, I'm starting to realize

I might not have anything she needs. I might not have anything at all.

Let's play family! Children on the beach, racing toward one another. Forming their little bands, creating order in the only way they know how. *You be the mommy. I'll be the baby.* Everything as simple as this: the designated role, the immediate alliance. And then, the easy dissolution: a real mother, calling, *Dinnertime!* And just like that, the family scattered across the sand.

My mom and I used to play like that on the public beach. I'd be the mommy, and she'd be the squalling infant, kicking her legs in the sand while I pretended to go to the bank. "I have to cash a check," I'd say, brushing the sand off my legs, "before we can get dinner." It took a few years before I realized why that made her sad. "Ana," she'd say. "Mija." Then: "Mommy. Just go to the grocery store. Just go buy everything, Mommy. It's pretend." But I refused. I would only play what I knew.

Sometimes my mom's friends from work would show up with their families, and the kids would all play together in the water while the moms and dads sat on beach towels and watched us. Big, rowdy families, kids spilling over one another in the water, our skin (tan, white, brown) goose pimpled when we'd get out, and our moms would wrap us in bear hugs and blankets. Those were the best times, when Mom and I pretended we were part of those wild and glorious families.

I've been playing family again. And soon, soon (maybe even now) I'll be alone on the beach with a bucket and a shovel and my single heart.

WHERE ADVENTURE AWAITS

There's a sign along the state highway leading out of town, just beyond the lumberyard and the Walmart. LEAVING GOLD FORK, it says in flowery font that only a city planner could have found attractive. COME BACK SOON. And then, in smaller font below, because it's clear that we were running out of space and there wasn't enough money in the town budget for a bigger sign: ADVENTURE AWAITS!

Adventure awaits. We want the Weekenders to believe this, to spend long months in the city thinking about the what-could-have-beens and the what-if-I-trieds from the summer before. We want them to think of Gold Fork as a place where anything can happen. Where anything does. Where the things that chain them during the year—uniforms and trig exams and failed movie dates that may or may not be dates—are released, and they break free just like the prisoner in the movie that may or may not have been a date and can be whoever they want every night of the weekend.

We want this for ourselves, too. Of course we do. And sometimes we get close enough to feel the giddiness of arrival as it shimmers around their shoulders in Grainey's on that first day of summer. Sometimes we can even pretend that a bit of it rubs off on our own shoulders, and we walk around tasting a new voice in our mouths, a voice like ours but with different things to say. We can pretend that we, too, will spend the fall thinking about our own what-could-have-beens and what-if-I'd-trieds.

We make believe, just like the Weekenders. The difference is, their wishes usually come true.

GEORGIE

"How about this?" Henry drives out of town with one hand on the wheel while he scrolls down on his phone with the other. "Pixies. 'Here Comes Your Man.'" He turns and winks.

"Good," I say.

He taps his phone and sets it on the dash. He doesn't put his hand back on the wheel; he places it right above my knee as the beat thrums through the 4Runner.

My whole body is on fire.

Outside there's a box car waiting . . .

"It was crazy," Henry's saying. "We'd never played a venue like that. The sound system was off the hook."

I try to ignore his hand on my leg and focus instead as he tells me about the band.

"When I listened to the recording later, we sounded like something between sandpaper and a hangover."

"I'd listen to that," I say. My phone buzzes, and I pick it up and look at the screen. Not a number I recognize. Sent to the number I created with my burner app. But I do recognize the message. *Beef.* Surprising, since he usually waits for me to get in touch.

I ignore it.

Henry looks at me out of the corner of his eye, turns right onto Bear Creek Road. The car rumbles over potholes and gravel. We're driving along the outskirts of town, passing log cabins that look frayed in the bright afternoon light. The sun is high in the sky, making the forest seem frosted. "Picnic lunch," he explains. "Don't let anyone say I'm not romantic."

"Remains to be seen," I say. But the truth is, ever since he kissed me after handing over a thousand bucks, Henry's been more romantic than most of the Weekender guys I've hooked up with in the past. If I were the kind of girl who cares about these things, I'd probably be flattered that he holds doors, calls instead of texting, *just because*. I'd be twitter-pated. Starry-eyed. Moony with the fucking sweetness of it all. But I'm not that kind of girl. If Henry were only that guy, I'd have been gone as soon as he pulled away from that first kiss and said, *I've been wanting to do that since I saw you.* Luckily, he's not that guy—or, at least, he's not *just* that guy.

The music swells around us. *You'll never wait so long.*

Henry bops his head in time with the song. "God. I don't know," he says. "Sometimes I think the only thing left for musicians to do is cover old Nirvana songs over and over in an endless loop. Like it's all been done, you know?"

I stick my arm out the window. "We can't think that way," I say. "What's the alternative?"

"Business school," he says, and laughs.

"Certain death," I say, and try to ignore the note of unease that creeps into my voice. Of course there are options for Henry if his band doesn't work out. He's already in college. He jokes about business school, but honestly? You never know. Could happen.

But that's not an option for me. The only option for me is

success. Because if I don't make it with music, I don't make it at all. That's why I haven't told Henry about my plans to drop out. We've been hanging out for a couple of weeks, and I feel like we connect in a way that I didn't expect, but still—I don't know what he'd say about my plan.

Right now, though? Right now I want his hand on my leg. I've only ever felt this kind of electric attraction to one other person. I want Henry's hand on my leg almost more than I wanted to lean in toward Erik, answer his question—*What? You've never?*—with a kiss that said, *Yes*, and *Always* and—

Stop it, Georgie.

Another text. *beef*

I write back: *Got it.* Then I burn the number. I'll create a new burner number for the next round of texts later today. My number, as well as Dodge's, will be untraceable.

The code was my idea. Beef: the city park, three thirty, tomorrow. Pork: the Dumpsters behind the campground on the lake, Saturday morning, eleven. So far it's worked pretty well. Except that lately, whenever Dodge has met me with a new delivery, he's given me more than I think I can unload.

I don't have a choice.

"Hey," Henry says, and takes his hand off my leg to squeeze my shoulder. "You okay?"

"Yeah," I say. "Just—work."

He smiles. "Living the dream."

Sure. On paper, Henry's basically the guy wearing the sandwich board that says: *Danger. Summer Fuck-Buddy Within.*

And I know that's how I'd see him, normally. How Erik would see him. But Erik doesn't know about how Henry and I can spend half a night talking about punk, post-punk, grunge. How he knows bands I've never heard of, and I thought I knew them all. How he listened to the disc my band and I made, the one I've never shown anyone, and said it reminded him of the Breeders, pre-"Cannonball." That I sound like Kim Deal. Kim. Deal. If Erik asked, I'd tell him this isn't a dinner-at-the-steakhouse-boring-movie-hold-hands-kiss-at-the-end-of-the-night kind of situation. Thank God.

If Erik asked.

Maybe in the city, you run into people like Henry all the time. Maybe in the city, it's nothing to find someone who likes the music you like, who sees the world the way you do and wants the things you want. Maybe it's all easier in the city.

But in Gold Fork, meeting someone like Henry is like finding the nuggets of gold that everyone swears are hiding around here somewhere.

The song's refrain is playing again, pop-y and sweet, just an ounce of sand stuck in the teeth. *Here comes your man. Here comes your man.*

"Hey," I say suddenly. "Don't fuck this up."

He nods, eyes still on the road. He slowly coasts to a stop, parking on a little half-moon of grass that's shaded by tall pines. "I won't, Georgie." He leans over and kisses me. "I promise."

• • •

Look. No one's ever said I'm an easy lay. You can't be, when you deal. I've had my share of Weekender hookups, sure, but I never made it, like, a *thing*. That's why, after Henry drops me off at home in the middle of the afternoon, I think about calling Ana. Going over to her apartment later with a bag of microwaveable popcorn and some cheesy movie that we won't watch. Telling her about Henry. About how we almost did it.

Did it? *Christ.*

But those were the words Henry used. Kind of. After we moved to the back of the 4Runner, after he'd pulled out a wool blanket all surprised like, *How did this get in here?* and I'd laughed at him because *come on*, after he tangled himself around me and our clothes started to come off like they were held around us with Velcro—first his shirt, then mine, then his pants, then my shorts—that's when he said, "Do you want to?" And I can't really remember if he said anything after, if he actually said "do it," because I pretended I didn't know what he was talking about. Almost naked in the back of a 4Runner, and I said, *What?* like there were a thousand other things we could be talking about.

Jesus, Georgie.

But maybe he wasn't going to say "do it." Maybe he was going to say "fuck." Which is worse, even if it's the same thing.

Now I wish I could call Ana. Explain how I don't know why I didn't just say "sure." It's not exactly reinventing the wheel, I'd say. Nothing I haven't done before. And she'd ask me why I didn't, then, why instead I said, "Next time?" and Henry said, "That's cool," in a way that made it sound like maybe it wasn't. She'd ask me why I didn't.

And *this* is why I don't call her. Because I don't know. Because it has something to do with the fact that I like Henry—like, really like him—and that makes me feel like I might as well be one of those Weekender moms who looks at some pregnant Gold Fork girl and starts talking loudly about Family Values and The Sacred Gift to anyone who'll listen. And also, who knows how Ana feels about *doing it*? But I think I know how she'd feel about *fucking*.

So I don't call her.

Besides. It's summer. Who knows what could happen in the next week? The next day? The next hour? I'm going to see Henry again in a couple of days, anyway, to give him the dub sack he asked for. ("A friend," he'd explained, when I laughed at him and said there's no way he blew through a QP this fast.) There's no point in giving minute-by-minute updates when everything might change before the text has even been sent.

Which reminds me. I pull my phone out of my pocket, where it's been all afternoon, and read Davis's texts.

Breaking: shetland pony escapes from fairgrounds in Lindy.
don't worry—they caught it
hello?
anyone?
bueller?

You have to laugh, a little. Davis has never been shy about his nerdiness. The guy doesn't even use emojis. Some of his texts are still in complete sentences. Hey. If you've got it, flaunt it.

I take pity on him.

Shetland ponies are hot right now

He writes back immediately. *They're the BMX of thoroughbreds.*

Den? I text. *Been too long*

Ana now: *Sure*

Erik: *When?*

Meet in twenty, I write.

Davis: *i've got my parents' boat at the marina now. gassing up. anyone want a ride?*

Until Dodge cornered me at Grainey's, I'd kind of forgotten that Davis has a boat. Honestly, I usually forget that he lives on the lake. You don't exactly look at Davis and think *rich*. But once Dodge told me I'd be doing boat deliveries, I remembered real quick. As I lock up my bike next to the marina's lakeside grill, I wonder why we're not all out on Davis's boat every damn day. Working on our tans. Reading crappy magazines. Getting high if we want, or, you know, just drinking fizzy water or some shit. Why not? We could be Weekenders without having to be assholes about it.

Ana and Erik are already there, sitting in the back, leaving the passenger seat to me. The boat's not huge—not one of those monster truck/speedboat hybrids that all the Weekender dads buy the nanosecond they turn forty. Compared to those boats, this one's a canoe with a motor. Davis has it idling in a slip, and he's already pulled in a couple of the vinyl fenders. I jump in, clap Erik on the shoulder, and move to the front. I can feel Erik following me with his eyes.

"Gang's all here," I say, fake-jaunty. Then: "How about you let me drive." I pause, then add, "Please?"

Davis side-eyes me, says, "Once we get out of the marina."

"Fine." I shrug, pretend I don't care. Think about the first couple of deliveries, me driving too fast, hitting Weekender docks with just a little too much force. Dodge yelling at me. "Just want to practice."

"For what?"

I punch him in the shoulder. "For shut up."

"Ooh," he says. "Tough. Don't worry," he adds. "It's easier than a car."

I think about telling him that I know, but I stop myself. They don't need to hear about Dodge.

Davis stands as he drives the boat, keeping it to a slow putter as we make our way out of the marina and toward the buoys. It's dinnertime, but no one seems like they're in a hurry to go in. We pass stand-up paddleboarders, a handful of kayaks with people our parents' ages in them. (Terrible sun hats. Kind of a safari thing going on.)

Erik's looking at one of the paddleboarders. She shades her eyes with one hand and watches our boat pass by. Raises the hand in a wave, which Erik returns. She looks familiar, and it takes me a second to place her without the sundress and beer.

"Wasn't that girl at Fellman's?" I ask Erik.

Another shrug. "Layla," he says.

"Ah." I watch him watching her. There's something different about the way he looks at her. It takes me a minute before I realize that's how he looked at me, right before he tried to kiss me. I squeeze my eyes shut, trying not to remember. When I open them again, he's staring at me.

"She's great," he says quietly. "Really." He smiles for a second, and I can see that there's something there. I'd even swear Erik looks hopeful. "She's not a typical Weekender," he adds. "She's real. She—" He shrugs, embarrassed. "She does pottery. Like, vases and bowls."

"Never knew you were an art lover," I say, and try to focus on the memory of Henry handing me the 2008 limited-edition Fun Pack from the Vivian Girls the other day—T-shirt, button, postcards, seven-inch vinyl record, all in perfect condition. "Spent all night on eBay to get this thing," he said. "Bubblegum dream pop. Not your typical sound. Even so, I thought of you." How, when I listened to the record when I got home—kind of a Beach Boys influence, with sarcasm and grit, nothing I'd heard before—I loved it.

Erik will know about Henry soon enough. It's Gold Fork. No secrets here. I wonder if he'll care, and if so, how much.

We're past the buoys now. Davis angles the boat away from the lake traffic and opens it up, the sound of the motor so loud that it's not worth talking. He drives with one hand on the wheel, the other in the pocket of his shorts, still standing, and for a second it's like, oh, I get it. Davis could, in one of those alternate universes he's always reading about, be maybe-sort-of edging toward cute. Then I shake my head. Chalk it up to a boat-driving thing. *Jesus.* Still. Maybe I should tell him—give the ol' ego a boost. I glance at Ana to see if she's noticed too. She's watching him, a slight smile on her face. When she catches me looking, she blushes and stares out at the lake.

Water sprays against the sides of the boat, misting our faces, as we head north. Davis takes the middle, leaving the shoreline to the water-skiers. I turn and look back toward town: the boats at the marina, the storefronts by the water. Everything tiny, everything perfect. And then I sit back and enjoy the ride, because it's not often I get to do this. It's not often I get to see Gold Fork they way *they* do.

Man, if I could see it this way all the time, I'd probably want to stay too.

When we're out in the middle of the lake, Davis slows the boat and turns to me. "Wanna try?"

I nod. "Sure." I take the wheel, start pushing the throttle. Easy, easy. Get her going to a nice speed, keep my eyes open for other boats (luckily, not many), any buoys out in the water (none). Piece of cake.

Of course, it's easier during the daytime.

I take us by Washer's Landing on the left, the scar from the Nelson cabin fire still visible in the late-day sun. I see some kids climbing on the cliffs below to dive into the water from twenty feet up. Shake my head. *Idiots.* No one's on the higher cliffs, but that's not surprising. Suicide rocks. I slow us down and then kill the motor.

"What?" asks Erik, who's been leaning back in his seat, face to the sun. He blinks at me. "Why'd you stop?"

I point up at the burn site. "Just checking in," I say. "I was wondering how you're all doing—with that last fire."

"Are you our therapist?" asks Erik.

"Shut up."

"People are talking," says Ana. "At the nursing home, I heard some nurses saying that whoever it is isn't going to stop." She looks down at her hands. "I wanted to tell them there's no way all three fires are connected—but I didn't," she adds quickly, when she sees my face.

"My dad says some people are pulling out of deals," says Davis. "Wanting to hold off on signing until they catch whoever burned the Nelson cabin. But I'm not too worried," he adds. "There are new clues." He crosses his fingers, holds them up to his lips. "Vault it."

We nod.

"A word on a piece of paper. At the site."

The boat bobs underneath our feet. No one says anything for a minute. Finally, Erik lets out a puff of air. "That's not much," he says.

"No," says Davis, "it isn't. But I'm talking to the Nelsons this week, so maybe I'll get more."

"When are they going to call it?" asks Erik. "I mean, it's kind of a failed investigation at this point, isn't it?"

But Davis shrugs. "What else do the police have to do around here? Make some drunk and disorderly arrests? They've got time." Davis has got this kind of interior look on his face, but he turns abruptly and takes the wheel. "Whatever," he says. "Let's go. I'll drive."

We cruise across the lake, the wind slapping our faces. The sun was just hitting the top of Washer's Landing when we left, and the lake has the black sheen of near-dusk. When we get close to the Michaelson estate, Davis doesn't hit it head-on. He turns the boat north and points over his shoulder, and I follow his finger: There's a boat at the dock below the Den. I look back at Erik and Ana. They're as shocked as I am. Davis drives us toward the campground at the north end of the lake, more canoes over that way, more party boats. Then he turns, and we start to double back down the east side toward the Den. He slows as we get closer, turns in toward a vacant patch of beach, and I realize he's going to park at a kind of shattered old dock below one of the more rickety outbuildings on the property.

Which he does without drowning us, thankfully.

We all climb out, basically tiptoeing across the dock to the beach, hoping a plank doesn't break under our feet. This dock is more splinter than walkway.

"What the hell." Erik is whispering, even though we're, like, a thousand yards from the main cabin. He catches himself and clears his throat. Speaks in a normal voice. "Where'd that boat come from?"

"No idea," says Davis.

"Huckleberry pickers, maybe," says Ana. "Someone else from town?" She bites on the fingernails of one hand and looks nervously in the direction of the big cabin. It's far enough from this little beach that we can't see it, but I'm jittery anyway.

"I didn't recognize the boat," says Davis, and I'm about to say something like, *What? Are you an oracle?* when I remember how we got here. Davis probably *does* know all the boats on this lake. That's how it works, when you're a Dockside.

Erik juts his chin at a little deer path that leads away from the water. "Only one thing to do," he says. "Let's spy on those fuckers."

"I—" I start to say, but Ana's already nodding and following Erik into the trees. I blink at Davis. "Are we really doing this?" I ask.

"Georgie," he says, "this can't be the most dangerous thing you've done today."

And I know he's talking about dealing, but of course he's right. I follow him behind the others and try not to think about Henry. *Do you want to?* he'd asked. And in that moment, saying yes felt more dangerous than Dodge, more risky than a bag of blow.

The path winds through the property, climbing a little through old growth. We step over moss, rocks, the random nail or board, some trash. We don't talk. It's been a while since I went on a hike through the woods (you take it for granted when you're surrounded by it), and I kind of sink into the walk itself. The property is so big and the forest so dense that I don't see the cabin until we're almost on it. It rears out of the forest like a surprise. Ana has to pull Erik back, because he's been looking at the ground and almost walks right into the open. We crouch behind a couple of dogwoods and look.

At first it's just the cabin. Our Den. The grill on the deck is the first giveaway. Stainless steel. I haven't seen it before. Has it been stored in the garage this whole time? Then there are the curtains that have always, always, always been drawn across the sliding glass doors. They're open, and—I squint— the dining room within has plates, silverware, a fruit bowl.

A fucking fruit bowl.

I'm about to say something to the others about it because *seriously? A fruit bowl? Does anyone actually use one of those?* But I notice Davis first. He's looking at something just off the side of the deck, eyes wide. Then he kind of swivels and grabs Erik's arm.

"Let's go, guys," he mutters, and is trying to turn Erik around. But of course, Davis isn't that strong, and Erik's wheeled back around and is looking in the same direction, whispering, "What the hell, Dav—" And Ana and I are looking at each other and she's mouthing, *What?* when Erik just stops. Just freezes. And that's when I see him too.

They look exactly alike.

ERIK

No. No no no no no no no no. Not possible.

"Erik."

"Erik."

They're talking to me, and someone is shaking my arm, but I yank it free and just stare.

He's attaching a hose to a sprinkler head. But he can't quite get the grooves to match. He mutters something, but I can't hear him. I can only see his lips moving.

His mouth is just like mine.

You're not supposed to be here.

"Erik."

As I watch, he finally gets the sprinkler twisted on. He turns and yells into the house, "Someone turn on the water!" He sets the sprinkler in a little patch of grass by the deck.

And then the sliding glass door opens and a guy about my age, maybe a little older, comes out and turns the spigot on the side of the house. Water arcs out of the sprinkler. "On?" the guy asks.

"It's good," says my dad.

The guy—tall, blond, messy hair, bullshit lip ring, combat boots—doesn't look like us.

Georgie's saying something, but it's muffled, and I get this crazy idea that she's talking into her shirtsleeve, and it makes me want to laugh—like, a loud bark that I can feel in the pit of my stomach. I swallow to keep it down.

You're not supposed to be here.

"Let's go." It's Davis, still holding my arm. "Let's go. Erik—no, wait."

I don't know what he's talking about until I realize that I'm already out of the trees and walking toward the deck. Again that laugh—so sharp I can feel it pressing against my spine—but again I swallow it back.

He turns when he hears me come closer, and the look on his face is surprise at first, like maybe he thought I was a bear. Then it's as if his cheeks kind of fall a little, and his mouth opens. He just stands there, breathing through his mouth for a minute.

I don't say anything. I don't know what to do with my hands.

"Erik?" he says finally. Shakes his head. "Oh my God. Erik." Then: "Hi." He glances toward the deck and then back at me. "How did you—"

I shrug. Put my hands in my pockets, where they coil into fists.

The sliding door opens and shuts.

I'm just looking at him. His face is tan, and he's shorter

than I've imagined. Not as tall as me. A little heavier. Chino shorts and a checkered button-down shirt, short-sleeved. Those rubber sandals that only dads and environmental science teachers wear.

You're not supposed to be here. You're supposed to be spear fishing in Mexico, or running some bar down in Bermuda. Someone new every night. You're supposed to be so far away and so different that the distance between where you are and where I am is nonnegotiable. You can't come back. That's why you haven't.

But the way he looks. There's nothing from Bermuda or Mexico. Nothing about the wild life he's led. The one he had to leave to live.

"I was just about to get in touch," he says, stepping closer. His arms are spread out a little, like he's going to hug me, but he stops right when he gets to me and lets them fall back to his sides. "I was about to call. Today," he adds.

"Kyle?" The voice from the deck doesn't belong to the guy I just saw. It's a woman's voice, and I turn to see the most ordinary woman in the world standing there. Ordinary brown hair. Ordinary face. Not a body to sprint for. Like an egg, really. Beyond ordinary. "Oh," she says, when she sees me. "Oh."

"Abby," he says, "this is . . . Erik." Almost like he has to think about it.

And all the things I thought I'd say when I finally saw him again (because of course I would—just *not here not here not here*) seem so fucking stupid now. It hits me like a shot put to the chest: I shouldn't be standing here. I have no right. But I don't know how to leave. My feet are deadweights on the ground. My hands are heavy in my pockets. I open my mouth, but nothing comes. *No way out no way out no way out no way*

"Erik, man." It's Davis, clapping me on the back, his voice attempting cool. I didn't even hear him walk up. "Thought I'd lost you. We gotta get back to the boat." He looks at my dad. "Geocaching," he explains. "Easy to lose the path. Sorry to, you know—trespass."

My dad squints at Davis and nods like he knows what the fuck he's talking about. "Great," he says. "I mean, no problem."

No problem.

Davis's hand on my back, pushing me toward the trees. Time to go. And I can feel my breath, a sprint gone bad, everything caught in my throat, my chest exploding with it, going to walk away just walk away and is this it? Is this fucking it?

From behind me, his voice again. "I mean, wait. Hey. Erik—you got a phone? Let me give you my number." I turn and pull out my phone, hand it over, watch dumbly as he plugs in a number. "Great," he says again. "Call and we'll catch up. I'm here for another month at least."

I'm turning, Davis's hand on my back still, urging me to *go, get out*, but I stop and look at my dad again. "How long have you been here?" I ask. It doesn't sound like my voice.

He exchanges a look with the woman on the deck. "Call me," he says. "I'd love to see you."

Then I'm back in the trees with Davis, and he's marching me down to the water, where Ana and Georgie are waiting. It looks like they've both been crying. Georgie's smoking a cigarette, and she crushes it under the toe of her shoe.

"Fucking hell," she says. "The whole fucking family."

I don't remember getting home. I remember how the wind and the spray hit my face as Davis drove back across the lake. A thousand little bullets. Georgie raging about something—saying *Henry, Henry*, as though that would mean anything to me. But I don't think I biked from the marina. Someone must have driven me. Because it's like I'm in the boat one minute and then I'm standing inside my door the next and taking off my shoes and wondering why I'm doing that at all—taking off my shoes—when the Beast hears me and comes out of the living room.

"You're home," she says.

I look at her, those slumped shoulders, that sweater with faded purple flowers that she throws on whenever it's anything less than eighty degrees out, hair that's graying at the roots, no time, no money for a trip to the salon. She's just standing there like a bag of potatoes that someone forgot to bring in from the garage. And the feeling that's been grating against my lungs since I saw him finally bursts out like a cough. I start laughing.

"What's so funny?" At first she smiles like she wants in on the joke. But her smile fades as I laugh and laugh, leaning over to hold myself against the wall with one hand. I'm barking. I'm howling. I couldn't stop if I wanted to—and I don't want to. "What's going on?" she asks, and it's a different voice for the Beast—smaller, a little afraid. "Is everything okay?"

The idea of telling her, of actually telling her, makes me laugh even more. It makes me laugh so hard that I'm crying. And once I'm crying, I can't stop that, either.

"Erik. Erik. Are you okay?" Her hand on my back, rubbing like she used to when I was little and couldn't sleep. When she would sing to me. When I would let her. Her hand's on my back, and then it's not. She rattles around me, talking. "This is strange," she's saying. "You're acting strange." Then: "You must be hungry." Then: "I've made dinner. Beef Stroganoff."

And I sob-laugh even harder. Beef Stroganoff! In what world?

"If you don't—" she starts, but I can hear her voice wilt. "Whenever you're ready," she says, finally, and retreats.

But I'm not. I can't. I can't follow her into the kitchen. When I think about a plate of beef Stroganoff—her plate—and a forkful of greasy noodles, meat that she got for a buck off at Toney's because it was about to pass its sell-by date, I want to throw up. I put my shoes back on. Stop sob-laughing as quickly as I started. Swallow once, twice. Test my voice in a little whisper: "I'm just going." Fine. Raise the voice, yell into the kitchen. "I'm just going out for a bit. Don't wait up." Let the door close behind me—don't slam. Don't raise suspicion. Keep moving. Whatever you do, keep moving.

And then I'm running. Away from our house. Back toward town and the condos on the water.

I don't remember him—not really. The others have never asked, but they're probably all wondering. I was three. I don't remember. Don't remember the day he left, whether he told the Beast he'd be back in a day or two, whether he told her where he was supposedly fishing, whether he packed a pretend fishing vest, pretend waders, a pretend rod. She won't say. Won't talk about it. *He found something better.* The only time we talked. The Beast on the sofa, a cold washcloth over her eyes. Me, small still, in the chair opposite. Asking questions I'd eventually learn not to ask. But for all my questions, only one answer. *Found something better.* Explanation enough, because that's all life is: use, replace, repeat.

Feet pounding on the pavement. Sweat dripping down my back. Can't get there fast enough.

Three is still cute. I see them around town—little kids at the community beach with their parents, their sunscreen. I see that they're still babies. They can't disappoint. Right? You don't look at a toddler, at a three-year-old, and think, *I can probably do better.* Right. Must have been her. Must have been her.

And then I'm here. Oh, thank God. I can stop I can stop I can stop thinking. The sweat drips off my forehead onto the grass in front of the lakefront condos when I pause and lean over, hands on my knees. Then I stand up and make my way to the unit at the end. I've been here so many times in the past couple of weeks, standing outside in the dark, watching the lights turn on and off, pretending that I live inside that warm glow, that I could find my way blindfolded.

But I've never been inside.

Layla opens the door when I knock. Her long brown hair is wet, like she just got out of the shower. "Erik," she says.

My mind is running intervals. Back and forth. Back and forth.

I focus only on her.

"I didn't know you'd be coming over," she says.

Back and forth. Back and forth. "Just passing by," I say. My voice still thin, still not right.

She hears it, too. "Is anything—everything all right?"

No.

"Just—bad day," I say. "The worst." I speak slowly so my voice doesn't waver. "The goddamn worst."

She leans against the doorframe. "Tell me about it," she says. And then, when I open my mouth, she adds, "I've been stuck inside all day. Mom needed 'family time' again. It's like, don't we get enough of that at home?" She grins at me. "But now you're here. So things are looking better." She's got a great smile. It starts off sweet and ends a little savory. Something about what she does with her eyes. *Hold on to it.*

"Yeah." I clear my throat. "I know what you mean. Like I said, I was just passing by. If now's not good—" I wipe my face with the hem of my shirt and wait for it. Sure enough, I feel her trace a line with one finger from my belly button down.

"You're sweaty," she starts to say, but then I hear a voice from inside the condo.

"Layla? Who is it?"

"Just a friend," she says over her shoulder. "He's not staying." She looks at me. Adds, "Not for long. I'm just going to lend him a book. For"—a wink—"his summer class."

I shake my head. Give her a smile. Try to ignore the way my stomach clenches. Summer class. A stupid lie. A lie about stupid.

But the voice from the back of the condo doesn't sound suspicious. "That's fine. Dinner in fifteen, remember. And let your brother know."

Another wink. So I let Layla lead me up the stairs to her bedroom, where she shuts the door and pushes me against it and then slides down to her knees.

If this is what stupid gets me, I'll take it.

When it comes down to it, I spend most of my time trying not to think about the things I've ruined.

But not thinking isn't without its benefits. *Hold on to it. Hold on to it.*

The light's on in the kitchen when I finally get back. I can't go inside. I can't face her yet. So, I take my time unlacing my shoes outside the door, pulling them off and knocking the mud off of them. I line them up on the doormat. *I'll text you,* she'd said. *We'll hang out.*

"Erik." Her voice comes from the kitchen. I can hear its quiet accusation through the door. "You're home."

Deep breath. I square my shoulders and go inside.

"Hey, Mom," I say, passing by the kitchen on the way to my bedroom. "Pretty tired. Think I'll just head to bed."

"Tired." When is the Beast of Burden *not* sitting at the kitchen table, waiting for me? She's got a mug of something—probably some new tea that tastes like bark—and she twists it in her hands. "Too tired to talk."

It's not a question, so I don't answer. The Beast is looking at me closely, trying to read my expression, so I give her my Cream of Wheat look: neutral. Bland.

She hunches forward over her mug. She looks either very old or very young. "You'd tell me if there was something wrong. Wouldn't you."

Over the past ten years, ever since I first noticed that the Beast was different, somehow, from the other moms, she and I have been carefully building and maintaining a mirage. Squint, and you can see the Perfect Son in the middle of it, holding his medals in one hand and his mother's frail arm in the other. What's that he's whispering? *One more year.*

Careful, Erik. Careful.

"There's nothing," I tell her. Then, because I have to give her something, I add, "Girl problems. I'm dealing with it."

"Okay." She opens her mouth like she's going to say something else, but she shuts it like a trap. Finally she says, "You'd tell me," and her eyes are piercing. "You'd tell me if there was something."

"Of course," I say. "You're my mom."

• • •

By the time I get out of the kitchen and up to bed, it feels like I've been running four hundred repeats—each one exhausting as a sprint, but drawn-out as a mile. I flop down on my bed and pull out my phone.

Georgie's texted three times since we got back from the Den.

Wanna talk?

Call me

Hey. Call me.

I throw my phone down on my bed.

My eyes rove around the room, skimming the dresser and the small box that I know is in the top drawer, waiting. My fingers itch with what I could do. No. Not yet. Not now. I'm looking for something different. Finally, I see it—a shoe box in the corner. Empty ever since I got the new running shoes for District. I'd taken them out and then left the box there in the corner, a reminder that I can have something new, sometimes.

I pick it up, bring it back to the bed. Slide Layla's headband off my wrist, where I wrapped it twice while she was in the bathroom. Blue and stretchy. A dollar-store find, except probably not. I'd pulled it off her head and she'd smiled up at me the way you smile at a toy, the way I'd smiled at my new shoes. And later, when she said, *Hey. Really. Is something wrong?* because I'd fucked up for a second and had started to *think* again—she must've seen it in my face—and I considered

209

telling her everything, of laying my head in her lap and letting it all just fucking *be* for a minute, I remembered that smile and said no.

I put the headband in the box and slide it under my bed. *Careful, Erik. Careful.*

She's a Weekender. Maybe even my Weekender. But if I want her (and oh God, I want want want just one good thing), I have to be careful. I have to keep all my secrets. I have to be okay.

Because Weekenders don't like broken toys.

WHERE THE MEN ARE

There are plenty of men in Gold Fork. We see them everywhere: lounging at the gas station with a hot dog in one hand and a cigarette in the other; listening to our hearts at the hospital and declaring us healthy; loading planks onto a flatbed truck at the lumberyard; helping Weekenders unhook their boats at the marina. They are thirty-four, fifty-seven, seventy-two. They all look familiar, even the ones we've never seen before. Gold Fork gives a cast to the skin, a bronze tint that the Weekenders' moms pay big money for in the city but that we get for free. On some men, though, the tint turns ruddy, like something flayed. An animal's wet hide. We look at some Gold Fork men and we think that they've always been more beast than boy. We can't imagine them as kids. Can't imagine playing ball with them in the small field behind the airstrip or getting ice-cream cones at the parlor that's only open from May to September and eating them so fast that we yell "Brain freeze!" at the same time and then have to shout "Jinx!" before five seconds are up. We can't imagine the sound that would come from their mouths if they ever opened them to laugh. Would it be a bear's growl, an extended hiss? What would they say, if they could speak to us? Would they say they're sorry? Would they mean it?

Sure, there are plenty of men in Gold Fork. There just aren't as many dads.

Gold Fork women are different. Even the girls. Look hard enough at a Gold Fork girl, and you can see the mom lurking within, waiting for her moment to clamber out from beneath the blush and eye shadow, the tousled hair. Sometimes she doesn't have to wait long. Every graduating class at Tri High's got a couple of new moms, girls who blinked and looked away at the wrong moment. We tell ourselves that's what it was—the wrong moment—because we don't want to believe that a girl might want this, after all: a shabby rental house by the airstrip, the bedroom just big enough for her childhood twin bed and a bassinet for the baby who is, even now, crying to be held.

Not a dad in sight.

DAVIS

I wake up at six thirty on Tuesday morning. Put on chinos, a button-down short-sleeved shirt that my grandparents sent for my birthday and that I swore I'd never wear. Rummage around in my closet for a pair of shoes that aren't sneakers. I'm ready three hours before I have to leave. I borrow my dad's car and spend a couple hours driving the lake road around and around, all seventeen miles of it, trying to make sense of what happened at the Den.

But I can't.

The Nelsons are having brunch when I get there. They said they'd meet me in the hotel dining room at noon, and I spot them as soon as I walk through the door: orange and floral in a sea of crisp white shirts. The Gold Fork Grand attracts a certain clientele—people who come to town because they read about it in a magazine and it seemed like a fun way to drop a couple thousand dollars in a weekend. People who probably do this kind of thing a couple times a month, in different hotels with different views but the same amenities: fluffy robes, fresh flowers, daily massages.

The Nelsons aren't like that. They have the sense of entitlement that practically oozes from the Grand, but without as much class. An orange polo. Floral capri pants. Not exactly crisp white shirts.

They don't stand when I walk over and introduce myself. They've each got a plate of food in front of them. He's got

213

a Bloody Mary, and she's drinking a mimosa. There are two empty glasses on the table from the first round. Mr. Nelson waves to a chair. "Go ahead," he says, which is either an invitation to sit or a suggestion to start talking, so I do both.

I flip open my notebook. "Are there any new leads on your case?" I ask. "Anything you can tell our readers?"

"You get right to the point, don't you?" says Mrs. Nelson. She's eating toast points, I notice.

I lean back in my chair, all pretend-casual, and try again. "It must have been a shock," I say. "The fire."

"Damn straight," says Mr. Nelson. He takes a sip of his Bloody Mary through a straw, and then pulls the celery out of the drink and bites it. "You leave for the week and come back to rubble. Cleaner shows up and there's nothing to clean. Not even a carpet. I'd say it was a shock." Tomato juice drips off the celery onto the white tablecloth.

"It sounds like there might be some new information pertaining to the case," I say, and wait.

"There was a footprint," says Mr. Nelson, "but that seems pretty thin. Most people wear tennis shoes around here. And what—the police are going to go around measuring people's feet? I don't think so." He takes another bite out of the celery. A server walks by, and he grabs at her sleeve, waving two fingers toward their drinks. "And one for the road," he says, chewing noisily.

The server nods, but I see her roll her eyes just as she turns away.

"Oh!" says Mrs. Nelson. "I almost forgot! The paper!"

I bring my notebook closer to my face, as though I'm reading. "I understand there was a legible word on it," I say, scanning the blank paper. "Something like . . ."

"Regret," she says quickly, filling in the blank. "It was 'regret.'"

"Doris!" Mr. Nelson puts down his drink. Looks at me. "That's off the record, son," he says. "Police don't want us sharing that, *Doris*. Might tip off the arsonist."

"Got it," I say, and close the notebook with a half-audible sigh. "Well." I don't know what Dan wants from this interview if anything worth reporting is confidential. So I settle for asking them about the items they lost in the fire ("Everything!"), what they'll miss most ("Oh God, *Everything!*"), and how plans are coming for the new construction (Mr. Nelson, this time: "Slow as shit."). Then they tell me all about the cost of marble countertops for twenty minutes.

These two make most Weekenders look like Buddhist monks.

But as I make my way from the Gold Fork Grand to the newspaper office to type up my notes, one word tumbles around in my head like a piece of a jigsaw puzzle that's fallen out of the box.

Regret.

When I get to the office, I turn on my computer and read through my notes. I can almost convince myself that I'm doing real work here, instead of just avoiding thinking about what we saw at the Den. The look on Erik's face when he saw his dad. Georgie's new boyfriend. And Abby.

I shake my head. Back to work.

Dan might have only asked me to talk to the Nelsons, but he didn't *not* tell me to do some other digging. I look at what I've compiled so far. I type up everything I can remember from the interview this morning—nothing good there. Just the Nelsons complaining about all their stuff. The fire inspector's report. Police reports. Amazing what a phone call and a mention of the *Roundup* can get you. I don't know why, exactly, I'm digging in here, but something doesn't feel right.

The police reports lay out a time line, and not much more. Fire must have started late enough that there wouldn't have been boats on the water to see the smoke. And, once it was lit, the place went down fast. Police are assuming the arsonist left by boat. No car tracks in the dirt, at least. Just a footprint (men's size eleven, nondescript running shoe) and the burnt paper.

I'm going to need more than this to go on.

My phone rings in my pocket while I'm glancing at the interview for the third time. Something about what Mrs. Nelson—or was it Mr.—said. Something there that I'm not seeing right now. I answer.

"Davis." It's Dan, calling from his cell. I can hear sounds in the background—a siren, the clang of a lid or a door. "There's been another fire." He speeds up, talking over my obvious questions. "Early this morning. Out at the skate park. Trash cans—two of them. Small-time. But intentional, it looks like." He pauses to take a breath, and I hear the tumbling roll of skateboards on concrete.

"Copycat?" I ask.

"Right now that's what we're running with," he says. "But there's nothing to link this to the Nelson fire. And the scale is all off, like it was at the brewery. Frankly," he adds, "it's probably some kids you might know." Another pause.

"Oh," I say. "I don't know very many people." Which is true, even if it's a little shameful.

"Ask around," he says. "That's all. Just ask around. You'll get more than I will."

"Sure," I say, though I know no one at the skate park's going to talk to me. My feet have never graced a longboard. I think Ollie is a good name for a cat. The kids at the park are going to see me coming and—if they know anything at all—they're going to stuff their secrets in their back pockets next to the American Spirits.

"Great," says Dan. Then he adds, "We might crack this case yet."

I hang up, laughing to myself about how Dan thinks we're private investigators or something. My phone buzzes—a text—and I wonder what he forgot to mention. Some totally useless clue, most likely. I glance down and see her name, try to ignore the little hiccup in my chest that's as confusing as it is sudden.

But when I read her message, I forget the hiccup completely.

Vera's in the hospital. Can you come?

I'm grabbing the keys to the car before I've finished reading.

Jane used to get headaches. Four or five at least in the two months we were together. (Two months that now seem more and more removed from my real life, like a dream that I never quite understood.) She never grabbed at her head and rubbed her temple, the way people do when they're faking. She just closed her eyes and told me she needed to be alone. *Find me a dark place,* she'd say. And I never knew if she meant a broom closet or a state of mind.

I should have taken her to the hospital.

I know, I know, hospitals are usually as bright and glaring as supermarkets. And in general, Gold Fork's is no different. When I get there, practically running through the entrance doors of the emergency room, I have to squint against the flash of a thousand halogen lights. But once the nurse gets my name and talks to someone on the phone and makes some note on her computer and leads me to Vera's room—that's when I realize that the hospital is one of the darkest places in town.

It's not just that the overheads are off or that the shades are drawn against the light, which they are. It's the air itself. So heavy and gray and hopeless that I feel like I shouldn't be breathing.

Ana looks up at me from where she's sitting by Vera's bed. Her eyes are red and empty.

"Hey." I think about taking a step closer. Touching her shoulder. My right hand tenses by my side.

"Hey." She turns back to the bed. Then she adds, "Thanks. For showing up." She's leaning forward like she's just willing life into Vera. "I'm kind of going crazy here. I didn't know who else to—just, thanks." Vera's hand is lying still on top of the sheet. Ana rests her hand on top and squeezes.

"Of course."

A nurse knocks on the door and bustles in, clipboard in hand. "Checking vitals," she says. Then, when she sees the look on Ana's face, she adds, "Totally routine. You'll see me again in an hour. Same song and dance." She's fluffing pillows, adjusting the IV drip. Bustle, bustle. "Here you go, Miss V," she says as she lifts one wrist and holds it, counting silently. "Let's bring that pulse up a bit, all right?" Her voice is too loud, and I watch Ana wince at the false cheer. "Don't you know you have visitors?" The nurse practically winks at us. "Rise and shine!"

Ana's jaw clenches.

"Uh," I say. "No offense, but I just got here. Can we have a few minutes to, um, be alone with our"—I glance at Ana in time to see her mouth the word—"grandma?"

She looks at her clipboard and then at me. Glances between me and Ana, taking in the difference in skin. Her eyes narrow as she tries to decide. *Is it possible?* Then, slowly, she says, "Sure thing. It's good to have company. Right, Miss V?" Her voice gets a little louder. "Right?"

Once she's gone, a couple more singsongy platitudes lobbed over her shoulder as parting gifts, I let my shoulders relax. "Wow," I say to Ana. "She sounded like cough syrup tastes."

Ana nods, and smiles—a first.

"Grandma?" I ask.

"Only thing that came to mind," she says. "And it worked at the information desk when I first got here. Wasn't sure it would. That's why they let you in too. But," she adds, "you and I don't exactly look related." She holds out one tan arm. Ana doesn't usually wear short sleeves, but it's warm in the room. The scar is dark in this light, like a river cutting through a canyon. She catches me looking at it and crosses her arms.

I glance away. "Cousins," I say.

"Cousins." She stands and walks over to the window. "You'd make a nice cousin." Shakes her head. "I mean . . ." She doesn't finish the thought.

It's a good thing her back's to me so she can't see my face.

"I don't know where Abby is," she continues, talking to the window. "She called to tell me about the stroke, but she wasn't around when I got here. And she's not responding to my texts." She moves away from the window, comes over to where I'm standing. Then she makes a sound like an engine puttering out. "World-class daughter."

We're standing next to each other, but we're both looking at the old lady on the bed. Vera's smaller than I remember. Her skin, loose and wrinkled, seems painted on from this distance. She looks like a doll. As we watch, one arm stirs, lifting slightly. Her mouth opens, and a low moan comes out. Ana jerks forward, says, "Vera?" but the arm falls back to the sheets and the moan becomes a quiet whistle. I watch the sheet over her chest move rhythmically up and down as she breathes. In, out. In, out.

"She seems okay," I say, even though she doesn't. I try not to focus on the warm pulse where Ana's shoulder is touching the side of my arm. "Have you heard anything from the doctors?"

"No one will tell me anything," Ana says. She's glaring at the side of the bed. "They'll only tell Abby. I'm not her child," she adds, drawing the last word out. "I'm just the help."

There's a light knock on the door, and another nurse pokes her head in. It takes me a second before I recognize Georgie's mom.

"Oh, Davis," she says. "And Ana. I thought"—she glances at the chart in her hands—"I was under the impression that there were family members in here."

"Hi, Mrs. Rowland." I haven't seen her in months, but she looks the same: graying hair, a permanent yawn tucked behind her smile. "We're family in spirit." I try my most winning smile.

It works, I think. "I'll assume that you've both gotten permission from the family, then." She holds up one hand before Ana or I can say anything. "I'll assume that's a yes." Then, looking down at the chart so she doesn't have to watch our reactions, she adds, "Because of course we all know that no one other than family or those with written permission from the family can enter the room. We all know that if someone without permission had gotten in here, they'd be in big trouble."

Silence. I move a little toward the door. Try to make significant eye contact with Ana. But she only moves closer to Vera and says, "You can go if you want, Davis."

"I'm staying," I say.

Georgie's mom smiles. "You're a good friend for being here."

Good friend. Nice cousin. What next? Neutered puppy?

"Does Georgie know about Vera's stroke?" Her mom pretends to read the chart, but I see how her chin angles up as she waits for one of us to answer.

"Yeah. I texted her," I say. And I did. As soon as I heard from Ana, I sent texts to both Georgie and Erik. He wrote back immediately, saying he was in the middle of something—the first I've heard from him since we saw his dad—but I never heard from Georgie.

"I'm sure she'd be here if she wasn't working." Georgie's mom is looking at me now, watching my reaction. "Those little kids sure take up a lot of time."

"Mmm-hmmm."

"Their parents must really like to go out."

"I guess." Georgie's told us about her fake job, but I've never had to lie for her. And I'm getting the distinct impression that her mom is a hard one to fool.

"What are their names again? I always forget." She stares at me now, and I have to look away. Then she must think better of it, because she says, "I'm sure Georgie can remind us." She opens the door. "You two take care. And, Ana"—her smiles softens—"I can tell how important this lady is to you." Then she leaves.

Ana sits next to Vera in one of those wood-and-burlap hospital chairs that look like they were fashioned out of someone's chronic depression. She pulls out her phone and looks at the blank screen.

"She's had a couple of hours to make the ten-minute drive." There are tears in her eyes, and she rubs at them, her hands in fists. She doesn't mention where Abby would be driving from. Doesn't mention the Den. Instead, she says, "Who doesn't visit her own mother when she could be dy—" Ana stops before she has to say the obvious thing.

"She's not," I tell her. "Look. She's had a stroke. Sure. But lots of people do. My grandma did. And she was fine."

"Really?"

"Really."

My grandma died of a heart attack before I was born.

"Have you—" I start, but I'm not sure how to ask. "Have you talked to anyone? Georgie? Or—Erik?"

She shakes her head. "No. And, Davis," she adds quickly, before I can say anything else, "I don't want to talk about it. I can't. It's too—" She rubs her face with one hand. "Too much."

"Okay," I say.

223

There's another tap on the door, and then it opens. I watch Ana's eyes light up with hope and then cloud over again when she sees the nurse who was here earlier.

She gives us a tight smile and looks closely at Vera's chart. "Grandma, huh?" Her cheery facade seems to be slipping. "Unless one of you is the forty-eight-year-old daughter I just spoke with on the phone, you have to go." She glances at her watch.

"I'd like to stay." Ana's chin quivers. "She's . . . I don't want her to be alone."

For a second, I think the nurse is going to turn on the charm again. Give Ana a hug or something. But then she says, "She won't be alone. She'll have me." Another horizontal smile. "And besides, I have to take her over to radiology anyway. Testing, testing, one, two, three."

"We're going," I say.

"I'll be back in the morning." Ana's glare is a challenge.

But the nurse isn't even listening to us. She's unhooking monitors and popping up the rails on the sides of Vera's bed. She doesn't turn around when we leave.

When we get outside, heat radiates off the asphalt of the parking lot. I shade my eyes with my hand. "I don't understand why the sun needs to be so relentlessly optimistic," I say. "Days like today, it could stand to tone it down a bit."

Ana shrugs—not exactly the reaction I was hoping for. "It's fine," she says, but I can see that she's sweating already.

"Need a ride?" I ask. "I drove." Flew, more like it. And, I realize now, I didn't even leave a note.

Ana looks around the parking lot as though just figuring out where we are. "Yeah," she says, "sure. Thanks." She runs a hand through her hair. "I was at Grainey's when Abby called. I think I ran here." Shaking her head, she adds, "Don't know why I forgot my bike. It's probably still in front of Grainey's."

"Bodies in motion," I say, remembering my own reaction to Ana's text. "You were probably halfway here before you knew you'd left the coffee shop."

Ana nods. "Right." She puts her hand on my arm. "Thanks, Davis. For everything."

I turn, pull her in for a quick hug. I wrap my arms around her back. "No problem," I say.

And as I open the car door for her, I try to think of Vera, alone in her hospital room, maybe surviving, maybe not.

I try to think about all this, but I can't.

I'm thinking instead about the hug, how I wanted to keep Ana there in that moment.

How it didn't feel anything like hugging Jane.

How different doesn't mean worse.

ANA

I don't want him to let go. I don't want him to, but he does. I slide into the seat. "Nice car," I say, trying to sound normal. "It looks like chinos and family suppers." Then I glance at his pants. Chinos. "Sorry."

225

Davis gets in and pats the dashboard. He clears his throat. "We call it 'I'm Not Giving Up; I'm Just Giving In.'"

I want to laugh, but all the worry of the past two hours has left me hollow.

We start driving away from the hospital.

"Want me to swing by Grainey's?" Davis asks. "We can throw your bike in the back."

"No," I say. "I've already texted my mom. She'll pick it up after work tonight."

He nods. "Okay." I tell him how to take the back roads toward my apartment complex. "Good thinking," Davis says. "Friday afternoon. We don't want to get caught in Weekender traffic."

"There's not a lot of traffic out by my house," I tell him. "There never is."

I still feel numb, the image of Vera in her hospital bed always a half second away from crushing me, but being here in the car with Davis is helping. There's a heat radiating off his body that's more comforting than the glare of the sun outside. I'm not alone. I'm not alone yet.

Davis looks at me out of the corner of his eye. "I don't remember when you moved here," he says. "Isn't that funny? It seems like we've known each other forever." He coughs, embarrassed about something.

"I was ten," I tell him.

"Where were you before that?"

I look out the window. "Where *weren't* we?" So many

years of trying first one town and then another, the cities getting smaller in direct proportion to my mom's dreams. Someone told her about an opening at the Grand, and we packed up and moved the next week. "I can still remember what it was like to walk around Main Street for the first time," I tell Davis now, "and how relieved I was to be somewhere with a beach. I'd never been to the ocean—still never have."

"Really?" He tries to cover his surprise.

I nod. "Yeah. The lake was just as good, though. I remember I loved the way the water lapped at my feet after boats went by. Just like the ocean—or at least, that's what I thought." I don't tell him about the other thing. How I felt like I could be anyone out there on the public beach. Just another girl building castles with her mom. Maybe they live in a house. Maybe they're visiting from out of town. Even then, I knew enough to know that this was something rare: a place to go that was free but didn't make us feel poor.

"Sounds nice," he says.

"You know," I say, "we talk about the Weekenders like there's a hierarchy. Toney's, Docksides—"

"There is," he interrupts. We've pulled up to my apartment building, and he puts the car in park. Neither of us gets out.

"Maybe," I say, "but you want to ignore the hierarchy when they're gone. You want to think everything is equal to the Dead Enders. And it's not." My mom's voice on the phone when I called her from the hospital and she said she

227

couldn't get off work to meet me: worried, anxious, guilty. Her time isn't her own—ever. I tap the cover of one of the books on the floor of Davis's car with the toe of my shoe. "This town is like a kingdom in one of these fantasy novels. The gates open more easily for some people. For others"—I lift my chin toward the apartment complex—"the gate can be a little rusty." I don't say it, but I know what would happen if real estate was crazy and Davis's dad—the neat freak in the house—was too busy and couldn't get all the cleaning done. They'd hire someone to help. Someone like Erik's mom.

Davis rubs his hands over his face. "You're right." Then he adds, "And it never ends. I mean, you know—Erik's dad." He looks at me again. I nod—I'm ready to talk about it. So he goes on. "The Dead Ender who got out."

"Married into another tier, it looks like," I say. "But at what cost?"

"Exactly. And Abby and Henry. And"—he pauses—"the Den."

"Do you think they're renting it?" I ask. "Or could they—"

"Own it?" Davis shakes his head. "Is Vera's last name Michaelson?"

"No. It's Whitaker."

"I doubt they're squatting," he says. "Not with that fancy grill on the deck." And I know he's thinking the same thing I am. From the little we know, Erik's dad could totally be a squatter. But not Abby. Not Henry.

Henry. I shake my head. "Wonder what Georgie thinks

of this whole thing," I say. "If Henry'd said something earlier, she'd have told us, right?"

"Yeah," says Davis, "I think so. With Georgie, though, you never know. She's kind of a vault."

"Has to be, I guess," I say. "But she and Erik are close."

"Yeah," says Davis.

"They've always had a kind of will-they-or-won't-they vibe," I say. I stick my arm out the window and feel the warm air on my skin.

"What? You think?" He looks surprised. "I've never seen it between them."

"You haven't been looking," I say, and blush. "Georgie is the only girl Erik actually talks to. On top of everything else, finding out that her boyfriend is his dad's stepson has got to really hurt. Although," I add, "he doesn't know that, does he? She hasn't told him yet."

Davis shakes his head. "Not that I know of." Then he adds, "You're always a few steps ahead of me. I get words, but you get people." Then he smiles. "Maybe you should help me at the paper—there's been another fire."

"Seriously?"

"Small one at the skate park. Probably nothing. But that's the thing—if there's something, I bet you'd get it, Ana. You'd see it immediately. That's just how you are," he adds.

I hold the compliment for a second like a lake-polished stone.

"I don't know how to read Erik," Davis continues. "A

thing like this—if it were you or Georgie, I'd know what to say, you know? But Erik . . ." His voice trails off.

"Erik doesn't react like the rest of us," I say. "He doesn't react like anyone I know."

Davis nods. "That's what scares me."

I don't want to lose my chance. "Davis?"

"Yeah."

"I need your help."

He turns to me. "Anything." And there's something in his voice that I want to trust, a tone that I want to believe is saying more than he's ever said before. But there's no way. Not Davis. Not me.

I take a breath. "I want to find Kathryn, Vera's other daughter. But I can't. Could you—is it possible to, I don't know, use your connections at the newspaper?" I laugh a little, embarrassed.

He does too. "What connections I have, I'll use. Kathryn Whitaker. Got it."

"Thanks," I say, and unbuckle my seat belt.

"Is it just me," Davis says as I open the door and climb out into the hot afternoon light, "or has this summer really taken a turn for the crazy?"

I rest my hand on the car door and lean in. "It's Gold Fork in the summer," I say. "Crazy is the just the beginning."

As soon as I get through the door, I take off my casual attitude and set it aside. I don't have to pretend not to feel the thing tugging at my ears, scratching at my neck, whispering, whispering.

Even though it isn't quite time for dinner, I make some pasta, shaking out the last bit of sauce from a jar that I find in the back of the fridge. It's still warm out, and the windows are open. Even this far from the lake, I can smell the water: clean and cold, with the vague, loamy scent of sediment. I've never liked the bottom of the lake out where it starts to slope down, never felt comfortable touching its thick underbelly with my toes. It's either the shore or the deep for me. I'd rather be out in the middle of the water, two hundred feet above the bottom, than standing chest-deep in it with the sand and gravel and algae and who knows what else creeping toward my ankles.

For some reason, it's that thought—algae, sand, suffocating water—that makes it all feel real again. Vera. Just lying there with tubes and monitors and silence. Not a word from her. But. Maybe she's suffocating in a way I can't see—a way no one can see—and crying out for help in her head. A prisoner in a frail, capricious body.

When I call my mom, she's concerned, but distracted.

"Did you see her? Is Vera okay?" A pause as I hear someone—probably sleazy Carl saying something in the background. "Sorry," she adds. "I'm between bookings."

For a second, I can't talk. I clear my throat, fighting down the sob that's been stuck there since I walked in the door. "Oh," I say. "Yeah. She's okay. No. Sorry. I just—just checking in," I finally manage.

"That's sweet." Then, "Is it all right with you if you're on your own tonight?" She doesn't wait for my answer—that's too risky—so she keeps talking. "It's only, Zeke wants to take me out after work. Dinner and drinks." I can hear her swallow. "So it's okay?"

There. There it is. I finally hear the little catch in her voice that says, *I know it's not but say it is.* That little catch is as familiar to me as the birthmark on her knee that's shaped like a crescent moon. *Okay that I stay late? Okay that I work all weekend? Okay that I miss the recital?* Now there's something else to take up her time. Someone else.

"Yeah," I say, "it's okay. I'm pretty tired anyway. I'll probably go to bed early." My cheeks are hot, and I can feel the tears welling, know that it's only a matter of seconds before the sob finally releases.

"Oh, well." Relief. "Don't forget to lock the door."

"I won't."

"Good night, mija."

When I hang up, I look around the kitchen. Everything seems pale, bleached of what little color or details my mom and I've added over the years: the potholders that we Jackson Pollocked with red and yellow paint; the postcards that we lined up against the back of the counter to hide the ugly linoleum backsplash; the chalkboard sign that we use to leave each other messages. An old message is still there from a couple of weeks ago. *It's not a chore if you enjoy it!* Smiley face. My mom's idea of a joke—she was making fun of other kids' parents, other kids' regulated lives and chore lists.

When I see that message, I let the sob loose. It's a wail that ricochets off the walls and fills the room to the ceiling. It's a cry for the chore lists my mom never made, the punishments I never endured when I didn't make my bed or clean my room because her parents were too strict and she didn't want to risk losing me the way they lost her. It's a cry for the only thing that's made me normal, the only person who holds me accountable, even if she doesn't always know it. I howl as I wash the dishes, shake and moan while I dry and put them back in the cupboard, let the tears roll down my cheeks and onto the collar of my shirt as I put away discarded socks, stack the magazines by the couch. *Vera, Vera, Vera.* I flip on the outside light over our apartment door. *Vera. My abuela.*

Finally, finally, it's over. I feel carved out. There's nothing left for me to cling to but a careful reliance on these systematic, mundane tasks. Leave a note for my mom, in case she comes home. *Taking the bus to the hospital.* I'll sleep in the waiting room if I have to. *Everything's fine.* Shut the door behind me. Both locks. Double-check.

I never forget, despite the fact that no one would ever break into our apartment. What could they hope to find up here? There's clearly nothing of worth.

JULY

WHERE THERE ARE NO EXCUSES

July is constant motion. It starts with the Fourth, but then it keeps going. A string of parties like the buoys that rope off the swimming area at the public beach: Not Beyond This Point. One, two, three, four, five . . . We are at the water every day, somewhere new every night. No more excuses now. All of Gold Fork is in on it. Weekenders and Dead Enders alike share the spoils of summer: perfect mornings, lazy afternoons. Frantic, unleashed nights. Every morning, we wake to a soup of remembered jokes, slight offenses, the sting of joy, the aftertaste of disappointment.

It's July. We think it will never end.

GEORGIE

I see them both at Jeff-the-Spastic's Fourth of July party. Of course. I've been ignoring one of them, and the other is doing the same to me. They saw each other at the Den, but Henry didn't see me. And Erik doesn't know—I don't think he knows—that Henry is *Henry*. As in, my Henry.

If he is my Henry.

Shit.

So it makes sense that I'd have to deal with them at the same time. And on a work night, too, no less.

Because I've been hustling. I'm bringing my A game. I'm working the summer party scene like a used-car salesman, all bravado and slick maneuvers. *You sure this will be enough?* I ask the unsuspecting Weekenders when I give them just as much as they ordered last week and no more. *There's that party at Jonesy's coming up. . . .* When they ask if I have any extra on hand, I scrunch my face into a question, let them worry. *I might,* I say. *But hey, don't tell anyone else. I don't have enough to top off everyone.* This does the trick. As soon as they pay me, they're running to tell five or ten of their best friends that if they think they're going to want more than normal this week, they'd better jump on it *fast,* because inventory's low and *Georgie doesn't have enough for everyone.*

I've basically got a line of anxious Weekenders waiting for me at every party. Fistfuls of money. A hand on my arm at every turn, pulling me into corners, asking, *Do you have extra this week?*

And Dodge in his boat, waiting.

What I'm saying is, I'm busy. And making money keeps my mind off other things, like the look on Erik's face when he saw his dad, or the look on Henry's face as he watched Erik through the sliding glass door.

Until I see them, that is.

Jeff-the-Spastic. Weekly with a place on the west side of the lake. I remember him from last summer: wide grin, windmilling arms, dub sack every couple of days, Molly for the parties. He hosted on the Fourth last year, too, and all the faces look familiar, even the ones I've never seen before. Davis and Ana aren't here—probably weren't invited. But Erik is.

He's got his arm around a small brown-haired girl as he weaves his way toward me through the crowd in the living room. When they get closer, I can see that it's the same one who was on the paddleboard the day we went out to the Den. She reaches up with one hand to pull his face toward hers, and I see that she's wearing one of those wrap bracelets that all the Weekender girls have this summer. Costs something around two hundred bucks. I shake my head as she kisses him and then heads toward the kitchen.

"Layla," he says, watching the door to the kitchen like she might pop out at any minute.

"She's still around, huh?" I watch him carefully, looking for any clue that he knows about Henry. Any clue that he's reacting at all to seeing his dad and his new family.

But he gives me nothing. Shrugs his shoulders instead. "She's still around."

"So the two of you are . . ." I raise my eyebrows, like, *We can be normal! This can be normal!*

He glances away so that I can't see his face. When he turns back to me, he's got a smile, but it's not his usual grin. It's a Walmart greeter's fake smile. "Yeah," he says, "we are."

"Okay," I say, but he looks jangled. Something's off, like his face has broken apart and been put back together with the seams not quite matching. "Erik," I say, and step closer. I can smell his shampoo—clean, a little minty—and I fight the impulse to reach over and touch his face. "I've been worried about you."

We stare at each other, the heavy beat of the latest pop-rap sensation thrumming around us. Everything we haven't said is reverberating in the room, making me dizzy.

"How are you?" I ask.

"Fine. Good."

"Come on, Erik."

"I'm good." He looks away.

"You haven't returned my calls," I say, and he shrugs. "Look. I know it's shitty—it's so shitty—but, what? Have you talked to him again? Are you going to see him?"

Erik holds up a hand. "Can we not?" He glances toward the kitchen. "I'm here to enjoy myself." When he looks back at me, his eyes are scrunched tight like he's in physical pain. Then he blinks and his face is clear again.

I nod. I know Erik. "Okay." I look toward the kitchen too. Let a beat pass. Then I say, "Layla. Pretty name. You sure she's tough enough for you?"

Erik shakes his head and smiles. "They can't all be you, George." He pauses. "Besides," he adds, "she's wilder than you'd think."

I raise my hand, palm flat in front of his face. "Stop. I don't need details."

"Suit yourself. Just thought you might want some pointers."

"Screw you."

"Anytime." It's our usual banter, but it feels off.

"You're a broken record, Erik." I turn and take in the scene around us, pretending everything's cool. He needs this from me, I know.

Small groups of Weekenders and Dead Enders are bunched around the cabin's living room, perching on the arm of the Pendleton sofa, sifting through Jeff's parents' record collection. (Davis says that having retro pieces like record players in one's cabin is a hallmark of Weekender design.) *God.* I was just at band practice this afternoon—the last one before half the band moves to the city. Our sound blows this trash out of the water.

I should be going with them. *Soon,* I remind myself. *Soon.*

Out on the deck overlooking the lake, there's a big group huddled around a bong. Someone brought fireworks, but no one seems that interested. A few people light sparklers and wave them around lazily before they burn out. I know what they're thinking. Fireworks are kid stuff.

"Erik, right?" Jeff-the-spastic is standing next to us, a microbrew in one hand, cigarette in the other. "Thanks for coming, man." He smiles at me. "I don't have to thank *you*, I know." His smile is just this side of charming—more condescending than friendly. He turns back to Erik. "You're the guy who got that local scholarship, right? Free college in a year, right?"

Erik winces at the word "local." "Yeah," he says. "It's a pretty sweet deal." I've seen that look on his face before. It's the look he has whenever he's with his mother. Bland. Cautious. Erik once said a conversation with his mom is like waiting in the trees while she stands on the porch with a gun, shooting into the dark.

Jeff takes a swig of beer. "My parents were talking about it. It's awesome that they have things like that, you know?" He shakes his head. "My dad was thinking about setting something up, too, you know, for more kids like you, but then he saw the price of tuition for my brother and me, and he was like, 'whoa.'"

"Whoa," Erik deadpans, but Jeff must be tone-deaf, because he soldiers on.

"Not that you'll need anything like that, huh, Georgie?" He kind of punches me in the arm. "You got it made here." He looks toward the sliding glass door to the deck. "Man, I'd stay here if I could. Fuck college."

243

"Yeah," I agree. "Fuck it." *Fuck you.* Then I remember that Jeff's going to need a refill after this party. "Hey," I add, "when do you want me to come by again? Or do you just want to load up now for the next week or so?"

"Oh, man," says Jeff, "sorry. This is it for me." He kind of dips his head, embarrassed about something. "My parents are a little freaked, right? About the fires? They're dragging me back to the city on Monday."

"That's fucked up," I say. "Talk about an overreaction."

"That's what I said," says Jeff, "but it's not just my parents. How many, now? Four? Half the lake's going to be gone by the end of next week." He shrugs, then looks at someone over my shoulder and tips his hand in front of his mouth, pretending to chug a beer. "Shit. I'll catch you all later, right?"

"Later," I say, trying to quell the panic that's rising in my chest.

"Prick," says Erik when he's gone. His face has gone kind of splotchy, and his fists are tight at his sides. He looks like he's about to explode. "I *bet* his dad thought about starting some sort of fund. I bet he fucking did. For about two seconds."

"Erik," I say, "did you hear him? They're all leaving. They're leaving." I can feel the drugs in my pockets, weighing me down like rocks. "How the fuck am I supposed to work if I don't have any customers?"

He stands there for a second. "You'll be fine," he says.

"Easy for you to say. God. I have to get to work. I have to unload this stuff before they all go home." And I want to scream, knowing what this means. More boat deliveries. More Dodge.

Erik looks around the room. "I hate these people," he says. "All of them."

Layla's walking toward us, a couple cans of beer in her hands. She smiles at me, but the smile is more of a question mark—*anything to worry about here?* I smile back: *I don't know, is there?* I look at her closely. She's pretty—I'll give her that. But is she enough for him? Can anyone be? He needs—

God. I want to kick myself. Like I'm in any position to be deciding what Erik needs. He's made his choices, and I've made mine.

I step back from Erik and look around. A few other kids are in various states of consciousness around the room, but there's a group by the bookshelves laughing loudly, talking with their hands. I've been at this long enough to know when people are getting restless. And a restless party is a prime market. "I have to get busy," I say.

"Sure you do." Erik shakes his head.

"Hey," says Layla. Her smile is genuine, with a touch of possession. "Georgie, right? I've seen you around."

"Yeah," I say. I don't have time for small talk. Especially not with her. I turn to go, and then look at Erik again. "But I'm serious," I say, my voice low. "If you want to talk."

I watch him turn toward Layla. His smile is wide, bright, and fake. He takes the beer from her. "Thanks," he says, not looking at me. "I'm good."

As I walk away, I hear her ask him a question. I can't hear what he says in return, but when I turn again she's stepped closer to him so that the bottom of her head touches his chin. I watch as he closes his eyes for a second. Then I look away.

I swallow. There's no getting through to him. Not here. And besides, I have too much to do.

Erik may hate these people, but I need them. $1,900 to go, and suddenly, what feels like a ticking clock. So, I spend the next hour working the room. I'm fairly successful, especially once I make it down to the beach. Turns out naked, swimming Weekenders want a top-off, something to keep them flying into morning. I do my best, but I'm still going to leave the party with some bud and a teener, a handful of caps. I stand on the deck and look out over the lake, where half of the kids from the party are swimming. It's dark, but I can still see that the beach is dotted with clumps of clothes. I consider just leaving my backpack here and going home, letting someone else find the stash. Happy birthday to you.

$1,900. $1,900. $1,900.

I can hear the sound of the fireworks show starting up at the marina in town. The pop before the color. Sure enough, the sky fills with bursts of red, blue, purple, white. It looks like it's raining fire on the swimmers below.

"This is my favorite part." Erik's standing next to me, peering down at the swimmers. "Wish I'd brought a flash-light."

"Remind me never to go skinny-dipping when you're around."

"I'll do no such thing," he says, and looks at me quickly, then away. His voice is missing some of its customary cockiness.

I look behind us, but I don't see her. "Where's Layla?"

"Had to go home. Something about early breakfast with her parents."

"Does she know?" I ask. "About your dad?"

"No." And before I can press it, he adds, "I don't want to burden her." Erik leans on the railing, and I can see that he isn't even looking at the swimmers. Instead, he's glaring at the lake itself, his gaze cast toward the far end, where I can see the lights from the bigger homes glowing yellow against the black. "I can't wait to get the hell out."

"Me too," I say. "In fact—" I pause, not sure if I should tell him.

"In fact?"

"I'm getting out."

He shrugs. "I know that."

"I mean, I'm getting out now. The end of this summer. Headed to the city with the band."

I watch him for a reaction, but he doesn't give me one. Instead, he looks out over the lake.

"What, nothing?" I say.

He's quiet for a second. Finally, he turns toward me. "I think I always kind of knew that, George," he says. "We're

247

never—this town was never going to be enough. So yeah. Go." He doesn't sound mad anymore. Just different. Sad. Then he smiles at me. "What is it you always say? Grit, guts, glory?" He nods. "You've got that. You'll be fine."

"Okay," I say. "Worst Case Scenario: Saskatoon."

"Where the fuck is that?"

"Canada."

"I'll take it."

"You wouldn't."

"I bet it's got decent restaurants, at least."

"Don't let Mr. Chin hear you say that." Then I add, "Don't worry. That's not going to be your only option. In fact, my friend," I add, scooting over and jostling him with my shoulder, "you're the only one with a guaranteed ride out of here. You're going—"

"Just stop, okay? Just stop." He glances at me and then looks away. "There's no scholarship."

"What?"

He raises his right hand, fingers pinched together, and then splays them open, mimicking a dropped bomb. "Bam," he says. "Gone."

"Bullshit," I say. "A scholarship doesn't just disappear."

"Doesn't it?" A hollow laugh. "Sometimes it just fucking does, Georgie."

"That's—" I start to say, but I feel a hand on the small of my back and hear a hoarse voice singing quietly.

"Four-alarm girl, nothing to see."

248

Shit. Shit shit shit. Erik can see Henry behind me, and I watch Erik's eyes widen with recognition.

And yet. And yet: *God, I love that voice.*

I turn to Henry and my stomach flips. He looks cuter. More punk. Less sure. And yes, it's only been a week, but a week in the summer is a month during the rest of the year. I've been ignoring his calls, responding to texts with one-word answers. He doesn't know that I saw him at the Den, and I don't know how to tell him. "Hey," I say, and my voice sounds thin and hopeful.

Jesus. This was not how I wanted it to go down.

I turn to Erik. Grip his arm, hard. "Have you met Henry, Erik?" Because maybe? Maybe I haven't wanted to think that it matters—that Erik's dad being Henry's stepdad is even a problem.

His eyes rake over mine, and for half a second I can see panic and fury and betrayal. I've been lying to myself. How could I think it wouldn't be this way? I hold my breath.

But then: "Not really, no." He holds out a hand to Henry, eyes now empty. "Hey."

Henry's less polished. "You're . . ." A pause as he chooses his words, like he's speaking through thick oil. "Kyle's son."

"Something like that."

Henry looks at me. I have to remind myself that he doesn't know. He doesn't know that I know everything.

"Erik's one of my best friends," I say, and I feel Erik's arm tense under my hand. "You were asking who my friends are.

249

Well. We've been friends for years." I let my hand slide down his arm until it finds his hand, and I squeeze. Then because fuck it, I can't help myself: "I'm surprised you two haven't met."

"Didn't know I existed, did you?" says Erik, just as Henry says, "The other day." He gives me a long look that's more of a question, and then he adds, "But I'd seen pictures."

"What?" Erik pulls his hand away from my grip.

"Pictures. Dad—your dad—has a few from when you were a little kid. So." Henry shifts from foot to foot and squints down at the water. His eyes are rimmed red. I didn't notice before. That's why this conversation seems like such a struggle for him.

"He has some pictures." Erik looks frozen, arms by his sides, legs planted. He looks like a warrior in the moment before battle. "I bet he does. What . . . ?" he starts to ask, and then stops himself. "Doesn't matter."

From across the room, Jeff yells a hello to Henry. "Man! You gotta get a taste of this!"

Henry steps away from me a few inches, raises his hand in a wave to Jeff. "Give me a minute," he shouts back. Then he turns to Erik. "Hey, man," he says. "Look. I didn't know—I didn't think—he said you'd probably moved, you know? Or I'd have . . ." He swallows. "I'm not a dick. I'm not the problem here."

My head snaps in his direction. "What kind of bullshit is that?" And I'm furious. Furious at him—for being stoned, for being part of this, for not-knowing but maybe-knowing that Erik was here all along. But I'm also furious at my body, and how it seems to move closer to Henry of its own will. God.

Henry reaches out and touches my arm. "I'm just saying. Our dad is complicated."

"You don't have to tell me what he's like," says Erik, his voice growing louder. "Okay? You don't have to tell me."

"I was just—" says Henry, but Erik's voice, now a shout, cuts him off.

"DON'T TELL ME!"

A few people in the water stop splashing one another. I can see their bobbing heads in the lake, turned toward the cabin. There's a whistle and a screech in the air, and the fireworks finale begins, the sky lighting up with sunbursts of color.

"Okay. Okay," says Henry, taking a step back. "Got it." Then he looks at me and says, under his breath, "Call me back sometime, would you?" He leans in like he's going to kiss me, but he stops and pulls back a little. Looks around and whispers, "I've missed you."

Shit. There goes my stomach again. Traitor.

Erik watches him head back inside. "So that's your hookup?" His voice catches and he shakes his head, runs a hand through his hair. He looks up. "What are you even doing with him, George? I mean, does it have to be him? Come on." His eyes are bright in the light of the fireworks. There's something else in his voice—something small and hurt. "Just don't let it be him."

251

I push back a defensive twinge. "That's, like, the least of it, Erik," I say, but it's not. I know it's not. I'm watching him carefully. His hands are balled into fists at his sides, and he's standing there, rigid, like a trap that's about to be sprung. "You okay?" I ask.

"*Okay*? No, I'm—" He takes in a long breath. "I mean— what? *Maybe Erik doesn't even live here anymore?* Was he even going to try to find me? We haven't moved. My mom and I—we haven't gone anywhere." His face kind of crumples for a second. Then he blows out another breath and says, "He'll be gone soon." Looks at me, pleading. *Make this all go away.*

Out in the water, everyone's forgotten about the shouting. I hear splashing, the occasional scream of protest, laughter that sounds like howls. We're such animals, when it comes down to it. Survival of the fittest. Fight or flight.

"I'm heading out," I say. "Wanna come? We could hit the diner or something. Talk—or not. Whatever you want." I'm supposed to meet Dodge down on the beach in a little bit, but he can wait. This is more important. Was Kyle really not going to get in touch? Christ. And I want to hear more about the scholarship—that kind of thing doesn't just disappear, does it? I reach out, put my hand on Erik's cheek.

"Erik," I say, "come with me." I try not to think about how angry Dodge will be—or what he'll do. I say to myself again, *This is more important.*

"No," says Erik. "Thanks." He moves his head so that my hand falls away from his cheek. He smiles at me, but his eyes

252

are empty again. "You should probably go find Henry. I'm sure he's waiting for you."

"Erik. It's not—" But I can't finish.

He nods back toward the living room. "Besides, you've got work, right? Aren't those the two things you care about—Henry and work?"

"And you."

He laughs quietly. "Yeah. Sure. And me." Erik reaches over and grabs me by the shoulders, drawing me toward him. I lean in until I can feel his breath against my forehead as he whispers, "To market, to market." Then he pushes me away gently. "Isn't that the way the song goes?" He laughs. "You can't take it all on, George. So don't try."

There's nothing to do. Nothing to say. I reach out and squeeze his arm, then turn. As I shut the sliding door to the deck behind me, I hear his voice follow me in a broken sing-song. "Home again, home again, jiggety-jig."

Dodge is waiting for me on the next dock over. It belongs to a little A-frame that's empty for most of the summer—owners are geriatric, I think—so it doesn't matter that he's tied the boat up there.

"Took you long enough," he says when I show up. He jumps in, jerking his chin toward me. "Hurry up." He starts the motor as I untie the boat. Then I get behind the wheel and putter out past the dock. Davis was right: Practice enough, and it's easier than driving a car.

"Where?" I ask. I don't want to speak more than I have to. This night has already sapped my ability to string a thought together, much less a sentence. Erik's voice in my head: *Just don't let it be him.*

"East side," he says from where he's kind of crouched beside me. "Tollefson."

To market, to market.

I nod and open it up on the water, skirting the gathering of boats in the middle that have thrown down anchor to watch the fireworks. They'll all be heading home soon, but right now they're still watching the show or lighting their own bottle rockets and roman candles. The sheriff does lake rounds at night, especially on the Fourth, but the little green light on the top of his boat is a dead giveaway, and I don't see it anywhere.

As I'm driving toward the Tollefsons', I think about Erik and Henry. The way Erik's voice sounded over the water, loud as a firecracker. How I could have stayed—should have stayed—and made him leave the party with me. I should have made him talk. Because if Erik's not talking to me, he's not talking to anyone.

But I didn't. I left to make money. Or maybe just to leave. To get out of the discomfort of staring down Erik's pain and saying, *It's okay*, even when it isn't. To get away from my guilt about not ending things with Henry as soon as I realized the connection.

The drop at the Tollefsons' is easy enough: a quick

exchange on the dock below their cabin, the youngest Tollefson glancing over her shoulder in case her parents decided to come down too. Easy hundred. I jump back in the boat, turn us around, start to head back into town, when Dodge says, "No. North."

"Another drop?" I ask, turning the boat slowly, scanning the shoreline for any cabin lights that might indicate our next customers.

Dodge shakes his head. "Something new. Campground." Then, when he sees me staring at him, he reaches over and pushes the throttle up himself. The boat lurches forward, and I have to grab at the dash before I fall. We're moving too fast for conversation, and he lets me take the wheel again, but not before he says, "Time to earn your keep."

By the time Dodge and I park the boat at the marina, the festivities are over. The lake is dark and quiet; it'll be dawn soon enough. I imagine all the Weekenders, safe in their beds, ready to wake and hit the water. I can hear them now, people like Jeff-the-Spastic, calling his friends in the morning to come over, start the party up again. *The lake's glass, man. You have to be out there.*

What bullshit.

Know what I want to yell across the lake on this perfect summer night? *How many of you have been driven in a boat to a crowded campground and dropped off with tiny Ziplocs of coke and Molly tucked into your bra? How many of you have been told*

255

to go to the largest group site, the one farthest back in the trees that has space for a couple of RVs, a handful of tents, five or six motorcycles, and ask the people there if they're interested in buying? How many of you have had to wait inside one of those RVs, shaking and trying not to, thinking about the gun that Dodge wedged in the waistband of your pants, the gun you'd never, ever, ever be able to shoot, while some guy with a tattoo sleeve and a beard the length of your hand sizes you up and down and says, finally, "How much"? And then, how many of you have had to stand and squeeze your way between the two guys guarding the door while one of them pretends like he doesn't know that his hand is brushing against you as you leave?

I didn't think so.

On my own, I've only ever sold to friends or friends-of-friends. My client list consists of a few adults, sure, but they're the adults I see on a weekly basis while checking out at Toney's or grabbing my sandwich at the diner or filling my truck with gas. When I sell to strangers, they're strangers who go to the same parties I do, and that makes them known to me, somehow. And terrible as they've been, tonight I realized that the boat deliveries haven't been that dangerous, either. Scary, sure, but at least I've always known that Dodge is there, sitting in the passenger seat like a very ugly bodyguard.

Tonight was different. Tonight I sold to the kinds of strangers you cross the street to avoid. By myself, in the dark. Dodge was back in the boat, probably snorting what he'd taken out of one baggie before he told me to step onshore, too far away to hear me if I called out. And what would he have done if I did? Nothing.

I knew I was stuck before. I just didn't know that what I'm stuck in is quicksand, and I'm sinking, and it's only a matter of time before I go under.

I have to get out. I have to get out now.

Survival of the fittest? Bullshit. Let other people fight. I'll choose flight. Always flight.

ERIK

I tried to avoid her, waking up early and getting dressed in the dark. Didn't even turn on the bathroom light to brush my teeth. I've got my hand on the front doorknob when the kitchen light comes on and the Beast appears like a ghost at my side.

"Where are you going?"

Quick, Erik. Quick. But I can't think of anything. "Breakfast." It's the truth, sort of.

"This early?"

I shrug. The doorknob is starting to sweat under my palm. "Meeting a friend."

She looks down. "I thought we'd have breakfast together."

There's a sick feeling in the pit of my stomach. *This must have been how he left. Early morning, everything still fuzzy from sleep. Her questions, always more questions. Those pleading eyes. The door right there—right there.*

257

"Mom," I say, "I—" But I can't say it. Can't tell her who I'm meeting. Can't think about how it must've been—that night, when she waited for him to come home. And all the days all the days all the days after. "A friend," I say. "I'm meeting a friend."

"A girl?" she asks.

I don't say anything. But like a warm hand on my cheek, I can see Layla as we kissed good-bye the other night. How I looked at her, touched her hair with my fingers, allowed hope to bloom like a stain.

And then her smile, a little surprised, when I told her she was amazing.

Why did I say that?

"Be careful," the Beast adds. "Those girls will try to trap you."

Ah. Here we are. Back on familiar ground. I watch as she pats her hair, which is still wrapped around curlers. Her night-time routine is the stuff of a sitcom. Minus the laugh track.

"They all want out. Who's the one you've been hanging out with all year? Georgia?"

"Georgie?"

She makes a sound in her throat. "That one. She seems especially troubled."

"Mom, she—"

"Watch her," she continues. The Beast's on a roll now. There's no stopping her. "She'll be wanting a piece of your scholarship."

"It's not a cake," I say. "You can't, like, cut it into slices." *Zero divided by two is still zero.*

She glares at me. "Even so. She'll try to come with you. I guarantee it."

I look at the clock on the kitchen wall. Not even seven, and I'm already done for the day. "That's a whole year away. And besides, no one's coming with me. Especially not Georgie." Ignore the jolt of pain—stupid to still feel it. "I promise." Another glance at the clock. "Listen. I have to go."

"Georgie?" Her eyes narrow.

"No," I say. And then, because I can't think of anyone else who won't attract suspicion, I say, "Davis."

She nods. "Good. He's a good friend." Starts to shuffle toward the coffeepot. "See you later. I'm home today—Westerfields canceled their cleaning. They're not coming up after all." She looks back at me. "Third cancelation this week." She sighs. "I'm getting worried," she says, and her voice is small.

I remember how upset Georgie got at the Fourth of July party when she realized that her customers were leaving. She looked . . . scared. I wanted to tell her that it's better this way. Better that they leave.

"I'm not worried," I say.

She looks at me, grateful.

"Really, I'm not." Because, I want to add, nothing matters to the Weekenders. Nothing ever gets in the way of their easy lives.

Except Layla. Her life may be easy, but she doesn't take it

for granted. Last night, talking about her pottery and why she does it: *I want to leave the world better than I found it.* How she laughed at her own earnestness. How I did too, but I watched her as she talked—glowing with the certainty that she can make a difference.

"Dinner tonight?" the Beast asks. "I was thinking pot roast."

"Sure."

Pot roast. As I walk downtown toward the marina, I think about how those two words sound like slow death.

There's no one at the marina. I knew there wouldn't be. Gold Fork always wakes up slowly, starting with breakfast at the Pancake Parlor and moving toward the water. In an hour, sure, people will start bringing their boats down for put-in. Fewer than normal—the highway out of town's been packed in the past couple of weeks with Weekenders, fleeing. But right now, the docks at the marina are all mine. Which is just the way I want it.

I walk out to the end of the closest dock and sit, crossing my legs and leaning forward so that I can peer into the lake. The water is green-black. It's like looking through a pair of night-vision goggles. Down at the bottom, I can see dark shadows moving lazily around. Gutterfish. Not worth a worm.

I've been coming to the marina in the mornings since a couple days after I got the call about losing the scholarship. The lake's always been the place where I can think. When

I'm staring down into its quiet darkness, all the noise from the day before just melts away. All the ways I've screwed up, all the ways I'll continue to screw up, just don't matter. The lake is ancient, formed by glaciers twenty thousand years ago. It's kept thousands of secrets. Some of them are mine.

I shake the thought away. Behind me, I can hear a truck beginning to back toward the boat launch. Meaning my alone time is up. Time to get back on the battlefield.

As I head down the dock, I pass an old canoe that's been tethered loosely to a cleat all summer. I've never seen anyone take it out. I kneel, glancing at the truck that's halfway down the ramp, its boat in the water. The driver's still in the cab, and I can see his silhouette as he talks on the phone. I take a closer look at the canoe. The paddle, old and splintered, rests in an inch of dirty water near the stern.

This town is full of forgotten things.

I've only got half an hour to spend at the library this morning, working on my résumé, before my breakfast. Thirty minutes to maybe figure out how to make "Fourth Place, State" look like anything but failure. There's not enough time in the world for that.

Which is why I'm not exactly pleased to see Davis at the library entrance. He's got a couple books in his arms and looks almost as mortified as I feel.

"Oh," he says. "Didn't expect to see you here."

"Why, because I'm illiterate?" I can't go in now. No way.

It's bad enough that I spent all last winter driving a snowplow around Gold Fork's loops and cul-de-sacs, keeping driveways accessible on the off-chance that a Weekender might come up once or twice during the ski season. But to have to admit to *Davis* that I'm afraid I might do that forever? Or—worse— that I'll be standing just inside the sliding doors at Walmart, greeting every Dead Ender who comes in? Am I going to ask for Davis's advice on the placement of my name and address at the top of the page, and whether I should list my athletic achievements before my job history? No thanks.

Skills:

Pushing snow.

Pulling docks.

Fucking up.

Davis shifts one of the books so that I can't read the title. But it's clear from the picture on the front of the paperback—a dragon, some sort of cauldron—that this is one of those D&D fanboy things. Not a surprise. "No. Just." He shrugs. "So, what are you doing here?"

"Nothing," I say, and realize how fake that sounds. "Just getting a book for my mom. But," I add, "I don't think I'm going to get it right now. Fucking card catalog. Too much work." I turn around, start back down the library steps.

I think I've left him behind when I hear him say, "They don't use that—" and then stop himself. Then he says, "Wanna get coffee? Breakfast, or something?" His voice goes all guidance counselor, and I know what he's doing. It's what Georgie tried to do at that asshat Jeff's party the other night. *We need to check on poor Erik. Lend him a shoulder/ear/tissue/a pair.*

No thanks.

"I've got plans," I say.

"Oh," he says. "Okay." He kind of looks like a musician from the early sixties with his square glasses and his kind of pointy nose—one of those guys who were always singing about puppies and waterfalls and girls purer than water. Lies, lies, lies.

Still. What must it be like, to see the world that way?

I take pity. "Next time," I say.

"Okay." He's still standing there, and I wait for what's coming. "It's crazy," he says. "How all of this, like, everything, is connected to your d—" He stops, tries again. "I mean, Vera—that old woman who Ana visits—she's Abby's mother. And Abby's your—"

"I know who she is," I interrupt. "Small fucking world." God. I can't get out of here fast enough. I glance at my watch, like I'm late for something.

"And Henry—" Davis pauses, and I can feel his eyes on me, checking for a response. So he knows about Henry and Georgie, too. So, fine. I nod.

"You doing all right?" he asks. "I mean, have you talked to your dad?"

I give him a look.

"Cool," he says, flustered. "Cool. Hey, though. I wouldn't say anything—if you wanted to talk. I wouldn't tell anyone."

He laughs self-consciously and adds, "My own secrets now? Too boring to share. They're an introvert's secrets. Subtle shifts in my emotional landscape. But I'm a good listener."

I don't say anything, but for a second, I consider it. Think about telling him everything. What would it be like, to unburden myself finally?

Then he says, "I'm basically a man of the cloth by proximity. None of the wisdom, but all of the platitudes." As he says it, the books fall from his arms onto the ground. "None of the dignity," he says, bending to pick them up.

No. I can't tell him. It wouldn't be fair. I squat to help, handing him books. I pick one up and start flipping through.

"That's not—" he says.

"This is your novel, right?" I ask him. "That graphic thing?"

"That's one way of putting it," he says, reaching for the book, but I pull away and look at it.

It's good. Lots of pictures of Jane, always wearing the same thing, always sitting and staring off into space. But good. He's actually really talented. I turn the pages, reading. *It was always you. . . . Like to live inside your head. . . . Let's blow this town. . . . When we're sixty-four.* "Pretty serious monument to something that lasted only a couple of months," I say. Then I look through the pages again. "Huh."

"What?" He makes a sound in his throat like he's swallowing gum.

"You only draw endings," I tell him. "You know that, right? Each of these"—I tap a page—"is a happy ending."

He looks surprised. "No," he starts to say, but I interrupt him.

"You're lucky. You can just rewrite your ending as many times as you want."

He stares at me for a minute. "Sure," he says, "but it's never going to be real."

"Happy endings never are. They're just dry paper. Empty scribbles." I shut the book and hand it back to him. "I don't blame you," I add. "It'd be nice to get a do-over. I don't blame you for trying."

I leave Davis on the library steps and walk to the Pancake Parlor. It's on the road that eventually leads out of town toward the city, so it's always crowded with people just arriving in or—lately—leaving Gold Fork, not to mention the families who basically make it a daily stop. At this hour, it's filling up.

He's not here yet.

I take a booth near the front, but not so close that I look eager. Roll my shoulders back. Scan the menu, printed on what's supposed to be old newspaper. Try not to look toward the door.

Even so, I know the minute he walks in.

I read the menu even more furiously. *Eggs: poached, scrambled, fried.*

"Erik." He's standing next to the booth, and I glance up, casual.

"Hey." Almost like I didn't expect him.

He slides in across from me. "Glad you called." Then, like he rehearsed it: "I was hoping you would."

Nervous, jittery, as I listened to the phone ringing. Waiting for him to answer. Would he see the area code and let it ring? And what would be worse—if he answered, or if he didn't?

"Yeah." I watch him. Today he's wearing another Dad shirt: a polo with the logo of some golf course on it. Two golf clubs, crossed, with what looks like a flower sprouting out of the middle. Who would wear that?

"Oh, Erik." Like he was surprised to hear from me. A beat— too long?—and then he said, "Glad you called."

"Well." He looks down at the menu. "What's good here?"

"I doubt anything's changed," I say.

"Right, right." He doesn't look up.

"Coffee?" A Latina waitress is standing over us, waggling a pot at us. I nod. So does he. She pours it into our mugs. "Room for cream?"

"Black," I say, still watching him.

"I'll take some cream," he says.

She waggles the pot again in the general direction of a small bowl of creamer packets. "Fresh as the day is new," she says.

"Gracias," he says, and I watch her roll her eyes.

"You guys ready to order?"

"Two eggs, scrambled, hash browns, bacon, toast— white—and an extra side of bacon," I say without pausing for breath.

"A pancake." He glances up at the waitress. "And fruit." Pats his belly. "Trying to keep my girlish figure."

"Great," she says, deadpan, and walks away.

He leans back and looks at me for probably the first time. "You're looking good. I hear you're something of a track star. Good for you."

This? This is what we're going to talk about? I take a slow sip of my coffee. God. What did I expect? How do you explain the past thirteen years? "Yeah," I say.

"Big scholarship."

"Not so big." I stare into my coffee cup. "Not anything, really."

"I wouldn't say that." A pained smile. "It's great." He pauses. "Your mom doing okay?"

I set down the coffee cup carefully. *Poached, scrambled, fried.* "She's fine."

A long pause. Then he says, "Hey. I'm trying. You're the one who called. You're gonna have to give me something, here."

"I'm the one who called," I say. "That's right. I'm the one who called." I place my hands on my lap under the table, gripping my thighs. I glance down. My knuckles are white.

"If this is going to be some sort of witch hunt—" he starts, but stops as our server sets our plates down in front of us.

"Good to go?" she asks, and we both nod.

We dig into our food, shoveling it in as fast as we can. For a few minutes, it's quiet except for the sound of our forks against our plates. Then he tries again.

"Let's start over, here," he says. "I really—I think there might be some misunderstanding. About what happened." And just like that, I can see the shimmer of tears at the corner of each eye. You can't fake that. . . . Can you?

"Maybe you can tell me." I watch him—his mouth, nose, even his hair just like mine. If you didn't know better, you might think he was my cool uncle, or even a brother—he the firstborn, me the mistake.

He pushes his plate to the side and puts his elbows on the table. "What you have to understand is, things weren't good," he says. "I mean with your mother. She was—I felt—she was suffocating. Like a rock."

The weight of her worry, heavy on my shoulders, pressing down. The way, every night, the kitchen gets smaller and darker until it's just the two of us, sitting at that table, exchanging plates. Actors on a stage at the end of a play. I nod. "I know," I say, just like a traitor.

"And you were, I mean, God, you were just a baby, a little kid, but damn, don't let anyone tell you kids fix things, because between the diapers and the crying, it's not going to fix a thing." He says this real fast, and then he smiles, like we're in on a joke. "Glad to see you're out of diapers," he adds. He must see something in my face, because he says, "It wasn't you. I know that's what the books say you have to say—*it wasn't you*—but it really wasn't. It was"—he waves his hand around—"this place. Everything."

"Worst Case Scenario," I say.

"What?"

"It's a game we play. Like, what's worse than Gold Fork? Nothing."

"Ah," he says. "Oh. Right. Good one." He shifts in his seat. "I'd have played that."

You did play. You played and you won.

"What about you?" I ask. "I mean, so you're married. So . . ." I'm hoping he'll pick up my thread, give me something. Anything. I'll take anything.

"I am." He nods. "That I am."

I take a sip of coffee. It's cold. I look around for the server.

"I just wanted to clear things up," he says. "Just, you know, to be clear about what happened." He shifts in his seat like he's going to stand. Like he's going to leave.

"It's too bad you never saw me run," I say suddenly, and it's like I'm watching myself in a movie, like the words have flown out of my mouth and I'm cringing as I watch, maybe even yelling at the screen, but I can't stop myself from going on. "I'm really fast." I sound like a baby, like a little kid. *I'm really fast. Stupid stupid stupid.*

He smiles. "I bet you are. I was, too, you know."

"In high school? College?" I allow myself a breath of relief. Maybe I don't sound as dumb as I think.

"High school. Could've gone to college—wish there'd been opportunities like your scholarship back then, but"— he raises a hand like he's lofting a ball in the air—"life. What are you gonna do."

"Yeah." I can't help it—I smile. "Life."

The server glides over.

"Could I get a re—" I start to say, but then he interrupts.

"Do I pay you, or up at the counter?" A side smile to me like, *I can't remember!*

"Counter," she says, and turns away.

"Ready?" He's already standing.

I look down at my plate. There are still a couple pieces of bacon, some toast. "Sure."

We weave through the restaurant. By now the Pancake Parlor is full. Families and large groups huddle around the hostess stand, craning their necks to see where they are on the waiting list. He's making small talk now, relieved to be done with the heavy lifting.

"Some pyro you guys have here," he's saying over his shoulder. "What's next—Toney's? Burn it down, I say." He laughs.

"Yeah," I say. "Burn it down."

"I bet it's a group of kids. Kind of thing my friends and I would have done." We're at the cash register, and he's fishing dollar bills out of a leather wallet. "I've got this," he says to me. "They're gonna catch 'em soon, though. You hear about the shoe print? Piece of paper? Regular crime scene here."

"Yeah." The sounds around us dull to a roar.

"Wonder if the piece of paper had a name. But then, they'd probably be knocking on doors if they had a name." He laughs, dropping a dollar in the tip jar. I see the server watching him, see her eyes narrow in disgust. "Knowing the police, they probably can't even read whatever the word is."

"Yeah."

He turns to go, and I reach into my back pocket, pull out some ones, stuff them in the tip jar while he's not watching. Then I follow him. I'm opening the door when I feel a hand on my arm.

It's Henderson. The guidance counselor. The last person in the world I want to see.

"Erik," she says, "how are you?" Her voice is dripping with sympathy. It's sickening to hear. She glances over at him and does a double-take, then focuses back on me. Probably making a mental note to add *daddy issues?* to my file.

I look over at him and roll my eyes just slightly, hoping that she doesn't notice. But then, who cares if she does? I don't owe her anything.

"Fine, Ms. Henderson," I say. "Keeping busy." I try to angle my body and take a step toward him so that he has to take a step back. If I keep it up, I might be able to basically push him out the door. "Well, nice seeing you," I say.

"Erik," she says, squeezing my arm. "I can't tell you how sorry I am. Bureaucratic oversight. I should never have let you apply. Have you thought about what I said? Have you considered other options—"

"I'm really running late," I break in. "I'll call you. But hey—thanks for asking. See you around," I say before the door shuts behind us.

Out on the street, he turns to me. "What was that about?"

"Typical guidance counselor," I say. "Everything's a crisis to her." I wave my hand around. "Troubled youth everywhere."

"Yeah," he says. Then: "Want a ride?"

I can tell by the way he's shifting from side to side that he wants me to say no. For a second, I think about saying yes, making him drive me home, see where he left us. But then I remember the Beast, home all day with canceled appointments, and my stomach turns. "Got some things to do," I tell him.

"Okay," he says. "So, let's do this again, right?"

"Right," I say.

"I'll call you," he says. "Okay? I'll call you."

He doesn't try to hug me. I stand there and watch him get into his car, pull out of the parking lot, and drive away.

BMW. Naturally. That Abby's got him set up good.

I start walking.

When I get home, I know I'll go straight to my room. I'll open the smaller box in my dresser and pick up its contents, nestled in the palm of my hand. And my heart will start to slow, and my body will feel steady and strong again.

Then I'll pull out my box of trophies from under my bed and hold each of them in my hands, one by one. Layla's headband. A beaded necklace. Small clay cup, its edges rounded and imperfect, a thumbprint just visible near the bottom. Little things I've taken when she's not looking that remind me that I can have this, too—I can have a good moment, a special girl. I can have a Weekender. It really can be that easy.

As far as I know, she doesn't miss her things.

Everything's replaceable in her world.

But not in mine.

There are traps everywhere. In my house, at some Weekender's party, at the goddamn Pancake Parlor. What was it my dad said? *There might be some misunderstanding about what happened.* But there's no misunderstanding. He was trapped. He flew. Easy as that.

I don't blame him for flying. You can't blame someone for doing what you'd do too.

The problem is, he forgot to take me with him.

DAVIS

I like words. This is no surprise. But there are a few I detest. Words that sound humiliating in your mouth: "moist," "snack," "raw." Words that tell you the thing you don't want to know: *You're just not quite* it. And then there's "almost." Almost is a useless word. A gray-area word. A word of rejected possibility. If there's any action behind it, it's the mental gymnastics of talking yourself out of your own life.

Almost is nothing.

Weekenders don't dabble in *almost.* In the words of Georgie, "They just fucking *do.*" It's the thing I envy the most about them.

After I brought Ana back home from the hospital two weeks ago, I ended up going on a hike in the late-afternoon light. The lake road goes all the way around, pavement turning to gravel turning to potholes and then back to gravel and pavement again. In the winter, you can't get much farther than Fellman's before you're stopped by a wall of unplowed snow and ice. But in the summer, when the campground at the north shore is open, the road gets a fair amount of traffic. RVs, mostly, but also camp wheels and the odd Taurus.

Specifically, my dad's Taurus.

I'm not giving up. I'm just giving in.

I drove the lake road to a hike that my parents and I have gone on since I was a kid, and I thought about Ana and her mother. As I climbed through the trees, holding on to branches for support, I thought about arriving in Gold Fork and knowing no one. Having to make it all up as you go. When I got to the top of the trail and stood at the overlook, peering down the length of the lake toward town, I wondered what it would be like to be each other's only people. And I knew it would be easy for me to romanticize that—crossing state lines together, a mother-and-daughter adventure team, probably a cool indie soundtrack, a *Thelma and Louise* sort of vibe without, you know, the dive into the canyon—but I knew that wasn't what it was like. I'd seen Ana's face as she talked about the places they'd lived before arriving here finally. Loneliness.

Now, as I cross Main and head back toward the newspaper

office, I remember that hike and how I thought about going back to Ana's house just to check on her. Bring her some Chinese food or something. See if there's anything she needed, anything I could do. Just swing by—no big deal.

How I almost did it.

I listen to my footsteps on the sidewalk. *Al-most. Al-most. Al-most.*

Dan's been giving me more work to do lately. Right now, for instance. I'm on my way back from the police station. Another fire, this one out on North Beach. Could've been a campfire that got out of control, could've been the GFP— that's what we're calling him or her now: The Gold Fork Pyro. It's not the most inventive name in the world, but it's catchy enough for headlines. *GFP Fires Again.* (That one was mine. Thank you, thank you.) Police weren't sure it was the same person. Then again, when I drove out to the site with the station captain earlier today, he pointed to the blackened clearing near the campground outhouses and said, "Tell me who builds a campfire next to the shitter." Not exactly quote worthy.

When I get to work, Dan's pacing the length of the "newsroom," one hand flapping around as he gesticulates and talks to what I have to assume is an imagined source in his head.

"Land-use restrictions?" he says. "What about permits? Who's issuing them?"

"Hey," I say, stepping into the room, but he just kind of waves in my direction and keeps going.

"Fire code. Parking." Then he turns to me. "Will they have to widen the lake road?"

"I—"

"Of course. And what about the Boy Scouts? Impact there. Interview camp director."

There's a pause, and I realize he's waiting for me to say—or do—something.

"Did you want me to—"

"Write it down. Interview camp director." He's pacing again.

I drop my backpack next to my desk and pull out my notepad. Take the note. Look up at him again. "Anything else?"

Dan flops onto one of the two sitting chairs that he has by the door. "No," he says, deflated. "That's all for now."

"What's going on?" I look back at the note I just took. "Are the Boy Scouts expanding or something?" That's all I can piece together from what he just said.

"Hardly." Dan sits up. "Confidential information, Davis. Anonymous tip. Keep this under wraps." He pauses for so long that I think he's told me what he's going to, and I'm going to have to decipher it like some ancient rune. But then he says, "Michaelson estate's been sold. Condos. No. More than that." He pinches the bridge of his nose and squints. "They're going to tear it down and build a club: condos, restaurant, activity house, the works. And a gate," he adds. "You better believe there'll be a gate around it all. Like the Citadel, only stronger."

"What, a club, like, where the house is now?" The Den. Our Den. Gone.

Dan nods his head. "As I understand it, they're going to raze the whole sixty acres and build up from there."

My hand is already in my pocket, wrapped around my phone. I just have to wait until Dan is gone, and then I'm texting the others. No way I'm not telling them about this. No way. "Who are the sellers?"

He looks at me. "Boyd. Original owners all along. Which reminds me—tax break implications." Dan keeps staring at me until I write that down too.

I talk to the notepad. "Do we know anything about these"— pause so it looks like I'm checking my notes—"Boyds?"

Ana said Vera's last name was Whitaker, didn't she?

"Only that it's the kids' doing. Owner is apparently here— has been all along—but is no longer able to make cogent decisions. That's their line, anyway." He scratches at his chin. "Might be worth tracking her down, just to see."

This is the last thing Vera needs. The last thing Ana needs.

Dan starts toward his office and turns. "Weird, isn't it?" he says. "Why they haven't used the house all this time. Place like that, you'd think."

"Yeah," I say. "You would."

"People don't know what they've got," he says. "Or maybe, in this case, they do."

When I get home, my parents are in the living room.

"Hey, Moose," says my mom. She's sitting on the couch next to my dad, a cup of coffee on the table in front of her.

I check my phone one last time before joining them. I texted the news to the others as soon as Dan left for the day, but only Erik got back to me, surprisingly. Classic Erik response, too. Short and direct. *WTF.* Nothing about his dad. Nothing about Abby. Just *WTF.* (Whenever I think I'm starting to get Erik, he goes and WTFs it. Like the other day at the library. He looked like I'd caught him shoplifting Viagra from the pharmacy behind Toney's. Like he couldn't get away from me fast enough.)

"What's the latest?" asks my mom. "Has the arsonist left a clue this time? A name, written in ash?" She laughs, but it sounds a little forced. The fires have affected everyone—my mom included. No one's coming to church. And those who do come want to talk about the chapel fire—a hard memory for her.

"The fires are the least of it," I say.

"Sounds serious," says my dad. He doesn't look at me, which is how I know he knows something. "Let me guess. It has something to do with ungrateful children." He stands and walks over to the mantel.

It should come as no surprise that the only person in my family who can play poker is my mom.

"Where's this optimistic outlook coming from?" my mom asks him. "I never knew you to be a misanthrope."

"Sometimes," Dad says, "making money isn't as fun as you think it'll be." He nods at me. "Davis knows what I'm talking about."

"Yeah," I say, "I do." I plop myself into an easy chair.

Mom stands and walks over to my dad, rubbing his back. "Trouble in paradise?" she asks.

"Something like that," he says. "Got an interesting call today. I've been asked to broker a deal for West Corp."

Mom grimaces. Everyone knows about the A. J. West Corporation. It's a group of developers who are constantly trying to build golf clubs on National Forest land and skyscrapers along the lakeshore—things like that. Keeping it classy. So far, all of their plans have fallen through, much to the delight of Gold Fork's residents. "What are they planning now?" Mom asks. "Who's selling Grandma down the river?"

Dad nods. "Actually, someone's doing exactly that. Right, Davis?"

I nod.

Dad continues. "West Corp's got an agreement to purchase the old Michaelson place and turn it into a 'members-only resort.'" He makes air quotes with his fingers. "Security guards, gate, dues like you wouldn't believe. West Corp even mentioned 'application interviews.' And we all know that's just code for polite racism. The owner's children—daughter, daughters, I'm not sure which—are all in. Can't get it done fast enough." He drums his fingers on the mantelpiece. "Anyway, huge deal. I guess they've been working on it all summer. Just needed me to do the final paperwork. It's a great commission for an hour or two of work."

Mom looks at him. Deadpans, "What price integrity?"

He sighs. "I know. I know." Turns a smile on her. "That's what I told them, too, when I said I wouldn't do it. God knows we could use the commission—sales have dried up since the fires started—but I couldn't do it. I told them this town doesn't need the kind of pollution that comes from 'members-only' clubs." He laughs. "They asked me what I meant by that. I said the stink of exclusion doesn't wash off." He claps his hands. "That was the end of that conversation."

"You're the anonymous tipster," I say. "You called the *Roundup*."

"Guilty." He smiles.

Mom pretends to swoon. "My hero! Look closely, Davis. Your dad might be the only socialist real estate agent in the whole country."

Dad thumps his chest with his fist. "Take from the rich and give to the poor."

"That's Robin Hood, hon," says my mom.

"They made lots of noise about how this is good for the local economy," says Dad. "But when you build an all-inclusive resort, people don't tend to hit the town too often. It's a sham."

"Wait. Did you say 'daughters'?" I ask. "Are they both on board?" Maybe there's a trail to Kathryn, the one Ana wants to find. I did some searching at the office a few days ago, but came up with nothing. How hard can it be to track someone down? Harder than I thought—but then, I was looking for Kathryn Whitaker, not Kathryn Boyd.

"Not sure," says Dad. "Did your editor know more about the family?"

"No," I say. "It's just sad, is all. I hope it doesn't go through."

"Oh, it will," my dad says. "Probably already has. Some guy on the ground's been showing West Corp around—another family member, I think."

My mom makes a strange sound in her throat, but then she clears it and looks away.

"Funny who comes out of the woodwork when there's twenty million dollars at stake," my dad continues. "If it's not me brokering the deal, it'll be someone else. Gold Fork's changing. People are saying it's the next Vail. And as we know, money talks."

"But only if someone's listening." Mom starts heading toward the stairs. "And this town is pretty good at plugging its ears."

Dad waits until she's all the way upstairs before saying to me, "Twenty million. Eventually, Moose, the noise gets in."

After dinner, I go upstairs to my room. I wish I could go back to the office, but chances are good that Dan's asleep in there, and I don't think I want to explain why I'm looking through old archives. I turn on my computer and text Ana while I wait for it to boot up, even though she still hasn't responded to my message about the Den. *Vera's daughters have a different last name,* I write. *It's not Kathryn Whitaker. We're looking for Kathryn Boyd.* Then I start Googling.

WHERE EVERYTHING'S AVAILABLE

There's another group of Weekenders whom we don't talk about much. Our parents talk about them, though. They talk about this group in quiet, confidential whispers at Grainey's, leaning over graphs and spreadsheets on the table in front of them. Sometimes our parents can't help it: They shout.

This group comes in the summer, sure, but you can sometimes see a couple of them in the spring, sometimes early fall, walking through the town with their phones and their iPads out, telling their lackeys where, exactly, to set up the surveying equipment. "That's not right," they shout into their phones. "Get me the right specs! Those numbers are jacked."

They care about numbers.

Maximum capacity. Fire code. Number of units, and how many people they can conceivably fit into each one. "But if there's a foldaway bed in each room," they might say, "we can get away with less square footage. The question is how much use each bed provides."

Everything is quantifiable to the developers, even sleep.

It's a small group, owing to the fact that Gold Fork only has so much land left to carve. Most of it's protected by the Forest Service. The land that's still available is objectionable in some way: too far from downtown, too close to the state highway, too ugly, too barren. The developers often have futility etched across their faces as they yell into their phones. Because, forget about the lake. There hasn't been land for sale on the lake in a decade, maybe more. And when cabins do occasionally hit the market, they're tiny, their parcels hardly big enough to develop into anything resembling a profit.

But the developers keep coming back. It's as if they know that someday, someone is going to strike gold, and the waterfront property on the lake will open its arms and pull them in.

ANA

There are times you can forget you're a Dead Ender. Like when you stay out all night and watch the sun come up over the lake, the sky gray and then pink, the air sharp and pure on your skin, in your lungs, and the lake feels as much yours as anyone's. Then, Gold Fork feels as magical and full of promise as it must to the Weekenders. Then, you feel your heart leap in the way that theirs do whenever they drive into town and see the lake for the first time. Leap and flutter.

But.

Sometimes Gold Fork isn't magical at all. Sometimes it's just a town that offers nothing, where people hurt one another and make mistake after mistake until it seems there's nothing but mistakes all around them. Until it seems like there's nothing to do *but* casually ruin everything.

I'm at the Royal Pines when they move Vera back into her room, and I'm amazed by how many people have to coordinate in order to transfer one ninety-pound woman from a van to a wheelchair to a bed. The whole process must take a half hour, but finally she's lying down, head propped up by pillows, one hand worrying the covers, the other resting on her chest. I've brought her a floppy stuffed dog, and the red of its fur looks garish and false next to her skin.

"Hi, Vera," I say in my brightest voice, pulling my chair next to hers. "I've been thinking about you. How do you feel?

285

Good?" Everything I say sounds false. I overheard one of the aides telling another under her breath as they moved her in that the doctors haven't ruled out more strokes. "Just a matter of time," she said, and then changed the subject when she noticed I was listening.

Vera looks over at me, confused. Then, like lightning, a smile. "Oh," she says, "how *is* he?"

"Who?"

"Your caller," Vera says.

"Who?"

"Your sweetheart."

"I don't have—" I start to say, but she lays her hand on mine and struggles to sit up in her bed.

"You think I don't see, but I do," she says. "That young man—he's been here before with you." She laughs quietly. "I had to refill the bowl of nuts!"

Does she mean Davis? I do remember when he visited her with me once and ate almost all the nuts in that bowl. I didn't have the heart to tell him how old they were.

"Sweet boy," she says. "He visited me in the hospital when you weren't there."

"He did?" I say.

"Sat quietly. A quiet boy." She peers at me. Her voice grows a little louder, more commanding. "There's no reason to withhold," she says, and squeezes my hand. "When you cherish someone, shouldn't they know it?"

"I—" I start to say, but she interrupts.

"Not many measure up. Lord knows my Lewis didn't. Should have left him when I had the chance."

"Oh." I'm about to say something like, *You don't mean that,* because she's never insinuated that Lewis was anything but wonderful, when she continues.

"Should've left him for Abigail's father." The nod of her head is barely noticeable, like she's welcoming an old memory. "Just one summer," she says, "but what a summer it was." Vera shifts around on her pillow. "And then Abigail came." She looks at me. "Children can be mysterious," she says. "Kathryn I know, but Abigail? She's always been such a mystery to me. Always a mystery . . ." Vera exhales, a thin whisper of breath. She closes her eyes. Then nothing. I'm suddenly listening hard, waiting for the next breath, my other hand fumbling for her call button, when she speaks again, her eyes still closed. "You don't always have to reciprocate," she says, "but don't dismiss it. What a gift—to know you're loved." I wonder if she's talking about Abby or Abby's father.

"Good. You're here." It's Abby, standing in the doorway in another billowing caftan. I study her face to see if she heard what Vera just said, but it's expressionless. She moves around the room, dusting her fingers along the top of Vera's dresser, now picking up an old Valentine's card I gave her, now touching the music box that we sometimes wind up so that Vera can listen and say, *Oh, this song. Now I remember.* "We have so much," Abby says, "and look what it reduces to. A bunch of crap. Ugly sweaters." She looks over her shoulder at me.

"Start making a list now of what you want to take with you, because if you don't, you'll end up with nothing from the life you've lived." She runs her fingers over the bib that hangs off of Vera's doorknob. "Or maybe it doesn't matter once you're wearing one of these." She raises her eyebrows.

Beside me, Vera is snoring softly. I don't answer for a minute. Then I say (*calm, keep calm*), "You're selling her house."

Abby's eyes widen. "News travels fast," she says. When I don't answer, she sighs. "Ana, I know you're angry. But these are . . . complicated things." She smiles at me and leans against the dresser. "Sometimes the right thing doesn't look right from the outside. It's time to cut the cord," she goes on. "Leave this place behind us." She pauses on "us," and I remember that she doesn't know that I saw her at the Den. Then she says, "And it'll be easier to have her situated near me in Chicago."

"You're moving her?" I say, my voice thick. "To Chicago?" I'll never see Vera again. I feel like I can't breathe.

"I'm a professor there," she says now, as though this explains something, "of art history."

I try to inhale, but it's more like a hiccup. Chicago.

"I've published books. About Man Ray," she adds.

Why is she telling me this? I don't care about her job. I certainly don't care about Man Ray, whatever that is—a type of sea creature? She's starting to sound like a little kid, pointing to a row of toys and saying, *Mine. Mine. Mine. Mine.*

"I can't believe you're moving her," I say, feeling hot tears that threaten to spill down my cheeks.

Abby pats the air like she's dribbling a basketball. "Calm down. It doesn't make sense to keep her in Gold Fork," she says. "Not with her health how it is." And she's back to that voice of hers, so regulated, so without feeling. "And these fires? Something's wrong with this town. I don't trust it."

"You don't trust the town."

"She can get better care near us."

"Us." I'm still trying to breathe. It feels like the room is filled with smoke. I'll never see her again.

"My family. You didn't think I have one?" She laughs drily. "You and Mother are more alike than you'd imagine. Besides, I'll be able to get in more often to take care of things."

"But not to visit."

She looks at me, eyes narrowed. "And to visit."

My phone buzzes and I check it. Davis. *Call me ASAP.* I set the phone facedown on my leg.

"But you won't," I say, and am surprised by how quickly the tears spill. It's dim enough in the room that I don't think Abby can see, and I blink. "I've seen it here," I add. "People always think they'll visit. But a one-hour visit turns into thirty, then fifteen, then five minutes, and then it's just easier to check in with the nurses. You don't want to bother her if she's sleeping, right? It's just easier to drop off a blanket or some slippers and ease back out before she sees you." My voice is high and I'm speaking fast. "After all, you're taking care of her, aren't you? Doesn't she need slippers? I mean, of course she does. You're doing what needs to be done." I wipe at my cheek. "She doesn't need slippers," I say. "She needs . . ."

"Stop it." Abby's cheeks are flushed, and her voice is a whisper-scream. "Just stop."

"Enough. Both of you." We whip our heads toward the bed, where Vera is sitting up, barely, and glaring at us. "No more of this nonsense. You've always fought like cats and dogs." She looks at Abby. "Go to your room." Looks at me: "You stay here with me. Help me with dinner." Vera scoots back down slowly and turns on her side, clutching the stuffed dog. She doesn't say anything else, and within moments, we can hear her deep, regular breaths.

When I look back up at Abby, her face is hard.

"That," she says, voice low. "That's how it was."

"She's confused," I say. The phone buzzes again, vibrating against my leg, but I ignore it.

But Abby shakes her head. Her laugh is hollow. "Tell me this. In all your sunny afternoons in the solarium, your little tête-à-têtes, did my mother ever tell you that I was 'never a great beauty'?" Her voice changes, becomes a tinny approximation of Vera's. "'Abigail's personality will have to work overtime.'" She clears her throat. "'Not graced with a face.'"

She blinks and looks at me, and I can feel the heat rise in my cheeks.

"I thought so," she says. "And how would you feel about a mother who spends your whole childhood telling you that only one thing matters in life, and—sorry to break it to you, kid—you ain't got it?" She runs a hand through her hair. "Would you want her to live with you? Would you even want to be in the same town, the same state?" Abby comes closer to the bed, leans over Vera, and brushes something off of her cheek. The gesture is tender, almost. "She never loved me," she says, her face just inches from Vera's. "Gave Kathryn all sorts of nice presents: dresses and barrettes and ribbons. Girl stuff. Kathryn didn't want any of it—threw it away first chance she got. The only thing I ever got from our mother was disappointment." She straightens.

Vera's voice is still echoing in my mind: *Should've left him for Abigail's father.* Did Abby hear her? "God," I say, and my voice is louder than I mean it to be. "Don't you think that's how everyone feels about their parents, to one degree or another? It's no reason to abandon her." *Grow up,* I want to add, but don't.

Abby walks over to the little sink by the bathroom and washes her hands. I watch her stare at herself in the mirror. Then she turns. "I bet she's told you all about her *sweet Lewis.* And he was sweet. Just ask his girlfriends." She shakes her head. "In my opinion, that's what marriage is: a constant looking-away."

Erik's dad.

"My mother went through twenty-five of their fifty years together with her eyes closed and a gin and tonic in hand."

I look at Vera, sleeping peacefully. None of this makes sense. It's not the Vera I know. A rock turns in my stomach.

On my leg, the phone vibrates again, and then again. Someone's calling me.

Abby keeps talking, but her voice gets rough, and she swallows often, as though she's choking on the words. "And, you know, that's the thing about being drunk all the time. You miss things."

Piano recitals. Soccer games. PTA meetings. All the things my mom has missed because of work.

Abby's looking down, but she turns her head quickly toward me, like she knows what I'm thinking. Her face is distorted by pain. "No. I mean, you miss things like one of your daughters taking the boat out during a thunderstorm even though—God—she's only fourteen, she shouldn't be driving the boat at all. Not hearing your other daughter yelling for you until it's too late, the boat's halfway to the north end of the lake, out of sight. Not calling the sheriff—not doing a thing about it—until you've had a chance to sober up, because God forbid anyone find out that you're a drunk, but by then it's too late and the storm is so bad no one's on the water anyway." She stops and rubs her hand over her face. When she looks at me again, her eyes are hard. "They never found the boat. The lake just"—she waves her hand—"swallowed her up." Abby moves to the window. "They might not have signed a death certificate, but I watched that boat fly through the storm. I know my sister is dead."

I push back the image of a boat, crashing. A boat, flipping. A girl, falling.

"Even then—even then—they didn't get a divorce. But we moved. Rented the house out for the first ten years to the Michaelsons. Nice family. Eventually, my dad just left it empty. He'd come back during some summers to make improvements, add things—the tennis court, new windows. Sometimes he'd make me come with him. I don't know why he was so obsessed with preserving the worst memory of our lives." She takes a breath and stands, moves toward the window. "It's like he was the curator of a museum of ugly feelings." She glances over at her mother. "When he died, she got sober. Took back her maiden name. Said she was done with her family. So. I let her. Be done."

Next to me Vera snores and shifts, her hand letting go of the stuffed dog to rest along the side of her face. It doesn't make sense. This doesn't fit. That person Abby's talking about? That's not my Vera. I turn from the image of the boat, the falling girl, and focus on *my* Vera. My Vera has no one— not anymore. And my love for her rises like a wave and crests over me.

"So why are you here? And don't just say 'business.' That's bull. Are you just going to keep punishing her for something she can't change?" I want to stand up and drag her by that fancy bedsheet she's wearing out into the hall and kick her out of the Royal Pines, kick her out forever. If Davis were here, he'd help. We'd bolt the entrance so that none of them could ever come back in. "That's not the Vera I know. She won't understand why you hate her." My voice catches, but I

293

keep going. "Most of the time, she won't even know who you are." I don't try to wipe the tears away from my cheeks where they're falling faster than the words I want to hurl at Abby. "You've come too late for vindication."

Abby takes a step toward me and I flinch, but then she rears back and sinks into a chair. Buries her face in her hands. I watch as her shoulders start to shake with each sob. She cries and I wait, listening to the soft whir of Vera's humidifier. When Abby looks up again, her face is red, eyes puffy.

"You always think there's going to be time to tell someone how they've hurt you," she says. "God. I can't tell you the hours I've spent, imagining what I'd say to her, how I'd phrase it exactly. And now"—she snaps her fingers—"that chance is gone." She starts crying again, but catches herself. Shakes her head. "I don't know why I'm here."

I'd feel sorry for her if I could, but I can't. Not right now. I don't know the Vera she's talking about. I only know the small, frail woman in the bed next to us, alone in the world but for me, and we're both surrounded by sharks.

Mom's still out by the time I get home. I putter around the kitchen, washing a few dishes, getting the coffee maker prepped for the morning. Two scoops for every cup, the way we like it. But I can't settle down, can't *sit* down. I wish Mom would get home. I need to not be alone with this.

By nine, I'm climbing the walls. There's only one other person I want to talk to.

"Vera?" He doesn't even say hi.

I nod before I realize he can't see me. "Yeah. Her daughter, actually."

"Listen," he says. "There's something—I found something."

"Kathryn?" I ask. "I know." My voice breaks, and I let out a little sob like a hiccup. And then I'm crying ugly, can't breathe can't talk can't stop sobs that ricochet off the phone and hit me from every angle.

"It's okay. Hey. It's okay." He doesn't sound scared, the way some people would—a girl crying on the phone like this. He just sounds . . . certain. He waits until I finish crying.

A long, shaky breath. Then I tell him all of it: Kathryn, Lewis, Abby's real dad.

"I found out about Kathryn last night," he says. "I wanted to tell you."

"I don't understand how it gets to this point," I say. "How you can just decide that your mom isn't worth it. Ever. End of story. Even if."

"Even if." Davis pauses. "I don't know," he says. "It's hard to imagine."

I wipe my nose on my sleeve and smile at the phone. "Says the golden child of golden people."

"You make me sound like a character in a fairy tale," he says.

"Exactly." And he is. The only person who doesn't know that Davis is the kid in the palace who wins every magical bet, vanquishes witches and evil sorcerers, saves the kingdom with a shrug and a smile, is Davis.

I hear him blow a sigh into the phone. "I'm lucky," he says. "I admit it. And so are you."

"My mom isn't anything like your parents." I can hear the bitterness in my voice.

There's a pause. Then he says, "It can't be easy, doing it all on your own."

"It's not," I say. "It's exhausting."

"I was talking about your mom."

"Oh." I sigh. "She's— It's complicated. We haven't exactly been connecting lately. She's got—" I almost tell him about Zeke, how she's been going out with him a few times a week, how everything's *amazing*, she says—and then decide not to. "She's been busy," I say instead.

"But she loves you." I can hear how embarrassed he is to say those words. "Remember after the fire? She was the only one who didn't try to forget what happened."

I do remember. Georgie's parents sent her immediately to a counselor, and then on to a three-week tennis camp in Lindy, the next town over (despite the fact that she doesn't play tennis). They acted as though being outside of a burning building was somehow just as dangerous as being inside. Erik's mom pulled him from the youth group—said it posed a threat. Side-eyed the rest of us whenever she saw us in town. Davis's parents were busy dealing with the loss of the chapel and the cost of rebuilding. But my mom sat next to me in the hospital as I got my arm stitched up. She sat there and didn't ask any questions. She just held my hand. Later, she invited Davis, Georgie, and Erik to a barbecue on the community beach. Fed us hot dogs, chips, watermelon. Let us just be. *Go through something like that together,* she told me later, *and you'll always know who your friends are.* She was the only one who saw how it changed things, even though she didn't know—couldn't know—that we were responsible for it.

"And—this is something I've been thinking about." Davis coughs and keeps going. "How the people you love most will disappoint you. It's inevitable."

"Glass half-full," I say.

"No, but," he says, "it's more what you do with that disappointment. Whether you forgive. Whether there's a reason to, I guess."

"Yeah," I say. "Fine. But Vera. She couldn't—" I can't finish. I can't imagine Vera not loving her daughters. Not wanting the best for them. I can't bear to think otherwise. Can't bear to think that she rejected her daughters the way my mom's parents rejected us.

But Abby's voice sounds in my head: *Not calling the sheriff, not doing a thing about it.* And then: *They might not have signed a death certificate, but . . .*

Wait.

"Davis," I say, "does your dad have the paperwork for the sale of the estate?"

"I doubt it," he says. "He turned them down. Why?"

"Can you find out?" I say. "There's something I want to check."

"Okay," he says. "I'll ask." Then he adds, "You going to be okay?"

"I don't know," I say. "I feel like everything solid is water."

"It really is," he says, "if you think about it." We both listen to the distant buzz of an airplane on his end, probably flying low over the lake. "Fucking tourists," Davis adds, and I don't know if he's talking about Abby.

GEORGIE

What do you do when everything burns? I mean the slow burn of desire. The reaching for each other in tiny ways—finger on wrist, slight touch of the shoulder, hips brushing hips as you walk. Everything bright, everything burning. The goddamn song of it all.

Being with Henry is really screwing with my music.

That's not all it's screwing with.

Because I can't stay away. Just like a character in a pop song, I'm addicted to Henry. Addicted to the way he makes me feel, the way he looks at me, the way his hands move across my body. Cue the orchestral accompaniment. We're a song I want to play. So even though I *mean* to end things after the party on the Fourth, even though I wake up most nights to the memory of Erik's face as he looked at Henry and realized how I know him—even though. I still can't do it.

And that's why I'm with Henry when I find out about the sale of the Den. Another afternoon tangled up in each other in the back of his 4Runner, my phone on silent, the only noise his heavy breath in my ear, asking the question.

This time, I don't hesitate. I bite his lip, pull him closer.

Yes.

Yes.

Yes.

But later, when I read the message and look over at Henry as he pulls on his shorts, his shirt still in a ball in the corner of the SUV next to a catcher's mitt—*why?*—I regret the yes. For a second.

"What the hell?" I say. "Your mom is selling the estate?" I almost say "Den," but catch myself in time.

He reaches into the back pocket of his shorts and pulls out a couple of pills. Holds one out to me.

"No," I say, waving it away.

Henry puts it back in his pocket and pops the other in his mouth. Drinks a mouthful of water before swinging his legs over the back and letting them dangle in the air. We're out at the Nelson cabin site, and the way he parked, I can see from the back of the 4Runner all the way to the Den. I imagine a scar instead of a house.

"Sorry," he says, lighting a cigarette, taking a drag, and blowing smoke away from me. "I didn't know what to say, you know?"

"How about this: 'Oh, Georgie. Almost forgot. There's

gonna be an exclusive club that none of you can join, taking up, like, a third of the lake.'" I pull my shirt over my head. "'Thanks to me and my family, Gold Fork's about to get fucked.'" I can't get dressed fast enough.

"Don't be so dramatic," he says, reaching for me. "It's just a club."

I shift farther away. "It's never just a club. And Davis told me the way it's planned, it's going to bring more fucking aristocrats."

"Aristocrats!" He laughs. Then, when he sees how serious I am, he says, "Come on."

"Don't you know what this means for the town?"

He looks at me blankly. "I'd imagine something good. I mean, all these fires haven't exactly bolstered the economy, have they?"

I lean forward. "This is exactly the kind of thing Gold Fork *isn't*. Other towns have resorts—gated communities and shit. Not here. That's never what we've been about."

"*We've?*" He smiles. "Aren't you a class warrior." Henry reaches over and tucks some hair behind my ear. "It's sexy."

"You don't get it," I say. "You can't." And I don't know why, but suddenly I'm thinking about Kelly, one of those Dead Enders that Erik used to hook up with, and I can just see her, down to the gray streaks on the apron that ties around her waist, standing over an industrial sink in the back kitchen of the club restaurant, hands submerged in soapy water. I can see her loveliness leach out of her, replaced with fatigue. Poverty. Not enough of anything, ever.

"Hey. Hey." Henry runs his hand up and down my arm. "Let's not. This was good. Let's just let it be." He puts his head on my shoulder. "This isn't us."

"It's not *you*, you mean. It's just your family." I jerk my shoulder so that he has to move his head. "Your family, ruining everything."

He sits up straight. "You think I don't know that, Georgie?" I'm pretty sure, but I'm not certain, that his lower lip quivers in the hazy light of the afternoon. My heart twists in my chest. Then he swallows and looks away. "Why do you think I go to State—and not some school closer to Chicago? I wanted to be close to this place. Until this summer, I hadn't been here since I was a kid. It's my family's only real thing, right?" For a second, it looks like he might cry. "Now I can't even have that. Kyle's basically been ruining everything ever since he and my mom met that one summer. He's a dick. He just is."

"I wish you could tell Erik that," I say. My cheeks are still bright with anger, but I can feel myself starting to soften.

Henry looks away. "You sure care about him."

I don't say anything.

"Fine," he says, and makes a sweeping-away gesture. "Do you get how little we can control any of this?" he goes on. "Our parents' jobs. Our parents' money. Look," he says, "I get that this club kind of sucks. I get it. But it's not going to ruin anyone's

life. And maybe with Kyle, that's the most you can hope for."
He touches my arm, and I let him pull me toward him.

"I know," I say, leaning in. It's not fair to blame Henry. He didn't make all of this happen. This isn't his fault.

Also, we just had sex. And I'm not, like, the kind of person who thinks that sex changes everything, but, okay, it changes *some* things.

So I drop it.

Henry lets me off downtown. I tell him I want to walk home from there, but the truth is, I don't want to introduce him to my parents. What's the point? I've never talked to them about these things, and I'm not about to start now—not when I'm this close to leaving. And okay, maybe there's a tiny part of me that thinks there might be space for Henry in my life in the city—a visiting-on-the-weekends sort of thing, a casual-until-it-isn't situation—but even if that ends up happening (and I know, I know, what are the odds, really), my parents don't need to meet him yet.

Besides, there's another reason I don't want Henry to drop me off at home.

I'm meeting Erik.

He texted me earlier, before I met up with Henry. *Got something for you*, he wrote. *Meet at the beach?*

And sure, it would've been easy to tell Henry—to say, "Drop me downtown. I'm hanging out with Erik." But I didn't say anything.

I don't really want to think about why I didn't.

He's waiting down by the water. There are families all around him: Noisy little kids in water wings hoist buckets of sand, their faces as serious as if they're building a goddamn church. Erik stands among all the kids like an elementary PE teacher. He sees me coming and smiles. There's something in his hand. A brown paper bag.

"Took you long enough," he says.

"I had a thing." I haven't seen him since the Fourth, and he looks smaller. Younger.

Then he says, voice sure and light, just like the old Erik, "I bet you did." There's the slightest pause, and I'm afraid he might shut down like he did at the party, but he smiles again, and it's genuine. "You been okay?" he asks.

"You're asking *me*?" I laugh. "I'm fine, Erik."

Erik nods. "Yeah. You're fine."

"But I mean, what about you?" I say. "The Den—"

He shakes his head. "Nope. This isn't about that. We're not going to talk about that." He holds the paper bag out to me. "Got a little something for you this morning."

I rub a hand over my face. "Okay." Then I open the bag and pull out a mug from the Pancake Parlor. Yellow, with brown writing—probably made in the seventies and still on rotation today. I raise my eyebrows at him. "Pancake Parlor," I say. "What are you, a Weekender?"

"I've been there a couple times lately," he says.

"By yourself?"

When he says, "I was there with Layla this morning," it's like biting into an orange with a cut on my lip.

"Surprised she didn't mind. Something tells me you didn't buy this."

"Not for sale," he says, and shrugs. "Doesn't mean not for the taking." He mimes slipping something under his shirt, and I see a brief wink of skin above the waistband of his jeans. "Layla'd already left." Then he laughs. "Look inside."

I do. The mug is filled halfway with dirt. "Thanks?" I say. "A reminder to wash?"

"From Twin Lakes," he says. "Remember?"

I remember. Early days in the youth group. Some death march to the top of a mountain, followed by an overnight at two joined lakes that, from the peak, looked like someone had drawn an infinity sign and colored it in with green water. It was so cold—cement toes no matter how many socks I layered—and then Erik pulled out this tinfoil blanket and gave it to me. Said that astronauts swear by it. *I don't need it*, he said when I asked him what he was going to do. *I'm a self-sustaining organism.*

Here's what else I remember: How much we laughed. How cold it was, and how beautiful.

This was a month before the chapel fire.

"Thanks," I say. "But shouldn't you be giving this to Layla, not me?"

"It's not a fucking promise ring, George," he says, and his cheeks get red. "Consider it a parting gift."

"Didn't know you to be a blusher," I say, leaning into him so that I can elbow him in the side.

He grabs my elbow and holds it for a second. "I'm a changed man," he says. Then he lets go and adds, "She wouldn't understand that." He gestures toward the mug. "But believe me, I give Layla plenty."

"How're things going with that?" I don't want to know—not really—but I feel like I have to ask.

"They're good," he says. "Really good." He pauses like he's embarrassed, and then he adds, "Who knows? Maybe I'll see you in the city in a couple years."

"What do you mean?"

"Just—things are going really well. Who knows, you know?" Then Erik looks away.

I almost make a joke about how every summer romance has a moment when you think it's going to last forever, but then I think about Henry, his body moving over mine, and how he looked at me like I was the best fucking thing he'd seen in a lifetime. How, afterward, he made some joke about visiting me in the city next year (because I told him—of course—about dropping out and just going), and how I laughed but thought, *Why not?*

Because: summer. Because: In Gold Fork, nothing and anything is possible.

"That's great," I say.

Erik glances out over the lake. A few boats drift near the buoys. We can hear someone yelling from a boat toward a friend on the beach: "Swim out here! Come on! We're hitting the cliffs!" And we watch as a kid—twelve, maybe thirteen—runs into the water, swims out to the boat, and pulls herself in. Then the boat—parent at the wheel, from the looks of it—speeds off toward Washer's Landing.

"Won't make it past the ten-footers," I say. "Once you're standing there, they seem a lot higher than they look from the water."

"Yeah," Erik agrees. "Twenty bucks says none of them jump."

And we laugh. Then I hold the mug up in the sunlight and turn it, inspecting.

"A perfect specimen," I say.

"That's why I thought of you."

I place the mug carefully back in the bag and tuck it in the crook of my elbow. "I'll love it forever," I say. "Seriously."

"Good," says Erik, turning from the beach and starting back toward Main Street. "I wouldn't want you to forget us when you're gone."

I stay on the beach. Then I raise my voice and yell, "Erik."

He turns.

"No one could forget you."

He looks at me for a long minute. "You'd be surprised," he says. Then he walks away.

ERIK

I'm pretending not to wait.

I'm always playing pretend.

The box under my bed is overflowing. So I get a bigger box.

Boxes, boxes. For things, for people, for hopes, for broken promises. There's a box for everything.

When the phone rings, I count to three before looking at it. I don't want to look too eager. I thought he'd call sooner, but . . . Well, never mind. The relief is a hot washcloth on my forehead. He's calling now.

I hold the stuffed rabbit from the box in one hand and look at the phone. *Not him not him not him.* I take a breath and answer. "Hey, Davis."

"Erik, hey."

Another breath. I cradle the phone between my ear and shoulder and begin to pull at one of the stuffed rabbit's ears. Layla told me it was her lovey when she was a kid and that she brings it with her everywhere she goes, even now. Funny that she hasn't seemed to notice it's gone. There's a thread loose where the ear connects to the rest of the bunny's head, and I scratch at it with my thumb.

"Didn't you get my texts?"

"Yeah." A few more threads have come loose now, and I'm pulling harder at the ear. I twist it first one way, then another.

"Another fire, if you can believe it. Near the airport. This is getting crazy."

"Any leads?" I ask.

"If there are, the police aren't telling the newspaper, that's for sure. Hey—" He sounds uncertain, a little flustered.

"Georgie wants to get together. And so everyone is coming over to my place."

"Yeah. I know."

"Oh. So, will you come? Listen," he adds, "my parents aren't home."

He tells me how to get to his house, and I pretend to be writing down the address, but the truth is, I know where Davis lives. I've known since we were in seventh grade and some of the guys and I threw dog shit at his door on Halloween and his mom came out and shouted and I swore she recognized me but maybe, just maybe, she didn't.

Obviously, I've never told him this.

"An hour okay?"

"Yeah."

I hang up the phone and look at the stuffed rabbit. One final twist, and the ear comes off in my hand.

There's a knock. I toss the rabbit in the box and kick it under my bed just as the Beast opens the door.

"You hungry?" She's in her house uniform: muumuu, slippers, sweater.

"Not really," I say. Look again at the slippers. "No work today?"

She looks at her hands. "Another cancelation." She walks into the room a ways and looks at the posters on my wall. "This is nice," she says, pointing to a poster-size panoramic of the lake. "Did you take this?"

I nod.

"What is that?" She moves closer, puts her finger on the poster. "North Beach Campground?"

"I guess." You can see almost everything: Washer's Landing, the campground, forest service land. The only thing you can't see is the town. I bought it back when things were easy and good.

"Well." She kind of dusts her hands on her dress and looks around again. I don't want her to look too closely. But she appears small, a little broken.

"It'll be okay," I say, and she looks at me, her eyes kind of squinting. "Work," I say, "and stuff. I think it'll be okay. These things pass over, you know?"

"I want to believe you," she says. She comes closer to me and stops. "No, you're right." She's kind of looking at my shoulder, not exactly in my eyes, when she says, "They're going to leave, Erik."

"I know."

"It'll be fall soon." The Beast turns and starts to walk out of the room. "Back to normal."

"Yeah," I say, staring at her head as she walks away. "Back to normal."

I don't want to be the first one there. Don't want to look too eager. But the fact is, when I park my bike along the side of Davis's house and knock on the front door (looking for any remnants of shit, though of course there wouldn't be now, it's been years, *Jesus*), I'm practically smiling. I've missed them.

309

It's been more than a month since we sat at the Den, just hanging out, thinking that this summer might actually be something. Something good.

Feels like years.

"Yo," I say, and glance inside as he opens the door wider.

"Glad you could—well. Whatever." Davis is trying to be casual, but I can tell that he doesn't know how to act around me. *Poor Erik.*

"Nice digs," I say as I walk in and look around. It's nice, but not too nice. Not nice like a place you live in only a couple months a year. Nice like a home should be, you know? Big comfy couch in the living room. Family pictures on the mantel. I catch a glimpse of Davis's twelve-year-old self, propped between his parents on a Ferris wheel, before he steps over to the fireplace and turns the picture facedown.

This house is a promise someone made and kept.

"The others are in the kitchen," he says.

It's at the back of the house, facing the lake. This kitchen's old, not updated with all the stainless-steel whatevers and useless gadgets that the Beast is always telling me about from the houses she cleans, but it's cozy like the rest of the house. There's a big table off to one side, and windows that look out over the trees that grow on the slope down to the water. Georgie's the first one I see, like always. She's perched on a counter, legs dangling, her heels knocking against a cabinet door. Ana's sitting at the kitchen table, drinking coffee. I just catch the end of what Georgie's saying to her when we walk in.

"—met when she was helping her father close the house up after the last renters—" She sees me and stops. "Oh. Erik."

"Don't let me stop you," I say. "One guess: the love story of Kyle and Abby, as narrated by Henry." I laugh, too loudly.

"It's not his fault," she says, and stands up, giving me a hug. When she pulls away, I keep one arm around her shoulder.

"I'll take a coffee," I say to Davis. "Black."

Ana's just sipping her drink quietly. I notice Davis tap her once on the shoulder as he walks over with my mug, and she looks up at him, gives him a sad sort of grimace. He nods, smiles down at her.

"What's going on?" I take another sip and gesture toward Ana as I lean back against a counter. "You look terrible."

"Thanks," she says.

Georgie shoots me a look. "Now's not the time, Erik."

"He'll hear about it eventually, anyway," says Ana.

"About what?" Have they all been meeting without me? I glare down at my cup. "Don't leave a guy in the dark," I say, and it comes out sounding more pathetic than I intend.

Ana shrugs. Looks at Davis. Says: "Long story short. Vera?"

"Yeah."

"She's sick."

"I'm sorry." And I am. Visiting a mausoleum every week's not my cup of tea, sure, but anyone can see that Ana loves that old lady more than most kids love their own grand-parents.

"And," she adds, "Abby—you know, Ky—your dad's

wife—is taking her back with them to Chicago or wherever, once the development deal is finalized."

"Jesus." I keep my voice light. "Lame."

Chicago.

"That's an understatement," says Georgie.

And she's right. Because what I really want to do is what I've wanted to do ever since I got Davis's text about the house being sold. I want to break shit. Hurl my coffee cup against the wall. Tear all the cabinets off their hinges and throw them in the lake. *Chicago.* The thing my dad conveniently forgot to mention when we had breakfast: where he lives. Fucking Chicago. I'm practically knocked over by the anger that's closing in. A familiar rage rises in my throat like fire, and I can't breathe. *They'll always win,* I want to yell—to the town, the lake, the rocks that have been here for thousands of years. *They're always winning. They take and take and give nothing back. It's the same fucking thing, every time.*

Chicago.

I'm clenching my fists. "I hope they burn," I say under my breath.

Davis looks at me.

I release my fists. Shrug, though it looks more like a tic. "Lame."

Davis blinks and shakes his head. "Wait until you read the letters in 'The Forked Tongue.'" They're pouring in. The best ones are from the Old Forkers. *Back in my day,*" he says in a quivering voice, "*we were lucky to have a tent. None of this gated clubhouse business.*"

Georgie laughs.

"Erik, has your dad—has he said anything about this?" Ana's voice is quiet, but she stares at me over her coffee, intense. "I mean, what's his story?"

I can't. I can't tell them that he hasn't said anything, because he hasn't called. I don't know what his story is, because he doesn't want to talk to me. I can't tell them that I didn't even know that he lives in Chicago—a place so far away, so fucking impossible, that I don't even really believe it exists. So I shrug—again. "What's he gonna do? He married a shitstorm. It's, like, his and not his, you know?"

Georgie raises her eyebrows. "Twenty million is going to be his."

And no one says anything, but in the silence, I hear it: *And maybe—someday—yours.*

My phone buzzes in my back pocket and I take it out, look at it. "Hold on," I say, and walk back into Davis's living room, staring at the number.

Big breath.

"Erik." My name is an apology.

"Oh," I say, "hi." I smile immediately and clap my hand over my mouth. Stupid. Like anyone can see.

"Sorry I didn't call earlier. I got caught up in some business." There's a car alarm going off in the background, and I hear him mumble, "Shit." Then the beep of the alarm being turned off. "Sorry," he says again, but I think he might be talking to the car.

"Sure."

"You up for coffee or something? Abby and I are heading to the city for a few days, but I thought we could get together after we get back."

"When?" I turn the picture on the mantel over again and stand it up. Davis's mom has her arm around him. His dad is holding on to the safety bar across their laps, and he's making this joking, *Here we gooooooo!* dad face.

"A week from Thursday or Friday? What works for you?"

Bothbothbothbothbothbothboth. I pause, like I'm checking my appointments. "Friday morning would work. Ten."

"Good," he says. "That place downtown, what's it called?"

"Grainey's."

"Yeah. Funny, the things you forget."

And then he's gone.

When I walk back into the kitchen, the others are still talking about the club.

"They'll start demolition next month." Davis is chewing on a fingernail. He nods at me.

"Probably call it 'renovation,'" says Georgie. "Not that they'll save anything from the original cabin. They never do."

"They don't appreciate what they've got," says Ana. "None of it."

Davis leans over and gives Ana an awkward side hug from where he's standing. God, he's as smooth as an elementary school principal. I shake my head and am about to give him shit for it when I see that Ana's got tears in her eyes.

"Assholes," she says, and it sounds a little foreign coming from her mouth.

"Assholes," we agree.

There's a minute when we just drink our coffee and kind of stare at one another. Georgie's chewing on her bottom lip. Davis pushes his glasses up his nose. Ana rubs at her eyes.

I can't handle the silence. Can't keep thinking about the Den. A week. I'm going to see him in a week. And—Chicago. For a second, so quick I don't have time to think about it, I see myself surrounded by skyscrapers. Walking somewhere with purpose. Passing beautiful women. Sun shining, wind in my hair. Nowhere to go but up. Then I snap back. "Don't tell me we're just here to talk about some business deal. I mean, what's done is done, right?" I laugh, like, *whatever!*, like I'm a goddamn cheerleader. "What about the party? That's the real question."

Ana looks confused, but Georgie gets it. "They'll have to relocate. I mean, there's the chance your dad and Abby wouldn't even notice, but still. Too risky."

"What?" says Ana. "What're you talking about?"

I forget. Of course she hasn't gone. It's not her thing. "End-of-summer party," I explain. "It's always been on the Den's property—but obviously not this year."

"Last year it was in the woods by the dock we parked at when we first saw . . ." Davis's voice trails off.

I pretend not to hear him. "I'll ask around," I say. "Location'll have been picked by now. I'm pretty sure I can find out."

We stand around for a few minutes, drinking coffee, talking about who might be there—who's still here, who's already left. If I close my eyes, I can pretend we're at the Den, and everything's still okay.

Georgie's hand is on my arm. "Erik," she says, voice low, "can I talk to you for a second?" Davis and Ana are leaning toward each other, laughing about something. It's a relief to see Ana smiling. Georgie jerks her thumb toward the small deck, and I follow her out the kitchen's back door.

The lake is sparkling. Water-skiers cut through it, the spray like diamonds behind them. I prop my elbows on the deck's thin railing and take it in.

"I've been using my mug," she says, and adds, "I put the dirt in a Tupperware. Don't worry."

"Glad you like it," I say.

The sun is warm on my arms. God. This is what life is like for Davis every damn day.

"You're a hard man to get ahold of," Georgie says, moving closer to me at the railing. "You never answer my texts anymore."

"I've been busy," I say, and stare at the water.

"I know, but—I want to talk about the scholarship. You said, at the party—"

"I was drunk."

"No, you weren't."

"Forget it," I say.

"But it's true, isn't it? About the scholarship?" She's trying

316

to look in my eyes, but I'm afraid of what she'll see. Georgie is the only one who would see my eyes and know.

I look away, off to the side. There's a noise in my head, coming from far away, hard to grasp. "So what? It wasn't that great, anyway. I can do better." She doesn't have to see my face to know that's a lie. The noise is getting louder. Too loud.

"But what happened?"

"Red tape. That's what happened." I turn to her, grab her by the shoulders. The noise in my head is a jangling cacophony, and I don't know what I'm going to do. I stare at my hands like they're two sticks.

"Erik." She reaches up, puts her hands over mine. "Tell me."

The noise subsides, moves away. I stare at the lake, a shimmering mirage. *Not for you*, the winking water seems to say. *Never for you.*

"I can't," I say. "I just can't." Then I turn and look through the window at Davis, who's watching us. And I realize that there's just a screen—no glass. He's heard everything. I take my hands off Georgie's shoulders and stuff them in my pockets. "Look like one of us isn't going anywhere," I tell them both.

AUGUST

WHERE THERE'S NOTHING TO LOSE

There's nothing like the sound of the lake at night in late summer. The wind in the trees is a white noise machine: *whsh-whsh-whsh*. It whispers, School's coming. Or, endings, endings. We can hear the docks knocking against the water, warning and invitation both. It turns cold now as soon as the sun is gone, and the lake is choppy and forbidding. We still swim at night, but we don't linger; we feel the depth of it, the boundlessness, and we pull ourselves up on the docks, scraping our bellies in our rush to get out.

But. For some reason, there's even more of a sense of possibility during these nights—a fall-is-coming-what-do-we-have-to-lose sort of feeling. Things no one dared try in June suddenly seem worth it. Why not? In a week, maybe two, we lose the cape. The magic slipper no longer fits. We are shorn—sometimes literally, with new haircuts that make us look younger, make us question whether the summer even was. And we don't want to forget. We want to have something to not want to forget. This is what Dead Enders and Weekenders have in common, finally: In the face of the inevitable return to our autumn selves, we're willing to go for it. We're willing, after a summer of mild to moderate successes, to risk epic, fantastic failure.

Most summer stories are made in August.

DAVIS

"Washer's Landing. Erik found out from Layla. It's next weekend. They're calling it Dance on the Ashes."

"Do these parties normally have names?" Ana asks. Her laughter comes through the phone as I turn on my computer and sit down at my desk. The office is quiet and dark; Dan must be out.

"I don't know—maybe? Erik didn't seem surprised by it when he told me. And they do like to name things," I say. "Classic imperialist strategy: You name it, you own it."

"Davis, you're hilarious." Her voice is lighter than usual. Brighter. I lean back in my chair and click on the newest file. It opens, and the piece I've started writing stares back at me. All three paragraphs of it. "Are you going?" she asks.

"Yeah," I say. "Who could miss it?"

"I could. I did. Every summer."

"Regretting your sane and sober approach to Weekender bullshit?" I say.

"I'm getting my fill of it now." Gone is the brightness.

"Any news there?" I imagine Ana—sitting at home, probably. But it's hard to think of her in some dim room. When I've thought of Ana lately, she's usually been in a sun-dappled meadow. Because I'm creative that way. Sun-dappled? Is she in a deodorant commercial? No wonder I'm not a famous writer yet.

She sighs. "Not really. I haven't seen Abby. I think they're planning on leaving in a couple of weeks, though. The nurses said something about starting to pack Vera's things." Her voice catches, and I hear her swallow. "Did your dad say anything about the sale? Did he have any paperwork?"

"He didn't have it," I tell her. "But I asked him to snoop a little, if he can. He said he'd see what he can do." I pause. "Why do you want to see it?" I pull a piece of paper toward me and start doodling.

"It's probably nothing," she says. "But I want to check the language. Just—a hunch I have."

"Cryptic."

"I'm an enigma."

I laugh, relaxing into the ease of the conversation. We've started calling each other every day—sometimes twice a day—even if we don't have anything to talk about.

"What are you up to?" she asks.

"Typical Friday. I have to read through some letters to the editor and pick the best ones." I don't think about what I'm drawing, but I can feel the pen moving in clean lines across the page. I close my eyes and keep doodling. "What about you?" I ask.

"Nada," she says. Then her voice rises a little, and she asks, "Want to get coffee?"

Yes. Yes yes yes. I clear my throat. "Didn't you just tell me you had three cups already this morning?" I ask.

"I could have more."

"Well, then. Sure," I say. Then, remembering—*shit*: "I mean, no."

Ana laughs. "You're the enigma."

"I wish." *God, how I wish.* "I just have to get this work done. Dan's coming in an hour, and I have to have the letters ready for print."

"Your loss," she says, and I think about how right she is.

When I get off the phone with Ana, I look at my document for a few minutes, reading what I've written so far. Observations about Gold Fork. A compilation of reflections, maybe. It's not an article. It's not even for my graphic novel. In fact, I don't really know what it is. But that probably doesn't matter. I doubt Dan will ever let me publish it.

At the bottom of the last paragraph I've written, I type, *We need them.*

I close the document and open the letters to the editor. Before I dive in, I glance down at my doodle.

Turns out, it's not Jane my hands want to draw. It's not Jane at all.

Ana's face stares back at me. Her hair sweeps across her chin in long, curved lines. Her eyes are bright. She's looking straight at me, not off to the side or down, like Jane did in all of my drawings.

Not my train, Jane. Not my fucking train.

When I get home around four, Mom's out front. Well, Mom's feet are out front. More precisely, her feet are sticking out from under the car, which is parked at an odd angle in the driveway. She must hear my shoes on the gravel, because she scoots out on her back and says, "Oil change."

I don't know anyone else who changes their own oil. But that's my mom for you. She calls it "a dying art," like it's on par with calligraphy or playing the pan flute. Suits up for it in a pair of coveralls straight out of a Bruce Springsteen video.

"Want any help?" I ask.

She gives me her look. It's the equivalent of a raised-eyebrow-slash-eye-roll without really moving any part of her face. The kind of look only a minister can perfect. "What do you need?"

"Mom." I try for indignant, and hit somewhere around apologetic.

She smiles up at me from the ground. "I'm almost done. But you could grab me a lemonade. Turns out the shade of a vehicle isn't so useful when you're stuck underneath one."

"Sure." I head in and pour her a glass. By the time I get back outside, she's standing and dusting off her coveralls.

"Thanks." We walk around the side of the house to our tiny deck and sit, looking out over the lake. "Summer's almost over," she says, sipping her drink. She glances at me, then away. "How's work?"

"Good," I say. "Not a ton of news."

"Any leads on the arsonist?"

I shake my head. "Not really. Just that shoe print and the scrap of paper. Just the one word." I look at her. "Keep a secret?"

"That's all I do," she says.

"'Regret,'" I tell her. "That's the word. No one's supposed to know, but Mrs. Nelson let it slip."

"Regret." She mulls that over. "A love letter? Bad breakup?" She laughs. "Not that I have an easy time imagining the Nelsons in a steamy love triangle."

I try to put that image out of my head as quickly as possible. "Thanks," I say. "Let's not go there."

"Agreed. Anything else? At work?" She leans back in her chair and rests her feet on the deck railing.

"I mean, it's mostly this new club. The demolition out at the Michaelson estate. That's all anyone wants to talk about aside from the fires, so that's what we're covering."

"And what do you all think of that?" I don't look over, but I can tell she's watching me. "You and your friends. Hasn't that been kind of your hangout?"

I turn to look at her. "I didn't know you knew about that," I say carefully.

"You'd be surprised what I know." Mom takes another sip of lemonade. "It's got to be particularly hard on Erik."

She's a subtle one, my mom.

"How long've you known?" I ask her.

"Davis," she says. "Plenty of people know about Erik's dad. This is Gold Fork, after all. A secret's only a secret until you come back to town. And Kyle . . . enough people remember when he left. A congregation talks, you know," she says. "It's more gossipy than a PTA meeting."

"How'd he go?" I don't even think Erik knows the answer to this one.

She looks at me like she's trying to decide something. Then she says, "Quickly. He went quickly. One summer." She does a little half smile. "The thing you might not realize—and, honey, I don't mean just you; I mean all of you, all kids, teenagers, everywhere—is that the dramas you see playing out between yourselves . . . They don't necessarily stop as you get older. The stakes just get higher."

"God," I say, "that's exhausting to consider." Then it occurs to me. "Does Erik's mom know he's back?"

"Yes." She doesn't even pause to consider the question.

"Oh, man." Just thinking about Erik and his mom having dinner or something, neither one thinking the other knows—it's like looking at an aerial photo of a village right before the bombing begins.

She puts her hand on mine. "You're a good friend to Erik. And he's going to need his friends."

I think about what he and Georgie were talking about the other day. How he lost his scholarship. And I wish, for the hundredth time, that we trusted each other. "I don't even know if he's been getting together with his dad," I say. "I mean, he doesn't really talk about him. He definitely doesn't talk to me. So, he might be fine." But even as I say it, I know it's bullshit.

Mom does too. "He's going to need you," she repeats. She glances at me, then away toward the lake. "How about other stuff? Your book, and"—meaningful pause—"other things? Anything eventful?"

"I know what you're asking, Mom," I say. "Real subtle."

She laughs. "Guilty as charged."

I should've expected it. The trajectory of all parental conversations ever.

So I say, "Don't worry, Mom. Your prayers have been answered."

"My prayers?"

"Yeah," I say. "You know, the gambler's prayer of parents everywhere." I make my voice go falsetto. *"Whatever you do, God, whatever it takes: Let nothing happen to my boy."* I look at her. "You should've stipulated that you meant nothing *bad*."

She's laughing too hard to respond at first. Then she says, "How are you *my* son?" She throws an arm around me and squeezes. "Love you, Moose. Love your crazy mind. And," she adds, "someone else will too."

"There it is." I smile. "The parental pep." But I feel something igniting in my chest for the first time since Jane said I wasn't *it*—something hot and bright and real. Hope.

Erik, telling me that I was only writing happy endings in my graphic novel. I couldn't believe it took me that long to figure out what it took Erik five seconds to see—that my whole book about Jane was just a fantasy.

And what a relief that was.

"Believe me or not," my mom goes on. "I'm not worried about you."

"No one ever is." I look out at the lake. It's a hot day, and a busy one. Boats everywhere. "I'm always surprised there aren't more crashes," I say, pointing as two speedboats veer away from each other at the last minute.

"People run into one another," my mom says. "It's inevitable." Then she says, "Oh. Your dad had to go to work, but he left something for you. 'Confidential,' he says, so it must be good. Envelope in the kitchen."

It's on the table—a manila envelope, legal size. I pull out the contract and look at it. "Mom," I yell through the screen door, "can I use your scanner?"

I send Ana a text. *Got something for you.* From what I can tell, nothing's out of the ordinary, but who knows what she needs.

And I'd love to be the one to have something she needs.

ANA

When I get there on Saturday afternoon, Abby's packing.

I stand in the doorway, watching her fold skirts from a pile on the bed and place them in a cardboard box. I'm clutching the printout from the document that Davis sent me yesterday. She looks up, nods at me, then continues folding.

"I didn't know you'd be here," I say. "Where's Vera?" Her bed is empty except for the pile of clothes, freshly made. Again the familiar panic, rising.

"On the patio, smoking with a nurse," she says. "They'll be back in a few."

Thank God. "Okay," I say. "Good."

She straightens. Gives me an odd look. "Would you bring that box over? This one's almost full."

I sigh. "Fine." I watch as she expertly pulls tape across the box she's been working on and writes in large black marker, *Boyd.* Then she opens the box I've carried over and lays a sweater inside.

"As though she needs this many clothes," she says. "She really wears the same four outfits—have you noticed?"

Of course I have.

"Let me know if there's anything you want," she continues. "Though I doubt there's anything valuable."

I know what I need to do. But I don't know how to do it. What would Davis say in this situation? Georgie? Erik? Sometimes I want to bottle up my friends, shake, and drink. Just to have an ounce of what they've all got.

But here's what I say instead: "I want her."

Abby looks up. And instead of saying the thing I expect, like, *Excuse me?* or *What do you mean?* she says, "No. You don't."

"You asked," I say, "and I told you. She's what I want. She's what's valuable." I walk over and take a shirt out of her hands. Carefully, I place it back on a hanger in Vera's closet. "It wouldn't be that hard for you to leave her again," I say, my back to her. "It'd probably be a relief."

"Kids," I hear her say. "You're all just looking for a cause.

331

Self-righteous. I'd admire it, if it weren't so misplaced." She raps her knuckles against the flaps of the cardboard box. "Everyone in this town thinks they know better." I turn around and stare, but she keeps going, her voice getting stronger, louder. "You, your friends, probably. Even the goddamn priest."

"Wait," I say. "What? Has Davis's mom—" But she talks over me.

"That's the thing about you people. You don't have the imagination to know what the rest of our lives are like. You think we appear one day, and one day we're gone, and the space between our arrivals is just a long pause. It's childish, really."

"What about you?" I ask. "We're not set pieces, you know. Not just extras in the great film of your Big Summer Vacation."

"Does this look like a vacation to you?" Abby grimaces. "Does this look fun?"

"It probably looked fun when you met Kyle," I say, and watch her expression shift. Her cheeks are red, and she blinks quickly. So I'm right about this. "Your very own Dead Ender. What was it, one of those summers you helped your dad get the place cleaned up? And how long, exactly, did you consider the fact that he had a family already?" I can see the effect I'm having, but I don't care. "Or were they just the extras you didn't see, like stagehands? So easy to ignore."

"You know nothing," she says. "Nothing. I can't believe I'm even—" She steps toward me. "How about this. Call me in ten years. Call me when you've gotten pregnant at some grad school party and your mother—your own mother—acts like this is all she ever expected of you."

"I—"

"Call me when you've got a little kid, a new job, no friends, and you haven't been on a date in two years." Another step toward me, close enough I can feel her breath as she speaks. "Call me then, Ana, and tell me what you *consider* when you finally fall for a guy who seems to see you more clearly than you've ever been seen before."

"People can justify anything," I say, but my voice is thin. In all of this, I never stopped to consider that Abby and Kyle might have actually been in love. She was, at least. I wonder if that's still true, or if, as she said, he only *seemed* to love her.

"I didn't expect you to understand," she says, turning back to the pile of clothes. "You don't know anything yet."

"I know that you need to forgive her."

"We don't know each other well enough to forgive."

I ignore that. "And I know something else, too," I say. "I know Vera better than you do."

"That's ridiculous." Abby picks up a skirt, looks at it, and then tosses it on the floor.

I walk over to Abby. Stare at her until she meets my eyes. "I might not know a single 'truth' about Vera's life before the Royal Pines," I say, "but I know the truth of her life now." I'm crying a little, but I'm not embarrassed. "She's hurt you," I say. "I can understand that. But if you can't be with her *now*—

as she is *now*—I don't think you should be with her at all."

"That's for me to decide." But her eyes are red, and her voice sounds husky. "I'm the one in charge here."

"You are." I step back, sit on Vera's bed, place the document next to me. "And you could decide to leave her here. With me."

"What's that?"

"The paperwork for the sale," I say, and raise my hand when she opens her mouth. "Doesn't matter how I got it. I have it. And there's something here I find really interesting." I peel back a few pages until I get to it. "'The owners are in full agreement with the terms of sale,'" I read. "Owners."

She looks at me, speechless.

"What was it you told me? They never declared Kathryn dead." I refuse to look away from her. This is my only chance. I have to be brave. "Legally, you need her signature. Oh"—another wave of my hand, dismissing the obvious objection—"I'm sure you *could* jump through all the hoops to have a death certificate issued. But I understand that takes time. And sellers don't want to wait. Summer's almost over," I add. "Gold Fork doesn't look nearly as promising in the off-season. Just ask Kyle."

Her voice is a whisper. "I can't believe you. This isn't—" Her voice falters. "It isn't right."

"Sometimes the right thing doesn't look right from the outside."

"Using my words against me." She walks over to the box

334

and picks up the skirt again. It's one I've seen Vera wear often: pleated blue, with satin ribbon along the hem. She folds it again and then holds it in her arms. She stares down at that skirt like it's got all the answers. Then she looks up at me. Her voice is a graveled, angry whisper. "Get out," she says. "Get the hell out."

"Gladly," I say. I open the door and step into the hallway. Before the door closes behind me, I hear her clear her throat.

"Ana," she says. "You're fired." Then the door clicks shut.

GEORGIE

The *Sun Rider*.

That's what I'm thinking about tonight.

Most summers, there's a pontoon boat that drives around the lake all afternoon, selling hot dogs and slushies to the Docksides. When the sun starts to set, the hot dogs morph into little baskets of chips and salsa, the slushies into margaritas. The woman who owns it, a hard-as-nails ski instructor named Hadley, says it's the most lucrative idea she's ever come up with, and she swears she thought of airport massage chairs first.

But it's not around this summer. (Davis reported that there was a problem with the liquor license.) Instead, the only boat doing dockside deliveries is much smaller, much faster, the customer service is shit, and the concessions are way more expensive.

Nine hundred dollars to go, and it's already August. I need every delivery to count. Now that I'm spending so much time with Henry during the day, the boat deliveries are my bread and butter.

Dodge is here, of course, sitting in the seat next to me. I wasn't supposed to work tonight—he was going to take his old truck. But I guess he changed his mind—wanted to go on the water. Who knows why. When I asked, he gave me a flat stare and said, "Ambience."

Trying to figure out Dodge is like trying to track a mosquito.

Not like I was doing anything. When he dropped me off after we left the Nelson cabin site the other day, Henry said he had something going on for the next few nights—something about family friends visiting—and what? I'm going to sit at home on a Saturday night with my parents and watch the news while they kind of obviously don't speak to each other? I'd rather make money. And so far, it's been fine. Easy. Four deliveries so far. Nothing to it.

"Last stop," Dodge says now. "Michaelson."

I almost stall the boat.

"Michaelson?"

"Don't act so surprised." He reaches into the small cooler that he keeps at his feet and pulls out a bag. I try not to watch as he pulls a smaller bag from within it and grabs a couple of pills, which he pops into his mouth. Throws his head back and swallows. "My. Cull. Son."

I drive the boat.

When I pull up alongside the dock, I don't see anyone at first. I tilt my head and stare up at the deck of the house, where there's music—something familiar, though it's far enough away that I can't quite make it out—pumping through a set of speakers. Then I see the glass door to the house open and a few guys come out, clear enough in the glare from the lights inside. College students, it looks like, from the insignia on one guy's baseball hat, the Greek letters on another's T-shirt. The Greek and the third guy, tall and kind of disheveled, make their way off the deck and come down to the dock. The third guy's got on a pair of combat boots, an old flannel. He looks different.

Oh, I recognize the music now. The Pixies. "Here Comes Your Man."

I've jumped out of the boat and am holding it against the dock with one hand. I raise the other as the two guys walk down the dock toward me.

"Hey," I say, and I watch Henry's eyes widen.

"Georgie. Hey. I didn't know you were working tonight." His face turns crimson. Nothing about *gonna call*. Nothing about *meant to invite you*. I can smell the liquor on him from here.

Greek T-shirt looks me up and down. "Well, hey, your-self," he says, then turns to Henry. "Man, you weren't kid-ding. Boat deliveries? This place is off the hook. Worth the drive, man."

337

Henry doesn't say anything, but as I turn back to the boat, I think I see him nod.

Wordlessly, I reach back and pull out a bag. Hand it over. Wonder how he's going to explain putting an order in for enough drugs to basically fill a piñata.

Sure enough: "Gotta keep the guests happy." But I know he's saying it for his friend's benefit, not mine.

His friend is still staring at me with something I like to call "resting letch face." "Yeah," he says slowly, the alcohol making him sound both sleepy and kind of dangerous, "what's it my dad always says? The customer's always right." And before I can step back, his hand is on my arm, pulling me. "Hey," Greek T-shirt says. "What about a different kind of order?"

"Fuck off." I look at Henry, but he's staring at the bag in his hands like it's the most interesting fucking thing in the whole fucking world.

From behind me: "Let's go."

From Greek T-shirt: "The girl might want to stay." Another tug on the arm, this one pulling me off-balance. To me, he whispers, "Get out of work early," his wet, boozy breath on my ears.

From Henry: "We should probably head back up." He shifts from foot to foot.

Greek T-shirt steps in so that my eyes are level with his neck. I can't breathe, and he's holding me so tightly that I can't move an inch away from him. "Hey, Henry," he says, and when he sways, I sway with him. "Don't you think we should get a taste of the local flavor?"

"Dick," I say, but my voice sounds small. Then, louder: "Asshole." I step in even closer, my chest against his, and he loosens his grip in a reflex. I bring my knee up once, hard, and then twist away, my back toward him as he doubles over.

"Bitch!" he yells.

I climb into the boat and turn. "Great to see you," I say to Henry. "Really great to finally see you."

He steps toward the boat and looks at me with a stricken expression. Just when I think he's going to apologize—though who am I kidding? What apology would make up for this?—he says, "College friends."

From next to me, Dodge's hiss: "The money."

"Right." I look at Henry, trying to keep my eyes empty. It's hard, though, because I can feel the tears building up behind them.

"College friends, right?" he says again, like that's all the explanation I'll need.

I hold out my hand for the money, don't say a word.

"Georgie," he says quietly, so his friend can't hear, "I'm sorry."

Except there's something so casual about the way that he peels off seven fifties from a money clip, flips the fifties into a small fold and holds them out to me, wrist steady, palm down. Like, this is still business. Like, this is the kind of thing he does often. Like, let's not forget: I'm working for him.

339

It's wrong. All of it.

"Henry." His name sounds strange suddenly. Like the word for a very exotic bat. "What the fuck."

He looks at me for a long time. His eyes are glassy, face already a little puffy. "Can you just—" He slurs a word and then starts again. "Can we just, like, talk tomorrow?" From behind him, I watch Greek T-shirt straighten up and move down the dock toward the cabin, swearing and stumbling. "Hey." Henry reaches out, misses my arm, stares at his hand. "Hey."

I turn and look out at the lake so he can't see my chin quivering. I glance at Dodge, who circles the hand on his wrist. *Speed it up.*

"They're only here for a couple nights." He keeps squinting like he's trying to get me in focus.

I nod. "So I'll see you later, I guess."

"Yeah. Georgie," he says, and points to the house. He speaks slowly. Trying so hard. "This isn't, like, a *thing*. It doesn't have to be a thing."

"You can say that again."

He looks at me, confused. Then he turns and heads back up to the house, practically sprinting.

When I get back in the boat, Dodge is looking at me.

"The QP," he says. "Thought he looked familiar." He sneers. "Not just a customer, after all. That explains it." He leans back in the boat's passenger seat.

"Explains what?" I turn the wheel slightly, heading back toward town.

340

"Strange that he reached out to me for the order. Guess he didn't want you to know how bad he wanted it." And before I can say anything, Dodge leans toward me, grabs the wheel, jerks it so that the boat careens to the right in a tight circle. The wake rushes over the side, splashing us both.

"Shit!" I yell, and pull the wheel straight again.

He grabs me by the neck. "How'd he know how to reach me? I don't take direct orders. This isn't some fucking artisanal shit. They go through you. That's the process."

I can't breathe.

"You're getting sloppy," says Dodge, jaw set. "Sloppy and reckless. And I don't care if you screw yourself over. But I do care if you screw me, too. I'm not going down because you couldn't keep your pants on."

Then he lets go.

By the time I park the boat, the sun's gone down behind the mountains. Main Street is packed with Weekenders in their sundresses and shorts, eating ice cream, laughing, making plans to go to the Pancake Parlor tomorrow, shouting across the street at one another. At the marina, boats idle just outside the buoys, no one ready to call it a night. One last drink. One last chance at something new.

It all reminds me of one of Gold Fork's slogans. *The city's playground.* Not that anyone actually says it. Because who wants to live on a fucking playground? Who wants to watch everyone leave, sit there as it shuts down at night, listen for the tweakers and the drunks as they make their way onto the swings, the forgotten slide?

Any asshole can use the playground. And if you live on a playground, any asshole can use you, too.

ERIK

"And then, I don't know, maybe art school."

Layla's sitting on her bed, winding and unwinding the leather wrap bracelet that she always wears. It's studded with what I have to think are fake diamonds—because even Weekenders don't bring their diamonds to the lake. I'm at the foot of the bed, putting on my socks.

"What if it doesn't work out?" I ask her. "The pottery. What if it's not what you think it'll be?"

She looks confused for a second. Then she smiles at me. "Oh, I know I'm not going to make money at it, if that's what you're asking. No one does." Then, when she can tell I don't get it, she adds, "But, like, art school would be this gift I'd give myself, you know? Just *time*."

"Time."

"Why are you smiling?" she asks, and leans forward so that she can push some hair off my forehead. "You look like you've got some inside joke."

"Time is an inside joke," I say. "It's what Week—it's what some people have and some don't."

"You're not making sense," says Layla, frowning. She

342

scoots back so she's leaning against the headboard. "We all have time."

"Never mind," I say. Georgie would understand. Ana, too. Even Davis, to a certain degree. They'd get that just the idea of buying time—art school or a year in Europe or whatever else the Weekenders do when they leave Gold Fork—is a joke to the rest of us. But I can't tell Layla that. I can't tell her anything. I reach over and rub her leg. "But first, senior year, right?"

"Yeah," she says. "God. It's going to be amazing." And she gets the far-off look that I've seen on her before, the one that reminds me of a shut door.

"Hey," I say, like the thought has just occurred to me. "What if I visited? Like," I add quickly, when I see her start to open her mouth, "I'll probably be in the city this fall for random things. So maybe I'll call? We'll hang out?"

"Sure," she says. "I mean, yeah." And there's something in her voice, something I haven't wanted to hear. Hesitation. And more. I've almost convinced myself I can't hear it. Then she kind of twists the bracelet on her wrist and looks down at it. There's writing on one length of leather—a name, I think, not hers—and I see things just as clearly as if she told me.

"You've got a boyfriend," I say. "In the city." I'm still holding one sock in my hand, and I look at it.

Layla moves so that she's sitting beside me. She runs a hand through my hair again. "No," she says. "Not a boyfriend. Not this summer. We agreed—" She shrugs. "On a break," she adds.

"But you're wearing the bracelet he gave you."

Her eyes widen. "Wait. Did I tell—" She shakes her head. "Never mind." Holds the bracelet up. "It's not about that. I like it. It suits me."

"Sure." The sock in my hand is plain and white. I could throw it away. There are ten more that look just like it.

"Listen," she says, still trying to salvage *this*—whatever it is. "It's not a big deal. I mean . . ." She pauses. Tries again. "Do you want"—she glances toward the door—"want to go out? Burgers, or—"

"I've got something," I say, and put on the sock and my tennis shoes. I speak to the laces. "But I'll call you."

"Yeah, okay," she says. And she smiles at me in that way that she has.

It's a smile fit for a Kelly. Except I'm the Kelly.

We kiss good-bye before she opens her bedroom door, but we don't talk about later and we don't make plans, because you only make plans when something is real.

God. I'm so stupid. When she talked about *leaving things better than I found them*, she was talking about me.

Well, I've got a platitude for her in return. If you love something, set it free. If it comes back to you, keep setting it free until it fucking gets it.

"I know somewhere we can go."

Kelly's looking at me with these big eyes, kind of like a deer, or maybe a frog.

344

"Oh yeah? Where?" I'm only half paying attention. Not sure why I called her, anyway, except I couldn't be home. Couldn't be alone.

"Some guys I met? College guys here for a long weekend? Party's been going since yesterday? That's what they said, anyway?"

I'd forgotten this about Kelly: She's one of those girls who can't just make a statement without framing it as a question. Her room is blue, with pink accents. Like she's never taken the time to change the sheets since she was twelve.

"Sounds awesome," I say, pulling my shirt back on over my head. "Really awesome."

But she doesn't hear the sarcasm in my voice, because she says, "It's out on the east side of the lake? Pretty cool, I guess. We could go? I mean, if you—"

And because I can't stand to hear her voice lift up in a question mark one more time, I interrupt her and say, "You drive."

God. This is going to be a long night.

Still. At least I'm not home. And ever since leaving Layla's this afternoon, I've been feeling jittery. Anywhere is better than nowhere.

We're driving along the east side of the lake in no time, my hand on her thigh even though I'm not really into it, and I'm wondering whether maybe I've had enough of these girls, whether maybe I should just call it and go home, call Georgie and see if she wants to hang out, when Kelly turns into the driveway of the Den.

I sit up straighter. Take my hand off her leg. "You sure this is the place?"

"Yeah. I mean, this is the address they gave me?"

And when we get closer to the house, I can see she's right. There are a few cars parked in front of the door and off to the side. The curtains are open. People are milling around inside, but most of the action's on the deck. I can hear them all when I get out of the car.

"Dude."

"Man!"

"No *way!*"

Bro-speak. I don't need to see them to know what they look like.

I'm not wrong. When she and I turn the corner onto the back deck, they're all standing around like the spread from the state university alumni magazine that I remember reading cover to cover as soon as Ms. Henderson told me about my scholarship. Messy hair. T-shirts with beer logos or Greek symbols. Baseball hats. Chino shorts. Really, I can hardly tell any of them apart. There are some girls, too, but not many, which explains why the one I'm with heard about it. Gotta keep the numbers even, I guess, even if it means dipping into the high school pool.

My dad and Abby are nowhere in sight. But then I remember that they're in the city.

One of the bros detaches himself from the group and comes over to say hi to the girl, and another one, tall, black hair, board shorts, is suddenly shaking my hand (like what, are we investment bankers or something?) and saying, "Hey, man. Grab a beer."

Like I need an invitation.

I'm on my second one when I finally see Henry. He comes outside, looks around, sees me, walks over. He's got this kind of electric look in his eyes, and I'm not surprised. I've seen the guys going into the house, two or three at a time, and coming out a little bit faster, a little bit looser. Kelly went inside at one point, too, and now she's sitting on the arm of an Adirondack chair (mine, I want to tell her, that chair's usually mine) and talking a mile a minute to some sorority sister who looks like she couldn't care less.

Georgie's been here. Or maybe just whoever she works for. Because I don't see her now, and I've been looking.

"Hey," Henry says. "Cool you're here."

"I didn't know I was coming." Fuck, that sounded stupid. I'm almost done with this beer. Take one last swig. "Where's Georgie?"

Henry crinkles his eyebrows like he's trying to put together some child's jigsaw puzzle. "She couldn't—I mean, this isn't really her scene, right?"

"But it's yours." I'm feeling a little buzzed, but it's nothing on him. Whatever Henry's taken must be some powerful shit, because he looks like he can't hold a thought together with a bottle of superglue. Blitzed. "What, you didn't even invite her?"

"Noooo," he says slowly. "I mean, kind of. I saw her yesterday when she brought the . . . appetizers." Then he adds, "But, like, these guys. You know." He waves his arm around.

"I don't."

Henry shrugs. "She's cool," he says. "She's cool with it." But he doesn't sound sure.

I could laugh. "Yeah," I say. "I bet she is."

Then Henry's face brightens. "You want a tour? Like, of the house?"

Is he serious? Or is this, like, the world's worst joke? Do I want a tour of the house my dad semi-legitimately owns and is now selling without himself ever actually inviting me inside? Do I want to see family pictures, a fruit bowl on the counter with any kind of fruit you want, laptops and gear and new shoes and enough of everything, always, breakfast dishes that no one put away, suitcases maybe even already packed?

"No thanks," I say. Where is the cooler? I can't do this without at least two more in me. In fact, if it weren't for my ride, who's standing up now and swaying to the music that's coming from the speakers, I'd have left as soon as we got here.

"Yeah," he says, "I guess not, right?"

Henry's acting nice but also too nice, like I'm some foster kid and his parents told him to keep an eye on me or something. I have to hold my hands steady at my sides to keep from punching him.

God. *Get it the fuck together, Erik.* This kind of thing is usually my scene. I look around again, hoping he'll just leave. Remind myself of what it takes. Drink a beer, flirt a little, see what happens. If not Kelly, then one of these other girls. I mean, that's the way it works, right? Anything to keep the demons at bay. The things I'd rather not think about, rather not remember. Like the thing that is staring me in the face and saying, "He's kind of a dick. Kyle. He's a real dick sometimes."

A beer. Where is a goddamned beer?

"Thanks for the PSA."

"I mean, you haven't missed much, is all." He's looking at me with this pitying expression. Face is puffy as shit, kind of plastic-looking from all the pills he's probably taken, but you can see pity in plastic. You can see it everywhere.

"I haven't missed much." I take a step closer to him. "You don't know a thing about me."

He tries to step back, but he kind of stumbles. Grabs on to my arm for balance. Some beer sloshes out onto the sleeve of his other hand. "It's not exactly easy," he slurs, "having a mom like mine."

"A mom like yours."

"Yeah. And Kyle—I've always wondered if he's playing the long game, you know? For the money?" He leans toward me. "Sometimes I wonder if you have it easier." He shrugs.

This. This is the thing about Weekenders. They are so fucking sorry for themselves all the fucking time. Too much money. Too many choices. Too much useless freedom. They don't know what to do with any of it.

I'd know. I'd know exactly what to do with it.

"I've got nothing to say to you," I tell Henry, then add, "Asshole."

"What did you call me?"

"Ass. Hole."

"Henry. Man. What's going on here?" One of his bros has come over and is swaying next to us, peering down at me. Guy's got to be over six-five, at least. "You need me to run interference?" And then, before Henry can answer, the guy says to me, "What the fuck are you doing here, anyway?"

Henry holds up one finger like he's silencing a crowd. "He's cool. Just—you know—leaving."

I'm about to tell him I'm doing no such thing, that he can go fuck himself, when his friend keeps going. First, he laughs. "What, are you, like, playing dress-up? Practicing for rush week?" He laughs again. It's a hollow sound. "Don't waste your time. Not quite college style, if you know what I mean."

"Milo," Henry says. "God." But the look he gives me, before his eyes turn all kind and sorry and pathetic, says he agrees. His hands on my shoulders, turning me around toward where Kelly is now lying on the deck, one wavering arm raised in the air, swearing she can see Cassiopeia, *right there*. "I think your friend needs a little assistance."

It's not a shove, not even a push. It's worse—a gentle tap on each shoulder. Like a butler handing me my coat and pointing to the door.

Before we leave, my hand clutching Kelly's car keys so

hard that I can feel the teeth of each one bite into my palm, I see Henry answer his phone. His head bows low like he's listening hard, or trying, at least, to make sense of what the person on the other end of the line is telling him. He holds the phone out and looks at it while rubbing at the back of his neck. Then he shakes his head and puts the phone back in his pocket.

Good. I hope he got some bad news. I hope it fucking ruins his life.

DAVIS

The case is going cold. That's what Dan told me this morning in the office. "All these fires," he said, "and not a single lead." Then he'd kind of laughed a sad little laugh and added, "Once the Weekenders go home, I bet you ten bucks we don't see another flame. Lose the audience, lose the will. So I guess we have to just wait it out. They'll be gone in the next week or so, anyway."

But that seems stupid. It seems, in fact, lazy. What are the police doing, if not trying to follow leads? I sit at my desk at home and look over everything Dan or I have found out about the Nelson fire. All of the small details from the other fires—four so far. I stare at the clues, trying to put something together. Anything.

Shoe print.

The scrap of burned paper. *Regret.*

The Nelson cabin: a notable lack of clues—no wiring problems, no exploding propane tank. Just good, honest arson. A quote from the fire inspector: *This wasn't a professional job, but then again, it doesn't take a professional to get the job done.* His theory? Dropped cigarette or match. *With the right fuel, that's all it would take.*

The phone rings. Ana.

"Hey," I say. "Glad you called." Am I ever. "What time are you headed to the party tomorrow night? I don't want to be alone with all those Weekenders at the last party of the year. Their sense of nostalgia can be a little smothering." I wait for the laughter, but it doesn't come.

"Davis," she says, "I was just at Grainey's. And I saw Erik there. With his dad."

"Ah."

"It didn't look good." Her voice is subdued.

"Why?" I ask.

"Just—a look Erik had. I couldn't hear them, and I left as soon as he saw me, but—Erik was kind of scrunched in the corner of a booth. His dad was talking at him. He just looked small." She clears her throat. "Not a way I've seen Erik before."

"Shit," I say. "I mean, poor Erik. Though he doesn't want our pity—that much is clear."

"His dad gave him something, right before I walked out. I didn't see what it was, but, Davis"—she pauses—"I thought Erik was going to cry."

"I wonder what it was," I say. "Have you told Georgie?"

"Yeah," she says. "I just got off the phone with her. She's going to call. And I've texted him, you know, just to check. But he hasn't written back." She pauses. "It really didn't look good, Davis."

"Okay," I say. "If he doesn't answer you or Georgie, let's make sure to talk to him at the party. My mom said something about it too." But I don't elaborate. It just doesn't seem right—all of us knowing that Erik's mom knows about his dad while Erik is still in the dark.

"All right," she says.

"Hey. You—I don't know. You want a ride? To the party? Or, like, to go together?" As soon as I say it I realize how awkward it sounds. I hold my breath.

"Yeah," she says, and I can almost hear the smile over the phone. "Yeah. I'd like that, Davis."

After I hang up, I sit at my desk, staring at the wall, replaying the conversation over and over in my head. What she said about seeing Erik. And: The way my name sounded, coming from her. Like something to hold on to. Like a gift.

Eventually, I look back down at my notes from the fires.

Skate park: some pebbles on the cement near the burn site, but that could have been anything.

Brewery: lots of trash—hard to tell if anything's a clue. Styrofoam cup, girl's hair band. Maybe connected, maybe not.

The campground, the airport: nothing. Not a single clue. All small fires that, taken alone, wouldn't mean a thing. Taken together, though, and you've got the highway out of town glutted with fleeing Weekenders.

What was it the fire inspector said? I glance back over my notes. *With the right fuel, that's all it would take.* I stare at the words. *Fuel.*

What if the fuel everyone's been looking for isn't gasoline or matches? What if it's something else, something having to do with Gold Fork itself, with the Weekenders and the way that we love the place we want to leave? I've only just started my new writing project, but I can already hear the voice of this town, and it's trying to tell me something.

The fuel isn't a thing. It's a feeling.

The plan is to go down to the public beach and write before dinner. Not for the book—I haven't worked on *She Woke Before Me* in weeks. There's the other thing I've started, but every time I sit down to write more reflections about the town, I end up thinking about other things. Erik's dad. The Den. Vera. And Ana. Always Ana.

I'm heading toward a free bench when I see Erik, standing on one of the little swimming docks that divide the swimming area from the marina. He's staring down at a rusty canoe that's tied up there. I walk out to the end of the dock and stand next to him. The canoe looks like it hasn't been used in a long time. Like it might sink if you sat in it.

"Considering a purchase?" I ask. "They should be giving that one away, from the looks of it."

He startles, then rolls his shoulders back to mask it. "Slow as shit," he says. "I'd rather walk around the lake."

"Good point. So. Anything new?" I look at the sky—gray. "Think it's going to rain?" The conversation with Ana is practically printed on my face—I know it, so I look anywhere but at Erik. I wish Ana and Georgie were here. They'd know how to ask Erik about the meeting with his dad. I can barely muster a sentence about the weather. Davis: playing it cool since never.

But he doesn't seem to notice my awkwardness. He keeps looking at the canoe like it's the answer sheet for a pre-calc final. Then he says to the canoe, "You think we'll ever count?" His voice is small—not Erik's voice, really. He still doesn't look at me.

And I start to say something like, *Of course we will. We already do!* But then I remember that this is Erik. This is his life. And I say, "To them? Probably not."

He's still talking to the canoe. "At best, we're just a name on a form. A mess to clean up. A stray dog that needs saving."

An image swims into my head and then out again before I can catch it. Something familiar. "What do you mean?"

He turns to me finally, looking away from the canoe. "Nothing." He scuffs the toe of his running shoe against the splintered wood of the dock. The sounds from the beach are a little muffled, even at this distance. I think I can hear a baby screaming, someone yelling, *Give it here!* and then: *Moooom!* "Nothing."

"We all need to be saved," I say. "From what, though. That's the question."

Erik looks out at the lake. He swallows heavily and wipes his forehead with the back of his hand.

"Erik." I tilt my head. "You okay?"

He kneels and picks up a pebble from the dock. Lobs it out into the water. "Yeah," he says. "Sure."

"If you want to talk—" I start, but he interrupts me.

"Sometimes I think everything started with the fire in the chapel, you know?"

"What do you mean?"

"Like, maybe if that hadn't happened, I'd be fine. We'd be fine," he corrects himself.

"But we wouldn't have this," I say. "I mean—the four of us. We wouldn't have that."

"I wonder if it's worth it," he says.

"Even Georgie?" I don't look at him, but I can feel the way he freezes when I say her name.

"She'd be better off without me." When I glance at him, he's trailing a finger through the water. Pulls his hand out and wipes the water on his shorts. "Whatever. Forget it."

"Bottom line: We're fine," I say. And then I add the thing we all said, over and over right after it happened, as though saying it could detract from the scar on Ana's arm. "No one died."

"Maybe not," he says, "but that's not always the worst thing that can happen." He pauses, then adds, "I'm sorry."

"What do you mean?"

"Just . . . I'm sorry."

I'm remembering the night the chapel burned. Erik standing outside, yelling. His mouth moving, though I couldn't hear him. Except now I think I can, and the words are ringing and clear. *Sorry. I'm so sorry.*

"You'll tell them that, right?" He's staring hard at the lake.

"Erik," I say, "the chapel."

He stands.

"You're right," he says. "No one died."

"But the chapel." *Sorry. So sorry.*

"Listen." He's already backing away down the dock. "I gotta run. See you at the party tomorrow."

"Erik," I say. "Come on. Let's get coffee or something."

He shakes his head. "I already had coffee." Then he wheels on his feet and kind of jogs back toward Main Street.

I glance again at the canoe before heading down the dock. It looks abandoned. Like a dog tied up outside a rest stop.

I wonder what Erik saw in it.

We're just a mess to clean up, he said. Why does that sound so familiar to me?

Something's been wavering at the periphery, just out of focus, ever since my mom joked about the Nelsons being in a love triangle. No way. And yet.

You leave for the week.

My interview with them. The way the sunlight poured into the dining room at the Gold Fork Grand.

Come back to rubble.

The thing that's been scratching at the edges all this time comes into focus. I can see the tomato juice on the white tablecloth, can hear Mr. Nelson's voice, dripping with condescension and righteous anger.

Cleaner shows up and there's nothing to clean.

Erik's mom. Of course.

Not a love triangle. But a third person, nonetheless.

I turn and scan the beach. Yell, "Erik!"

But he's gone.

ANA

Mom's home when I get back from the Pines on Saturday. I've been visiting Vera at odd times, hoping not to run into Abby, and so far I've been mostly successful. Today, though, her car was there when I pulled up on my bike, and I had to turn around and head home. I fought tears for the whole ride. I wanted to see Vera today before the party for some reason, and now I've got this sad, sick feeling in my gut. It's irrational, I know, but I needed to see her—to tell her about Davis, and how he kind-of-maybe asked me to go with him. It's not real unless I've told Vera.

When I walk in, Mom's in the kitchen, cleaning—a first. And there's a heavy smell in the air that I can't quite place.

"Querida! Good! I was afraid you had plans. I'm making roast chicken for dinner."

So that's the smell. I walk over to the oven and pull it open. Sure enough, a small chicken is roasting in a deep pan, herbs and veggies surrounding it. The smell is heavenly. "I didn't know you knew how to cook a chicken," I say, ashamed at how brittle my voice sounds.

Mom looks down and then back up at me. "I thought we deserved a nice meal together. Place mats, even." She laughs a little, embarrassed. "I haven't seen much of you lately, and . . ." Her voice trails off.

"Whose fault is that?" I ask. I know how I sound, bitter and mean, but I can't help it.

She puts down a spray bottle of cleaner and sits at our little table. "Mine." Extends a hand to me. "And I'm sorry. This is me saying I'm sorry." Her eyes squint a little.

I stop myself before I say something like, *No thanks,* or *Sorry's not good enough.* Because really, what am I going to do? The chicken smells incredible. And I've been waiting for weeks—months, maybe—for her to notice me. What was it Abby said? *We don't know each other well enough to forgive.* Well, I know my mom. I take her hand and sit down too. "Is Zeke coming?" I ask.

"Oh, Zeke." She waves her free hand in the air. "Fun for a time, but not the real deal. We just decided to let it be what it was—a good time. Not everything has to be forever, you know." She smiles. "Not everyone is the Better."

"I thought you really liked him," I say. "You sure spent enough time with him."

"Ana," says my mom, "I know you've felt left out. But I didn't want to bring someone into our life unless I knew he was worth it. And—" She shrugs. "He wasn't. Almost was, though. Maybe the next one will be." She pats me on the arm. "Because, mija," she says gently, "I get to have a life, too, you know."

"I know," I say. "I just—I miss you."

She nods. "Me too. You'd be surprised at how much I think about you—how often I ask myself what you'd do in a situation." She laughs a little. "Maybe I've learned a thing or two from my daughter."

"What do you mean?"

She unwinds a scarf from around her neck, hanging it on the back of the chair, and sits down. "No one's going to break your heart," she says.

That's when I lose it. Everything that's been building up since Vera's stroke comes out in a rush of tears. If I thought I was alone before, it was nothing compared to how I feel right now. Is there no one in the world who can see me? I stand there shaking and crying, and my mother springs up and pulls me to her, wrapping me in a hug.

"Shhh, shhh," she says to the top of my head.

"My heart *is* breaking! It's been breaking for weeks!" I sob into her shoulder.

Mom continues to hold me, making comforting sounds like she did when I was a little girl. "Oh, mija," she says. Then she asks, "Vera?"

I nod into her shirt.

"She's been wonderful for you," says my mom. "She's the grandmother I'd have imagined for you. And—" She laughs lightly. "Can I admit I've been jealous, sometimes, of your bond with her? Who wouldn't want that?" She kisses the top of my head and then asks, "What can I do to help?"

"There's nothing you can do," I say, swallowing another sob. "Unless you can go back in time."

"I can't do that," she concedes.

We stand there for a minute, my mom's arms wrapped around me.

"What I said about no one breaking your heart? I didn't mean it in a bad way," she says softly.

"There's no other way to mean it!" I cry, pulling away. "You mean that no one's going to break my heart because no one's going to love me!" My hands are curled into fists at my sides, and they hang there, useless.

"No. No." She shakes her head, and I can see tears forming in her own eyes. "Not at all." She pauses, searching for the right words. "I meant that no one's going to break your heart, Ana, because when you really choose to love someone, he—or she—will be worth it. And that person will never hurt you willingly." She pulls me into another hug. "Ever since you were little, I've seen how people are drawn to you. People with good hearts." She pauses, then adds, "You have the capacity to love so hard, Ana. Anything less will stand out like burlap in a bed of silk."

I let myself sink into her embrace like I did as a child,

when I'd wake from a nightmare and inhale her scent, which has always reminded me of vinegar and strawberries. "Where have you been?" I ask.

"Here," she says quietly. "I've been here. Ana, I know I disappoint you." She pauses. "And sometimes I let other things—work, worry—get in the way. But that doesn't mean I'm not watching you. Always, always. I can't protect you— and I don't want to. My parents tried, you know, and look where it got me: I had a baby on a Greyhound." I can hear her laugh into my hair. "Wouldn't change it. But you—you're smarter than I ever was, than I'll ever be. I figured out pretty early that I'd need to let you do your thing. But, Ana, if you need help, I hope you know I'm here."

The oven timer goes off, but we let it ding.

"I do need help," I say.

"Good." She holds me out at arm's length and smiles. "Let's have some dinner and talk about it. We can come up with a solution—whatever it is," she says, as I open my mouth to protest. She smoothes my hair behind my ears like she used to do when I was a kid. "Ana, there's always a solution."

I sit down at the table and look around the kitchen. Notice the fresh flowers, the magnets on the fridge holding up old elementary school photos. All the little ways she's shown her love. Am I only just noticing now? What else have I missed?

I'm pouring a little oil into the bottom of a pot when she calls after dinner. The phone chirps in my pocket, and my mom looks up from where she's stirring hot chocolate into two mugs.

"Wanna ignore it?" she asks.

"Yeah," I say. I reach for the bag of popcorn, pour a little into the pot, and cover it with a lid.

But . . . it could be Davis.

"Hold on," I say, and pull the phone out. I look at my mom. "It's Abby."

She nods. "I'll watch the popcorn."

I walk into the living room and hold the phone to my ear.

"Ana." She doesn't wait for me to say hello. "I want to apologize."

Not what I was expecting. At all.

"I did some thinking after I saw you last week. Some serious thinking. I'm sorry that you're wrapped up in all of this. It's not fair to you." It sounds like it's hard for her to get the words out. "I wonder if we could—" She clears her throat. "Do you have time to come by the house tomorrow? I want to discuss the . . . paperwork. I think we can come up with a solution."

I glance back into the kitchen. My mom is holding the lid on the pot and shaking it by the handle. I can hear the kernels jumping against the sides. I'm still thinking about everything she and I talked about. There's a buzz of possibility in my chest. Maybe this will work after all. "I can come tonight. Now."

There's a pause. I can hear a car door slam. "Okay."

My mom is standing in the doorway, and I mouth her a question: *Can I borrow the car?* She nods. "Fine."

"Good. Come over whenever you like. We're just heading home from dinner. And, Ana," she adds, her voice a little gruff, "the thing is, you love my mother, and I haven't taken that into account. I haven't—thanked—you for that."

Mom is pouring some popcorn into a baggie when I come back into the kitchen. "For the road," she says, smiling.

I walk over and lean toward her, hugging her around the neck. "I'm going to tell her what we talked about," I say. "About handing over the power of attorney to you, in case of emergency."

She squeezes my arm. "Good luck. Tell her she can call me if she has any questions."

"I will." Then I add, "I'll probably be late. There's a party tonight."

She sighs dramatically and smiles. "Okay," she says. "Try not to have too much fun."

"Don't worry," I say. "It's just some party. Nothing ever happens beyond the predictable."

Mom sips her cocoa and laughs. "You'd be surprised, mija."

I get into Mom's car and pull my phone out again. I'm nervous to tell Abby about my plan, but that's not what's causing my stomach to jump and twist, my breath to come jagged and quick.

A text, to Davis. *I'll have to meet you at the party. Abby called—headed to the Den. Cross fingers—I think it worked.*

He writes back immediately. *Can't wait for details.*

Can't wait to tell you. Then I write, *Can't wait to see you,* hit send, and put the phone facedown on the seat beside me.

Vera's voice, in my head: *When you cherish someone, shouldn't they know it?*

It's time to stop letting the fire control me. It's time to be brave.

GEORGIE

August is always a bittersweet month. Everyone can see the specter of school hanging there in the distance like some tropical storm, moving closer day by day. And each day feels like the last: last time on Jonesy's dock, last ride around the lake in Blake's dad's speedboat, last paddleboard to North Beach, last party. Except it's never the last. There's always another last party.

August is the best month for business.

If it weren't for that—for the seven hundred still dangling in front of me like a carrot, seven hundred between me and my new life, my *real* life—I wouldn't be here. I'd be home with my parents, listening to them go over the monthly food budget and quietly fight about whether we can afford new snow tires this year. I sure as shit wouldn't be standing by myself at the last party of the year. I don't have to be alone—I know this. And there are enough people up here already that if I wanted to party—like, really wanted to—I'd just have to say the word. But, God. That's the last thing I want to do.

I'm just here to make money and get out.

They finished clearing the burn site last week. Tore down the fireplace, brought in a Dumpster. Everything gone now but the foundation. I hear that the new cabin is going to be even nicer than the one that went up in flames. Money is no object. Right now, though, it's a blank slate, a slash at the top of Washer's Landing, like an effect of Divine Punishment— the sort of bullshit that Davis is always going on about. The perfect place for a party.

It's early still—maybe nine—but it's already fairly crowded, considering how many people have left Gold Fork early this year. Even so, people keep showing up, streaming through the woods between the cabin site and the road beyond. Two guys lift a keg between them as they walk. Someone else carries a box of wine on each shoulder. Everyone's got something. It's the ultimate potluck. The air is humid, heavy on our shoulders as the light dims, sinking below the mountain behind us. The dusk makes weird shadows on the Nelson cabin's foundation—mottled gray splotches, shapes that resemble the furniture that burned. People hop up and down from the foundation like it's a game. Duck, duck, goose. Some sit on the edge, legs spread out before them, and drink beers while they talk and watch everyone else. From the foundation, there's a perfect view of the lake, and to the south, the lights of downtown have started to sparkle and wink. There's music, but I don't know where it's coming from.

Last party of the year. Last party in the world I want to be at.

Last time I was here, it was with Henry.

Last, last, last.

What is it Erik says? *Ain't no party like a pity party.*

Where *is* he, anyway? And where are Ana and Davis? I called everyone half an hour ago, but no one picked up.

I've been trying to get ahold of Erik since Ana called me yesterday to tell me about seeing him with his dad at Grainey's.

Remember when he lost State? she said. *Remember the way he looked, when he didn't know we could see him?*

I did remember. We'd all gone to watch him race. And afterward—fourth place, still good, that's what we thought—we went around to the tent where the athletes left their stuff to surprise him. Only, we saw him before he saw us. He was just holding his water bottle and looking at it. Totally broken.

This was worse, Ana said.

Erik. Where are you?

"There you are."

Shit.

I thought I'd see him coming. Thought, at least, I'd know when he got here—the quick burn up the spine. Or maybe the way all the birds stop singing when there's a snake in the woods.

But I felt nothing. And I feel nothing, still, when I turn and look at him and say, in my most neutral voice, "Henry."

"Very professional." He laughs, leans in, puts both hands on my shoulders. "Hel-*lo*, Georgie."

So this is how he wants to play it.

I pull back.

"What?" he says. "Come on." He watches me, and I search his eyes, looking for—what, exactly?—dilated pupils, maybe. The familiar glaze.

Sure enough, there they are.

"Couldn't wait for the party?" I ask. "Or were there just too many leftovers at your house?" I think about what was in the bag I delivered to his dock. A freaking Thanksgiving dinner.

"You're still mad about that? Georgie," he says, swaying just a little and catching himself, "I told you. Those guys were just—you know, like, they showed up. Here for a couple days, and then they went home. What was I going to do? I seriously thought you wouldn't want to come, you know?"

I want to tell him that I don't care about the guys, or the fact that he didn't want me to meet them. Not the first night, and not the second, when Erik texted to tell me Henry had another party. It's not that, really. It was how I felt when his friend hit on me and Henry didn't step in. The way he pretended we didn't know each other. The way he slid the money into my hand. Professional. Expected.

Dope dealer.

Pill lady.

Hookup.

That's what I am first. Anything else is just an adjective.

And I want to hit myself for not knowing it. For thinking I could be anything else to him, this Weekender of Weekenders, a tourist even in his own summer home.

But I say, "Just showed up? They drove all this way without an invitation? I'm sure you were *really* surprised."

He looks down at his boots and kicks the dirt.

"And what's up with ordering behind my back? What, you didn't want me to know how much you do?" I cross my arms in front of my chest. "That was shitty."

"Was it shitty because of that, or because you didn't get a commission?" He stares at me. "Admit it, Georgie. I'm your best customer. Maybe that's all I am to you."

"Bullshit," I say, but I feel a little sting on my neck, a moment of recognition. I shake it off.

"Come on," he says. "What's the big deal?" I'm really killing his high. So what.

"That's the thing, Henry. You keep asking that. I mean, does any of this matter to you? Kyle, the house, your grandmother? Or is it just noise?"

There's a moment of pain in his eyes, a flash of real sadness. But then he raises his shoulders in a shrug, and I'm too mad to care.

"You know," I say, "I'm starting to think that's all there is to you: a big fucking question mark." I step back, look around.

There's Jane, leaning against some Weekender with a look on her face like she can't believe her good luck. As I watch, her Weekender stares over her head at another girl, who stares back, smiling. She jerks her head toward the woods, raises her eyebrows in a question. Jane's Weekender smiles. Typical end-of-the-summer party. Nothing matters anymore. If they haven't done it yet, everyone knows this is the last chance to blow up their lives. The sentence that's been ringing in my head like feedback ever since I saw him down at his dock comes out. "Henry," I say, "let's just call this."

He stares at me for a long minute. "Sure," he says finally. "Whatever."

Whatever.

Then: "Screw this." He stuffs his hands in his pockets. "You know," he says, "you think you're different from"—he waves his arm around—"all this. *Them.* But you're not. Not really."

"God," I say, reaching around behind me and pulling my shirt away from my sticky back. "That's all you've got? Some cliché?" I shake my head.

"They're clichés because they're true."

"Maybe," I say. "And you're probably right. I'm not different. I belong here. Unlike you."

Henry looks around at the party, probably so he doesn't have to look at me. It's almost dark now, and some people can only be seen in outline as they tip their heads back and drink. I can't see his eyes clearly, but they're glinting a little with what I can almost believe are tears. "You've blamed me for Kyle—for everything shitty my family has done. I should've known you wouldn't get it. I should've known you'd always protect him."

"Who?"

"Erik." Henry glares at me. There are no tears now, if there ever were. "I mean, do you even know what it was like to come back here? To his town? Where he's, like, the prince of fucking everything?"

I want to laugh. Henry, jealous of Erik? What bullshit. "Sorry that was hard for you, Henry. Sorry you can't win at being the most abandoned. Christ."

"Don't spin it that way," Henry says. "He didn't get his crappy dad. I did. Lucky me. He got other things."

"I'm sure Erik would love to know what he won."

Henry mumbles. "He got this place." Pauses, then adds, "He got you."

"Bullshit."

He rolls his eyes. "Took me about five seconds at the Fourth of July party to see how much he wants you. And how you'd basically cut someone if they hurt him."

"It's not—" I start to say, and stop.

Because it's not. But it also is.

"I can't wait to leave this shithole town," Henry says. "Go back to Chicago. Back to the real people."

I laugh. "Oh, fuck you, Henry," I say, and it almost sounds like an endearment. "There are real people everywhere." I picture Erik, Davis, and Ana sitting on the deck of the Den. Laughing. "You don't even know," I say.

"Shouldn't have even tried," he continues, almost like I'm not here. He's talking to his hands—more fucked up than I thought. "Should've just kept my head down, like Kyle said. 'Don't engage, don't engage.' Like this is a war zone or something. I told him that was bullshit." He looks up at me, and for a second, his eyes clear and I see him again, the real him: long drives and the right song and conversations that hit like drumbeats in my rib cage. The newness of him, like nothing else I'd found in Gold Fork. I'm about to say something when he adds, "Kyle was right. It's a place worth leaving." Then he turns and walks, stumbling only once, toward the keg.

I watch him pour himself a beer. Guzzle it without pausing to take a breath. Give some guy a high five. Pour himself another.

Rinse and repeat.

And I know this isn't the real Henry. I mean, it can't be. The real Henry had to have been that other guy—the one I wanted to spend hours with, the one I slept with, the one who made me feel like more than just a Dead Ender. Not this guy. Right?

What is it Ana said once? She'd been talking about Vera, I think. *Amazing how mysterious people can be. Mysterious even to themselves.*

Maybe the only true thing I need to know about Henry is this: I thought it would hurt more. I'm standing here, alone, watching him get drunk, also alone, and it doesn't hurt like I thought it would.

I turn in a slow circle. Recognize some clients over by the trees. Do some calculations in my head. Good for a hundred, maybe two. A solid start, if I pitch it right.

If I pitch it right. I'm suddenly so exhausted by all of this—the work, this place, Henry, Dodge's threats, my inability, it seems, to ever be free of any of it—and all I want, all I really really want, is to go home.

I know everyone here. I know no one here.

Clouds have moved in, and I can't see the stars anymore.

But I also know this: I'm not going anywhere until I see Erik. Ana's words from yesterday ring in my head: *This was worse.* I'll wait here for him, and then I'll go.

So I do what needs doing: I wave at the group by the trees and head toward them.

Anything to take my mind off the fact that there's something whispering *wrong wrong wrong* up and down my spine.

ERIK

We all need to be saved, Davis said the other day. *From what, though. That's the question.*

The developers, taking everything they can, breaking it and wrapping it in tinfoil, handing it back to us like a present.

Mom at the dinner table, holding her plate out to me.

Layla. How easy it was to take her things, put them in my

backpack to look at later, try to decipher what they mean in the story of her normal, perfect life. Like panning for gold.

My dad. Picking me up, looking at me, turning me one direction and then another. Deciding I'm not worth it.

Throwing me away.

I take the small box out of my dresser drawer.

The canoe is still tied up at the marina. Forgotten, just like when I took it to North Beach. I'm paddling away beyond the buoys before anyone would even see me kneeling there, cutting it loose. Maybe I'll return it. Maybe I won't. If you don't care enough to protect your things, you lose them. Sometimes even when you do everything right, you still lose. I learned that the hard way. So can they.

I've come prepared. Socks stuffed with moss. Water bottles filled with gasoline. And my lighter, safe in its little box.

I pull the canoe out of the water next to the old dock. Take the trail that winds through the property—the same one I walked with Davis, Ana, and Georgie when we first saw them here. Seems so long ago now. I hide in the bushes below the deck. From here, I can see the dining room. No one's there.

Well, they shouldn't be. What did he say yesterday, when we were having coffee? . . . *Dinner at the steakhouse with Abby tomorrow. She loves their mashed potatoes.*

I step out of the trees.

It's easier than it was the first time, because I've done some prep work already. Biked out here this morning and waited until they went to the Pancake Parlor for breakfast. Thought about their cozy family meal—bacon and eggs, flapjacks, bottomless cups of coffee—as I stuffed moss in the gutters. Jokes and laughter, everything easy, *More coffee, sir?* as I placed socks filled with dried sticks between the notches of wood on the outside of the cabin. My dad looking back into the restaurant as he got up to leave, tipping just a little less because maybe it doesn't look like the kind of place that deserves a good tip, not like those places *back home*, as I poured gasoline along the corners of the cabin that are hidden by bushes so they wouldn't notice the smell. An arm around Abby's shoulder, a hand on Henry's, steering them both outside, *Pretty good summer, right?* as I placed fireworks under the deck.

See? I'm a good Boy Scout. I know what makes perfect kindling, what will flare up as soon as I flick the lighter. I know just what to do to burn it all down.

I climb up onto the deck, edging my way across, my back to the log siding of the house.

First, the grill on the porch. Open the lid, twist the valve all the way, lefty-loosey. Turn each burner on high. Then into the house, quiet, quiet. Pull the sliding door open, lifting it slightly so it doesn't squeak. Though, who cares? There's no one here.

I'm in the dining room for the first time.

The Nelsons' cabin was concrete countertops, floor-to-ceiling fireplace, iron beams crossing the length of the house.

375

Everything top of the line. This is shabby. Comfortable. Dusty. A grand old family cabin. The image comes to me, suddenly: the party. Henry's face as he took me by the shoulders on the deck and turned me around so gently, like he was shooing a toddler out of the room. I close my eyes. Shut down the part of me that hurts. Open them again.

There's the fruit bowl on the dining room table. There's the paperback book, facedown by an easy chair. Into the kitchen now. There's the sheaf of papers, real estate contracts probably, on the counter. I pick one up, see the signature, hold the lighter to it, watch it curl into itself, drop it on the linoleum floor.

There's a creaking sound from upstairs—like a floorboard. I freeze. But then—nothing. These old houses with their old bones—everything creaks.

There's a bedroom off of the kitchen—old servants' quarters, probably.

A man's sweater, folded on the bed in the master.

Probably wouldn't be a good idea. It's a big city. More dangerous than you'd think.

Hairbrush with a few strands of long hair in it. Forgotten toothbrush. Old compact, jar of hand cream.

I wouldn't have much time. And I'd feel bad about that.

Scuffed dock shoes in the closet. Lube in the bedside drawer.

Abby and I've been having problems. She's not—Careful what you wish for, right?

No photographs. No diaries. Nothing lasting.

What I'm saying is, it's not a good time. But this has been nice, hasn't it?

Gasoline on the curtains, on the rug, poured in a figure eight across the bed. I douse the moss-filled socks with gasoline and wedge them under the mattress.

Great to catch up. Next time. Next time.

Finally, I reach into my backpack and pull out the necklace, the cup, the stuffed rabbit with one floppy ear. All the things I took from Layla this summer. The things I took to remind myself that I mattered—that I was more important to her than these *things*. I hold up the lighter, and can just make out the words that are etched onto its side: *Gold Fork Grand*. It's the first thing I ever stole.

I place the items on the bed.

But hey. Here's a little something. College expenses. All I can do.

It was then—the minute he gave me the check for three thousand dollars with a sort of apologetic shrug—that I knew for sure he was never coming back. I'd never see my dad again.

All I can do.

I think about the check, cashed and divided into two envelopes on my dresser at home. Then I light up the pile on the bed. I walk out of the guest room and through the kitchen to the sliding door, closing it behind me, shutting it tight.

The first time was easy. More of an experiment, really. Walk back into the chapel when no one else is looking. Drop a match on the ground, next to a pile of old hymnals. Walk out again. Wait and see.

To be honest, I didn't really think it would catch. And I didn't know about the cat, or that Ana would go in after it. I didn't know—how could I—that the ember would hit the tent where Chrissy Nolls was sleeping.

If I'd known that, I never never never never would have done it.

But it was useful, in its way. When I saw the flames licking at the chapel's stained-glass windows, I'd felt powerful. It was the first time I felt like I could control something other than how fast my feet were moving. And I liked it.

And after that, I used fire to settle myself when things were stressful. Bad track meet? Burn a piece of paper in the sink. Not hitting my target time in practice? Light up some twigs and sticks out at an abandoned campsite. Never anything lasting. Never anything big. Just a way to let things go.

But at the Nelsons', I didn't know what I was doing. I was nervous. I moved quickly, but I was sloppy, and that cost me time. Didn't bring enough kindling and had to go out scrounging around the Nelsons' cabin for sticks and things like some lame pioneer. Added the letter at the last minute—rookie mistake. By the time I was ready, I'd been there almost two hours, and I knew the Beast would be wondering where I was. Every minute was one more minute in which someone might knock on the door—a caretaker, maybe. Friendly neighbor. Not the cleaning lady. I knew she cleaned the place on Wednesday mornings.

378

The first curls of smoke were barely visible over the trees as I jumped on my bike and rode away. *You get what you deserve,* I thought. *You get what's coming to you.*

The call had come a couple of days before. The phone wasn't for me—it was for the Beast. But she wasn't home. I was.

"Erik, hi." Ms. Henderson sounded surprised that I answered. Surprised and a little nervous. "Is your mom home?"

"She's working." I didn't tell the guidance counselor that the Beast would be back any minute, actually. I held the phone to my ear and looked down at our kitchen counter, an old laminate speckled with gold. I remember thinking that, just like everything else in the house, it was trying to be something it wasn't.

"Oh." There was a pause. "Could you—There's something I need to discuss with her. Tell her, actually."

For someone whose entire job has to do with communicating, she was doing a pretty crap job of it. So I didn't say anything. I waited her out.

"Well, the thing is, I don't know if I should tell you." Then, like she was speaking to herself, she added, "Not that you won't know, or shouldn't know. It's your future, after all."

The thing is. The thing is. This was too much. "Ms. Henderson," I said, "can you just tell me what's going on?" I had to struggle to keep my voice calm, flat. But my chest had seized like it does in the minute before I start a race. "Have I gotten in trouble for something?" I was thinking, *shit,* pregnancy, Kelly or Mischa freaking out and going to the guidance counselor. Thinking about the chapel, the cat, Chrissy. Stupid. No way, not after all this time. Nothing I can't handle, I told myself.

Henderson sighed. "Sure. Okay. The thing is, Erik, I know you were told you won the athletic award. And you did win it. I mean, you earned it." Her voice went down an octave when she said this, and I knew that whatever she was about to say, it was worse than knocking someone up. "But the bylaws stipulate that the winner can have no previous financial connection to the donors, and the couple who funds the scholarships, the Nelsons . . ." Her voice trailed off.

"The Nelsons."

"Yes. I mean, generally, they don't advertise their role, but when the committee got back to them with your name, they recognized it and . . ."

"Yes." Gold-colored flecks on beige plastic. That's all I could see.

She kept talking. "They'd have figured it out sooner, but they were out of the country. And by the time they came back, it had been announced. You already knew."

"Yes."

"I asked them if there was a work-around. We all feel so horrible. I even suggested—I know this wasn't my place, but forgive me—that your mother could quit cleaning for them. That maybe this wasn't what the bylaw meant." She sounded like she was going to cry. "But they're adamant. Oh, sympathetic," she added quickly, "but adamant."

Our car pulled up to the curb. I watched out the kitchen window as the Beast of Burden got out, put one hand on her back, grimaced, stretched before opening the trunk and pulling out the vacuum.

"I'll tell my mom," I said. "It'll be better coming from me."

"Erik. I don't know what to—"

"It's okay." She was almost to the front door. "I understand. Rules are rules."

I could hear Henderson sigh over the phone. "A letter will arrive," she said. "To make it official." Then: "Come in and see me before classes get out. Let's come up with a plan B."

"I will." The creak of our screen door. "Thanks." The doorknob turned. "I have to go."

"Remember, Erik—" Henderson was still talking when I hung up the phone and turned toward my mother.

"Who was that?"

"High school reporter. They're doing an article about me." I smiled at her, though everything looked blurry. I could only see her outline: frizzy hair, slumped shoulders. Failure embodied. "It's not every day a Gold Fork kid gets a full ride."

Two days later, I burned the place down.

I'm down at the broken dock. The air is filling with smoke now, and I know the cabin is burning. Just for a second, I think about hiking back up to watch, but I know how reckless it would be. Time to go. I'm about to step into the canoe and push off when I see a boat coming toward me.

It's coming in so fast that I jump back onto shore. The boat slows suddenly, sending waves over the dock, and Davis is jumping out and tying it up even as the wood is still rocking under him.

"You didn't!" he's yelling. And, "You couldn't!" And something else that I can't make out.

There's a noise behind me, a sort of hollow popping sound, and I know from the Nelsons' that it's a window exploding.

He's running toward me and I think for a crazy second that he's going to hit me. But he swerves and starts up the path. I can hardly hear what he's saying, but then what he's been screaming makes sense. He turns and shouts again, "Ana's in there! Ana's in there, you crazy fuck!"

DAVIS

He just stands there. For a half second, he starts toward me. Then he looks at me, his eyebrows pulled together in a question, his mouth open like he's going to say something. He stops. Looks down and shakes his head. Turns, and steps into the canoe.

"Come on!" I yell. My voice sounds unfamiliar—high and screechy. "Come on!"

But he pushes off with one paddle, gliding across the lake, and I don't have time. I don't have time. I turn and run toward the house.

I'm flying through the trees. Stumble over a root. Something scratches my cheek—quick flash of heat—and I swipe my hand across, smear of blood, keep running. *Ana.*

It's already—oh God, it's already on fire.

Can't wait to see you, she'd texted, and I'd felt a wave of hope.

I remember putting on a clean shirt. Thinking maybe tonight I'll finally tell Ana how I feel. Maybe I matter to her the way she matters to me. And I remember thinking, suddenly, of Erik.

Think we'll ever matter? he'd asked on the dock.

One window has burst in the kitchen, and flames reach out for me as I start toward the porch.

The shoe print—a running shoe. Erik's mom, working for the Nelsons. *Just a name on a form.* And the conversation I overheard between him and Georgie: *Red tape. That's what happened.* Something clicked. It just took a phone call for me to put it together. Just the right question, just a follow-up, really, about whether the Nelsons had any other connections to their cleaning lady besides the usual. All of it coming out quickly, then. Mrs. Nelson's sympathetic voice: *Such a shame. But the scholarship language was very clear. Would have looked like we were showing a preference to our cleaning lady's son. And we can't show a preference.*

After I hung up the phone, I grabbed my binoculars and stepped onto my deck, training them on the Den. Scanned the water below—nothing. Glanced toward the house. Remembered Erik, once, talking about—who? The Weekenders? His dad? Was he talking about his dad? *I hope they burn.* God.

How did I not see it? At the marina: *I'm sorry. You'll tell them that, right?* As I watched through my binoculars, a small curl of smoke rose lazily out of the house like an afterthought.

That's when I jumped into my parents' boat.

The porch explodes. A burst of light throwing me back, heat so searing I can't see. The whole porch gone, just a wall of fire now.

"Ana!" I can't even hear my voice over the noise. It's like being in the middle of a wind tunnel. "Ana!"

I stick to the trees, run around to the other side of the house. And I see them there—Erik's dad, Abby. They're sitting on the gravel in the driveway, a few hundred feet from the house, and Erik's dad has his phone out and is jabbing at the screen with his finger. They look stoned, almost comatose with confusion.

"Where is she?" I scream over the noise, running toward them, looking around. "Where is she?"

"Let me just—" Kyle hits the screen again. "Why isn't this working?" It's as though he can't hear me.

Abby looks at me. She's crying, and her arms are hanging loose at her sides like a rag doll's. "She's inside. We were upstairs—giving a tour. She'd—gone to the kitchen to get a glass of water. I'd said, 'Glasses next to the sink,' let her go herself, and then—" She shakes her head. "We got out through a window."

But I'm not listening. I'm running back toward the house, heading for the door, opening it, yelling, "Ana!"

The heat.

The smothering heat.

It sucks the breath out of my lungs.

And I almost turn around, fresh air right behind me, so close I can still feel it on my back. God. So close.

But I can't. I push into the house, arm over my mouth.

"Here!" Her voice. Small, strong, clear. "Davis! I'm here!"

I head toward the kitchen, the blaze of it. The living room is starting to light up, but I make it through, skirting furniture, drapes that are moving with the heat.

She's sitting, back against the doorway between the kitchen and the dining room. Her arm is bleeding as it wraps around a knee.

I'm picking her up, my arms under hers, before she says, "I fell. There was—what? An explosion?" She looks around through the smoke like she can't quite place where she is.

"Come on," I say.

"Did I pass out?" She struggles to stand, and I stumble forward, one arm around her waist, the other across her front, a sideways waltz.

The door is ahead of us, things crashing behind. I hear another window pop, a whooshing sound, and then the fire pushes us out the door—an insistent, searing hand on our backs. We tumble to the ground, crawling toward the gravel on our hands and knees.

When we're clear of the house, I take a long, cold breath of air. Like drinking water in a desert. I can't get enough of it. I can hear Ana gasping next to me. Five, six, seven breaths. Then I turn to look at the house.

The whole thing is blazing. It's not even a house. I can see the skeleton of it through the flames, and I know there's no saving it now.

"Davis." Ana is panting, but she looks at me, clear-eyed, perfect even in the smoke. "We just almost—" Her breath catches and I reach for her, pull her toward me. I press my cheek to the top of her head, run my hand down her arm.

I want to hold her like this forever.

"Fire department is on its way." Kyle's voice, above us. "Sons of bitches can't get here faster?" Nothing about us. Nothing about death.

I stand, legs shaky. Ana stands, too. "We're fine, thanks," I say.

"Thank God." Abby's voice. And it sounds genuine. She's still sitting, but she makes this kind of ridiculous wave with her hand in our direction. "This feels like a dream. Like a— thank God," she says again.

Ana's hand on my arm. "How did you know? How did you know there was a fire?"

And I remember the look on Erik's face as he registered what I was yelling to him. How he stepped into that canoe and pushed off. How he knew everyone would know it was him. I stumble, take a breath, and move toward the water, pulling Ana after me. Kyle says something, but I can't hear him over the sound of the fire, and besides, I don't care.

"Wait," Ana says, panting. "The fire department. The

police, probably. Right? We have to stay." She's tugging on my arm. "Davis. Where are you going?"

I stop in the trees, far enough away from the smoke and heat that I can talk. "It was Erik. Ana, we have to get to him. He thinks you're still in there." I point back to the burning cabin. "He thinks he's killed you."

"Erik?" Then: "Erik." She looks at me. There's a second when I think she might lose it, but she takes a deep breath. Coughs and nods. "Where is he now?"

"I'm not sure," I say as we start running down through the trees again, feet hitting dirt, then rocks, then the sand of the small beach where my boat is tied. I look across the water. Small pinpricks of light flicker at the top of Washer's Landing, where everyone we know and mostly people we don't are dancing on the ashes of everything Erik ever wanted. Georgie's up there somewhere. The one person he'd run to. "But I have a pretty good guess."

ANA

Erik.

Davis guns the motor and we're roaring across the lake, the water choppy beneath us. He tries to steer into each wave, but we still pitch back and forth, hitting the water with hard smacks. It's too loud to talk at first. I sink into the seat beside Davis, who stands at the wheel. The air is cold on my cheeks.

Blessedly cold.

It happened so quickly. I remember getting the tour—room after room of beds covered in Pendleton blankets. Abby saying to me as I headed for the stairs, "Glasses next to the sink." I remember going to the bathroom and washing my hands, taking time to smell the expensive soap in a little silver dish on the sink in the bathroom. I think I remember turning on the faucet for water in the kitchen, think I recall the feel of the glass in my hand, but I'm not sure, because there was something in the corner of the room, something flickering from the doorway of a bedroom off the kitchen. That much I remember. And this: When I realized what was happening, saw the flames coming toward me, I turned and—slipped.

At least, that's what I think happened. For a second, I saw the cat, curled around her kittens, crying softly. I think I moved toward them—or maybe I didn't. Because then I was on the floor, and fire—the blistering cloak of heat— disoriented me. Everything after that flashes back to me as Davis drives across the lake: an explosion outside, crawling toward the sound of people yelling, terror replaced with—crazy—intense fatigue, leaning my back against the doorframe, thinking—why on earth would I think this—that I needed to rest for just a minute.

And then Davis.

I look over at him as he drives the boat, his mouth set in a hard line, eyes peering across the dark water. Davis's arm around me, picking me up. Davis pushing us both through the door before the whole house went up in flames. The moment I wanted to stay in forever: his cheek on my head, arms around me.

I stand in the boat, holding on to the edge of the windshield. I touch his back and yell into the wind, "You saved my life."

He shifts his weight toward me, touching my shoulder with his own. "Good."

I laugh. The breath catches in my throat, and suddenly I'm doubled over, coughing. My lungs are burning.

"You okay?" His hand on my back.

I stand. Take a few practice breaths. "I think I need to go to the doctor," I yell. "After we get Erik."

He nods.

There's no one else on the water. I scan the lake for the telltale green light of the sheriff's patrol boat, but even that's been docked, I guess. The dark water crests and falls, crests and falls against itself, and we cut through it. Together, we watch as Washer's Landing becomes more distinct against the black sky. The flickering lights that we could see from the Den are larger now, small bonfires at the top. I can't hear it yet, but I know there's music.

I turn to look at the Den. From here, it's a bright orange glow against the black sheet of water and sky and trees. Have they seen it yet? Do they know what they're looking at?

Touching Davis's arm again (it's all I want to do), I yell, "What are we going to do? About Erik?"

"I don't know," he yells back, the wind swallowing the ends of his words. Then he adds, "He did the Nelsons', too."

"What?"

"He's done all the fires." Davis looks pained. "Starting with the chapel, I think."

"We all started the chapel," I say, but Davis shakes his head.

"I'm not so sure. Because when you went back in there, he was yelling—and I didn't remember what he was saying until today."

I wait, the wind cutting across the bow of the boat. Washer's Landing is getting closer now.

"Sorry," says Davis. "He was yelling that he was sorry, so sorry. He thought he'd killed you then. And now . . ." He leans forward, pushes the throttle up even higher. The boat jumps across one wave, smacks the water, hard. "We've got to get there," says Davis. "He has to see that you're all right."

I'm watching Washer's Landing. We're almost there now. The cliffs are obsidian walls. It looks like a fortress. And then—

"Davis," I say, grabbing his arm. "What was that?"

GEORGIE

Henry's long gone. And I don't mean that he's *gone* gone, scared off by my rejection. I mean that he's gone in the way that all Weekenders like him are gone at the last party of the year. I catch glimpses of him over by the keg, eyes glassy, Gumby arms. Geeked out. Gone. Once, when I glance over, he's hitting on Kelly. I watch him lean over to whisper at her face, and I can see her step back and move away.

Gone.

It's getting colder, and people look annoyed. They hug their arms, drink more, give me money for just a little something extra, even if that's not what they planned to do tonight. I'm probably going to walk away with four fifty, and it's all bullshit, all of it. I'd tell someone if I had someone to tell. But the others aren't here. And I can't tell if the bad feeling I have is because of that or something else.

I'm just finishing up a deal when I see him.

Erik's standing in the middle of the cabin's foundation, his arms at his sides. People step around him almost like they don't see him. He's not moving. And when he spots me, his face crumples, just for a second—the face of a broken boy. He reaches his arms in my direction and takes one, two, three steps toward me.

When we're finally face-to-face, I can see that he's been crying. There's a dark black smudge by his hairline. He smells like a campfire. His hands are shaking.

"Erik," I say. "What did you do?"

Someone's put Neil Young on—one last shout-out to their summer, I guess—and the speakers crackle as he sings, *"Out of the blue, and into the black. They give you this, but you pay for that."*

"What did you do?" I ask again, but he doesn't answer. The party roars around us like an ocean, and I focus on his face. There's moss in his hair. Dirt on his cheeks. And that black smudge. "Where were you?"

"I'll show you," he says, and starts walking away from the party, toward the cliffs.

Erik weaves through the trees, carving a steady diagonal. I step over rocks, fallen logs, trying to keep up. We can still hear the party—we're not that far away—but it's just static.

Finally, he stops.

We're at the highest cliff. The one that no one jumps from, not only because the rocks below it jut out too far from this angle, but because it's sixty feet to the water. The ledge here is wider, probably ten feet total, and there are small rocks and pebbles scattered around. In the middle of the ledge, looking out over the lake, is a small circle with some burnt logs and sticks, the makeshift campfire of some Weekenders looking for a place to screw and spend the night. The trees on either side of the ledge are dark soldiers, hemming us in. The sky is black now, the stars obscured by heavy clouds. I smell rain.

"Let's go back," I say. "Erik? Let's go back to the party."

He smiles at me. "Nah," he says. "You can go. I'll stay."

That's when I see the fire.

At first, it looks like one of the larger cabins on the lake has all its lights on. Floodlights, the works. I shield my eyes with one hand and squint. That's not what it is. The lights move. They flicker. And they're orange—red, even. As I watch, the redness kind of gels together, fuzzing at the edges. Taking over.

"Holy shit," I say. "Erik. Look." My hand is in my pocket, closing around my phone. I pull it out, start punching numbers. "I'm calling 911."

"Don't." His voice is quiet, and my head snaps up. Erik has a tear running down each cheek, but he's smiling. "Please don't," he says.

I drop my phone on the ground. "Oh shit, Erik." The look on his face tells me everything. I watch the fire burn across the lake. I can almost hear the pop as windows shatter. The red glow gets steadily stronger, and from behind us, at the party, I hear a few screams, some shouting. "We have to—" I start to say, but he interrupts me.

"Gold Fork."

"What?" I'm staring at his heels, which are scuffing backward. Little shuffle dance.

"Worst Case Scenario. I don't even get Bismarck, right? Omaha is out." He shrugs. "It's just fucking Gold Fork."

"Not true." My voice is high and nervous, and I try again. I keep my eyes focused on his. "Not true, Erik. You always have a choice. You can always go."

"*You* can. Davis can. Ana—" He stops. "You can all go. Not me." He glances behind him, and I don't know if he's looking at the cliff or the inferno beyond. "Better to burn out, George." He swallows, and I can see, for a second, that his chin is trembling. He looks like a little boy, and I want so badly for him to come to me, to run away from all these demons.

"It's okay," I say, and step forward.

"No," he says.

ERIK

"No," I say, and she stops coming toward me.

I shift my gaze out over the water, to where the Michaelson estate is lit up like a torch. I think I can make out the distant sound of sirens screaming through town. "I want to watch my show," I say.

She follows my gaze. "Is that—" Her voice catches in her throat. Georgie leans forward. "The Den?"

I nod. "Was."

Another gasping breath. "You didn't." But she doesn't say anything else.

"Sure I did. Don't you know?" I point out at the flames, sparks popping in the sky. "It's Independence Day."

"Erik." Georgie's crying. "What did you do?"

"I fixed it." I have to fight the sudden burst of laughter that starts somewhere low in my gut. I swallow. "It's okay now."

It's okay it's okay it's okay it's okay.

Davis running toward the cabin.

Ana.

Davis running toward the cabin.

Ana.

It's okay it's okay it's okay it's okay.

Georgie points across the water. Red and blue lights flash around the burning cabin. Her voice, when she talks, is high and frantic. "Oh shit. Oh shit. You didn't— Wait. Did you do the Nelsons', too?" She looks at me, and I nod. "But why did you—" Georgie leans over, dry heaving. Her arms kind of sway next to her. "Oh God. This is so fucked."

Rain starts to fall—fat drops that splash against the ledge and seem to bounce in the air.

She doesn't know that Ana's in there. Maybe the others, too. She doesn't know, and I don't want her to. Not yet. She can hear about it later. Right now, I just want her to understand me.

"Because he deserves to lose too." I feel calm. Calmer than I've felt in months. "They all do. These people, they come in and take anything they want. And they promise us that if we just play our parts, we'll get something in return. But they're lying. They're not going to give us a damn thing. They'll just keep taking, and taking, and taking." My cheeks are wet, and I swipe at them. Funny, I don't feel sad. Just still and calm.

"What are you talking about?" Georgie takes a deep breath.

She's looking just beyond me, and I turn and notice how close I am to the edge of the rocks. I shrug, walk away from the cliff a few paces, watch her relax a little. It's raining harder now, and I have to raise my voice over the sound.

"Where's it gonna be, George? Where's it gonna be? Nowhere. That's where."

"I don't understand."

"This whole goddamn summer," I say. "My whole goddamn life. Everything. You think they were going to let me out of here?"

"You can still go. You don't need a stupid scholarship."

"Never gonna happen. And that place—" I look back at the fire. "They might call it a private club, but we know what it would really be. A prison."

"Erik, you're not making sense." Georgie's voice is quiet and even. "Erik, I think we need to get some help here."

So she doesn't understand. Well, I shouldn't expect her to. But I have to try to make her see what I see. I shake my head. Too late to think that way.

"Not a prison for them," I tell her. "For the rest of us. Most people can't get in. But if you *are* in, like my mom, like me— you can't get out. Just cleaning up their crumbs and their piss for the rest of your life. And even then they'll think they're doing you a favor."

"That's not how it has to be," she says. "Erik, listen, your dad's a dick. So what? Let's just take a minute. Okay?"

Her voice is still so even, and I glance behind me, notice that the edge of the cliff is close. Again I step toward her.

"We have to forget all of this," Georgie says. Her voice catches, but she keeps going. "No one has to know about . . . the fires."

"They'll figure it out," I say. I look toward the fire and see the boat coming across the water. Even though it's dark, I can see Davis's outline. And next to him, a figure. Ana.

Thank God. Oh, thank God.

And I laugh a little, before my voice breaks and the sob comes out. "This isn't like the Nelsons'. There's more, Georgie."

"Erik," Georgie says. "It's okay. Listen to me. We can explain this."

"We can't." For a second, the weight of it all threatens to pin me down. "You don't understand. There's no way out of this."

"Let's talk. Let's get help. I can help you."

But everything's starting to sound muted, like I'm listening from far away, and I just smile at her. "I know," I say. "I know."

And I *do* know. I know what's waiting for me at home, her anxious hands folded, always folded, around some mug of tea as she sits at the kitchen table, waiting. I know what's waiting for me next year, and the year after that, and the year after that. The same kitchen. The same table. The same hands. The same me.

"I wanted someone to take me with them," I say. "Anyone. But especially you."

She flinches, remembering the party at Fellman's, how I asked. I don't want her to remember how she laughed—she doesn't need this, it's not fair to her—but I watch her squeeze her eyes shut and then open them again. "You wanted me." I can't see her face too clearly in the rain, but something passes over it—something beautiful and sorrowful and too too late. "Come with me, Erik," she says. "Come with me. Wherever I go, you go."

And the thing is, it feels just like I thought it would. The words hit me in the gut, a warm, safe, *finally* feeling that moves up my neck, over my face. Like arms around my waist. Like a hand on my cheek. *Finally. Finally.*

"Thank you," I say. I step closer to Georgie and I smile through my tears, through the rain. I'm trying to tell her everything.

Because then I spin around and I'm running, faster than I've ever run before, my feet wheeling under me so that I don't even feel it when they leave the ground and I'm in the air, the night so dark and perfect and I'm flying straight into it, arms out, nothing behind me because I know, without a doubt, that they'll never catch me now.

We all get out, one way or another. To leave Gold Fork is to pack a bag that includes only what scares you. Nothing else will serve. Leave everything else behind.

The people we'll meet wherever we're going won't understand. In dorm rooms and barracks, at art galleries and gyms, we'll tell them about Gold Fork and will hear the way we've turned it into a place as mythic and magical as Atlantis, hidden beneath the water. And they'll listen to us and will say, "I don't get it. Isn't it just a town?" because they come from "just a town" themselves, and can only imagine their home as a place to return for obligatory holidays, not the thing they've lost forever.

Because we have lost it. Even if we come back from time to time, drop our bags at the door and yell, "I'm home!" even if we stay for a whole summer between graduating from college and starting that internship in New York we never thought we'd get, Gold Fork is gone. It's no longer the place we grew up, stretching our arms above our heads as though reaching through the sky to something different, something that we were sure would be better than the endless cycle of waiting for Weekenders and enduring the rest. We lost Gold Fork the minute we left.

Of course, most of us won't leave. Most of us will stay, our feet seemingly encased in the drying cement of the new sidewalk along Fourth and Main, or stuck in the thigh-high mud next to the fishing pond. Every day, as we walk to work at the diner or the post office, as we lug cleaning supplies or fresh linens from one Weekender's home to another's, we'll feel the cement drying, the mud cracking around our knees, and we'll feel the impossibility of escape. But we'll be wrong. Eventually, everyone leaves. Perhaps: Old and wrinkled, our heads on thin pillows, we'll take our last breath of Gold Fork's piney air. Perhaps: Browsing through the books at the drugstore, we'll feel our heart click and whir and, grabbing our chest just like in the movies, we will tumble in a slow-motion fall to the ground.

Perhaps. Or perhaps the lake will claim us as it has always

399

promised, and we will live beneath the water-skiers and paddle-boarders, far beneath even the fish, our hair wrapped in algae and our hands clutching the pebbled sand of our only and true home.

DAVIS

Georgie is scrambling down the rocky path from the top of the cliff as we anchor the boat. It looks like she's flying. She's screaming, but I don't need to hear her to know what she's saying—we saw it too.

And then we're all in the water, diving down, popping back up, diving again. The rain is coming down hard, the waves so high that they splash our faces whenever we come up for air so that it feels like we're drowning even as we rise.

We have to pull Georgie out.

And then clawing our way back up to the party, the three of us running, slipping, falling in the gravel, screaming at the Weekenders to call, fucking call someone. Waving down the first truck we see on the road (finally, finally) and screaming for the cops. For anybody. And the driver, a logger just down from a clear-cutting operation on the mountain, making the call on his CB radio and running back down to the water with us and tossing off his boots and flannel and jumping in himself, yelling for us to wait there, wait there.

Ana's lips: a blue line across her face.

My hands: an old woman's tremor.

Georgie: crawling to the edge of the rocks, cupping her

hands around her mouth, and screaming Erik's name. She jumps in again before we can stop her.

It's the logger, finally, who grabs her under the armpits and swims her back to shore. "Fucking crazy!" he's shouting at her, and then he glares at Ana and me before turning and diving back into the water. We can barely hear him over the rain and the thunder. "You want to lose two of your friends tonight?"

Before she can try again, I throw my arms around Georgie. She fights and shakes, cursing me, cursing Erik. It takes me a while to realize that the shaking is involuntary. It racks her whole body so that it feels like I'm trying to hold on to a jackhammer. "She's too cold!" I yell at Ana over the thunder that cracks above our heads. "In shock or something!"

She looks at Georgie, looks at me. Takes off her shirt.

I blink.

"Davis."

She's beautiful.

"Dammit, Davis." She jerks her finger at me. "You too."

And then I understand what she wants us to do, and I take off my shirt as Ana takes off Georgie's, and the two of us wrap ourselves around her and hold on. My arms reach around Georgie to grab Ana's shoulders. Her hands meet my ribs. And we stay like that, sandwiching Georgie between us, looking at each other and rocking back and forth, until the ambulance arrives far above with the first lightning strike.

GEORGIE

There is nobody in the water. Correction: no body. That's all they could say, after a six-day search. Divers, a scope. Early on, a net dragged carefully through the water in front of Washer's Landing, though the net went down only sixty feet and we all know that no one's been to the very bottom. Or, if anyone has, they haven't risen back up to talk about it.

And now, three weeks later, it doesn't look like anyone will.

"He doesn't know how deep it is," I tell Davis, "because he's not down there." Davis doesn't answer. He's sitting on my bed, watching me pack. I grab a sweater from my floor and turn it over in my hands. Then I fling it back onto the rug. "He's out there somewhere, living the dream. Don't you think this was part of his plan?"

"What plan?" His voice is quiet. "Georgie," he says, "it's been two weeks. Don't you think—"

"I'm sure he had one. Erik always had plans."

But I remember what the policeman told my mom at the station. They hadn't been able to get back in the water until the lightning stopped. By then it had been hours. "It was never a rescue," the policeman said, before he noticed me sitting there in my standard-issue wool blanket. "It was always a recovery."

Bullshit.

I'm throwing T-shirts and jeans into a duffel, stuffing

them in until it looks like it won't zip shut. I reach down beside my bed and toss a couple of books and a notebook on top of the pile. Then I grab a smaller black notebook, fling it at Davis.

"Want it?"

I watch him leaf through. Read the names. Next to the names: dates, prices, measurements. "What is this, a cookbook?"

I raise my eyebrows.

"Hey, Betty Crocker," he says, throwing it back at me, "burn this."

I laugh a little. But it hurts, like trying to swallow something sharp.

I pick up my swimsuit from the floor and toss it at Davis. He catches it before it hits his face. "That comes with," I say. "Where I'm going, it's nothing but sun and sand. I'm a snowbird now. Just me and the retirees, drinking mai tais by the pool." I try to smile, but it looks as real as Silly Putty.

"Your working days are over," he says.

"You can say that again. Looks like I'm out of the game for good." And there's a sudden and familiar sting in my chest that I try to ignore. I reach down and pick up the mug Erik stole for me from the Pancake Parlor. I hold it for a minute before wrapping it in a shirt. I tuck the mug in the duffel, safe in a cocoon of clothes.

"What about the band?" Davis asks. "Are they going to . . . wait?"

"Would you?" I ask him.

He looks down at his hands.

"It's Gold Fork," I tell him. "No one can afford to wait. Besides," I add, "I've talked to them. Told them not to." And I don't say it, but we both know: I'm not coming back.

When the ambulance arrived at Washer's Landing, so did the police. And it didn't take long before someone found my jacket with all those useful zippered pockets.

I didn't care. They arrested me, and I didn't care. Threatened me with years in jail, huge fines. The book, thrown. Mom: crying. Dad: silent. Didn't care. Didn't care. Didn't. Care.

The rest of it is fuzzy. Mom and Dad emptying their savings to pay for the lawyer from the city. The lawyer earning every penny—a Weekender, naturally, swooping in and saving the day. Again. I'd have resented it if I didn't feel so grateful.

And what did all of this cost me ultimately? My savings are gone, obviously, eaten by fines and fees. Dodge is in jail— thanks to my lawyer, a plea bargain, and my detailed knowledge of his business dealings. My parents will never look at me the same way again, but they don't have to look for long. I'm getting out, but not in the way I wanted.

"I bet there's a music program at the school," says Davis.

"Sure," I say, throwing a couple more T-shirts in my duffel, "if you like campfire songs. Keep it wholesome. Speaking of." I reach over to my nightstand and pick up the Vivian Girls record that Henry gave me. I throw it over at Davis. "You might like this. Bubblegum pop with an edge."

"You don't want it?" he asks.

"I'm over it. Besides, I don't think they've got record players at the school."

Davis chuckles. "I'd pay money to see your face when they talk about the Love of Learning! at orientation."

"Meeting Challenges Head-On!" I say.

"Excelling for the Sake of Excellence!"

We're both laughing, or trying to, but it feels like acting. "It's going to be such bullshit," I say, but the fact is, I'll take it. I'll take some therapeutic school in the desert where they check my possessions once a day over staying here and being reminded of Erik everywhere I go. My punishment—the school—is nothing compared to the punishment of the rest of my life.

As if he can read my mind, Davis says, "It's not your fault."

"Easy for you to say. I should have figured out what was going on with him."

"We all should have."

"Yeah, but I should have seen it. He was trying to tell me, in his way." I sit down next to him on the bed. "Sorry I wasn't at the memorial. I just couldn't do it."

"I know. It was packed, though. He'd have liked that."

"Would he? I'm not so sure. Erik hated most of those people." Even just talking about him in the past tense feels like betrayal.

Davis's laugh is quiet. "True. But they should've set aside a whole wing of the church for his Dead Ender girls. What a show. It was like they hoped that the volume of their sobs was in direct proportion to how much they meant to him." He adds, "I kind of hope one of them was right." Then he squeezes my arm quickly. "Anyone could see what you meant to him."

And that sharp pain again in my chest. Erik on the cliff. Me stepping toward him. The way he smiled and spun and flew. I take a breath. I can't talk about us—if there was ever an us. Because there's no us now. "How'd his dad look?"

"Like he had unspeakable remorse," says Davis. "Which is too good for him."

Neither of us says anything about Erik's mom.

"The Nelsons were there," Davis adds, almost in apology. "He'd have hated that."

"Screw them. I bet they don't feel responsible for any of this." Then: "Isn't it funny," I say. "No one seems to care that much that he did the fires."

"It only seems to make him *better*, somehow," agrees Davis. "More noble. The whole town's son, in a way."

"The only one with the guts to *do* something," I agree.

"Our Spartacus. Our Che."

"Now, *that* he'd like." I pick up the little black book. Flip through, looking at old orders. They almost look like numbers written in a foreign script—a language I'll never use again. "It could've turned out differently."

"Maybe," says Davis. "But maybe something like this was inevitable. Maybe he was going to"—he pauses to choose the right word—"go, no matter what."

"Least he could've done is write a fucking note." My fingers are flipping roughly through the black book, making little tears in the pages. "You know, before his magnificent escape."

Davis nods. I know "escape" isn't the word he'd use.

I wave my hand in front of my face, one-two, one-two. "Now you see us, now you don't." Us.

"At least you'll visit," says Davis.

"Don't be so sure." I set down the book. "But listen. If he comes back—" I put my hand on his shoulder. "Davis. Seriously. If he comes back. You'll tell him how to find me." My breath catches in my throat. "You'll tell him where I am."

"Of course."

I need to hear this from him. I need to think he believes it's possible, too, even though I know he agrees with what one of the divers said after they called it off. *No one could survive that.*

"Yes. Of course I will," he says again, and I let out the breath I've been holding.

I use my hand on his shoulder to push myself to standing. I stare down at him for a minute. "Thanks," I say. Then I turn back to my duffel. "The thing is," I add over my shoulder, "even after his miraculous return?"

"Yeah?"

"He'll probably want a fucking medal."

SEPTEMBER

WHERE SOMETIMES YOU LOSE

September is loss.

They leave in the opposite order they arrived: First, the families, hurrying to pack up the Tahoe and get back to the city in time for school to start again. Always forgetting something: the cooler, dog food, portable DVD player. Always saying, "We'll pop back up sometime this fall to get it." Always forgetting. They leave, and the Monday after they've gone is a day of hunger and listlessness. Then the families with toddlers and babies, taking their time because they have to work around naps and bottles and one hundred tiny snacks. But they, too, leave for jobs and playdates in the city.

Finally, it's just the retirees. They fill the diner in the early-September mornings, decked out in fleece jackets and moisture-wicking pants. Most of them have already been out hiking or bird-watching at that early hour, and their day is half over. They look at us with our backpacks and schoolbooks and they mutter about truancy and tardiness. They wonder about us as we wonder about them. What does it take, we wonder, to get to this point: ordering the egg plate, extra bacon, sitting back and sipping at coffee, taking their time because time, finally, is theirs again. We would ask them how they did it if we could, but they don't speak our language, and their answer, if they gave it, would confuse us. But finally they go too, called south by the warming sun. If you stand on Main on the right day in September, you'll see a flock of RVs, sides folded in like wings, lifting over the small rise from the lake road and soaring soundlessly through town.

And then it's over. They're all gone. The town is ours again, but also not really.

The construction companies hustle in, tearing down old cabins to prep for the spring building season. The sounds of jackhammers and bulldozers blaze across the lake. Rubble everywhere, it seems.

The dock builders come back with their hired hands, using pike poles and tugboats to take apart the docks, pushing them onto the beach in sections. They'll rest there like stranded whales as the water levels fall around them, and the walkways, their sturdy pilings sunk into the ground on shore, will lead to nothing.

We go to Toney's after the Weekenders have gone, and we check each item carefully before we put it in our cart. Yogurt, orange juice, milk. These things have usually just passed their expiration dates. And who can blame Toney's for keeping them on the shelves and hoping we don't notice? Who can blame the grocery store for trying to stave off the losses of the next nine months?

Who can blame any of us for trying?

DAVIS

The letter, if you can call it that, took up the whole newspaper the day after the memorial. Dan said it was worth it. Framed it like a brochure. Said everyone in town would understand once they read it. "They'll see themselves in the pages," he said. "They'll think about what led your friend to that place. They'll consider their own responsibility for the fires. What more can an editor ask for?"

A lot, I told him.

But he was right. To say it touched a nerve would be like calling appendicitis a slight tummy ache. The Weekenders seethed and left, though not before writing three or four newspapers' worth of letters for "The Forked Tongue" that basically said either *No, really! We're just like you!* or the less attractive, *You'd be nothing without us.* Dan printed a few, and then shrugged and ignored the rest. "They'll be back," he said. And of course, he's right.

But here in Gold Fork. If I thought being the son of the town minister wasn't legacy enough. Phone calls—to the newspaper, to the house. The guidance counselor on my doorstep, holding a brand-new college guide and tearing up as she handed it to me. Even the library started a reading group to discuss "Gold Fork Is" (Dan's title, obviously). I'm the—gasp—invited speaker. Some people agreed with what I wrote. Some didn't. Depending on who you talk to, I got Gold Fork completely, utterly right or completely, utterly wrong. My parents, proud in their typical we'd-be-proud-of-you-no-matter-what-but-okay-maybe-we're-slightly-prouder-of-this-than-of-that-ex-girlfriend-book-you-were-working-on way, joke that I need a publicist. Our mayor, looking like he couldn't tell if this opened up a healthy dialogue or broke the seventh seal, gave me some sort of made-up certificate that I guess is only twenty-five steps removed from getting the key to the city.

I'd tell someone that—the thing about the seventh seal—but I have no one to tell.

I haven't talked to Ana since the memorial. She stood in the middle of one of the pews at church and held on to her mom's hand. I hadn't noticed until then how much she looks like her mom. And I said . . .

Hey.

And then I shuffled my feet or something equally idiotic, and she looked at me with those thoughtful, somber eyes and didn't say anything, and I just kind of walked back to where my dad was sitting near the front.

I called once, but when she didn't call back, I dropped it.

If she leaves too . . . If her mom decides that this town has done enough damage, or she—I don't know—follows Vera to Chicago. Or something.

There are a thousand ways to leave.

I can't even think about it.

Small-town journalistic fame aside, it's amazing how quickly things become normal-ish. School starts up again, with the

414

predictable essays about What We Did All Summer and the equally predictable lectures about Making Our Time Here Count and Seeking Help When You Need It. Some stores close until May; some stores close for good. The weather starts to turn, little by little, and suddenly we're all wearing jackets in the mornings over our T-shirts.

People talk about Georgie and Erik as though they're both dead, even though Georgie hasn't left yet, and maybe that's for the best. Maybe all we can hope for is a way through this, each of us dealing with it on our own.

Maybe.

When Ana finally shows up at my door one Saturday evening in mid-September, I don't know what to say. I've seen her at school and have even tried talking to her, but she's seemed folded into herself somehow.

I don't blame her.

But I miss her.

"Davis," she says. "Hi."

"Hey," I say. She's standing in the doorway like it's nothing, and all I can think about is the old fisherman's sweater I'm wearing over my long-sleeved tee and why, oh God, why? I glance behind me toward the kitchen, where my parents are finishing dinner.

We both stand there for a minute, unsure of what to say. Finally, Ana says, "I was just biking around. Thought I'd stop by." She shrugs. "But maybe you're busy."

"I'm not busy," I say, too quickly. Try not to look directly at her. Then I add, "Wanna go down to the water?"

She nods, her expression unreadable.

I lead her down the side path to our old, weathered dock. We walk out to the end and sit down. Ana takes off her shoes and dips her feet tentatively in the water.

"It's cold," she says, and then plunges them both in to her shins. I hear her inhale. "Wow."

"Brave soul," I say, but I roll up my pants and do the same. The water feels sharp against my skin, little needles pricking at the soles of my feet, but then they start to numb and it's manageable. "How've you been?" I ask.

"You know." She looks out across the lake. "I've been okay." She glances at me out of the corner of her eyes. "You?"

"Same. It's weird," I add. "Everything feels normal, but totally alien at the same time."

"Yeah," she says. "You're right. Whenever I think about it . . ." She stops.

"It's like you want to climb out of your body," I say. "Like you can't stand to sit there in your skin, remembering."

"Exactly," she says. "I keep thinking there must have been a moment when I could have changed things. If I hadn't been at the Den. Or if the boat had gone faster." There are tears in her eyes. "But more than that. All those moments when we were just hanging out, the four of us, and we could have been—I don't know—saving him."

I nod. "It's what I wake up thinking every morning." I don't tell her about the stomachaches I wake with every morning, the constant state of nausea. The fear that things will never be right again. "But you can't control how other people are going to act." I laugh self-consciously. "Mom's words."

"Pastor Davis." She nudges me with her elbow. "I know that. And we can't spend all our time just reacting, either. That's just as bad. It's—it's dangerous." She wipes at her eyes with one hand.

"Yeah," I say, and pause. Erik, who felt like reacting was all he could do. And then also—dumb to think about it now, but—Jane. Me fumbling, trying to keep up, never quite *it* and knowing this, knowing it all along. Always just reacting to whatever little hints or bread crumbs or thinly veiled insults she'd throw my way. Never saying, *You know what, Jane? I'm out.* When I was with Jane, I was just one reaction away from losing myself completely. I thought that was real—I thought the fantasy of Jane was as much as I could hope for.

There was nothing real about my relationship with Jane. I'm sitting next to the only real thing I'll ever know.

The sun's going down across the lake, rimming the mountains pink. Ana shivers, and before she can say anything, I take off my sweater and hold it out. "Here," I say. "The epitome of style."

"You sure?" she asks. I nod, and she pulls it on over her shirt.

I can't believe I thought that sweater was ugly.

"Thanks," she says, and she unconsciously tugs on the sleeve where her scar is.

"You always do that," I say, pointing to the sleeve. "I've noticed how you try to keep it covered."

She looks away. "I didn't know it was that obvious," she says.

"No," I say, "that's not what I meant. I didn't mean to—I don't think it's bad. I just—I think the scar is beautiful." I blurt the last part out.

Her head whips around to me. "It's not beautiful," she says, though her voice doesn't sound angry. "Not at all."

"It's beautiful the way relics are beautiful," I say. "The way they represent a time that's passed, a way of being in the world. The scar does that too."

She looks at me for a long time. Then she nods, touching her arm. She pulls the sleeve up, and we both look at the beautiful river of it. "Before and after."

I reach out and touch the scar. "Before," I say, following its path down her wrist, "and after."

She shivers, and I pull back. I can't read her expression, so I say, "I don't really know what to do with Georgie gone."

"What do you mean? She hasn't left yet." Ana shifts in her seat, covers the scar again.

"I know, but she's going soon. And she's not in school. I just—I don't know how to handle my time. What to do with myself." I don't tell Ana what I've actually been doing, which is driving around, looking for her. Parking in front of her apartment building and not knocking on her door. Bringing her name up on my phone and never hitting send.

Ana nods. "I know what you mean. I guess I didn't really

know how much she planned our days. How in charge she was of everything."

"I keep waiting for you to leave too," I blurt out before I can stop myself.

"What?" She smiles and looks at me.

"I thought maybe . . ." I shrug. "Everyone else is doing it."

"Where would I go?" She laughs, and then her expression turns serious. "Besides, there's someone here I would never leave."

ANA

I watch him for a reaction, but I can't quite read his expression. For a second, he seems like he's going to lean forward, but then he kicks his feet in the water, making tiny bubbles.

"She's not going?" he asks.

Vera. He thinks I'm only talking about Vera.

Okay.

"Nope," I say. "Abby agreed to leave her here. With me." I lift one foot out of the lake and watch the water drip off of it before letting it fall again with a slight splash. "Turns out all it took was a little . . . pressure."

"That's awesome," Davis says. "But is that . . . ? Can you take all of that on?"

"My mom and I have it all worked out," I tell him. "Abby's transferring the power of attorney to my mom. She's going to help. If things get . . . as Vera gets older." And I remember the way Vera looked at us when I brought Mom to meet her, finally. *Sisters are a gift,* she'd said, and we didn't correct her. Before we left, Vera touched my hand. *You're her world,* she said. *Anyone can see that.*

Davis nods. "Will Abby visit, do you think?"

"Honestly? No," I say. "She says she will, but, I mean, how could they now? Besides, the sale's still going through—the buyers were going to tear it down anyway."

The image rushes back, as it does ten times a day at least: the house burning and Erik falling. Falling as we watched. I close my eyes. Will this haunt me forever? "It seems pretty final," I say, and I'm talking about more than just the sale. Then I add, "I don't know. Maybe." I look at him out of the corner of my eyes. There are so many things I want to tell him. So many. About Erik, and Georgie, and the summer. About us. "You got it, you know," I say, pulling my feet out of the water and sitting cross-legged. I cup the tops of my feet in each hand, warming them. "The letter. Article. Brochure. Whatever you want to call it. You got Gold Fork." A water-skier goes by in a full wet suit, backlit by the sunset, and the wake makes the dock bob and sway under us. "It wasn't always nice, but it was honest. You let the town talk," I say. "And it was my voice. Ours." Then I add, "Everyone's."

I read it twenty times.

"Thanks," he says, and stares hard at the water. "That means a lot."

"You sure didn't hold back."

420

"Yeah," he says, "but it was a letter, you know? That's easier, in a way. Removed from the action. At least you call it like you see it. You've never been afraid to tell people when they're being assholes." He shakes his head a little. "I don't know anyone else like you—like that."

"Thank you, I guess." I laugh and turn back toward the lake. "It certainly hasn't won me any love, that's for sure."

"I bet it has."

I keep my eyes trained on the mountains across the lake, the lengthening shadows of trees on the far shore. I've hardly let myself hope until now. But. Something in his voice. The memory of the chapel comes back to me, but this time, it's not smoke and flames that I remember. It's the two of us, standing together in the chapel, shoulders touching, the whole world a bright, flickering spark of possibility.

I turn to him quickly. "The Better," I say, and let out a shaky breath.

"Are we speaking in code?" He makes a show of looking furtively left and then right. "Are we spies here? Because I can see it: you all beautiful and shit in a trench coat, me trying too hard in a dark hat. Rainy streetscape, dim light. I could start another graphic novel, this one about how, minus any superpowers, the two of us fight for good and truth and—"

I laugh. He doesn't get it. Of course. And I'm tempted to drop it, to go back to our casual way of being. But. "No," I say, "you. You're the Better. Something my mom said once." I keep my eyes on him. Take a big breath. "If I've learned one thing this summer, it's that we don't have time to keep things hidden. And—" I take a deep breath. "And I need you to know how I feel. In case there was any doubt."

I watch him get it. He looks confused for a second, eyebrows knitted together like he can't trust what he's hearing, and then his face just kind of clears—washed clean with certainty. He smiles at me. "Well," he says, lifting his hand and staring at it a moment before letting it fall gently onto my shoulder, "your mom's a wise woman."

His hand moves from my shoulder over to the back of my neck and rests there, and everything inside of me seems to lift up at once and answer the touch.

"Besides," he adds, "we can learn a lot from our elders."

"Like what?" I keep my face turned toward his. My voice sounds in my ears like I've just sprinted a mile to get here. And we both have, really. Miles and miles and miles.

"One," he says. "Always offer guests something to eat." He leans closer, moves his hand up so that it's cupping the back of my head. "Two." His forehead touching mine now, and it's not clear whose skin is hotter, mine or his. "You never know when someone's going to surprise you. It'll hit you like a truck."

"And three?" I bring my hand up between us like a wish and rest it on his cheek.

"No three," he says, so close that I can smell his hair, and it's spruce and wood smoke, and I know that this is the one thing I'll never forget, not in five years, not in fifty. "Just two."

WHERE SOMETIMES YOU WIN

When we talk about it, we say that Gold Fork is a four-season resort town with only two that matter.

But that's just something we say to make sense of this place. Because we know that sometimes, sometimes there's a fifth season. It might be as long as a week, as short as the breath that passes between two people. And most years, we miss it—turn our heads at the last second, lean over to tie our shoes, and it's gone. Those are years of regret and chill, everything doused in gray. But when we do catch and hold and see it for what it is, we understand that no other town has it, and that, for this week or moment or breath, we're the lucky ones. We hold it in our hands, there in the curve of our palms, and we feel the intensity of it burn clean through.

Our season.

The air: clean, cold, bright.

The sound: a lake lapping against the shore, geese lifting off together in one lilting spray.

And the smell: wood smoke. Spruce. Vinegar. Strawberries.

GEORGIE

I'm alone when the doorbell rings. I'm sitting in my room, feet propped on the duffel that's been packed for weeks. My flight leaves tonight, and my parents are at Toney's, stocking up on toothpaste and deodorant, as though maybe the place where I'm going doesn't have basic necessities. When I hear the doorbell's chime I whip my head around. Try to suppress the hope, a sudden plucked string. *Maybe.* I run down the stairs, two at a time, and throw open the door.

It's not him.

She looks at me the way you look at the cashier who's given you the wrong change. Doesn't say a word.

"Hi," I say.

She steps inside the house. Looks around. "I expected nicer," she says. She's wearing a thick coat that reaches toward her knees, even though it's not even cold enough for a sweater today. Her hair is messy. I can see where she tried to put on lipstick and missed—a red slash at the corner of her mouth.

When she still doesn't say anything else, I start rambling. "I'm sorry I wasn't at the memorial," I say. "I heard it was nice." I sound like a recording of someone who's paid to say nothing real. But I've never really talked to Erik's mom. I don't know how to begin now.

She ignores me and reaches into the deep pocket of her coat. I watch her hand fish around for something, distracted. "This is yours," she says, and hands me a thick envelope.

My heart trips. There's my name, in his chicken-scratch handwriting. I glance at her.

Her glare is a challenge. "I thought about it."

"I'd have read it. If it were me."

"Don't worry. He left one for me, too. With—" Her voice cracks, and she swipes at her face with a puffy coat sleeve. "Do you know where he'd have gotten two thousand dollars?" She shakes her head into her sleeve. "I don't even want to know. I don't even—" She sobs once, quickly—a heaving, gasping sound—and stops just as suddenly.

"He must have saved it," I say. "For you." It's a lie, and we both know it, but I don't know what else to say. I never understood Erik's relationship with his mom, but I'm looking at her, tiny in that huge, ridiculous coat, and I know she will never be okay again. Normal—whatever it was—is over. The anger I feel is sudden and hot. How could he not see what this would do to her?

"I'd have brought it earlier." But then she doesn't say anything else. Instead, she turns to go. Stops right outside the door and looks over her shoulder at me. "I never knew what he was doing with any of you."

And I know she means all the girls, but I say, "He was one of us."

She starts down the walkway, then turns. "Then you should have taken better care of him." I watch her as she walks with uneven steps to her car and gets in. She doesn't look at me again.

I close the door. Davis told me that Erik's mom knew his dad was back in town, and she and Erik never talked about it. She's right. We all should have taken better care of him. All of us.

But especially me. Especially, especially, especially me. And, like it does a dozen times a day, the crushing weight of this—the fucking *endness* of it—presses against my chest with a force that almost knocks me over. Ana and Davis will be okay. They'll live with this, and eventually it'll sew itself into the fabric of their memories, a strand of something that was beautiful, once, before it was awful. But I'll always know that there were a million moments when I could have been brave. I could have tipped my face toward his that night at Fellman's— feels like years ago now—when the air crackled around us and it was all still possible. I could have held on to him. I could have made a million different choices—for Erik, for myself.

But I can almost hear him now, in that voice that was always resting this side of a joke that only he got: *Stop taking yourself so seriously, George. It's not all about you.*

I open the envelope. Money falls out: hundred-dollar bills. Ten of them. I stare at the money, run my fingers over it. Gather it together in my hand, feeling the insubstantial heft, the uselessness. Slowly, I curl my fingers around the money until it's crunched together in a misshapen ball. I lob it toward the garbage can. Then I reach into the envelope and pull out a wrinkled sheet of paper. The handwriting slants across the page, written in a hurry, dashes everywhere. My name, then a dash.

GEORGIE—
YOU NEVER QUITE GOT IT—

I stop reading and look up. Take a deep breath. Swallow, and start again.

YOU NEVER QUITE GOT IT—
WHAT I ACTUALLY THOUGHT—OF YOU.
I'M OKAY WITH IT—NO, REALLY—I CAN SEE
YOU SHAKING YOUR HEAD—BUT I AM. IT'S
EASIER THIS WAY. ONE LESS MESS.
IT'S FUNNY BECAUSE I DON'T KNOW
WHERE I'LL BE WHEN YOU READ THIS.
DON'T KNOW WHAT I'LL BE.
THAT'S FUNNY, ISN'T IT.

BUT IF YOU'RE READING THIS, YOU KNOW
ABOUT THE FIRES. ALL OF THEM—PROBABLY.
(YOU'RE NOT THE ONLY ONE TO HAVE A
SECRET STASH, IT TURNS OUT.) HERE'S
WHAT I WANT TO TELL YOU—I HAVE TO
TELL YOU.

I NEEDED SOMETHING TO ANCHOR ME.
ALL THAT WIND. ALL THAT NOISE. I NEEDED
AN ANCHOR—YOU UNDERSTAND.

428

BUT I'M GLAD YOU WEREN'T THAT ANCHOR.
YOU'D SINK WITH ME.

I CAN'T LIVE HERE, GEORGE—NO MATTER
WHAT—I CAN'T LIVE HERE. AND NOW I
KNOW I CAN'T LIVE ANYWHERE—THERE'S
NOWHERE THAT'LL HAVE ME. ALL I'VE EVER
HAD IS THE ABILITY TO LIGHT THINGS ON
FIRE AND WALK AWAY.

BUT YOU'RE BETTER THAN THAT. YOU'RE
THE FLAME THAT PEOPLE ARE DRAWN TO.
I KNOW I AM.

THERE ARE SO MANY THINGS I WISH I'D SAID.

LIKE—THAT NIGHT IN THE CHAPEL. I WENT
BACK IN. I DROPPED A MATCH. JUST TO
SEE, RIGHT? BUT ALSO BECAUSE IT FELT
SO PERFECT, SO RIGHT, THE FOUR OF US
IN THERE. YOU PROBABLY THOUGHT IT WAS
JUST ANOTHER NIGHT, ANOTHER CHANCE
TO PARTY. BUT TO ME IT FELT LIKE—HERE
ARE MY PEOPLE, FINALLY. THREE PEOPLE
WHO DON'T CARE IF I RUN OR WALK. HE
WOULDN'T BELIEVE ME, BUT YES—DAVIS, TOO.

I THOUGHT, FINALLY I BELONG. AND I DIDN'T
WANT ANYONE ELSE TO HAVE THAT. TIME
RUINS EVERYTHING. I WANTED THAT SPACE
TO CRYSTALIZE, BECOME A PERFECT ARTIFACT.
GEORGIE, I'VE MADE SO MANY MISTAKES.
SO MANY. AND I'VE LIED TO EVERYONE—

BUT NEVER TO YOU.

SO HERE'S THE TRUTH. I'M NOT WORRIED
ABOUT YOU. NEVER WAS. YOU'RE NOT
GOING TO BURN OUT. YOU'RE GOING TO
BLAZE BRIGHTER THAN ANYTHING, AND
EVERYONE WILL WANT TO STAND IN YOUR
GLOW. I ALWAYS DID.

ADVENTURE AWAITS, GEORGIE. WE ALWAYS
THOUGHT THAT WAS GOLD FORK'S BIGGEST
LIE. BUT I'M STARTING TO THINK IT'S THE
ONLY TRUE THING ABOUT THIS PLACE.
IT HAS TO BE. FOR YOU.

—E

I'm crying as I fold the letter carefully and place it back
in the envelope. I know I'll take it with me to my new life.

430

I'll read it thousands more times over the next few years, maybe by the light of a flashlight in my bunk at the therapeutic school after everyone has fallen asleep, maybe in a dorm room at college, maybe even in a small apartment in the city, my guitar leaning against the wall, friends—yes, maybe friends—knocking at the door. I'll read it to remind me of what I had, and what I lost. What—if I ever find it again—I have to protect with everything I've got.

I'll read this letter every night, scanning the words for clues, some sense of why and how and maybe, maybe, where he is. Because I refuse to think he's at the bottom of the lake. I refuse to think he lost so absolutely, so definitively. There has to be a version of this story in which Erik is taking plates of food out to customers at a restaurant, or sitting behind a desk at a bank, bored out of his mind. There has to be a version—there just has to be—in which he's running across a ridgeline, the wind at his back, in front of him only mountains and space and freedom.

GOLD FORK IS

In the end, Gold Fork is everything I've made it out to be: fantasy, refuge, opportunity, impossible problem. Mirage or love story—take your pick. It's all of these things, and none of them. The town is woven into our lives so intricately that even we can't see it clearly. We have to leave to get the perspective that only distance and time can offer. We have to leave so that we can return.

But what happens when you can't leave? What happens when the only way to go is to leap into the dark?

People will talk about this summer for years. They'll wonder what we could have done differently. They'll try to unpack the tangled contents of What Happened and Why. But maybe all they need to know, finally, is this: We were Gold Fork's four-chambered heart. We beat for the town, for what it can and should be. We even beat for what it is, its heartbreak and joys. But a heart sometimes skips a beat. The rhythm gets lost; something shuts down.

Because.

When you love a place, you sometimes hate it too. Sometimes you feel strangled by your love for it—your complicated, grueling, enduring love. And all you want is to forget it. To get away. Forever. But when you love a place like we love Gold Fork, you're never far from it, even when you are. Gold Fork is your firsts: first step in the lake, first sip of coffee at Grainey's, first midnight swim, first kiss on the dock. The Weekenders get some of those firsts too, but not all of them, and not in the same way. That's the thing the Weekenders will never understand, and what we're here to tell them: You think you own this place, but you don't. We don't either. It owns us. And for those of us who really live here, no matter where we go, Gold Fork will be our lasts. Last memory, last word, last breath: home.

SUICIDE PREVENTION AND AWARENESS RESOURCES

National Suicide Prevention Lifeline
1-800-273-8255
suicidepreventionlifeline.org

Crisis Text Line
Text HOME to 741741 in the US for free 24/7 support.
crisistextline.org

National Alliance on Mental Illness
1-800-950-6264
nami.org

National Center for the Prevention of Youth Suicide
suicidology.org/NCPYS

Youth Suicide Warning Signs
youthsuicidewarningsigns.org/youth

ACKNOWLEDGMENTS

I wouldn't have been able to complete this book without a team of childcare providers to love and nurture our daughters while I worked. So, from the bottom of my heart, thanks to: Brenna, Amanda, Sophie, Hannah, Natalie, Peggy, Nicky, Gabby, Alexa, Kristal, Jayme, Megan, Jessie, Lauren, Nicole, Phoebe, Yohanna, Shane, and Vida, and everyone else at Bambini's, Missoula Community School, and ASUM Child Care. Huge gratitude to Liesa Abrams, Sarah McCabe, and Jessica Smith, who saw the story in the messy draft(s) and carved to set it free, and to Denise Shannon, who found the right home for this book. And for the support I received from others: Cheryl Klein, who provided an early, thoughtful response to the book; Natalie Peeterse and the Open Country Reading Series; Maria Dahvana Headley, who gave the right advice at the right time; the Montana Arts Council; everyone in the Davidson Honors College and the English Department at the University of Montana; Alex and the

Parents Lloyd, who provided my Austenian writing room in Tenants Harbor, where the first sentences of this book arose; Drew and Aja, who heard those first sentences; MJ, Sierra, Caroline, and Alexa, my first readers; Daisy and Gillian, the Gucci Gucci Yamas; and Morgan, Emily, Will, Tom, Mary Pat, Jake, Kate, Emma, Megan, Kelly, and Christina, who all provided emotional support in the form of delicately posed questions and/or coffee, and/or whiskey. Thanks to Those Who Speak the Language of Music and Guitars: Tracy, Brendan, Sara, and Kevin; and to Those Who Answer Questions About Potentially Incriminating Things About Which They Have No Firsthand Experience: Tait, Marielle, Andy, and Elwyn. I'm grateful for my supportive family: my parents and my sister, who believed in me before I wrote a single word; and Tom and Sue, who provided a writing room in McCall and gave me crucial information on the science of dock maintenance. But finally, my love and respect and gratitude go to Rob, who did all of the above and then some. Rob, you're the Better.

This book was written in memory of Miriam Shea, the original pipe-smoking spitfire. She was lucky to have a family who cherished her, and I was lucky to be folded into that family through my friendship with her.